Aberdeen Stories

Aberdeen Stories

Growing Up Right in Small-town America

Steven C. Stoker

Writers Club Press
San Jose New York Lincoln Shanghai

Aberdeen Stories
Growing Up Right in Small-town America

Writers Club Press
an imprint of iUniverse.com, Inc.

For information address:
iUniverse.com, Inc.
5220 S 16th, Ste. 200
Lincoln, NE 68512
www.iuniverse.com

ISBN: 0-595-19653-5

Printed in the United States of America

This collection of stories is dedicated to the citizens of Aberdeen, Idaho. It is the people that make a community so memorable, and there are no better than they who touched my life as I was growing up in that wonderful little town. It is the influence and interaction of the people of Aberdeen that helped to make me who and what I have become—whether good or bad!

Nor knowest thou what argument
Thy life to thy neighbor's creed has lent.
All are needed by each one;
Nothing is fair or good alone.

—Ralph Waldo Emerson (Each and All)

Foreword

How do you rediscover your youth? Where do you look to find the values that once were important to our society? For me, it was reading about the daily activities of a family in the town of Aberdeen. I was intrigued by the name immediately because I was born in Aberdeen…Mississippi. The adventures Steve encountered in **his** Aberdeen weren't much different than the ones I experienced in Mississippi. We lived far apart in distance, but were on the same wavelength as children. I played with rough and tumble cousins that taught me how to ride a wild bronco (a mop handle), pilot a spaceship (a cardboard box) and save anyone needing a super hero.

Steve's stories from Aberdeen bring out the best in a person as he shares his life experiences. In a world that sometimes goes terribly wrong, these stories show how it did and can still go right. Take a journey through a simpler time brought to life through the eyes of young boy who grew up to be a wonderful man I'm proud to call my friend.

—Ann Farmer (former Alzheimer's Caregiver)

Preface

In the early 1990's, I began a special topic on a bulletin board of a national computer service. The purpose of that bulletin board was to provide support, information, and even distraction for some very special people—Alzheimer's caregivers. They are those remarkable people who give up so much of their lives to face the burdensome task of caring for loved ones suffering from Alzheimer's Disease.

I was urged by many of the regular users of that support medium to post some short stories. The purpose was simple—to help take their minds off the frustrating duties they face every day as caregivers. I thought about what I might entertain them with, what might distract them and amuse them at the same time. I decided to write some short stories based on events that took place during the years I spent as a boy growing up on a farm in Southeastern Idaho. I used real events to outline the stories, but took liberties in combining events and embellishing facts as I struggled to remember details. In the end, I must admit that the stories are only about 90% true. I hope, however, that they have stayed true to their purpose—to entertain!

I began posting these stories, little more than vignettes, and the response was nothing short of amazing. I soon received e-mail requests to post them on other areas of the support board. They, too, responded positively to the stories.

The chief sysop for the bulletin board ultimately decided to give me my own "area" in which to post my stories. That allowed people from the entire service to read the stories if and when they chose to. Sadly, however, after many months, the postings ended and the original caregiver group disbanded.

I have continued to write these stories, and sometimes sent copies to people on request. Many who read some of them asked how they might order the book, often including comments about how the stories have triggered happy memories of their own lives.

Until now, **there has been no book**, but now the first of these stories will be available to anyone who wants them. Although they are somewhat fictionalized accounts of real events in my childhood, they seem to have broad appeal in all parts of the country. Older readers seem to enjoy the nostalgic value, while younger people seem fascinated by the lifestyles and values of a time gone by.

I continue to write these stories, for the writing has a therapeutic effect on me and the remembering takes me to such wonderful places. I hope every reader can draw something just as enjoyable from reading them.

Acknowledgements

I would like to express my gratitude to and admiration for those cyber-friends that have done so much to encourage me to write these little stories. Although I have not met them face-to-face, their interest and support were paramount in bringing each story to fruition.

I regret that I am unable to remember all the names of those good folks, for some were but transient visitors to an Alzheimer's Caregiver's Support board. However, some names stand out. Among them:

Ann Farmer
Linda Palmer
Donna Lindsay
Carol Treptow
Anne Wood
Don Tester

I would also like to acknowledge the support and tolerance of my better half, Peggy, and my two girls—Kimberly and Chris. Without their help and assistance I never could have spent all those hours on and offline!

Lastly, I'd like to formally recognize my extended family, whose lives were so intertwined with my own. Without my brothers, sister, parents, grandparents, aunts, uncles and cousins it would have been a boring life indeed!

Introduction

This collection of stories is a work of love that came about almost by accident. Some friends on a national computer bulletin board are responsible for its beginning. I was asked to include some stories on an Alzheimer's Support Board to help people to take their minds off the problems they encountered as caregivers for that most terrible of diseases.

Without much thought about what to write, I began to post small vignettes about my own experiences as a boy.

These short stories are based on events in my life. I prefer to describe them as 90% fact and 10% fiction, for I have taken liberties in order to compile some events. I also used some embellishment to help me reach points that might not otherwise have been reached.

I tried not to be derogative or insulting in any way, for I look back on my days in Aberdeen with only fond memories. I would have preferred to **not** change names of most people because I feel they deserve to be recognized for their contributions to the sense of community that I celebrate. On the other hand, I realize that in this day and age a person's privacy might easily be compromised. I tried not to be unkind to anyone, but if I have been, I apologize in advance.

I would like to express my thanks to computer friends who encouraged me at every turn, to family that made it all possible, especially my parents. No boy ever had better!

I would also like to thank the people of Aberdeen for making it the town that it was then, and still is today.

Steven C. Stoker

Contents

1

Getting Started

There are other Aberdeens. The largest is in Scotland. There are Aberdeens in Washington, Indiana, Mississippi, Montana, and even South Dakota. In fact, there are at least a dozen states that can boast of having an Aberdeen. However, it was the great state of Idaho that provided **my** Aberdeen, the community that provided the rich, nurturing environment where I grew up. Things did not start smoothly though. There were a few years of turmoil before I was able to settle permanently in my Aberdeen home.

I was born in December of 1946, nine months after my father's return from Okinawa, where he served during World War II. He and my mother had married shortly before he left for overseas service, but they barely had time to really get to know one another. When the war ended, they were eager to start their life together in earnest. I like to think of myself as part of that eagerness.

I was reluctant to emerge into the midst of an Idaho winter, and fought hard to remain where I was. Later, when sharing a bedroom with four brothers, I would delight in making a "punny" statement about it being the last time I would ever have a womb of my own.

It was less than a week before Christmas and Santa Claus didn't even know about me. I wanted to wait and give the old elf more time to plan for my first Christmas. My mother was a strong and stubborn woman, however, and though I held out from the onset of labor on the fifteenth until nearly dawn on the nineteenth, she eventually won the battle and there I was.

I waited anxiously for some relief from the noise and irritating lights of the hospital nursery. I was happy to finally leave the small hospital in American Falls and travel to the less conspicuous side of the Snake River—to Aberdeen.

My parents seemed happy that I was there. They lived in a small rented house at the edge of town. It was near the highway leading southward toward American Falls. They had fixed it up nicely, turning it into a cute little home for our small family. Of course, it had some drawbacks as well.

Mom had to cook on a stove in the basement whenever her hot plate wasn't sufficient for meal preparation. The house did not have an indoor toilet. My parents had to go to a small structure in the back to satisfy those most basic needs. Neither problem affected me, however, for I had yet to experience my mother's cooking. I had no use for an outhouse either, for I learned that if I had to go, I could just go, wherever I happened to be. Mom was always there to make me fresh and lovable again.

The cute little home on the south highway was not to remain my home for long. My father tried valiantly to scrape out a meager living for his small family. He worked first as a plasterer, but a plasterer was in no danger of becoming wealthy in a stagnant farm town. He also worked in a Utoco (Utah Oil Company) service station, and made many friends. However, a poor economy forced dreams of better things and he finally moved the family to Spanish Fork, Utah.

Dad bought a brand new home, and began working in a steel plant. He and Mom were doing well, and even added another son to the family. My brother Mike was born in January of 1949. As I got older, I enjoyed the outdoors, though I was a bit restricted by the tether that kept me attached to the clothesline in the yard. I even learned how to use the new telephone. I could call my Grandpa Jack, Dad's stepfather, all by myself and listen to him laugh as I counted to ten and then sang my special rendition of *You Are My Sunshine*.

Life was good for a time, but it became apparent that the job at the steel plant would not last. My parents saw the writing on the wall, and sold the new home. Dad got another job, and we moved to the Tooele Ordnance Depot (TOD) west of Salt Lake City, where we lived in a small housing unit.

My brother, Mike, was just a baby and offered little as a playmate. Perhaps that is why I got bored and looked for excitement elsewhere. Mom tried to keep me occupied by buying a *Little Golden Book* for me each time we went to the store, but that wasn't enough. I needed more.

Dad built a fence in the back yard to try and keep me in. However, it posed no major problem for my secret "Houdini skills" and I easily escaped. Usually, I was soon found and reunited with my mother. But once I stayed away too long. My parents were frantic, and even had the police searching for me. I could not understand the chaos that ensued when they located me down by the tracks, throwing rocks at the passing trains. I did not know why they were so upset. I was not lost! I knew where I was the entire time! But the incident frightened my parents enough to influence one of their life decisions. They decided to move again!

In 1950, Mom's brother, Uncle Gordon, drove an old red Dodge truck from Idaho to TOD Park and helped Mom and Dad load up the family's meager belongings. We were returning to Idaho. But this time, things would be different. Dad was to run the farming operation of my mother's stepfather, Grandpa Frank. It was a permanent job, and offered the promise of a permanent home on one of Grandpa's three farms.

Once again, we were in Aberdeen!

2

Aberdeen

Aberdeen, Idaho, in the 1950 census, managed to muster a grand total of 1,486 residents, but only by counting the farmers. Farming was the mainstay of the Aberdeen economy and farms dotted the landscape, from the Bingham County line south of town to the village of Grandview several miles to the north. The east and west borders were natural ones, provided by the Snake River to the east and barren lava beds to the west.

Aberdeen was a small town, even by Idaho standards, and subject to the same jokes about its size as were thousands of other small towns. Residents shared these humorous exchanges, but were quick to anger when they heard such attempts from outsiders. There were few such incidents, however, for very few outsiders ever **found** Aberdeen.

The main line of traffic across the state could be found on the highway that connected Twin Falls and Pocatello, and that highway was on the opposite side of the river from Aberdeen. The only outsiders that found Aberdeen either had relatives living there or they were pheasant hunters from Pocatello that got lost on their way to Pleasant Valley. And **they** only came during the open pheasant season in October.

We used to joke about the "Entering Aberdeen" signs being on opposite sides of the same signpost. They weren't really, but the joke always got a laugh from someone, usually the teller. To be honest, the signs were more than four blocks apart, and on opposite sides of Main Street.

Between those signs was the city center, consisting of several business establishments. Among those businesses were the Rexall Drug Store; Landvatter Motors; an IGA grocery store; First Security Bank of Idaho; the Valley Store; the People's Store; Wiebe's Clothing Store and a blacksmith shop. There was also the Idaho Power Company (with it's cute little logo of Reddy Kilowatt), the post office, Aberdeen Hardware, Tarpeel's Utoco station and the Aberdeen-Springfield Canal Company. The Rainbow Bar and another pool hall with no name were also on Main Street.

For serious medical care, Aberdeen residents had to travel to American Falls, where they had a small hospital, Schiltz Memorial, and a doctor or two. American Falls also had the only mortuary in the area, snugly nestled in the rear of the store at Davis Furniture & Mortuary.

Of course, there were other business establishments in Aberdeen, but they were on side streets, concealed from the rest of the world. Those streets had names, but since most streets were not posted, no one knew the names, with the possible exception of Mrs. Kidd, the town librarian.

Aberdeen did have one claim to fame. For as long as I can remember, there was a story circulating about how Aberdeen was once mentioned in a *Ripley's Believe It Or Not* column because of its churches. There were supposedly twenty-seven different religious congregations in Aberdeen. I never could figure out **all** of them, but I could rattle off most of them if asked. Had the meager populace been evenly distributed, there would have been about fifty-five people per church, but there was **not** an even distribution. The majority of the townspeople were divided among the Presbyterians, the Methodists, the Mennonites, the Mormons, the Catholics, the Assemblies of God, and the Lutherans. Those groups all had their own meetinghouses. The Mormons had two.

There were many smaller groups that met in warehouses, stores, or even in private homes. There were the Friends, the Seventh-Day

Adventists, the Plymouth Brethren, and others that had no names as far as I know. I was always very proud of the religious distinction that set us apart from the other towns in the area.

Our new home was a magical place for me. There were eighty acres of running room, barns, sheds, a chicken coop, a granary filled with pigeons, and a huge yard. There was another house on the property, located across the driveway. It was used to house seasonal workers who helped with my grandfather's farm. My parents called it "the shack."

I was not yet of school age, but kept very busy. I spent my days exploring, riding my imaginary horse, Thunderhoof, and teaching my chubby little brother how to push me up and down the driveway in our bright red Radio Flyer. It was the finest red wagon available. I would steer with the handle, using it as a tiller as Mike pushed from the rear, constantly questioning me about when his turn to ride might begin. I rode most because I was the oldest.

Mike still wore diapers and cried for his pillow. In fact, the small pillow was always with him, except for the times when Mom would wash the "kid crud" out of it and hang it on the clothesline in the front yard. Mike would scream and cry and try desperately to reach the pillow, but could never quite reach that high. I took great delight in the knowledge that he could have stood on the wagon and retrieved the pillow easily, but he was unable to see such an easy solution to his problem. And I was **not** about to help.

The rose bushes across the back of the house were covered with yellow blossoms. They were nice enough, I guess, but the real treats were the bees they attracted. Mike and I picked them off the blossoms by their wings, placed them in Mason jars and kept them in our bedrooms until they died. It was a long time before we learned the secret of punching holes in the lids to give them air—and even **that** didn't work most of the time.

The holes were not a very popular idea with my mother either. She could never seem to understand that jams, jellies, fruits, etc. were rather boring contents for bottles that might best be utilized for bees, dragonflies, butterflies, and any number of other interesting bugs. Even frogs were better than raspberry jam!

My dad had hung an old tire from a big tree in the yard for us to play on. He tried his best to keep our play restricted to the yard, afraid that we might fall into an irrigation ditch or even worse. But we were not to be denied. I dragged poor Mike and his moldy old pillow from one end of the farm to the other. My mother was constantly retrieving us—not an easy task, for she had another baby, my sister Rebecca.

Becky was a girl, and therefore not at all interesting to Mike and me.

3

The Cow Toss

When I was very small, I longed to accompany my father as he did various tasks around the farm. He would have none of it, though, not wanting to have the additional task of keeping me in line while trying to do his work. However, there was a very special day when he announced that I would be permitted to accompany him as he fed the cows. I was excited! I was frightened of the huge beasts, but knew that the rail fencing would keep them in their place as I tagged along behind my dad.

I struggled to tear off sections from the hay bales as my father cut the twine and called the cows. He called each of them by name and they poked their massive heads between the slats on the feeding troughs. I scrambled to hoist the hay into the trough, trying desperately to prove to Dad that I was a valuable asset to have in the barnyard. He laughed as he watched me, but it was in no way derisive. He just enjoyed the fact that I was trying so hard.

"Come on, Daisy. Come Chloe. Here Mabel." Each cow in her turn stepped into place and began to munch on the hay. I was very conscious of just how close they were, and tried to hang back a bit as I filled the trough.

"They won't hurt you, Stevie. They're big, but they are just as tame as can be!" I believed him. I really did. But these animals had great big eyes that didn't look very friendly. They also had a very disconcerting habit of poking that very large tongue into each nostril, first one side, then the other, then back to the first. Mom would have had a fit. She was always scolding Mike when **he** tried to do that!

We watched the cows eat for a few minutes and Dad told me how to tell each of the cows by name. Daisy had a black eye and a white eye. Mabel's head was all black. Chloe was the biggest and had a blue tag on her ear. Frieda was different than the others. She wasn't black and white at all. She was kind of a golden brown, like the one on Becky's bib.

When Dad rose from the bale of hay he'd been sitting on and began to stretch, I knew it was time to leave. So I started for the end of the haystack, back the way we had come. But Dad called me back and said we would climb through the rails and cross the corral. He crossed through and then reached over and lifted me across. I hung onto his neck for dear life. I did not want to be in the same place as the cows and I was terrified. Dad just laughed as he broke my death-grip and set me down beside him.

"Look," he said. "They are eating and won't hurt you."

I was dubious, but I clutched his hand as we started across the corral toward the corner closest to the lane that led back to the house. I kept looking back at the cows. At first they seemed to be occupied with the hay, but then Chloe pulled her head out from between the slats and swung it in our direction. Then she started to come toward us. I tried to pull away and run, but Dad held on and laughed, "You're OK. Take it easy!"

I know now that Chloe loved my Dad and must have been very nervous about my taking so much of his attention. She came up behind me quickly and, the next thing I knew, I was flying through the air. I landed in a bed of straw nearly ten feet away and immediately began crying. Dad lifted me up, checked me over, and then started to laugh again, which only made me cry all the harder. Then he slapped Chloe on the rump and she took off back toward the other, better behaved animals.

As we made our way down the lane to the house, my mother heard my wailing and emerged from the house to investigate. I quit crying as Dad began to tell her what had happened. He was still laughing, and now Mom was smiling, too. I needed to set them straight. I tried to give them a more accurate version of what had transpired. I was excited and animated as I covered the whole story from my point of view. By the time I finished, both of them were in stitches. I did not understand. **They** did not understand! Chloe had tried to kill their son and they were laughing!

My mother would write of this incident in her journal. But her account held nothing about the imminent danger I had been subjected to, nor did she exhibit any sympathy for me whatsoever. Her account seemed to dwell on the fact that I could not yet make an "r" sound, and had closed my description of the adventure by saying, "I went wound and wound like a fewwis wheel!"

4

The Circus

To the casual observer, Aberdeen was just a sleepy little farm town. But there were some very special occasions that increased the level of excitement to dizzying heights. One such event was the traveling circus that came to town every year. It was not a regularly scheduled thing by any means, but always seemed to show up when it was needed the most.

I guess that by most standards, these circuses were small. But to the Stoker boys, they were the things that dreams were made of. And Mike and I were blessed with one additional advantage. We lived just a couple of hundred feet down the road from the "rodeo grounds," and that was always where the circus would set up.

The circus folks usually avoided the "townies" and kept to their own little world, just setting up tents and booths, and putting on a couple of shows before tearing everything down again and moving on to the next town on their circuit. They usually didn't even visit town, choosing instead to sleep in their trailers and eat at a huge cook tent at the edge of the midway entrance.

There was, however, one very important variation to this routine. There were many animals, from horses to elephants, that needed to eat. The circus was not equipped to carry much feed for these animals and so, was faced with getting it along the way. Because of the close proximity of our farm, they came to my dad to purchase hay and grain. As they would wheel and deal with Dad, they would befriend the two big-eyed kids that stared at them from the side—Mike and me! And, more often than not, they offered free passes to the show in the big tent. Dad would accept them on our behalf and Mike and I would run off into the yard and plan for the big event.

There was another advantage, too. We would often walk back to the rodeo grounds with the animal keepers, sometimes even using our own well-worn Radio Flyer, making several trips in order to transport food for the animals. That was hard work, but worth it when the show folks would treat us as if we were show folks, too. We'd stand in awe and watch as they all did their part to pull the whole thing together. Each had so much to do! And we could hardly wait until show time.

Dad always let us go to the show but would never give us money for side shows. He always called them "gyp joints," and said they were always filled with gimmicks designed to separate stupid kids from their money. He was so adamant about our staying away from the gyp joints that Mike and I never even considered going against his wishes. Except for once!

Mike and I were amazed at the huge banner over one of the side tents one year. It had an amazing painting of a two-headed boy. We stared at it for the longest time and then, when we returned home, we hid in the granary and made plans to defy my father's wishes.

The only solution I could see—the only way to get both of us into the tent to see the two-headed boy—was to do something that I knew in my heart was absolutely horrible. I sneaked into the house with Mike and while he watched the door, I climbed up on a chair in the kitchen and reached the clear glass piggy bank that my Aunt Kathleen had given me for my birthday.

I knew there was almost forty cents in it, cause Grandpa Frank gave me a quarter the same night I got the bank. And he had given me two nickels since—one for spotting a pheasant from his old DeSoto as we drove over to Uncle Bill's house, and the other for keeping quiet about the bottle he kept in under the canvas in the back corner of his garage. There were also some pennies that Mom had put in there when she came back from the store.

We carefully transported the bank out to the granary and used a lava rock to break it open. Mike and I counted the money several times. I had been wrong. There were sixty-seven cents—a small fortune. We were going to have a very good time. We already had passes for the main show, and the "freak show" only cost fifteen cents apiece. That would leave thirty-seven cents for cotton candy and maybe even a cup of ice cold *76* soda pop!

The day of the show came and Mike and I hustled across the road, passes in hand. I had wrapped my coins in a hankie so Mom and Dad wouldn't hear them. We went straight to the side tent and paid our money to a tall guy with whiskers and bad case of booze-breath, and went into the dark tent. There, under a lighted table, far back from the retaining rope, was a large jar with something in it. It looked very strange, and there **were** two heads, but it looked more like a sheep than a boy. We stayed there for the longest time. Then Mike looked at me and said, "gyp joint?" I just nodded and we left for the main show so as not to miss the opening parade.

We had a good time, and we ate cotton candy and had sodas. When we returned home that afternoon, I still had seven cents burning a hole in my pocket. I guess it was burning one in my face, too, because I knew by the expression on Mom's face that she had discovered the fact that my bank was no more.

When Dad got home, I got spanked. Mike didn't get spanked because I was supposed to be taking care of him. I was the oldest! The spanking wasn't a bad one at all. In fact, I considered it worth the crime. But the worst was yet to come. The next day, as we met Aunt Kathleen in the church foyer prior to church, my Mom made me tell her about breaking the bank she had given me for my birthday. Aunt Kathleen never gave me another birthday present.

5

There Is Good In Good-bye

The same people always occupied the small house on the other side of the driveway from ours, but seldom for long. Grandpa Frank offered it to the transient labor people who worked for him during the various seasons. In the summer, there was usually a family of Navajo Indians, sometimes even more than just a single family. They would come from New Mexico or Arizona during the summer to thin beets.

There were usually a lot of children with them, and Grandpa Frank would not allow anyone under twelve years of age to work in the fields. Therefore, there were always lots of kids around the house. Mike and I took full advantage and played with them from sunup till dark. It did not matter that they seldom could speak English. We could always make ourselves understood.

The beautiful turquoise bracelets and necklaces the Navajo women wore fascinated me. And the brightly colored velvet outfits were just as impressive. I always wished my own parents had shiny clothes but, except for the seat of Dad's suit pants, it never happened.

I loved to watch Grandpa negotiate with these folks. I do not know if he could speak Navajo for real, but I was impressed by his ability to grunt and gesticulate along with the best of them. He would always come away with a scowl on his face, but eyes that smiled his satisfaction with whatever had transpired.

Every season, Grandpa would present the occupants of the labor house with a sheep or two to slaughter. It was considered a great honor to receive such a gift and it was always done with a great deal of ceremony. Mike and I would go out to the east pasture and stand by as they butchered and divided the hapless animals. It was a gory sight and we were held spellbound through the entire process. Nothing was wasted. The Indians had a purpose for every part of the animal, and even spent days afterward processing the hides until they were dried, stretched, tanned, and chewed into a finely textured lambskin.

Sometimes, when Mexicans occupied the house, Grandpa would give them a sheep as well, but he always seemed aggravated at them, for they would take but a small portion of the beast and leave the rest for the dogs or magpies to scatter around the pasture. Grandpa never said anything directly, but I could tell that he admired the Navajo people for their frugality.

There was a very special couple that lived in the house for nearly two years. They were Mexican and, though they had no children, they had a very smart cocker spaniel. That dog was a constant source of entertainment for Mike and me. We played with it often, and even hitched it to our wagon on more than one occasion. Goldie, as she was called, tolerated just about everything we could think of to include her in our play, but began to get fat and nasty tempered. Soon, she just stayed in the house and we were not even allowed to see her for several days. One day, the lady motioned for both of us to come over and, as we looked on, she removed a burlap potato sack from an old tire near the incinerator barrel at the far corner of their yard and revealed five small puppies.

Goldie had become a mommy. As she lay there suckling the pups, I thought that I would burst with wanting a puppy so badly. So I asked for one. I was told that they were much too small to leave their mother. I was devastated. I went home and told mom about the pups and she tried to explain why I could not have one. For the next few days I talked of nothing else. I must have driven the poor lady crazy asking about when the pups would be weaned, for she began to duck into the house if she saw me coming.

One day, during dinner, there was a knock at the door and they were there to say good-bye. They were moving to Wyoming, and I hadn't even known. I left the table and hurried across the lane to say good-bye to the dogs as they chatted with Mom and Dad. But the dogs were nowhere to be found! I raced around the house, searching frantically for some sign of the puppies, expecting to see them romping toward me at any moment. I even checked to see if they had been locked in the outhouse, but it was empty. I searched everywhere I could think of. But they were gone!

I started back to my side of the lane and heard a bark. It was Goldie! She had been packed into the old Studebaker with several boxes and suitcases and she was frantic, trying to get someone's attention. I put my face up against the glass and peered in, hoping to see the pups, but they weren't there. My throat hurt and I could feel the tears welling in my eyes as I re-entered the house. I even let the screen door slam, hoping Mom would say something so that I could unload about my loss. But she just kept talking. I pushed by the grownups and went to the room I shared with Mike. I threw myself onto the lower bunk and started to cry—as quietly as I could, because I did not want to talk to anyone.

I was still there when I heard the Studebaker start up and chug out of the driveway, belching smoke like it always did. A few minutes later, Mom called me and I went to join the rest of the family so we could finish dinner. I told Mom that I didn't want any more to eat. I think she knew I was disappointed.

"It's too bad they had to go, Steve." Mom hesitated, then went on. "They have been very good friends. But Pete got a much better job and they have to move far away. They will write to us and tell us how they are doing."

I looked into Mom's face and could see that she just didn't understand. I had just decided to force myself to gulp down another spoonful of peas when Mom spoke again.

"I know what will make you feel better! How about some peaches for dessert? Steve, will you go in the back room and get a jar of peaches? Get one of the two-quart jars. We'll have big bowls tonight—with cream!"

I loved Mom's canned peaches, and I even thought that they might ease the pain. I went out to the mudroom at the back of the kitchen where the canned goods were stored neatly on their shelves. The room always smelled like sheep, though, 'cause that's where Dad hung his coveralls before he came into the house.

I pulled down a big jar of peaches from a shelf that was about a head higher than I when I felt something rub against my leg. In fact, I was so startled that I almost dropped the peaches, but Mom was there to grab them. Dad and Mike were there, too. They were all smiling at me as I recognized the little black spaniel puppy that was trying to climb up my leg. All my misery disappeared as I realized that, when they had given away Goldie's pups, they had saved the very best for me.

I felt like the luckiest kid in the world. In fact, that's what inspired me to name my new dog—Lucky!

6

Our Country Kitchen

Mealtimes in our humble country kitchen were always an event. My mom worked hard to make certain we children were provided the best possible diets. As her eldest, I felt compelled to resist her at every turn.

I learned at a very early age that my mom would do all she could to ruin my meat and potatoes with other, less desirable items that she called vegetables. Now I know that a potato is technically a vegetable, but we did not call it that. It just didn't fit. Potatoes tasted good! They were called spuds—a harmless enough term. But "vegetables" were to be avoided at all costs. They did horrendous things to the taste buds and could not be tolerated.

First, there were peas. These things were always grown in our garden and in Grandma's garden, and as near as I could tell, had only one useful purpose. They gave everyone something to do with their hands as they gossiped about everything on Grandma's back porch. Even the kids would participate in stripping the little green balls from the pods they grew in. You could turn a huge bowl of pods into a few peas that would barely cover the bottom of a second bowl. My two uncles, Dean and Dwight, would munch on them raw. These guys needed help. Peas were not fit to eat—especially raw ones!

There were also green beans. Those things didn't even warrant the same attention the peas got. They weren't even extricated from their pods. They were just broken into little sections about an inch long and cooked right in the pod. This made no sense to me, for both vegetables, even when cooked, had no redeeming value. Instead, they gave me the impression that I was trying to choke down a group of tiny sandbags. I truly hated them. The only thing worse were tomatoes!

Tomatoes were the terrible things that destroyed good soups and stews. They consisted of a slimy pulp that triggered the gag reflex of every self-respecting young lad. It was especially puzzling for one trying to understand why his mother could not seem to master the culinary arts to the satisfaction of her children.

Thankfully, my mom would make my helpings of these ghastly articles as small as she could reasonably make them, and with extra milk, I could normally coax them past my taste buds rapidly enough to avoid the misery. But sometimes, Dad would get angry and make me sit until I ate every item on my plate. And if I balked at the "veggies", he would only add more and make me sit until they were eaten. And the worst thing—he made me chew and swallow, without the normal milk wash.

Milk was my friend. I loved it. It was raw and refreshing, having been removed from our cows the night before and cooled in the refrigerator. In the morning the cream was skimmed from the top and kept in a separate bowl for special things. The milk was then ready to drink. And I drank it. Lots of it. It was the only thing I can remember that I could have any time I wanted it. All I had to do was ask mom and there was a cold glass right there.

After meals, I would sit at the table with Mike while Mom cleared the table and washed dishes. We would laugh at Becky, sitting in her high chair and taking forever to eat. She always got more food on the floor and in her hair than she got into her mouth, and Mike and I took delight in every aspect of the mess she made.

One day, after lunch, I was looking out the kitchen window and saw Grandpa Frank carrying his shovel along the ditch bank out by the beet field. I thought he was standing there talking with someone and asked my mother who Grandpa was talking to. She looked out the window and then got a funny look on her face. Then she asked me to look again and say who I thought it might be. I told her that I did not know the man.

The next day, Mom took me on a trip to Pocatello and my eyes were examined. At the tender age of five years, I got my first eyeglasses. All because I didn't recognize the fence post near my grandfather as he irrigated the sugar beets!

7

Grandma's House

Visits to Grandma's house were frequent and fun. Her house was atop a hill on 40 acres to the north of Aberdeen, just outside the city limit. It was an enormous house, especially to a little boy.

There were three rooms upstairs that were shared by my aunts—Ann, Nancy, and Kathleen. I was not supposed to go up there at all, but I did. My Uncle Dwight was nine months older than I, and we always managed to do whatever we were not supposed to do. We could never seem to sneak up the stairs for long without being discovered. It always seemed as if, as soon as we had attained the goal, a scream would ring out, "Mooooooom. The brats are in my room. Moooooommm!" And Grandma would appear at the foot of the stairs and order us to retreat to the basement. It was always a kind order, but firm enough so we knew that compliance was not a matter of choice.

We would slink to the basement, where the boys slept, and harass Uncle Phillip or Uncle Dean. Neither of them called for Grandma when they found us in their private realms, but instead, took matters into their own hands. They physically removed us before we could break their model airplanes and cars or mess up their beds with our rambunctious play.

Sometimes, when Phillip and Dean were in the right frame of mind and their tolerance level was high, they would let us sit and watch as they piloted their Lionel trains. Dwight and I watched as the trains chugged their way around the huge plywood city that occupied a large table near the endless shelves of canned fruits and vegetables behind the furnace. More often, though, we would play outside, and what a wonderful place it was!

The house was surrounded on three sides by beautiful lawn. The back of the house was even better, an immense garden, where we could go and sneak a snack whenever we chose. There were dozens of mature apple trees at the north end of the garden, separated from the rows and rows of vegetables by dozens of raspberry bushes. On the north side of the house, across the lawn, stood a well-stocked chicken coop and a playhouse for the girls. To the east of that were many more apple trees, some crabapple, and a swing that was hung from a large bar of steel wedged between two of the trees. There was another "monkey bar" nearby that served as a jumping off point when we climbed into the trees to sit and eat green apples.

At the far end of the orchard was the garage. The lawn in front of the house and to the south made a huge L-shaped playground, bordered by trees and purple lilac bushes that were so fragrant when they bloomed that it would make the eyes water. These two sides of the house had porches, too. In front, a small enclosed porch containing a hammock that Uncle Gordon had brought back from the Navy, and on the south side, a long, rambling porch covered with lattice work and flowers.

It was in this beautiful setting, that I learned how to play croquet, tag, baseball and a myriad of other games over the years. Just a short walk down the gravel road toward town was the slough, a large, deep man-made creek that served as a drainage ditch for all the farms in the area. Next to the road was an artesian well that spewed its cold, delicious water into the slough every minute of every hour of every day. It was merely an open 8-inch pipe, without even a valve, and its supply of water was infinite, as far as I knew.

Dwight and I would often walk along the slough and hunt for frogs and tadpoles, and sometimes, in season, we would cut cattails from the banks and take them home to Grandma's house, where we would use crayons to decorate them. They were always received with excitement by our parents and displayed for weeks afterward, but I never knew if there was any practical purpose for these objects of artistic expression.

The frogs we collected were, unlike the cattails, very useful. They could be used for jumping contests, races, and on very special occasions, for getting back at Uncle Dwight's older sisters when they aggravated us too much. We became very adept at sneaking up near the top of the stairs and "planting" a frog or two in Nancy and Ann's underwear drawers. We were never there to see the looks on their faces when they came across these gentle little amphibians, but the effect was global, and therefore just as entertaining. There was great deal of personal satisfaction in hearing them bounding down the stairs yelling, "Mooooooommm!" We just couldn't help but giggle!

When I was five, Dwight started school and my trips to Grandma's house became very boring unless they were after school or on the weekends. All I could do during those school-day visits was sit in Grandma's kitchen and listen to grownup talk. Boring. But there was a bright spot in this dim picture. Grandma always had fresh bread, scones, pies, and cakes to keep young hands occupied and young mouths quiet. And the cookies! And the fudge! There were many terrific smells in that kitchen. In a way, it was the hub of my small universe and I can close my eyes, even now, and almost smell the odors permeating Grandma's kitchen!

8

The School Bus

As summer came to a close during autumn of 1952, I finally was allowed to start school. Aberdeen did not have a kindergarten program. It may have been too expensive a luxury—I don't know. But I like to think an overwhelming majority of its citizens believed that kids need time to be kids before they are shuttled off to classes.

Even before I reached my first grade class, I could barely contain my excitement. I would finally get the opportunity to ride the school bus. It seemed as though I had watched it speed by the front of our house forever, never stopping. It fascinated me. I thought it would be so neat to ride through the countryside with a busload of kids. I was right.

My bus driver was Reverend Luke from the Methodist church. He was a roly-poly little man with a permanent smile etched into his red face as though it were painted there. He had a soft voice that he never raised to the kids, even when he had reason. And he had plenty of reason. Every time he finished his morning run, there were bus seats piled in the back of the bus and empty seat frames everywhere one looked. He must have been irritated at having to reassemble the seats every time he returned to the bus yard.

The route for Bus #4 was in two parts. The first part was south on the main highway toward American Falls, then west on the airport road, south to Death Corner, and then back to town on the highway. After dropping off a full busload at school, the empty bus would start its second leg. It would go east on Beach Road all the way to the lake, then backtrack to the city dump, where it would turn north to the Kendall farm, then west past the cemetery and back into town past the water tower and the grain elevators.

I was the very first pickup on the second leg, so I had the middle seat at the end of the aisle at the very back of the bus. It connected the two window seats and had no seat in front of it, only the aisle. There was a very important reason to get that particular seat, for as the bus did its backtrack on Beach Road, Bobby Litten and I would pop the seats loose from other frames and put them at least three high in the back. This was done in preparation for the mile stretch between the dump and Kendall's farm. The roads were of gravel, but that particular stretch had three "thrill hills" that were a result of lava ridges that had not been blasted away. They were considered safe enough for cars to traverse, but with a bus, especially a bus on a tight schedule, they were better than a Disneyland ride.

We approached the hills, knowing full well that we in the back of the bus would be thrown aimlessly into space. The anticipation was almost more than we could take. The ultimate goal was to bump our heads on the bus ceiling, and we were seldom disappointed. This morning ritual went on day after day for the longest time.

I was in third grade and still doing the "thrill hill" bit when Kathy Pershing had her lip cut open by a flying first grader. The school authorities, alarmed at the sight of blood, warned Reverend Luke about his driving. He slowed down and the fun ended. Only then did I realize that the good reverend had been participating as much as the rest of us. From that time on, every time we came to the "thrill hill," and the kids clamored for more speed, he lifted his foot from the accelerator and his ever-present smile disappeared for just a flicker of a moment.

9

First Grade

Aberdeen Grade School was a remarkable piece of architecture. It was the tallest building in town, with three stories. It was an old building of red brick, and its greatest features were the two fire escapes. Those fire escapes were a remarkable work of engineering. They were steel tubes, oval in shape, and they angled from the third floor, across the face of the building to the ground.

During fire drills, everyone on the second and third floors would slide to the ground on the outside of the building. It was a fast and extremely efficient way to empty the building quickly. And the ride was better than all the playground equipment put together. However, during the normal school day, only the third and fourth graders were permitted to exit the building that way for recess. The younger children were not permitted to use them. Perhaps that is why the younger children were always assigned rooms on the first floor or in the basement.

Mrs. Lancaster's room was on the southwest corner of the first floor. It had its own hallway, where coats were hung and lunches were stored on shelves at the end of the hall. And just in front of the shelves, a huge grating stretched the width of the hall. It was a return for the ventilation system and would become very significant to me when I reached fourth grade.

I had the third hook from the door and would hang my coat and, later in the season, my snow boots (Mom called them galoshes, but they were boots) from that hook. There was a piece of masking tape with my name above the hook. Another piece of tape marked my spot on the shelf where I would place my pride and joy, a Roy Rogers lunch box with a real thermos. It also had my name on it, painted so large on the outside that it covered up half a mountain and some cactus. My name was also on the inside of the lid. In fact, my whole address was on the inside, though I didn't think it likely that the box would have to be returned to me at some later date by strangers. As it turned out, I left the lunch box with my jacket as I rode the "Ocean Wave" after school a few weeks later and never saw it again. From that time on, I carried a brown paper bag with my lunch in it and my name written on it by my mother. And each bag had to last a week, so I had to fold it and store it in my coat pocket after lunch.

The room where I spent first grade was neat. It had five rows of desks. Each desk had an inkwell that was never used. There was a shelf underneath the desktop where each student would store his supplies. There were snub-nosed scissors, tablet (big lines with a dotted line between), a box of 8 Crayolas (we were not allowed more), a pencil box (mine was a cigar box that Mom tried to disguise as a real pencil box. I hated it!), and our *Dick and Jane* readers.

I sat near the middle of row 2. My desk had lots of neat carvings burned into it that had the names of others who had "owned" that desk in previous years. It was neat to have such a history, but the grooves in the wood were a real problem when they would make my pencil jerk off line while I was trying my best to do neat work for Mrs. Lancaster.

Mrs. Lancaster was beautiful. I thought she was the prettiest woman I had ever seen. And she was so short. It was nice to have a teacher that you could talk to without having to stretch your neck. The only thing she did that bothered me was that she adjusted the blinds—constantly. Because we were on the southwest side, the sunshine through the windows was a constant problem. Each window was equipped with two black blinds, an upper and a lower one. Mrs. Lancaster spent the best part of each day opening and closing all of them, trying desperately to let enough light into the room for the students while not permitting even a hint of glare on any face or desk. I think now that perhaps she was obsessed with those blinds.

As I said, I liked my desk. But I didn't like its location. It was in front of the desk belonging to a girl, Barbara. She was the snobby daughter of the guy who published The Aberdeen Times, our local newspaper that came out every Thursday. Barbara was evil. She was the nastiest person in my class, and she had the whiniest voice I have heard ever. She used to hit me in the back of the head with her pencil. Not just any pencil, but the big, fat pencils that Mrs. Lancaster handed out. It hurt, too. And I wanted to hit her back, but Dad always said never to hit a girl. I tried to get Mrs. Lancaster to stop her, but Barbara always whined "I didn't do anything." I hoped that someday Mrs. Lancaster might see an attack from the corner of her eye as she adjusted blinds, but it was futile. Barbara was never caught in the act!

One day, as I returned to my desk from reading group, I slipped on a crayon and fell against a desk, cutting a half inch gash in my lip and causing me to bleed profusely, much to the enjoyment of the class. The next day, with a face swollen to the size of a football, with stitches to match, I was able to finally convince Mrs. Lancaster to let me move my desk to the front of the first row. After all, the evil Barbara was the owner of that well-planted crayon.

10

Second Grade

My first day in second grade brought some very rude awakenings. The most important of these was a major difference in my teachers. Mrs. Lancaster had been one of the most beautiful, nicest, and kindest people I knew. Mrs. Manford, my new teacher was mean. She wore all black. Always. And she had black hair pulled tightly into a bun on the back of her head and held there with black netting and something that looked like my grandma's knitting needles. She had piercing dark eyes—unkind eyes that, when focused in my direction, made me want to run. Her face was out of place anywhere but in a Halloween poster. Her manner was one that gave the impression that just beneath the surface lay a serial child killer.

Another major change for me was that now my schoolroom was in the basement. We still had windows, but they opened to concrete wells outside and little light filtered down into the room, especially since now we were on the east side of the building. We might have had morning sun for awhile, but that was blocked by the shadow of the fire escape just above our window wells. All in all, the room was like a dungeon, and Mrs. Manford was our dungeon keeper.

There was a drinking fountain in the back of our room, but the teacher would not permit us to use it. It was just there, making us aware of how thirsty we were. But Mrs. Manford said we were given recess for drinking and going to the bathroom and it would not be done during class time.

There was also an allotment of playground toys, mainly large rubber balls, about the size of a basketball and used to play "keep-away." Every class in school had these supplies and the balls were marked clearly with room numbers. I don't think anyone ever saw the ones with "Room 4" on the playground, for Mrs. Manford did not believe recess was for playing ball. It was for drinking and going to the bathroom.

My best friend, Lester Larkin, had the unenviable position of having his desk in the left front of the class, right next to the teacher's desk. She could reach across her desk with her pointer and hit him on the hands or head any time she felt like it. And she felt like it often. My desk was in the right rear of the class, nearest the door. She had separated Lester and me as much as she could. I was lucky, though, for it was not as easy for her to reach me with the dreaded pointer.

There was a time, however, when I was victimized. Mrs. Manford had been called to the principal's office and the class was left alone. Lester quickly seized the opportunity and wrested one of the dusty rubber balls from the top shelf behind the desk. He hollered "Heads up!" and threw the ball clear across the room at me. I caught it and threw it back, much to the delight of the class. They began to laugh and giggle, egging us on to greater glory.

We passed the ball back and forth several times, showing off the best we could. We were the center of attention, demonstrating our bravery by defying the class rules that had been so rigidly adhered to in the past. Just as I made a truly impressive catch and was about to return it to the front of the class, a huge shadow loomed behind me just as Lester slipped back into his seat.

Mrs. Manford had returned! She leapt in through the door and grabbed my arm, her grip stopping all blood circulation in my arm. It would have made no difference. I think my heart had stopped anyway.

I was lifted from the floor and dragged to the front of the class, where she demanded that I place both hands on her desk. I complied, knowing the futility of trying to resist. As the long pointer whistled through its arc toward my hands, I flinched. It only served to make her angrier than ever. Somehow, she stopped the downward motion of the stick and prepared to launch a second attack. She warned me not to flinch again.

I mustered every ounce of will power I had and held still. The end of the stick gave a resounding crack as it struck the desk, but the bulk of the stick raised ugly red welts on my hands. The pain shot up the length of my arms and tears welled up in my eyes. I looked toward Lester and he was smiling. Smiling! The fact that he was enjoying my misery made me so angry! I drew strength from that anger and resolved not to cry and not to show any response at all.

I had been bestowed with incredible courage from some unknown benefactor. I was in control of the situation. I knew it, my classmates knew it, and Mrs. Manford knew it. That knowledge only served to infuriate her more. She struck me a second time. Then a third! I held still and tried as hard as I could to hold my face expressionless.

The fourth blow hit me right across the top of the head. The stick broke into three pieces. The sharp rubber tip bounced between a nearby row of desks. The business end flew over the class and glanced off the chalkboard in the back of the room. The handle remained in the white-knuckled hand of the teacher. She was livid! She was so angry that she shook! She dropped the remainder of the pointer and stormed out of the room. The class was mesmerized. There wasn't a whisper.

Only then did I venture a slow and exploratory investigation of my scalp, rather surprised that there was no blood. It hurt terribly.

In a few moments, Mrs. Manford returned with the principal, and I was removed from the room. I sat for a long time in the principal's outer office and waited till he was ready to see me. He was very solemn, but nice to me, and we discussed the course of events. He examined my hands and my head and lectured me about "proper class behavior."

Then he had me return to my seat in his outer office and sit until lunchtime. When Mrs. Manford finally released the class for lunch and came to the principal's office, I was told to go to lunch.

That afternoon, Mrs. Manford was almost nice. Not quite, but almost! The next morning she announced that we would be allowed to use the class playground equipment for the remaining few weeks of the year. And for the rest of my second grade year, Mrs. Manford never hit anyone again. She didn't even get a new pointer.

During the following summer, my mother, who never knew of the beating, told me that Mrs. Manford had died. She explained that Aberdeen had lost a great teacher. Perhaps! But I did not mourn her!

11

The Junkyard Trip

I had another brother, David, who was born after I started school. My dark-haired little sister and the baby took up most of my mother's time and energy, so Mike and I were permitted to play a lot on our own. We were inseparable. And we longed for an adventure!

During the summer after I finished second grade, we had one. We went on a great excursion! We loaded up the Radio Flyer wagon with food and water that we smuggled from the kitchen when Mom wasn't looking and we set out on our adventure. We went out the driveway onto the thick gravel of Beach Road and headed east.

It was a long way to go, but I had seen the city dump from the school bus day after day, and longed to get a closer look. To me, it was a wealth of treasures that obviously warranted further investigation. I don't think Mike had ever seen it, because he had not yet started school. However, he trusted my judgment and went along willingly, as excited as I was.

The road was difficult and the gravel often made the wagon hard to pull, but we trudged along, undaunted, taking turns pulling the wagon. The large hill just east of Bobby Litten's house forced us to pull in tandem. We huffed and puffed and struggled and finally got the wagon to the top of the hill. From there, we could see the dump and our pace quickened. When we reached the dump and left Beach Road, the going was much easier.

We turned off on a dirt road, packed to almost pavement hardness by years of use. There was a mound of grass growing between the tire tracks, but it was easy to pull the wagon over it as we moved from one track to another, inspecting the treasures along the way.

The lane, lined with sagebrush and lava rock, wound around the rusty, skeletal remains of old cars and farm machinery. There were other, less-used lanes that forked off and circled around huge stashes of debris, only to return to the main thoroughfare a few yards farther down. We stayed on the main path for the most part, except when there was something that diverted our attention.

As we made our way into the depths of the junkyard, we began to accumulate valuable items in the wagon. These were the booty of a successful trek, though I am certain that an adult would see no value in such things. Mike and I discussed various uses, both imaginary and real, for each and every treasure. There were some great cans for storing other treasures in. Hardly any rust on them at all! And the bottles—every shape and size—an absolute necessity for boys who needed to store insects. Especially boys whose mother put so much misguided value on her Mason jars.

There were nuts and bolts and washers and small pieces of farm equipment. All would serve well as other things when properly installed on the dirt pile behind the house where our Tonka trucks hauled dirt and debris from one end of our Tonka world to the other.

I found a toaster that, while it didn't look new, was far shinier than the one Mom used at home. Mike found an old crescent wrench, rusted into one position, but still useful for prying other treasures up. Once or twice, we even managed to loosen real nuts with it. Mike tucked it into his belt and became a cavalry officer, leading a supply train through Indian country. I was the scout, riding ahead and searching for unseen danger.

We had used up our water on the way, but we stopped near a large cedar tree for lunch. It was in the shade and there was a seat from an old car for us to sit on. Mike had made the sandwiches and he was only five, so there was a large clump of butter and jam in the center of each sandwich and nothing at the edges. I broke a branch off the nearest sage and got a stick so I could spread the innards of our sandwiches a bit better. We ate quickly, trying to get more of our lunch than the flies and the yellow jackets. Besides, the smells coming from the center of the dump were not good smells.

Soon after we ate, it was time to start for home. The wagon would hold no more. It had been a fruitful day, but the trip home was not easy. Our load was very heavy and, once we got back onto Beach Road, almost impossible to move over the gravel. It became necessary to carry some of our stuff in our arms. We did manage to get it all home, though, except for the broken rear view mirror from an old DeSoto. The rough ride and shifting load caused its breakage. We were sorely disappointed at its loss, but we went on without it.

When we turned into our driveway, we decided to go straight to the rear of the house and unload. We carried the toaster into the house and presented it to Mom. She accepted it graciously, but seemed more concerned with our having baths immediately, so she could wash our clothes.

When Mike and I emerged from the bathtub, squeaky clean, there was Mom with our pajamas ready for us to put on. We had not even had supper yet, but Mom wasn't about to let us dirty another set of clothes on the same day! We watched Captain Video on TV as Mom hung out the unexpected laundry and then, as she tried to poke strained carrots into David's mouth faster than he spit it onto his bib, we told Mom about our day. She asked us never to go there again, saying that it wasn't safe. We both promised not to, but we both had our fingers crossed behind our backs.

That night, Mom told Dad what had happened and showed him the terrific toaster we had brought for her. Dad looked it over with interest.

He even plugged it in, but nothing happened. When Mom tucked us into bed, she thanked us again for the fine gift, but the next morning it was gone. Our terrific toaster had disappeared during the night!

Dad said that maybe junkyard gremlins came in the night and took it back. Mike believed him, but I didn't. I was seven and a half years old and I was big enough to know that junkyard gremlins couldn't get into our house through the locked doors and windows!

12

Third Grade

Third grade brought several milestones with it. First, I was in Miss Bartholomew's class and it was on the second floor of the school. I was finally permitted to use the fire escape at recess. It was a long-awaited honor, and worth every second of the wait. The thrill of using the fire escapes was everything I had hoped it would be. It was even faster than it looked.

After Mrs. Manford, I had not expected to ever again compare a teacher to a witch, but Miss Bartholomew was the spitting (and I do mean spitting) image of the Wicked Witch of the West in The Wizard of Oz. They might have been twins. Even the hunchbacked walk was identical. But to give credit where credit was due, Miss Bartholomew was a good teacher—hard, but fair. But her "wicked witch" voice and her ability to spray the students as she talked proved quite distracting. There was a paddle hung on a nail at the end of her desk and she talked often of taking students "out behind the woodshed" for a spanking. As far as I know, though, the paddle was never used.

Mike was going to school now, too, and now that I was older, I convinced Mom to let us walk to school instead of riding the bus. That way, I could stop by Lester Larkin's house and walk with him the rest of the way. And if Mike had to tag along, then so be it. We walked straight out our driveway and just kept going, all the way past the Olsens', the Lewis', the Jensens', clear to the Reese's before turning left and going west toward the school, which was on the other side of town.

We had to pass the Nealy Honey Company on the way. It always smelled so good. Sometimes, old Sam Nealy, a tall gruff-looking man with a long beard, would motion us onto his loading dock and we would scramble up the ramp on the end and into the open bay door. As we gathered round the first vat, old Sam would nod his OK and we'd dip our hands into the waxy combs that were being churned up by the wooden paddles. Each of us pulled out the largest piece of honeycomb we could grab. Mr. Nealy would lean back and laugh as we left and continued on to school, sucking the honey off the comb as the stickiness ran from our chins and down our arms and elbows. By the time we reached our destination, we had to go right to the bathroom and wash up or be faced with the prospect of sticky desks, books, and bodies for the entire day.

We always dawdled on the way home, too. No matter how many times Mom told us to hurry home, we always had perfectly legitimate reasons for taking our time, not the least of which was Mrs. Jensen's orchard!

Mrs. Jensen was an elderly lady that lived alone in the house next to the Abercrombies', which was next to the Lewis' home on the corner. We might never have found out about her orchard had we not taken a "short cut" through the alley behind the honey company. It was not a well-traveled alley by any means. It was overgrown with vegetation. In fact, most folks would not even know of its existence, for even the turn off the main street was covered with grass and thistles.

Lester, Mike and I took this route, not because it was a real shortcut to anywhere, but because it was so overgrown that it was like entering a cave with a winding, dark path. Our imaginations ran rampant the first time. When we first saw the fruit-laden boughs hanging across the old wooden fence it was as if reality had decided to join us in our game. Lester and I were "Knights of the Round Table." We were Tom Sawyer and Huck Finn. We were the Hardy Boys. And there before us, in the darkest part of our forest, was a feast.

At first, we were hesitant to partake of the forbidden fruit, but logic told us that what hung outside the property of Mrs. Jensen was fair game. We filled our pockets with green apples and pears. We opened the buttons on our shirts and filled them, too. We had found a gold mine!

We took fruit every day after school as we took our "tunnel through the woods," until all the overhanging branches were stripped of fruit. We weren't aware that we had taken so much. It had seemed like a never-ending supply. Now we had to face a new truth. We had to forget about the fruit or we had venture over into the "forbidden zone," Mrs. Jensen's back yard. We peeked through the dilapidated fence and into the yard. It was as overgrown and ungroomed as the alley itself. It was obvious that Mrs. Jensen could not even **walk** in her orchard, let alone make use of its fruit.

And thus, we justified to ourselves the action we were about to take. We were not thieves, but to harvest unwanted fruit from an ill kept orchard seemed like an honorable thing to do, not theft at all. And so the three of us retrieved an old 50-gallon drum from behind the Lewis' house that had been used as an incinerator. It was rusty, but the bottom would serve as a stepping stone to the top of the fence. We rolled the drum on its side to a point where the back fence could not be seen from Mrs. Jensen's back porch. When turned upside down, the drum made it an easy task to reach the top of the fence. From there, we had but to launch ourselves into the trees.

We could climb through the entire orchard like monkeys, never having to touch the ground. We each found a special perch, where every afternoon we would sit and eat pears and green apples. We had even taken to carrying small Morton salt shakers to school. They were invaluable when eating green apples. Life was grand! It was said that "an apple a day keeps the doctor away" and we were stockpiling weeks and months of perfect health with our after school antics. But our good fortune was not to last.

One day we were high in the apple trees, eating and talking, just as we had so many time before, when our little world turned upside down. The first indication that something had gone awry was when Lester grabbed his left ear and yelped. Something had hit him! Then, as if his yelp was being answered, two large dogs were barking and snarling on the ground below us. They were trying to leap into the trees with us, and as we scrambled to reach the safety of the alley, they leaped at us, snapping and snorting. I am certain that, had any of us fallen, we would have been consumed as if we were green apples.

As we shinnied across branches and scurried toward safety, we were also being bombarded by "shellfire" from Mrs. Jensen. She was standing on her porch, shooting at us. We were terrified! She was a crazy lady! It seemed like forever, but we finally reached the safety of the alley. I had been hit in the rear and so had Lester. Mike hadn't been shot. The dogs began throwing themselves against the fence and were causing quite a furor, so we hurried on toward home.

We said a quick good-bye as Lester ducked into his house and then Mike and I ran the rest of the way home. We checked each other out to see if any bloody wounds needed attention, but all I had to show for my painful gunshot wound was a red spot. We decided we had been attacked with a BB gun.

For several days, we cut through the alley, but upon closer scrutiny, could see Mrs. Jensen, sitting in her rocker on the back porch, her gun at the ready. And her dogs sat expectantly nearby. We elected to stay out of harm's way. A few days later, the fruit was gone. Someone had taken it all. Mrs. Jensen's siege was over. She had won. Her crop had been saved!

13

An Eye for Football

Miss Bartholomew had the largest class in the history of Aberdeen Elementary. There were forty-four students crammed into that classroom. It was like having two classes in one most of the time and with its size came typical problems. One of those problems was a high noise level and Miss Bartholomew sometimes had to resort to desperate measures to maintain order in such a large class.

One day she, like other teachers before her, used the playground equipment as a tool for discipline. She reacted to a particularly rowdy class by suspending equipment privileges over the upcoming lunch hour. Notes were passed around the room about the sudden loss of our football. For several days, we had been playing football at lunch and were not prepared to give it up because of Miss Bartholomew's latest decree.

Plans were made for a covert action as soon as the bell rang for lunch. Gary Ramer was to race for the fire escape, Lester Larkin was to divert Miss Bartholomew's attention, and I was elected to steal the football from the rack beside her desk and toss it out the window to Gary. We were certain the plan would work and Miss Bartholomew would never know. It almost did!

Just before the bell was to ring, Lester approached Miss Bartholomew with his arithmetic assignment. He put on his best 'Dennis the Menace' face and pleaded for help as only Lester could plead. Miss Bartholomew fell for the ploy—hook, line and sinker! She was not about to pass up an opportunity to tutor Lester. Such chances were rare indeed! So she set about to make the best of the moment. Just as she had him sit down at her desk, the bell rang. She didn't even look up. I was home free!

I grabbed the football undetected, held it to my side with a perfect NFL quality fake, and moved quickly to the window in back of the room. One glance and I could see that Gary was waiting, hands apart and ready. I tossed the ball out the window and turned quickly away, trying to look as innocent as possible as I joined the stragglers who were heading for the door. It had worked!

I gave Lester a "thumbs up" signal as I passed behind Miss Bartholomew and then waited for him in the hall by the drinking fountain. He soon joined me and, with the help of the fire escape, we were soon on the playground, looking for Gary. He was nowhere to be found!

There must have been ten or twelve of us searching for Gary Ramer. All of us had arrived late and neither he nor the football had been seen. We were very puzzled. And when Mrs. Boatman came and asked me to report to the principal's office, I was even more puzzled.

As I sat in the principal's waiting area, Lester passed by several times in the hall, peering into see what was happening. He was as curious as I to find out what was happening. We were completely in the dark and it was not a good feeling. Finally, Mr. Nelson's door opened and out came Miss Bartholomew, followed by a sniffling Gary Ramer, whose dirty face had been marked by tears—tears that streamed from the blackest, most swollen eye I had ever seen!

Mr. Nelson, who had followed the others from the inner sanctum, instructed Miss Bartholomew to call Gary's parents and have them pick up Gary. And to provide a school insurance form for them to use when they took Gary to American Falls to see Dr. Harms. Then he focused his attention on me. And he did not look friendly!

I sat in Mr. Nelson's office for the rest of the lunch period and into the next class period. I listened quietly as he screamed at me about maturity, responsibility, safety, and stupidity. I had tried, early in the meeting, to explain Gary's part in the plan, but Mr. Nelson did not care to hear any explanations. There were no excuses! I had thrown the football from an upper floor window and it had hit Gary in the eye! There were no excuses! Not a word about how stupid it was to get hit by a football that he saw coming at him! There were no excuses! Not a word about how he had been part of the plan from the beginning! There were no excuses! Not a word about how he ratted on a classmate when he could have reported his injury without revealing its cause. There were no excuses!

By the time Mr. Nelson was finished with his tirade, I had lost my playground privileges for two weeks. Instead of spending recess with my friends, I had to walk with the teacher who had playground duty. I could not even play. It just wasn't fair!

As I walked home that afternoon with Lester, we made a pact. We vowed by all that was sacred to us, from our marble collections to the Los Angeles Rams that we would never again play football or even speak with Gary Ramer again! It was a vow that we both honored—at least for the rest of that week!

14

First Love

I first saw Connie Conklin in church. She was the prettiest girl I had ever seen and I couldn't help staring at her. She and her family had just moved to Aberdeen from Pocatello. Her father, Bernard, was to manage one of the hardware stores in town. Not the Western Auto, of course. Everyone knew the Ralphs family owned that one. But the other store, the one that went through three name changes in as many years.

Bernard's wife was named Dahlia. Connie was their only daughter, but they had three sons. Bert and Chris were both older and in junior high. Kip was two years younger than Connie. Connie was a year younger than I.

My parents rapidly became very close friends with the Conklins. The quick rapport was helped, in part, by square dancing. A couple of times a month, my parents would get together with Larry and Orpha Lewis, Bernard and Dahlia Conklin, and Harold and Jessica Lowell for the purpose of square dancing. They usually met in the Lewis' basement recreation room, but my mother always provided some of the music. She had an entire collection of 78's that had been given to her by my grandmother. They were the only records we had, and I often listened to them, trying to keep up with what the caller was saying. It was like listening to a Greek auction, but I enjoyed it.

I had no inkling of what "allemande left with the old left hand" meant, but they seemed to do that a lot. They did a lot of bowing, too, which I thought was rather funny. I couldn't picture Dad bowing to anyone, not even Mom.

I became more and more curious as I listened to the refrains of Red Wing and San Antonio Rose. I just couldn't figure out what it meant when you were told to "promenade her" or "serenade her." I suspected that perhaps it was some of that grownup stuff that made Mom blush, so I did not bother to ask.

One night, though, Aunt Nancy came to baby-sit, and I was permitted to go and witness this ritual dancing. Lizzie Lewis was there, because it was her parents' house. My best friend, Lester, was there. And so was Connie. She was wearing a pretty green velvet dress with puffy shoulders and white lacy stuff around the collar part. I couldn't even talk to her. She was just—just—neat!

I was so bashful, and I was sure I appeared somewhat twitterpated to all in attendance. I sat on one end of a long couch and Connie sat on the other end. We watched the grownups do their square dances over and over and over again, until it wasn't interesting anymore. Lester was playing the records and Lizzie went back upstairs to entertain herself, so there I was, sitting so close to Connie, and yet so far away. I think I was staring at her, except for the times she would glance at me and look down, just as I looked away. She was as bashful as I was.

I finally mustered up enough courage to ask her if she'd like some Kool-Aid and cookies. When she nodded, I valiantly strode to the table near the stairs and grabbed a napkin full of Mom's oatmeal cookies and two paper cups of grape Kool-Aid. I forgot to get an extra napkin for Connie and had to set everything down and start over. I was Cary Grant, Sir Walter Raleigh, and Adolph Menjou all rolled into one. I think I actually "sauntered" back to the couch. I smiled at Connie as I stood over her, offering the gifts from the snack table. She smiled at me, too—the sweetest, most genuine smile I had ever seen. Geez, she was beautiful!

The smile disappeared quickly though, as I tripped, emptying both cups of grape Kool-Aid onto the front of her green velvet dress! She began to cry as I made a hasty retreat to the far side of the room. The music and dancing stopped abruptly, and Dahlia sped to the couch to comfort her daughter. Her voice kept saying, "That's OK. No harm done," but the sidelong glances she shot at me belied her true feelings. I didn't want to go near her. In fact, I wanted only to find a hole to climb into. What little confidence I had attained had been shattered in one clumsy act, and I did not want to be there anymore.

That night, long after everyone else was sleeping, I lay awake and thought of the lovely Connie and the sweet, sweet smile that had been all mine for just an instant.

15

Marbles

Adults used money. Indians used wampum. But the currency used in the Aberdeen Elementary School in the early 50's was neither of these. It was marbles.

They were everywhere. Most of the boys carried them in leather bags attached to the belt loops. Mine had a rawhide tie-string and, I must admit, held an enviable collection. I had a variety of the marbled orbs pass through my hands during this time, and each one was a valued and individual commodity. But the marbled orbs were becoming less common. They were being replaced by the "cat's eye", which was clear glass with a strange and beautiful colored center, a center which came in thousands of possible color combinations. Less common than the "cats-eye" and marbled marbles, were the "clearies," which were clear and had no centerpiece, but were tinted different colors. Some of the deep blues and reds were equal to the beauty of rubies and sapphires as far as we were concerned.

There were a variety of games that were played at recesses and at lunch that served to move these treasures from one person's ownership to that of another. I was adept at most, but by no means infallible. There were many great marble players in Aberdeen. Lester was better than I. And both of us were better than most. Some of our games were so popular that they attracted crowds of onlookers, especially when the stakes became high. I won many of these showdowns and reveled in the thrill of the victory, the excitement of the new acquisitions that I dropped into my bag. But, I think the thing I enjoyed the most was the crestfallen look on the faces of those who had just lost their treasures.

I did not always win, though. Sometimes, I felt the crushing blow of defeat as it removed the wind from my sails. There were even a couple of times when my losses were so great that I would slink off to be alone, not willing to let anyone see the tears that welled up in those disappointing moments.

During the latter part of this great marble period, a new and valued utility came into prominence—the "steelie." They were, as the name implies, made of steel. Their value was unquestionable. The extra weight of a "steelie" made it much easier to knock a regular marble from the ring. They became the "shooters" of choice. "Steelies" could not be acquired through any store. They were, in fact, ball bearings, and once I had acquired that knowledge, I made plans to acquire some.

The average "steelie" was slightly smaller than the average marble. They were not to be scoffed at, but they hadn't near the status of a "steelie boulder," which was more than an inch in diameter. It seemed to us, Lester and me, that to get the biggest ball bearings, we first had to find the biggest machine that used ball bearings. After a bit of secretive and private brainstorming, we both knew where we had to go—the blacksmith shop.

On the way home from school that day, we stopped at the blacksmith shop to talk with the owner. He was a rough, tough, tall and muscular man who was famous locally for inventing a new type of potato digger. He had a very prosperous business, from what I could see. And he had a lot next to his shop where he sold used farm equipment. Among these exotic pieces of equipment were a couple of huge grain combines. Such machines had tires taller than my dad. It was those tires that inspired us to ask the owner of the shop for help.

He listened to us as we tried to make him understand what we were trying to find. He took one of my prize "steelies" and tossed it back and forth, from one hand to the other, as he listened. Then he told us flatly that if we wanted some of the largest "steelies" we would ever see, that we would have to work for them. Both of us agreed to report to him after school the next day to do some odd jobs around his shop.

The following day we hurried to the blacksmith shop quickly, anxious to be finished with our work and receive our prize. We went right to work. We stacked old tires at the side of the shop. We swept floors, emptied trash, sorted nuts and bolts and washers into boxes, and hung tools on hooks in the pegboard wall at the head of the garage. We worked so hard, we hardly had time to look at the picture of a naked woman on the bulletin board calendar.

When the owner was ready to close for the evening, he came out to give us the reward for which we had worked. He gave each of us a small box containing five brand new ball bearings. In addition, he gave each of us a two-dollar bill. We were ecstatic! The "steelies" were, indeed, the largest we had seen. They were very heavy, each of them about an inch and a half in diameter. And with the extra bonus of cash, we were able to run over to the IGA Food Store and buy goodies before going home. I bought an Idaho Spud candy bar, a Cherry-O-Let, a Black Cow, a Sugar Daddy, and something else I had always wanted—a box of 24 Crayolas! Mom had always given me 8 or 16 (one row or two), and I had coveted a three row box. I was able to buy that first three row box with the first money I had ever earned! It was a very dear box of crayons!

16

The Star Theater

Across from the Texaco station, and right behind Landvatter Motors, just off Main Street, was the Star Theater. It was the hub of all the pre-adult social life in Aberdeen. It was buzzing with activity every weekend. There was always a matinee on Saturday afternoon, and in the evenings, the teenagers took over the place, along with the Star Sweet Shop next door, which was connected with the theater through an open door in its lobby.

The Star Theater had nice clean bathrooms, too, but they were upstairs. The upstairs lobby was a small anteroom that provided access to not only the restrooms, but also three other areas. You could always look in and see the projectionist and all the equipment in the projection booth. I always wanted to go in and look out on the floor below through one of those little square windows.

There was a crying room on the one side of the projection booth, where mothers could take their babies and still watch the movie through a large glass window. There was a small balcony on the other side of the projection booth and that was where the teenagers took their babes. Both areas were off limits to kids my age.

The Star Sweet Shop was a place for music and dancing and sodas and malts and all kinds of activities that the goofy older kids seemed to enjoy. My favorite thing, however, was to go to the matinee on Saturday. In fact, our matinee trips were almost ritualistic in their regularity.

Mike and I would go to Grandma's house and walk to town with Dwight and sometimes Dean. Grandpa Frank always gave us each a quarter. It cost twenty cents for the movie ticket, leaving us a nickel for popcorn or candy. I almost always had popcorn because you could get so much of it for a nickel. Mike got popcorn, too, but Dean and Dwight always liked candy better.

Sometimes there were very special events during these matinees. I looked forward to them as much as the movie, because often there were real live celebrities promoting the movie of the day. We didn't often see big and famous stars, but I must have met and shaken the hands of every western sidekick in the business, except for Gabby Hayes. I thought Andy Devine was the most famous, but my personal favorite was Smiley Burnette.

Smiley Burnette held a drawing for a real live pony during the intermission and it was won by one of the kids from Springfield or Grandview. I didn't know any of those kids. They had their own schools, so I had no real opportunity to meet them, except on rare occasions when my father's softball team played their fathers' softball teams.

Once they had a very scary movie where they gave an insurance policy with the tickets. Nowadays, I would recognize it as pure hype, but I was certainly impressed at the time with such a thoughtful gesture. The name of the movie was *Macabre.* I had to look it up to find out what it meant.

My favorite thing, though, were the 3D movies. It was so cool to put on the special glasses and have Indian lances and hatchets come right out of the screen! I always had trouble with the special glasses because of the fact that I already had glasses. I always had to use one hand to hold them on, and that made popcorn eating very difficult. Still—I wouldn't have traded the experience. It was so neat!

The Star Theater was the hub of community activity for Aberdeen holidays, too. On Easter, after the egg hunt in the city park, all the kids would gather at the Star to open those Easter eggs with "special prize" slips inside so we could see who won the new bike. I never did. In fact, I never even got one of the "special prize" eggs.

Every Christmas, the lobby of the Star Theater had the best Christmas tree in town. It took up the whole left side of the lobby and had the most marvelous of decorations. My favorite things were little bubble tubes of various colors that reminded me of the marquee out in front.

After the movie was over, we would walk through town until the sidewalk ran out, then onto the gravel road passed the slough to my grandparents' house. On Friday nights, I would be allowed to spend the night at Grandma's house. Most of the time we slept in the basement, but sometimes Dwight and I slept in one of the bedrooms on the main floor, in a bed that had funny metal swanlike things on the tops of the corner posts. More often than not, though, we could not sleep there because our noise would disturb my grandparents.

After Saturday matinees, Mom was always waiting for us at Grandma's house and we were whisked home for the weekly ritual of bathing, shining shoes, trimming hair, etc. in preparation for Sunday school. Then we had to wait an entire week before we could go to the next show.

I shall never forget that wonderful theater! It was to be a special place to me until I finished high school years later—even when a poor economy limited it to opening only on weekends. The year that I left Aberdeen, a horrible fire destroyed both the theater and the soda shop. Neither was ever rebuilt.

17

When My Mother Was Sick

On my eighth birthday, as was the custom at my house, we had a party. You see, with my birthday being six days before Christmas, and Mike's being on January fifth, my mother thought it prudent (and convenient) to celebrate with one "shared" birthday party. Such parties are not something I would recommend. You see, having a birthday so close to the Christmas holiday puts a definite damper on gifts. And to be forced to have a "shared" party only compounds the problem. It provides the parents an excuse to buy "shared" gifts. A person's birthday should be a special day for just that one person. After all, did you ever try to split a book, or a dart gun, or a Tonka truck with a younger brother? It can't be done. It only makes you wish to split the lip of the brother.

Three days after Christmas, my mom went to the doctor's office in town to see Dr. Rock and returned with another baby boy. I now had three brothers. This one was named Dorian.

A few weeks later, Mom developed a fever and suffered from flu-like symptoms. She became so sick that Dad took her to the hospital in American Falls. I listened to the talk between Dad and Grandma and knew that she was seriously ill. I didn't know how bad it was, but she had a temperature of one hundred and seven and was hallucinating. Pneumonia developed. I didn't understand all that medical talk, but was shocked when Dad said that her hair had fallen out from the high fever.

The strain on my dad was awful. He was faced with visiting Mom and worrying about her, while doing his best to keep up with farm work and take care of five kids. It was too much for any man to deal with, so Grandma took the baby and agreed to take care of Mom when she got out of the hospital.

David and Becky went to stay with the Kings, a very nice family who went to our church. They had a whole bunch of their own kids and lived on a farm about five miles southeast of town.

Mike and I were taken to Provo, Utah, to stay with my paternal grandparents, Grandma Vera and Grandpa Jack. Grandpa Jack was my dad's stepfather. He was a fun-loving old guy who loved all his grandchildren and spent hours entertaining them. My brother and I were in good hands. Grandma Vera used to nag the poor man half to death about spoiling us, but spoil us he did.

It started with breakfast. It was here that I developed my lifelong favorite breakfast habits. Grandpa loved to eat eggs that were cooked "over easy" and then he'd use his heavily buttered toast to sop up the runny yokes. Grandma would chastise him on his terrible manners each and every time he did it, but it did not deter him from the task at hand. He taught me the same habit—a habit I still have to this day.

Another thing Grandpa did was to allow us to watch television until it was quite late. Grandma would send us to bed and Grandpa Jack would say, "in a few minutes, Grandma." Then we would continue to watch television, totally ignoring the edict that sent us to bed.

My grandmother's favorite show was Lawrence Welk, and when it was on, Grandpa would mimic the performers, driving poor Grandma to distraction. It was fun!

Grandma's house was interesting in that she had knick-knacks everywhere there was a space. My favorite was a small ceramic bottle with an etched country boy with a straw hat, plaid shirt, cutoff jeans, and no shoes. He was peeing into a stream. There was a caption that said "Don't Drink the Water." Underneath was a label that said "Bryce Canyon

National Park." I thought it was the funniest thing I had ever seen. Mike liked it, too.

With all of the trinkets scattered around the house, my Grandma was in dire need of one item that was missing—**toys**! She had no toys! Mike and I were bored beyond measure.

Grandpa tried to make things easier for us by offering a dime for each dirty joke we could tell. We struggled to try and remember every dirty joke we had ever heard, but still ended up inventing our own, much to Grandpa's delight. The dimes were always awarded in front of the grimacing face of my grandmother, who was convinced that Grandpa Jack was leading us both into the depths of hell with this practice. But to us, the jokes meant nothing. They were but a means to an end, for after we had our coins, we were given permission to link hands and cross the street, then go by ourselves around the corner to the supermarket, where we promptly purchased comic books.

I preferred *Superman Comics* and, when I had exhausted the available supply, I substituted other action Heroes. Mike was more of a *Little Lulu* and *Nancy* fan. It made no difference, though, for we swapped them back and forth, and read them until they were dog-eared.

We spent about three weeks in Provo, and on our last weekend there, my cousins and uncle from Spanish Fork joined Grandpa, Mike and me, and we went up into Spanish Fork Canyon on a camping trip. It was loads of fun and cooking our own food was a special treat. We had hot dogs and burgers and marshmallows—everything a good camper could want. And we had lots of soda pop, except for Uncle Max and Grandpa. They had beer. And the more they drank, the funnier they became. It was a terrific trip.

When we returned to Provo, Grandma asked how the camping trip went. We told it all! She exploded when we got to the beer part. She was very angry with Grandpa. And he was very angry with us. We did not know the beer was supposed to be a secret.

Dad picked us up a couple of days later and we went home. We had missed our mother very much and were happy to see her, even though we were surprised that she hardly had any hair. In fact, every night she would take out a glass appliance of some kind that had small glass tubes and looked very much like a hairbrush. She would plug it in and brush it over her head as it crackled and spit out strange purple lights from each tube. Mom called the purple lights ultraviolet rays. They were supposed to stimulate the follicles and speed the return of her absent tresses. I don't know whether it worked or not. Her hair returned after several weeks. But I still remember the fun I had watching my mother do the "Frankenstein trick."

18

The Gonzales Family

Across the gravel road from my grandparents' house was a much smaller and much older house. It was the home of the Gonzales family, and it was a stark contrast to Grandma's house, for it had no yard at all. There was nothing between the house and the road but a woven wire fence and a wide variety of weeds. The area around the house was decorated with old cars that no longer worked, and old machines with origins as mysterious as their purposes.

There was always smoke pouring from the chimney of the house, in summer as well as winter. But the most noticeable thing that poured from the house were the marvelous, titillating odors—odors that served to kick salivary glands into overdrive. They were aromatic treats that wafted into my grandmother's yard and, without fail, brought comments from someone.

The Gonzales family had three children. The oldest was Manuel, who was in his mid teens. Then there was Maria, barely a teenager, and Raymond, who was my Uncle Dwight's age and only a year older than I.

Dwight, Mike and I would spend a great deal of our time with Raymond. We played for hours at all kinds of games. Raymond was a slim, tall boy—a natural athlete. He was especially adept at baseball. I envied him such skills. In fact, I was quite jealous of them. Any boy would be.

Manuel was, to me, an equally amazing and talented person, for he could shoot arrows from a bow as well as Robin Hood himself! Time and time again, we stared open-mouthed as we watched Manuel shoot at the targets we would create for him in front of the haystack. And we were delighted to retrieve his arrows for him. It would have been degrading for such an archer to chase his own ammunition. Sometimes, though, the arrows would get lost in the cracks between the hay bales. In such cases, the appetites of the cows determined when their redemption would occur.

Manuel became bored with target shooting and took his talents to the slough to hunt real game. He allowed those of us who were younger to accompany him as long as we stayed back out of the way. We would watch as he stalked quietly through the cattails and reeds, searching for whatever game was there. He used an arrow with a small line attached behind the feathers to become a master "frogger." He also brought home muskrat on several occasions.

What his family did with his trophies, I never knew for certain. We often were invited to eat at the Gonzales home, and I often wondered if Manuel's "kills" might not be the staple ingredient in many of the unpronounceable dishes that were offered.

Mrs. Gonzales was always cooking, which explained the constant chimney output. Her food was completely different than the things from my grandmother's kitchen. I learned to appreciate Mexican cooking and loved to try any and all of her creations. Sometimes, we were treated to something as simple as hot buttered tortillas and sometimes much more complicated concoctions. I could not pronounce most of them, but I could and did eat them. And they were marvelous!

I believe Mrs. Gonzales enjoyed it when we ate her offerings. She seemed to be as delighted as we were when we cleaned up plate after plate. In fact, my mom was the only one who didn't seem to approve. Something about ruining our dinner, time and time again. I don't think Mom ever understood that I was, and still am, completely capable of downing more than one dinner. I could never understand the concept that one meal could be ruined by another.

One day, the Gonzales family left and moved away. It was a great loss, for they had become very close friends, not only to the kids, but to my grandparents as well. There were some very sad good-byes.

Shortly after the Gonzales' home was vacated, a bulldozer destroyed it. Construction began on a new brick home that would become the home of Warren Hollingsworth, a man who would become a very close friend of my father.

Life goes on in small towns like Aberdeen, and in some ways they never seem to change, but change they do, sometimes in the subtlest of ways.

I wonder whatever happened to my good friend, Raymond Gonzales.

19

The Labor Camp Vandals

Grandpa Frank was a field manager for the Utah-Idaho Sugar Company. One of his duties was to manage the scheduling and placement of the transient farm workers that flooded into town every summer. There were a few Mexican and many more Navajo Indian work crews that came to thin and hoe the thousands of acres of sugar beets in the area.

Thinning beets is an arduous task. The planting machines, which are pulled behind farm tractors, plant row after row of beets, creating long rows of what will become tiny beet plants. As the plants begin to sprout and grow, they are in such close proximity to each other that they cannot grow into large and healthy sugar beets. The only remedy for this is to have them "thinned."

The thinning process requires that hand-held hoes be used to remove most of the plants, leaving six to eight inches between plants. It requires skill and experience to do a proper job. Lazy workers might hack away with a long handled hoe and still do a fair job, but the best thinners use short handled hoes and their fingers to do a meticulous job, never leaving a double plant, nor a long empty space with no plants. Such thinning was back breaking work, requiring hours in a bent over position in the heat of the day.

Good crews worked hard to build and maintain good reputations. Then when they returned the next summer, they were in great demand and could also elicit a better fee from the farmers.

Grandpa Frank was always in the middle of the negotiations for work. He also was in charge of the labor camp—a long, L-shaped building where the work crews could live during the "thinning"season. The labor camp was on the west side of the rodeo grounds, just up the road from my house. There must have been two dozen separate units in the building, and each was always filled during the growing season. Grandpa assigned the units to the crews and families. He arranged for trash to be picked up. Sometimes he even arranged transportation.

During the summer, the camp was a beehive of activity, always crowded with children that were too young to work in the fields. There were always a few women that did not go to the fields, but spent their days watching children, cooking, doing laundry in big washtubs, and hanging out clothes on several clotheslines that had been installed. The Navajo women fascinated me, the way they strapped their babies to boards that they wore on their backs as they worked, just as they had done for centuries. Grandpa used to love to tickle a "papoose" and cause a smile as he walked by. Those babies seemed to be the happiest babies of any I had seen.

During the off season, the camp was empty. All that remained of the families that had been there were a few items left in the haste of their preparations to move on to other work or to their permanent homes in the Southwest. Eventually, Grandpa would hire someone to go in and clean up each unit, and the grounds, to prepare the camp for the next season. It was during this off-season period that I made one of the greatest mistakes of my young life.

I had a very good friend, Danny, who lived in town. His family was related to Grandpa Frank in some distant way and I suppose that made us sort of related to each other.

Danny and I wandered over to the labor camp to explore and to see if anything of value had been left behind. The place had not yet been cleaned up and, for a couple of young boys, the possibilities of finding some sort of treasure seemed very real indeed.

We explored from one end of the place to another. We looked in tin cans, under shelves, in every nook and cranny, but whatever treasure there might have been eluded us on that day. It was obvious that further searching would be fruitless. We did, however, in the course of our intensive examination, make a discovery. The interior walls of the camp were made of Celetex, a type of cheap fiberboard.

The two of us discussed the possibility of making improvements on the property. We assumed that it might be nice if each of the units had an internal access to the neighboring units. Then the people who lived there would not have to go outside to visit each other.

The more we discussed it, the more sensible it seemed. So we decided to make the appropriate changes in the architecture of the place. With a long piece of lead pipe and a two-by-four, we knocked holes in each wall. By the time we finished, even a grownup could walk from one end of the building to the other without going outside. We had done a fine job!

As we left, Danny stepped on a board and ran a rusty old nail far into the heel of his foot. He screeched like a banshee and headed for home. I went to my own house. It was little more than an hour before my very angry-looking grandfather drove madly down our road and into our driveway, leaving a half mile of dust settling slowly behind him. He drove right past the house and to the barn, where Dad was milking. After a few minutes, he left again. I had no idea why he was so angry that he didn't even stop to say hello to Mike and me.

When Dad finished milking and came into the house, I found out—the hard way. The first thing he did was to spank me. He said that he was doing it just to get my attention. Then he said it was to pound the "stupid" out of me. As he yelled at me, I began to get a distinct feeling that everyone had not appreciated the renovation of the labor camp. In fact, Dad called it vandalism! I didn't even know what vandalism was, so I was a bit confused. He said that Herschel Vergus had been called and was coming over to take a report. Now **that** got my undivided attention. There wasn't a kid in town that didn't know Herschel Vergus. He was the sum total of Aberdeen's Police Force.

That evening, I cowered in the corner of the kitchen, feeling very guilty, but not quite knowing why. Dad was talking with Herschel. When they had finished talking, Dad had agreed to pay $40 to match the $40 he had received from Danny's parents. The money was to be used to repair the damaged walls. My dad and Danny's father agreed to do the repairs once the materials were delivered. After Herschel left, Dad took great pains to make me understand that I was to work off every single cent of the money, and then some.

I saw Danny at church the following morning. He was limping around, expecting sympathy for his injured foot and for the tetanus shot he had received as a result of our adventure. But he got no sympathy from me. I was angry at him for running right home and telling the whole story. It seemed to me that the medical attention he received would have been just as adequate had he told a good lie. And it wouldn't have interfered with near as much of my playtime for the next few weeks.

20

Opening Day

My father was always up and working long before sunrise, and continued to work until after sundown. Farming, after all, is a harsh taskmaster. Because of my father's dedication to keeping the good life good, many of the "firsts" of my boyhood came as a result of a proxy—Grandpa Frank.

Grandpa included me in many of his activities. Dwight and I would often accompany him as he rode around the countryside, visiting people for the Sugar Company. Even after he retired, there was not a farmer in the area that did not seek out Grandpa Frank's opinion about how best to raise sugar beets.

As we traveled the back roads of Bingham County in his old DeSoto, he would encourage us to sharpen our hunting skills. With the promise of a nickel for each pheasant spotted through those dusty car windows, it did not take long before the cry, "A nickel for me. I spy" was heard over and over. Each time, the excited spotter would point at his subject and gloat as all eyes looked in an effort to dispute the sighting! Except for an occasional quail or grouse, though, the sightings were legitimate and the money was paid. As we grew older and more adept, Grandpa became less likely to remember the debt. But we didn't mind. The real thrill was in the victory over the other kids.

One of the most memorable days of my life was the day that I became elevated to the status of fisherman. Opening day of fishing season had come and gone before, and I had been relegated to the position of a mere listener. I heard fish stories from everyone, but I'd had no opportunity to create any of my own. Until that special day!

It was planned in advance. I was invited to join Grandpa, Dean and Dwight on the annual trip to Springfield Lake for opening day. In order to be prepared, I had to first go to see Joe Darvik, the pharmacist who was the owner and operator of the Rexall Drug Store.

I think the drug store was at the very center of Aberdeen, if not physically (though I think it was), then by its importance. Joe Darvik was a friendly, balding man who concentrated on business while carrying on personal conversation with each patron. I always admired that skill. He seemed equally comfortable whether preparing a prescription, making a malt behind the counter along the south wall, or checking off the inventory when the Aberdeen Valley Stage stopped in front of his store.

The stage was not a real old-fashioned horse-drawn stage like in the movies, but it **was** very interesting. It was a very long car, with about three rows of seats behind the driver's seat. It was similar to a limousine, but didn't quite have the style of a limo. And it stopped regularly outside the Rexall Drug Store to drop off packages, and on some occasions, even to pick up or drop off passengers. I am not certain of its route, but I suspect that Pocatello, Blackfoot, and American Falls were primary stops, with Grandview and Springfield being secondary possibilities.

One of Joe Darvik's collateral duties was the issuance of fishing and hunting licenses, probably because of his central location and devotion to civic duty. I bought that very first license from him, and heard his comments about it being my very first time. He teased me about being afraid of worms. The last thing he said as I left the store was that he had lost a boot in Springfield Lake the previous year and would I please "catch" it and bring it back to him? He was a nice guy, but his wit was in dire need of some serious honing.

I spent that night at Grandma's house. That way, Grandpa could get us all up and moving at the same time and would **not** have to go across town to get me in the morning. In the evening, before retiring, we carried a shovel and a couple of MJB coffee cans to a damp ditch bank out beyond the barnyard. We spent the time well, wresting earthworms from their homes while jabbering excitedly about the successes that were to be ours the following day.

That evening, it was almost as hard for me to sleep as it was on Christmas Eve. I kept taking the license from my pocket and looking at it, as if I was expecting it to do something magical.

When Grandpa rousted us at four the next morning, there was no sign of the previous evening's exuberance. Instead, Dean complained about having to get four fishing poles into the car and sticking out the rear wing window all in the same direction. Dwight complained that he was tired. I complained that I was hungry. Grandpa just laughed and encouraged us to grin and bear the misery we all felt.

Less than an hour later, we had found a place for the DeSoto along a gravel road at the north end of the lake, along with about a thousand other vehicles belonging to ten thousand anxious fishermen. Or so it seemed.

We carefully untangled the lines, hooks, and poles that had been jostled into a mess by the efforts of Dwight to stretch out for a bit more sleep. Finally, as the light of day began to appear, we left the car with poles, bait cans, creels, and two grocery bags from the bait shop in Springfield where Grandpa had made a last minute stop for salmon eggs and Twinkies. There were also a few cans of Nehi Orange Soda for washing down the Twinkies.

As we left the road on a well-beaten path, we immediately had to cross a fence. Grandpa had showed his boys in previous years how to cross a fence with a fishing pole. You don't. Instead, you place the pole on the other side and then retrieve it after carefully crawling between the wires.

I had not received this tidbit of information and promptly tangled my pole and line in the barbed wire. Grandpa helped me free both the pole and myself. He spent the time as well to give me a quick lesson in how to **not** be a dummy. We soon resumed our trek and hurried along the path in search of a likely "hole" that hadn't already been taken by the "early birds." Miraculously, Grandpa's favorite fishing hole was unoccupied. We quickly took up temporary residence and prepared to fish.

When the edge of the sun became visible in the east, we were ready. Hooks were baited, coats were laid out on the bank for sitting upon, and we had planned our strategy. Grandpa put down his own pole and showed me how to "cast." Once my line was in the water, he was free to fish for himself. In a matter of moments, we were all fishing!

I learned a lot about fishing that day. First and foremost, I decided that I liked it. I liked the early morning air, and the sounds made by the water birds nearby and the meadowlarks in the distance. I enjoyed the sounds of excitement that came across the lake when unseen fishermen on the other bank would catch something and then the quiet as they resumed their quests. I learned that patience is a virtue, and that a fisherman who is constantly shifting position or changing bait will go home empty-handed. I learned that, when learning to cast, a boy should check carefully behind him to avoid the massive guilt that he feels when he hooks his Grandpa's ear, then unknowingly tries to jerk it from his head.

But most of all, I learned what it felt like to be a beginner who was able to show his Grandma and parents a rainbow trout that weighed nearly four pounds, while the experienced fishermen who went with me could only manage small fry of less than two pounds.

It had been a marvelous day of fishing—the first of many!

21

The Aberdeen Public Library

Just off Main Street, behind the Utoco station, was the only city building in town. The major part of it housed the community's only fire truck, an old red classic that had been purchased in the late 40's and had seen better days. There were a couple of small offices off the garage that were used for city business. One was where the mayor could shuffle through paperwork whenever he got bored with his regular job. The other office was where Glory Wilde, the traffic judge, passed down her edicts for traffic tickets. She also gave tests for driver's licenses.

Behind the offices were a couple of small jail cells that saw very little use. There was an occasional drunk placed in a cell for safety until he sobered up, but the main purpose of the jail was just to give the place an air of officiousness.

The most important part of the city building to me, however, was to be found in the small wing on the north side. It was the library.

Aberdeen's Public Library was very small and quite new addition to the town offices. But it had been stocked well, with donations from the school and from many of the citizens. The hours of operation were erratic but I could usually count on its being open after school.

I began to stop at the library as part of my daily ritual. My library card was one of my most prized possessions. Mrs. Kidd, the gray-haired lady who ran the place, became a good friend. At first, she suggested some very good books for me to read. Soon, though, I was reading every book I could get my hands on. I was determined to read **all** the books that were there. I began with *The Hardy Boys*. Joe and Frank Hardy became my very best friends, and I couldn't wait to go with them from the end of one mysterious adventure into the next.

When I had read them all, I read *The Black Stallion*. Walter Farley became my favorite author. I read several books in the *Black Stallion* series and then the *Island Stallion* series. I became a horse nut! I talked horses. I slept horses. I drew horses on everything. My school notebooks were so horse-heavy they could have eaten hay!

Another boy, Richard Hagarman, was as enamored with the new equestrian phase as I. Both of us enjoyed confusing the other kids with our new vocabulary. Everything from fetlock to withers brought confused looks from most of the other kids and we loved it.

The major difference between Richard H. and me was that his family had real live horses. My family only had Half-pint! Half-pint was a Shetland pony. He was a very beautiful chocolate brown, with long white mane and tail. As a pony, he was one of the prettiest I had ever seen. But he had the temperament of a cornered badger! He had a nasty attitude, especially around me. I have no idea what Half-pint had against me, but there could be no mistaking it. The animal was out to kill me!

I was usually on opposite sides of town from the pony, for it usually resided in Grandpa's barn. But one summer, Grandpa elected to move this "demon" to the farm where we lived. At first, I thought it would be a great experience. I was excited. There was a saddle, bridle, and blanket with him, and the thought of galloping up and down Beach Road just served to increase my excitement.

My dreams of rodeo quality horsemanship were soon dashed with the discovery that Half-pint was possessed. There was an evil in the animal that only I could see. His bulging, hate-filled eyes followed me closely whenever I was around him. At every opportunity he would kick at me. On several occasions, he swung that big head around in an effort to bite me.

By the end of the summer, I could saddle and ride Half-pint, and he would go where I wanted him to go. But it just wasn't much fun, for he was an ornery animal. And I wanted not only a friendly mount, but one that had intelligence, and a flare for excitement. I wanted something more along the lines of Thunderhoof, the imaginary horse that I rode for so many years.

22

Traveling Salesmen

Most of the time, our days on the farm were quite predictable. We were not visited often by anyone other than family. There were however, some notable exceptions—the traveling salesmen.

By today's standards, I suppose these visits were quite frequent. The Fuller Brush man came on a regular basis, even though he seldom convinced my mother to purchase anything. In retrospect, I think he must have been a very bad salesman, for my mother seemed to listen to other salesmen all the time, not wanting to appear rude by shutting the door on them before they had said their piece. But the Fuller Brush man always got the brush-off!

There was a wide variety of products offered by these smooth talking peddlers and, in most instances, Mom was able to listen politely to the entire gamut of reasons why she should have these marvelous things in her home before sending each of these fellows on his merry way.

Heaven help them if they happened by while Dad was in the house, for they would not even get the chance to launch into the well-practiced spiels that they seemed to rattle off with such aplomb. Dad thought nothing of closing the door when they were in mid-sentence. When that happened, they seldom knocked again, so I must assume they were aware that Dad was not interested in their product.

There were exceptions to the rule, though, and on a few occasions Mom would find herself genuinely interested in what these folks had to sell. It was during these times that I became interested.

I loved to listen to the fast talkers' pitch their products. It was as entertaining as anything I can think of that happened on that farm. To begin with, the clothes they wore were unlike anything I had ever seen. They were usually dressed in brightly colored suits, as if it was some kind of uniform they had to wear. Some even had checkerboard patterns. They looked like clowns. And except for an occasional bald guy with bright red sunburn where his hair should have been, they all looked like they had used an entire bottle of Wildroot Cream Oil on their heads!

If my mother was interested in the product, she made these poor guys work for the sale. She repeated the same questions over and over again. She had questions about the product, the financing, the warranty, the reliability, the follow-up service, the brand, the color, and even the competition. If they balked, even a bit, at any of her questions, she went on an attack that would have made any soldier proud. She turned these guys into blithering bubbles of flesh on the verge of leaving without completing their sales. It was a sight to behold!

I think perhaps my mother made such an issue of everything in order to keep them talking until Dad came home, for she would buy nothing without discussing it with Dad. And when he entered the house, he knew instinctively that she wanted whatever the guy might be selling. He would listen attentively as the pitch was repeated and then feign a complete lack of interest. My mother would then shrug at the salesman and the whole thing would begin again. It was a highly refined game of cat and mouse. I thoroughly enjoyed watching these marathons.

I remember one man, in his effort to sell my mother a "Fine Filter Queen Vacuum Cleaning System," did a one-man Spring cleaning job on our house. He made the sale, but was not amused when Dad remarked that, "with such a clean house, we probably didn't need it after all."

There was an encyclopedia salesman that worked for hours to sell a set of books to my parents. When they convinced him that their kids were too young to make much use of *Grolier Encyclopedia*, he went to his car and wrestled an entire set of *The Book of Knowledge* into the house. Mike and I perused volume after volume, enjoying the smell of the new pages, fascinated with their content. The salesman relished the moment, quickly pointing out the dire consequences of depriving any child from such books. Mom played the game.

Another trip to the car and we had every volume of *Popular Science* spread around the living room. More guilt. And Mom played the game.

A third trip to the car and the *Grolier Encyclopedia*, every volume, was at hand for our appraisal. There were sheets of paper everywhere with estimates of various combinations worked out. And Mom played the game.

One last trip to the car yielded a cardboard box with a bookshelf in it that was designed to hold every book in all three sets, with additional space for the annual updates. Of course, Mom had to see the shelf assembled. She just "couldn't get a picture of it" in her mind. By the time Dad came in, the bookshelf was placed on the wall of our living room with all books carefully ordered on its shelves. When Dad inquired about the price of the set, the answer made him laugh out loud. The poor salesman was a wreck. He gave Dad such a pathetic, sad, pleading look that I thought my father a very hard man for seemingly ignoring it.

About an hour later, the salesman left. The books were ours. The shelf was ours. The game was over. The salesman had left with much less money than he had sought, but he had a small check, a book box full of canned peaches and pears, and a used tractor battery.

The entire family used the books during the next few years, and they were a source of pride to my Mom, who had played the game well!

23

Moving the Sheep

Several times a year, the sheep had to be moved from one farm to another. They spent the majority of their time at "the lower place."

The lower place was an eighty-acre farm a few miles southwest of town, out near the airport. It was one of Grandpa's three farms and had a house on it where my Uncle Gordon and Aunt Iris lived with their family. It also had all the lambing sheds and a huge red barn. The sheep always wintered there, but during the summer they chewed the pastures down to almost nothing and had to be moved to new pastures on the farm where we lived.

None of us looked forward to moving the sheep, and for very good reason. With the possible exception of the turkey, there is no animal as stupid as a sheep. It is also important to note that, contrary to reason, putting several hundred sheep together in a herd does **not** raise the overall IQ of the group, but lowers it to no intelligence at all.

Now I must give credit where credit is due, for there are reasons to keep sheep. Every Spring we could look forward to extra income from the wool. And the lambs were fattened up and taken to Blackfoot to the auction. According to my father, that provided enough money to support the raising of the sheep for one more year. Then the whole process was repeated.

When the time came to move the sheep, it didn't require a lot of planning, for to plan what sheep will do is a futile exercise at best. We merely collected everyone who could walk and wave a stick and then jumped right in, hoping for the best.

All the kids were sent out initially to round up the sheep and try to get them to move toward the corrals near the lambing sheds. This process usually went smoothly. Perhaps they thought they were being taken in to the corrals for a treat of rolled oats or something, for they were almost cooperative at that point. But once in the corral, we knew that the good part was over and that chaos was about to come with a vengeance.

The proper rails were pulled out of the way and an open path created between the "woolies" and the driveway that led to the gravel road out front. However, an open path meant nothing to a sheep for, unlike horses and cattle, they do not follow a leader. They just scatter—in every direction except for the open path that was created for them. In but a few short seconds there are sheep everywhere; in the back yard of the house, on the porch, running around haystacks and outbuildings. They are trying to climb fences, hiding in the garage, trying to crawl into the six-inch windows of the old chicken coop, trampling the rose bushes, and even trying to go back into the corral from whence they came.

Everyone races around, trying to adjust to each new emergency as it occurs in an effort to get the sheep to move toward the road. Finally, one by one, two by two, or whatever, they are moved onto the public road and headed in the right direction. If everyone pays close attention, the sheep can be held in a tight group and "eased" in the right direction and slowly moved down the road. Time and time again, one will break out of the pack and head for parts unknown, but its direction can be altered quickly if each person remains diligent and alert.

On a good day, persistence, dedication, and an immense expenditure of energy would result in a successful move. The sheep, tired and ready for a respite, would slowly wander into their new pasture and begin to graze quietly on the lush grass. But good days were rare. Usually, the sheep had to be re-grouped time and time again as they were startled by traffic on the road, or by barking dogs in the yards of homes we had to pass by, or by butterflies, or birds, or by nothing at all. They just took off in several directions at once and, as my Grandpa Frank renamed them, those of us who were younger would race to catch up with the wayward beasts and head them back in the right direction.

Grandpa used words during these drives that even a sailor wouldn't repeat. Even so, he kept the best of his curse words for those drivers who, having not the patience required to wait out the herds' passing, would "help" by honking their horns. Then, infuriated beyond description, Grandpa would forget all about the sheep as he "got neighborly" with the wide-eyed drivers. When they finally resumed their journeys, they were quite repentant.

When the sheep were finally safe and secure in their new environs, we would all gather at the house and drink our fill of water or Kool-Aid. We would make comments about what a great job we had done as we tried to clean our shoes so we would be presentable enough to re-enter our homes.

24

Our First Television

I remember the day that Dad first brought a television set into our home. It was so big that he could hardly carry it in. It had a small circular screen and when he plugged it in for the first time, I was fascinated with the "snow" and the noise of the static as it warmed up and began to cast an eerie light into our living room. It reminded me of some exotic instrument from Frankenstein's laboratory, spitting out mysterious rays of energy for some unknown purpose.

Mike and I watched with interest as Dad, with a reverence I did not understand, began to flip through the channels, one at a time. With each flip of the switch, the screen went dark for a second and then the strange light returned just as before.

Dad seemed pleased at the bright screen. He stood back and watched for a moment, then walked around the room and observed the screen from different vantagepoints. He seemed quite happy with this new thing and struck up a conversation with my mother about where it might best be placed in the room. I just stood there with my younger brother, curious about what to expect next, but content to just stare at the strange light that emanated from the box.

Once the decision was made to leave it right where it sat, Dad went to the car and carried in a large box and a paper bag. From the bag, he pulled out a big roll of brown flat wire and began to unroll it. Soon he had one end connected to the back of the box and was trying to get the other end fished through a gap between the window panes of one of the double-hung windows on the east side of the house. He had quickly routed the wire along the baseboard of the living room, under the throw rug in the kitchen doorway, and behind the sofa. It was taking much longer to poke the long wire inch by inch through the gap in the window. It seemed to take forever.

Once the wire had been pushed through and was lying in a heap at the outside of the house, Dad opened the box. He said it was an "aerial." When I asked what an aerial was, he explained that it was required to catch the television signals and had to be mounted high on the roof to catch the best ones. Mike and I ran outside and gazed at our roof for the longest time, trying to see if we could spot one of the signals that needed to be caught. I remembered that Dr. Frankenstein had some sort of thing on **his** roof too, but it caught lightning. I was beginning to worry just a bit, not wanting my Dad to be catching anything as ominous as lightning.

Once the assembly was finished, Dad made two trips up onto the roof of our back room, which was much lower than the rest of the house. On the first trip he took the aerial, and on the next, he carried a long metal pole and some tools. After he hammered and nailed and bolted for awhile, he came back down and got the rest of the things from his bag—little bolts with eyes in them, some black tape, and a roll of steel wire.

Soon Dad had finished mounting all the bolts at different points on the house and connected steel wire from them to the end of the pole. Then he connected the funny looking aerial to the same end and lifted the entire pole into a special holder at the highest point on the house. He went around to the other bolts and pulled the steel wire tight, until there were four tautly stretched wires holding the tall aerial in the right place. He folded and taped the excess brown wire to the bottom of the pole and then hollered down for us to go and get Mom.

When Mom came out, Dad told her to go inside, turn on the switch, and watch for a picture. Mike was to stand in the doorway. I was to stand at the corner of the house. We were to relay messages back and forth between my parents as Dad turned the aerial and Mom switched through channels. It seemed to take forever, but finally everything on Mom's end was "just right." Dad then tightened up one last thing and came down from the roof. We went in to the house together.

Mom and Mike were sitting in front of the television, watching a real picture. It was so neat! It didn't **do** anything, but it **was** a real picture. Dad called it a test pattern. It was a big CBS in the center, surrounded by a bunch of squiggly lines and the words "Idaho Falls" on the bottom. There was a big "3" in each of the four corners of the picture, but parts of the 3's were cutoff because of the round screen.

Dad turned off the set and said that Mr. Ralphs at the Western Auto Store had told him that no programs came on until five o'clock. It was only a little after two. We had nearly three hours to wait, and to me, it was the longest three hours I had ever lived.

Dad went out to "change his water" and Mom went back to her ironing. She told us to go and play, but we couldn't seem to leave the room for long. Even when we went outside, we would come in every few minutes just to look at the box and see that it was still there. We didn't even know what we were waiting for, but the waiting seemed endless.

By the time the clock on our kitchen stove said it was five o'clock, Dad had returned from his work and we were all gathered in the living room to see TV for the first time. Dad turned the set on. It took forever to warm up again, but finally there was the test pattern again. Nothing was happening! a couple of minutes passed and still nothing happened. Two more minutes. Nothing!

Just as I was about to lose interest altogether, the high-pitched noise of the test pattern stopped. Then it was replaced by music. Mike and I looked at each other with wide-eyed wonder. Something was about to happen. We couldn't even breathe. Then the loud voice of an announcer came on and began to recite a bunch of junk about thousands of watts and something called the FCC and authority and hours and times—a bunch of stuff I didn't understand. Then the screen went black for a moment before the very first TV program in our home began. It was a show called Captain Video and was the same kind of science fiction I had been reading in my library books.

No one talked. We just watched. It was the most amazing thing. Movies coming right into our house!

Two hours later, our national anthem was played while a picture of the American flag waved on the screen. When the anthem ended, the test pattern returned. Dad turned off the switch and the set went black.

We had watched Captain Video, several cartoons, and a show called "Stump the Organist." "Stump the Organist" was a show that was produced locally in Idaho Falls. The sheriff of Bonneville County, Sheriff Dean, sat at an organ as members of a live audience made requests of various musical pieces efforts to "stump" him. Whenever a request was made that he was unable to play, the audience member received a prize, usually some sort of gift certificate for some Idaho Falls business. The show was fascinating, and Sheriff Dean knew a lot of songs. I'd heard songs that I had never heard before.

It was difficult to wait until five the next day. We all were anxious to turn on the TV and watch again. As weeks turned into months, and months to years, more and more programming was added, especially on the weekends. When a new station in Pocatello began to broadcast programs from a different network, we were ecstatic! We actually had to refer to the newspaper and make a choice about what to watch.

By far, though, the most exciting thing we watched on television was the World Series. Even Dad scheduled his farm work around the baseball schedule. I watched in awe as the Brooklyn Dodgers and the New York Yankees battled for the championship of the world. And when it was over, names like Duke Snider, Roy Campenella, Whitey Ford, Mickey Mantle, Roger Maris, Bobby Richardson, Pee Wee Reese and

Yogi Berra became part of everyday conversation at school. From that time on, baseball became a role-playing game as we each took the name of our favorite player and fantasized about hitting the home run in a stadium filled with adoring fans. Very few people knew that Ebbetts Field was also a pasture on the east side of the Stoker home in Aberdeen, Idaho.

25

BB Guns

In many ways, life on the farm was remarkably good. There were, however, some things that were difficult for a young boy to deal with. One of those things was having to face the fact that money "was not," as my father said, "something that grew on trees." It was a constant struggle to make ends meet and, while hunger was never a problem, I often envied the extra luxuries and amenities enjoyed by many of my friends.

There were rare occasions, though, when the dreams we dreamed came true. One of those times was during the Christmas of 1955. I had wanted a Red Ryder air rifle. Dean and Dwight, my two uncles, had BB guns. Their guns were, of course, inferior models to the Red Ryder carbine, but at least they had something that would shoot BB's. My friends had BB guns. At least, that's what I told Mom and Dad as I pled my case.

But the matter was taken clear out of their hands on that snowy and memorable Christmas, for Santa Claus himself had intervened on my behalf. Regardless of the reluctance of my parents, that great Christmas elf had delivered a shiny black Red Ryder carbine and an ample supply of ammunition. As if to flaunt the fact at my parents, he left an identical gift for Mike.

Mike and I waited anxiously for an opportunity to try out the new guns. Christmas day crawled by, as it always does. The two of us played with a variety of substitute toys on hand, but we were unable to keep our attention on anything for very long. We wanted to go outside and shoot something. Anything. Just to make sure the guns worked and to feel the power of having a firearm of our very own.

Unfortunately, a typical Idaho winter storm raged on throughout that day and the next. Mom would not permit us to go out in such cold and snowy conditions.

It was the third day after Christmas when the sun finally peeked through the clouds with the promise of a mild day. It was a day that brought unseasonable warmth. It also brought our first opportunity to play outdoors after nearly a week of blizzard.

We stumbled out the front door, weapons in hand. We must have looked like miniature Eskimo hunters, for we were bundled up in layer after layer of clothing to the point where movement was hindered. We hurried to get out of sight of the house so we could shed some of the clothing, especially the mittens. No one can shoot a gun with mittens on his hands. It just can't be done.

With our heavy coats, mittens and scarves securely hidden in the granary, we were ready to shoot. We found a couple of rusty tin cans and set them on a fence post and then loaded the new air rifles from the same red cardboard tube of "ammo." For a time, we shot at the cans. Our skill in loading and our marksmanship both improved rapidly. When the cans began to fall with every shot, we became bored, and began to look for other targets.

One corner of the corral was a covered shelter. It had been covered first with woven wire fencing and then covered with straw, probably several years before. The straw was old and had a definite musty odor, especially strong on that day, as the snow on top melted and seeped into the thick bed of straw. On the underside of the shelter, the straw was riddled with holes, holes that had been made by birds. They had found the roof of the shelter to be an ideal nesting place. These birds became our new targets, and as they came and went to and from their homes, we fired at them.

Soon, though, we became bored with shooting at the birds as well. It was then that we got a brilliant idea. We decided to play army. Mike and I became opposing armies, and we spent the next hour scampering around haystacks and corrals. We took turns hiding in the potato cellar, the granary and the barn. We even used the old chicken coop, the old farm machinery. The entire place became our battleground. And as we rousted each other from our hiding places, we fired BB's at each other, often finding our mark and causing a stinging sensation when we did. We were having a ball.

The stupidity of our actions seemed to evade us, until I spotted Mike peeking around the corner of the haystack and I shot at him, striking him right between the eyes. He screamed in pain and I rushed to see what had happened. He was bleeding from the bridge of his nose.

The game was forgotten, and we ran to the house. Mom met us at the door and in a few moments, had calmed Mike and administered first aid to him. She also removed a BB that had traveled under his skin from the bridge of the nose to the corner of his eye.

When she finished, her ears were red. I knew she was angry! She turned on me and began to lecture me. I quickly learned how losing one's eyesight is possible amid the idiotic practice of shooting at each other with BB guns. I had no defense. I suppose I had known how dumb it was to shoot at each other, but it seemed like fun at the time. When Dad returned that night, he took away our guns and hid them somewhere on the other farm. I never knew where. We didn't see them again for months. In fact, he didn't return them to us until the following summer had almost ended. And even then, we had to prove to him that we understood gun safety before we got them back.

I realize just how lucky I was that my younger brother wasn't blinded that day.

26

Spring Hollow

The American Falls Reservoir was created many years ago by the construction of the American Falls Dam. The dam was designed to hold back a large portion of the Snake River. With the dam, came many changes. For one thing, the huge concrete grain elevator that had graced the old riverbank was now a concrete island in the midst of a great lake, a monolith symbolizing what had once been. It became an almost obscene object d'art, a gathering place for graffiti—graffiti that seemed to constantly change between the red and white of American Falls High School and the orange and black of the Aberdeen Tigers.

Also with the dam came hydroelectric power, a fish hatchery, irrigation canals to aid the farmers and one of the largest bodies of fresh water in Idaho. The catwalks below the dam were extensive, and offered a fascinating view of the dam from a very unusual perspective. The spillways were right above the catwalks, and fishermen on the catwalks could feel the mist from them as they tried their luck from the catwalks.

There were many small inlets and coves created by the new lake and they always changed with the seasonal changes in water level. One of the most significant of these in the American Falls Reservoir was called Spring Hollow. It was a large inlet from the lake that extended far in to the western shore. Even the highway between Aberdeen and American Falls dipped sharply into the ravine and bridged Spring Hollow with a very narrow bridge before climbing back up to the normal land level. It was a break in the terrain that was not often seen prior to the feeling that the bottom had dropped from under your car as you dipped into the ravine.

Most of the time, the inlet was full of water, bounded by small shrubs and sagebrush. But when the level of the lake fell, usually in late autumn, the water level in Spring Hollow fell to the point of mere mud.

Each year, as the level of the lake began to fall, local kids began to use Spring Hollow on a regular basis for normal respite from the summer heat. It was not uncommon to see kids almost anytime of day, taking a pleasant dip in the water. And I remember well the year that they used the old wrecked car for a diving platform.

For most of the summer, the car hadn't even been visible, for the water hid it completely. But as the level dropped in early autumn and the roof of the old car poked its way above the water, it became a popular spot, providing a kind of makeshift diving barge out in the water. The kids were drawn to it as if it had some other significance than just a protrusion from the water on which they could play "King of the Hill" or "water tag."

For several weeks, things stayed the same. The water levels did not change, and the roof of the old car caved in and rusted as it was used and abused by the local swimmers. Then, late in the season, the level of the lake fell again, revealing the windows and the hood of the old car. The slime-covered windows remained intact for a time, and the kids used the hood for a diving platform instead of the roof. But as might be expected, the windows could not remain whole for long. It was just too much of a temptation. Finally, some kids could no longer hold back, and the windows became the targets for lava rocks thrown from the shoreline. Even so, it is no wonder that it took so long to discover that there was a dead man inside the car.

Once the windows were broken, the odor revealed all. Authorities were notified and the car was pulled out of the hollow with a winch.

With rags tied over their faces, the men pried the door open and reached in to remove the long lost corpse from its Detroit-made sarcophagus. The story circulated for months about the man who grabbed and pulled on the corpse, only to have the outside layer of the man's arm slip off in the rescuer's hand. The story got juicier and more gore-filled each time it was told.

As it turned out, the man was identified as a transient worker that had disappeared about eight months earlier. After a night of drunkenness, he had missed the narrow bridge crossing Spring Hollow and launched his car into the ravine, where it remained hidden for months. The man's family had long since returned to Texas, having no idea where father and husband might have gone.

Spring Hollow now sports a wide, level highway and a new bridge. One scarcely notices they are crossing a bridge anymore. But I still think of that summer when a dead man occupied the hollow and no one knew.

27

More Than Just A Chicken Killing

Among the great events of growing up in Aberdeen were the family celebrations. They were many and varied, but always delightful. Sometimes, for very special occasions, some of Grandma's chickens were sacrificed for the sake of event. I found this entire procedure to be fascinating. And what a procedure it was! It was not at all for the faint of heart!

Grandpa would select the bird. With his experience and quick hand, he would soon be holding his choice upside down as he held its legs. He quickly placed the head of the hapless chicken on the top of the well-worn tree stump that served as a chopping block. One swift arc of the hatchet, and the head was severed. Grandpa would toss the headless carcass onto the lawn, where it would flip and flop around, spewing blood from that stub of a neck, until finally it would lie still. I was more fascinated with the heads, which lay in one place, with mouths and eyes opening and closing—fast at first, then slower until they were finally still.

Grandma sat on the back steps and plunged the carcasses of the chickens into scalding water. Then they were pulled from the water and plucked as quickly as possible. Some pinfeathers were always left after this process and holding the chicken over an open flame burned them off.

Once the birds were feather-free, my grandparents would cut and slice with the expertise gained with their years of experience. The innards of the fowl would slip into a bowl and be sorted for other uses, and the rest of the chicken was subjected to a final rinse before being battered and basted on its way into the frying pan.

In addition to the slaughtering of the chickens, there was always much more to do as we prepared for those great family get-togethers. Children were assigned kitchen tasks, preparation of table and chairs and cleaning. Some were assigned to harvest fresh vegetables from the garden. Some of the kids might be assigned to dig some potatoes or to harvest some rhubarb. Some might pick corn from the tall stalks at the far side of the garden or pick peas from the rows and rows near the center.

I always enjoyed the husking of the corn and the removing of peas from the pods. I suppose I enjoyed this because of the fact that these processes were much more than just a job to do—they were a social event. Some of the greatest philosophies of life and the finest and funniest jokes I ever heard were heard over a partially filled pan of peas. And though I always felt quite adept at the skills of "shelling" peas and "husking" corn, I could **never** hope to match the skill of my grandmother, whose hands fairly flew through the pea pods as she talked of other things. No matter how hard I tried or how deeply I concentrated on the task at hand, I could barely cover the bottom of my bowl before my grandmother would be starting her second.

I shall always have a deep appreciation for the love and life that went into those huge family meals at my grandmother's house. The food was always plentiful and remarkable in its goodness. It was at my grandmother's table that I learned that the "horn of plenty" is filled with love, cooperation, and hard work.

28

Fourth Grade

Fourth grade brought a couple of new wrinkles. For one thing, there were no more upper classmen at Aberdeen Elementary School. We were it. The elite! The oldest! And of course, the best!

We also had unrestricted use of the school fire escapes, an honor for which we had waited a very long time. What made this even better, was the fact that I was assigned to Mrs. Boatman's classroom. Mrs. Boatman was firm, but fair and I liked her most of the time. By being in her classroom though, we were right next to the fire escapes and therefore, always first to the playground when the bell rang for recess.

You really need to understand the concept of sliding down an enclosed slide and entering the playground like a cannonball shot from a cannon. Most kids learned not to walk casually in front of the fire escapes. Sometimes though, the momentum of kids emerging from the fire escapes would cause collisions with other kids that had inadvertently ventured into the "discharge path" of the fire escapes. Such cases usually resulted in no worse than isolated bruises and scrapes, though there was an occasional demand for real medical attention.

The ultimate conquest in fire escape bravado, however, was the "return." The "return" meant that a guy had to climb into the end of the fire escape and climb up the inside, against all odds, until he reached the upper floor and was able to scramble out of the tube to the safety of the hall. Now this may not sound like much to most people, but the risk here was not insignificant.

At any time during this effort to climb the slippery surface, there was a chance that some unsuspecting third or fourth grader, with no knowledge of the climb in progress, might come careening down the tube at maximum velocity, and crash into the climber. Such a risk was very real, and the fear of such a collision gave powerful meaning to the dares that prompted such irresponsible activity. It provided the grist from which the sticks and stones that little boys are made of might be formed. And I, being as anxious as the next to prove my bravery, was more than willing to risk life and limb for a moment of glory.

The secret of a successful "return" lay in the timing. To be successful, a kid had to be fast, agile, alert, and very, very lucky! And on one particular day, at one particular time, I was none of those things! Oh, I began my conquest of the fire escape in fine form. I listened at the mouth of the beast and heard no sounds from above. I scrambled quickly into the tube, planted my Keds firmly against the sides, and began to worm my way upward.

The first fifteen feet went quickly. I was fresh. The adrenalin was pumping. I was an athlete on the move. Then I slipped. I lost my footing and slid nearly five feet before catching myself. The shiny, butt-polished metal seemed to take on a life of its own as it sought to destroy mine. I slipped a second time, then a third. I was making no headway at all. I was not going down, but I was not climbing either. I was stuck, and exhausted. And then I heard it! Someone high above me had just entered the fire escape and was hurtling downward.

If I'd had a moment, I might have decided to let go and take my chances on a backward landing on my belly on the concrete below. Or I might have used that moment to turn my back to the oncoming threat. But there was no moment—no time at all, just the crunching collision and the pain. That terrible pain!

I awoke on the concrete. I was lying there, with someone's jacket as a pillow. My nose was bleeding. My head was bleeding. My arm was bleeding. My lip was twice its normal size. Both of my knees hurt terribly. There were teachers and students alike, standing around and watching. I wasn't the only injured party, after all. There on my left was Big Larry. He had a knot over his eye that was rapidly turning into a mean looking purple and black. He did not look happy. i just sat there, wondering why I had such good fortune all the time. Geez, Big Larry, the only kid in the entire school that could boast that he weighed in excess of two hundred pounds. What were the odds that I would be bowled over by the biggest fourth grader in the history of Aberdeen schools?

29

The Rabbit Drive

It was quite common in a close-knit town such as Aberdeen to see neighbors helping neighbors. It was not uncommon to see scores of neighboring farmers gather at the home of one who was sick or injured in order that they might provide whatever assistance was needed to do those things that needed to be done.

Weather, season, markets, and a myriad of other variables dictate a farmer's schedule. Whatever the situation, it is imperative that much of the work be done at exactly the right time. Hay needed to be baled and stacked according to a timetable. Grain needed to be cut and processed at just the right time. Beets and potatoes had to be harvested when they were ready, not before nor after.

It was refreshing to see man helping his neighbor. Usually, a few friends could handle any problems that needed handling. There was one situation, though, that required the cooperation of the entire community. It was the rabbit drive!

One of the great curses of the Idaho farmer was the jackrabbit. Now, understand from the beginning, these are definitely **not** the cute little Easter bunnies that everyone knows and loves. I am talking about the ultimate pest, a rodent so destructive as to be able to destroy a man's life overnight, leaving him destitute and bankrupt.

Every couple of years, armies of jackrabbits would come in from the desert to the west of Aberdeen, destroying haystacks and feed supplies as they came. The hordes could remove a haystack from the skyline overnight, and still manage to eat tons of grain from the storage bins in nearby barns. Not even doors or water could keep them out of the food supply—a food supply that was supposed to keep livestock thriving, not rodents.

The only solution to this problem was something called a rabbit drive. It was another special event of great import, involving the entire community, from store clerks to businessmen to migrant workers. It began with posters, newspaper ads, and even flyers! Everyone was called to help and all who could responded. It was a matter of financial security for the entire area, and everyone knew it!

The purpose of the rabbit drive is singular—to destroy as many jackrabbits as possible. The procedure was always the same. Hundreds of yards of lathe fencing are removed from trucks and unrolled into the sagebrush. The fence is then held up by a long line of townsfolk, a line of people and fence that might stretch as far as a mile to a mile and a half. They stand patiently, each person holding his own section of fence, while hundreds of people "beat the brush" by whooping, hollering, and beating sticks together in a massive effort to drive the rabbits into the fence.

As the din grows, and rabbits begin to run in the direction of the fence, the ends are slowly brought around and moved in toward each other in order to entrap the hapless animals. Once the trap is sprung, dozens of people enter the ever tightening ring, swinging sticks and clubs, trying to destroy the thousands of screaming rabbits. The noise is deafening! Time seems to stand still as the slaughter progresses!

Finally, the gore is completed, and the drive is over. Thousands of carcasses are piled and burned. The fence is rolled up and taken away to be stored until it is needed again. The only sure thing is **that it will be needed!**

The brutality of a rabbit drive is shocking! It is a process that would be difficult to explain to an outsider, yet such action was an absolute necessity to the preservation of the economic stability of that little Idaho farming community.

30

Broken Glasses

There is nothing quite so difficult as telling one's parents that your glasses have been broken—unless it is telling them how the glasses were broken—especially if they were broken as the result of something stupid.

Now, when my glasses were broken, I knew that my family not only had to cover the expense of repair, but a trip to Pocatello was required, for their are no optometrists in small farm towns. And a trip to Pocatello was an all day affair. The whole process was an extra expense as well as a pain in the neck, so I expected my parents to be somewhat upset when they heard the news.

Dad had a more "matter-of-fact" attitude about the glasses. I figured that he knew that rough and tumble sons were prone to such bad luck—that part of growing up a competitive sportsman was to risk broken spectacles. And most of the time, I was willing to show off my bruises or scrapes and just tell the tale of how my rough play had resulted in broken glasses.

But there was that one time—that one embarrassing time. And no matter how hard I tried, I could not cover it up.

I was strutting around the playground at lunchtime. My buddies were by my side—my own little gang. We were showing off as best that we could. My own attention was focused upon the beautiful Connie Conklin, the love of my elementary school life. On a dare from my friend Lester, I planted a kiss squarely on her mouth. As I drew back, ready to see the surprise and admiration in her eyes, she hit me with a roundhouse that would have made Jack Dempsey proud. I was knocked to the ground. I was not hurt, but I was definitely surprised. After all, I had not expected the lovely Connie to become hostile. Was I not her knight in shining armor? Did she not share in my dreams and fantasies? How could she not recognize such love and devotion as I had to offer?

I picked myself up, my feelings hurt, my pride hurt, but otherwise intact. My friend Lester put the remnants of my glasses in my hand. They were beyond help. In addition to a broken bow, the left lens was in two pieces. I was definitely in trouble. Something had to be done.

During the last recess of the afternoon, I picked a fight with Tony Valdez. I figured that if I showed that I had done battle, then Dad, at least, would show some sympathy if I explained how my glasses had been broken while defending myself against insurmountable odds. It made perfect sense. It was foolproof. I was dirty, disheveled, even had a small cut on my cheek (from a fingernail, I think). I was ready.

The ride home on the bus was spent perfecting the story I was to tell, thus wrapping up loose ends. But there was one loose end that I hadn't counted on.

Connie told her mother what had happened! And Dahlia, true to form, had already spoken to my mother. So everyone in Aberdeen knew that I had my glasses broken by a girl. What's worse, it was a girl that I kissed.

The humiliation was without equal. My father laughed at me every time he looked at me. Of course, without my glasses, I couldn't tell for sure, but I felt it.

I was very uncomfortable that evening, and the next day as my mother explained to the eye doctor in Pocatello what had happened. I don't understand why he had to know. The story wasn't **that** funny!

For the next several days, I took a lot of ribbing about kissing Connie and having my glasses broken when she hit me. I took the teasing like a man. I ignored it. Eventually, it was forgotten, except by me and, strangely enough, Connie, who would refer to the incident more than ten years later, on the occasion of the last time I kissed her. But that's another story.

31

Steve, the Cereal Killer

Store-bought toys were few in those early days in Aberdeen, partly because money was scarce and partly because of the isolation that is inherent to small farm towns. Such limits were not a normal topic of conversation. In fact, no mention was made of it. We just improvised, as best we could, with what was available.

Instead of a colorful swing set, we tied an old tire to the branch of a tree. Instead of porcelain dolls with perfect ringlets of hair, the girls in Aberdeen settled for rag dolls with locks of yarn and gunny sack dresses. Blocks of wood became cars. Larger ones were trucks. Old spoons became steam shovels. An old broomstick and a piece of twine became a horse. The only limits were the imagination itself.

There was one thing, however, that was the same in the largest city or the most remote of one-horse towns—the same from one end of this country to the other. It was the breakfast cereal—and those delightful promotional items that were packaged in each and every box. The cereal premiums in those days were treasures, and always a source of excitement. They were always terrific, and they were always changing.

There were small plastic scuba divers, dolphins, and submarines. Each needed only a smidgen of baking powder from Mom's kitchen cupboard to force them to dive, surface, and dive again. And the larger the jar of water, the better the effect. It was great.

There were terrific things hidden in those boxes back then. There were secret code rings with real codes to learn and to use. There were imaginary wrist radios that didn't really work, but who cared. They had a secret compartment for keeping spy notes and microfilm, depending on where your imagination took you.

Sometimes there were games or cards to collect. And for an investment of a couple of box tops and a three-cent stamp, you could join clubs for Red Ryder, Hopalong Cassidy, or on a really good offer, Roy Rogers. There were tiny "magic slates." There were puzzles. There were even small books of riddles that were good for one time around the school and then became rather useless. There was no end to the variety of gimmicks that the good people of Kellogg's, Post, and General Mills crammed into those boxes.

Even my mother had a premium. She collected the premium coupons for silverware on some of the boxes, so it was obvious that there was adult appeal as well as kid's surprises.

I emptied the treasures from hundreds of cereal boxes, sometimes not even waiting until they were empty. I'd spill cereal all over the table in an effort to reach the elusive toys in some boxes. My mother was beside herself when that happened, usually having to clean up the mess after I successfully retrieved the goodies and high-tailed it out the door.

There were rare occasions, when a very special series of items would come out in cereal boxes. I remember one series of items especially. The boxes contained small, round metal plates, about four inches in diameter. There was a small hole at the top of each circle for mounting with a nail or even hanging it on a string. Each of these terrific metallic circles was meticulously painted with elaborate examples of aeronautical instruments. There were a variety of things, from compasses to altimeters, from airspeed indicators to turn-bank indicators. There were more than a dozen of these things, and I collected them as fast as I could, even if it meant eating extra.

I was fascinated with the possibilities afforded me by these little metal replicas of airplane instruments. I'd had my face buried in science fiction books and was the leading fourth grade expert on outer space, our solar system, and space flight in general. And while I was aware of the fact that the metal disks from the cereal boxes did not accurately portray the intricate requirements of space flight, I was also aware that they were as good as anything else I could expect. So with Mike's help, I set about creating a very special vehicle—a space vehicle extraordinaire!

We worked diligently to build our vessel. Of course, the greatest part was the gorgeous control panel. The disks were organized and reorganized until a consensus was reached. Then they were nailed permanently in place, ready to report their normal measurements along with anything else the new pilots might require from them. There was also a "microphone" for making certain that contact with our home planet was always possible. There were "special" seats designed to decrease the effects of extra atmospheres of pressure.

Mike and I hammered and nailed and sawed for several days until we had everything just they way we wanted it. We reached a point where we both knew that our "spaceship" could not be improved with our limited resources. We had exhausted the scrap pile that my dad had allowed us to use. We were finished at last.

All that remained to be done was to name her and take her out on her maiden voyage. I chose the name, and using the greater part of a black Crayola, I painstakingly printed it on each side of our "ship." The name I chose was "Skylark 24". I do not know where the name came from, but it seemed to fit.

It was remarkable to note how the installation of wheels might have made Skylark 24 appear more like a large wooden boxcar instead of a space vehicle, but imagination, thankfully, dulls one's sense of esthetics.

For an entire summer, Skylark 24 carried us throughout the galaxy, its cereal box instrument panel working overtime as we escaped from bad alien life forms and transported interstellar diplomats to imaginary conferences. Protective shields prevented damage from asteroids and giant ray guns, but it only took one careless season outdoors in an Idaho winter to put that wonderful spacecraft into mothballs, its cereal box instrument panel rusted and unreadable. No one seemed to notice as the weeds grew up through the floor and eventually removed Skylark 24 from sight, sealing its fate. It would never fly again!

32

Spud Pickers Extraordinaire

I had my first legitimate job in the potato harvest during my eighth year. Oh, I had made money before, but I always wondered whether I was being paid or just getting handed a gift for being a kid. That first real job, though, was work. It was hard work.

Grandpa Frank came by early one morning and Mike and I piled into his old DeSoto, excited to be going to work on a real farm job. My two rowdy uncles, Dean and Dwight, were already in the car. We rode along the back roads, always alert for pheasants, on our way to Grandpa Frank's "lower" place.

When we arrived at the farm, we didn't go to the house, as we usually did. Instead, Grandpa parked on Airport Road and we all climbed the fence to gain access to the potato field. Uncle Gordon was already there, driving the tractor that pulled the spud digger.

Grandpa led the way to the pickup that was parked in the field and rummaged around in the back, collecting the gear we needed to pick potatoes. He gave each of us a pair of gloves and a picker's belt.

The gloves were of a brown cotton fabric that was common for farm work around Aberdeen. Mine were a bit big, but they stayed on, even though the tips of the fingers flapped a mite too loosely for my taste.

A picker's belt was a wide leather strap that had two large buckles in the front. The most important part of the belt was the "sack hooks", which were large steel hooks about three inches wide. The large burlap potato sacks, which we called "gunny sacks," were hooked on those two hooks and then the sack was dragged down the row of potatoes between the legs of the picker. The picker stayed bent over and kept both hands in motion as he picked the potatoes and shoveled them into the sack. It was not difficult in the beginning, but as the weight of the spuds being dragged increased, it took its toll on the picker's back and legs.

Dwight, Mike and I were a bit too small to drag a sack until it was full. Each sack was to weigh approximately a hundred pounds and since that was heavier than we were, it became necessary for us to unhook the sacks from our belts and place them in an upright position on the row. Then we had to carry potatoes to the sack until it was full. This method made for a lot more legwork, but there was no other way for us little guys to do the job.

As we worked, we were very careful to avoid getting potato vines into the sacks. Even harder were the clods, for they were often mistaken for potatoes, especially when working at a very fast rate. Sometimes, we had to stop and reach into the sack to retrieve a clod that was thrown in before the rhythm of the task could be interrupted. And those "clod retrievals" interrupted the rhythm even worse. It was hard work.

As the hours wore on, sacks full of potatoes accumulated behind us. We had only to glance over our shoulders to see that we were, indeed, doing the job. We felt quite proud of ourselves.

Grandpa walked the field, supervising the digging, often stopping the process to adjust weights and levers on the digger, compensating for different soil conditions. The rest of the time, he watched us pick, marking each completed sack on a tally sheet in his notebook with the little yellow stub of a pencil that he carried on his left ear. We were careful to make sure our sacks were tallied, as we knew that was the way our pay would be determined. We were to receive seven cents a sack for our picking. As we worked, our minds filled with the images of wealth that we were accumulating. The math alone was enough to boggle the mind.

About noon, Grandma and Mom parked behind Grandpa's car and brought peanut butter and jelly sandwiches for our lunch. They also brought a couple of Mason jars with ice water to help us wash down the sandwiches. Mom made jelly sandwiches special for me 'cause she knew I didn't like peanut butter.

After our lunch, the hauling crew joined us. This was a group that included my dad, who was there with the other tractor and a large flatbed wagon. They drove along the rows we had already done and loaded the full sacks onto the wagon. It was impressive to see those guys toss the sacks onto the wagon to be stacked by another guy. They worked quickly and never lost a spud.

It wasn't long before the wagon had made a couple of trips to the cellar and had caught up with us pickers. The digger was getting too far ahead of us. It was obvious to Grandpa that fatigue was slowing us down, so he stopped the digging for the day. We continued to work.

Grandpa had wanted to clear that field in one day, but it was not going to happen. We were much slower pickers than he had planned on. He was not a happy farmer as the sun went down and it became too dark to pick anymore.

The following day, we finished the field, but not until early afternoon. Grandpa Frank informed us that he had hired some high school kids to pick the other fields. We were just too small and not able to maintain the pace. He went over his tally sheet as we looked on and then dug into his overalls for our pay. I had picked eighty-nine sacks. Grandpa gave me seven dollars, pay enough for a hundred sacks. He told me that I was getting extra for "severance pay." I didn't know what he meant, but I was not going to argue about it. It was much more money than I had ever had at one time.

In the space of a day and a half, we had been hired and fired—by my own grandfather. But we didn't mind the firing. We were exhausted. Besides, we had money and needed time to go into Aberdeen and shop. I could hardly wait until I could get to the Rexall Drug store and spend my loot.

33

Nothing Vented, Nothing Gained

Lester Larkin and I had been in all sorts of trouble throughout our short school histories, but our crowning moment came in the middle of the fourth grade. We did not **deliberately** get into trouble but it did seem to seek us out.

It was a pure and complete accident when Lester and I discovered the hidden access hatch to the school vent system. To be honest, we were paying close attention to the Coffey twins teasing Jan Thornhill and we just leaned too hard on the sill of an old boarded up window. The plywood splintered and gave way, revealing a second window frame, about ten inches inside the first.

Lester and I, making certain that we weren't being watched, worked the rest of the plywood out of the way, creating a box about three feet by two feet and, as I said, about ten inches deep. At first, we just took turns leaning back and looking up into the blackness above the opening we had created. We wondered if perhaps there was more to that blackness than met the eye. Lester climbed into the opening and I held the plywood piece in front so that he could not be seen.

Seconds later, Lester tapped on the piece I had jammed back into place and I removed it so he could jump down. He came out, squinting at the sudden immersion into the sunlight. He grinned from ear to ear.

"We found a gold mine, Stoker," he said as he pulled the plywood piece back into place. "Wait until the lunch period. We'll both go in." He was excited, and it rubbed off on me, but we hadn't time to discuss his discovery. The bell had rung and we were dangerously late.

We took the steps to our class two at a time, all the way to the third floor. We made it to class just in time to avoid a confrontation with Mrs. Boatman, but not quite fast enough to avoid the stare. She gazed at each of us over the top of her glasses, a habit she had that had a way of making you squirm even if you were innocent. We took our seats, but said nothing. For the time being, we were safe.

The morning seemed longer than usual. I could tell that Lester was excited about something he had seen, and I was curious as to just what it was. I even tried to manipulate things so that Lester and I were able to go to the bathroom at the same time, but Mrs. Boatman wasn't fooled by that old trick. There was no way that both Lester and I were going to be allowed outside the room at the same time. Mrs. Boatman knew us too well.

Finally, the lunch hour arrived. Lester and I "marched" out with the lunchroom group, as required, but skipped out the door and into the playground as soon as we reached the first floor. We ran around the corner and removed the plywood from the old window frame. Lester told me to go first and I climbed into the niche in the wall. As I raised to a standing position, Lester told me to push on the wood at the top. When I did so, it opened. It was a hinged door.

I lifted the "trap" door and looked inside. There was little light, but enough to tell that we had gained access into the vent system. It was certainly worthy of further investigation.

Lester prodded me onward and I pulled myself through the hatch and into the vent. I held the hatch open until Lester had pulled the plywood cover into place behind him and climbed in with me.

As our eyes grew accustomed to the gloom it became apparent that we were under the floor grate that was located in the hall outside Mrs.

Lancaster's first grade classroom. We could look up through the grate and see the coat hooks and the cabinet where the cold lunches were kept. There were no children in the hallway. They were already outside for noon recess.

We were in some kind of junction area for the entire school vent system. The space was big as some bathrooms I had been in. As I said, overhead was the grating in the floor outside a classroom, and on one side was another grate that was located on the wall near the ceiling of the lunchroom. We could look through it and down about twenty feet to the lunchroom floor. It was way too high for anyone to be able to see us from the lunchroom. We weren't sure whether anyone could spot us from Mrs. Lancaster's hall, but we didn't think they could because it was so dark where we were.

On the wall opposite the lunchroom grating was a small hole, about three inches across. There were a couple of electrical wires going through it, but we were unable to tell what was on the other side. The rest of the space consisted of smaller vent distribution channels, and they looked like they went through the whole school. Some looked big enough to crawl through, but others were not.

Lester and I were very quiet, using sign language and whispers to communicate, thus avoiding detection. I saw a reflection in the lint at my feet and bent to check it out. It was nickel. As I picked it up, I swept away another pile of lint that had accumulated on the floor of the place and found a dime and two more nickels. When Lester saw what I was picking up, he joined me and we both squatted, moving lint carefully and retrieving coins. It was apparent that a lot of first graders had lost their lunch money down the grating over the years. Now Lester's comment earlier took on a different meaning. We **had** found a gold mine!

We spent the entire lunch hour in our new hideout and, by the time we left, each of us had more than a dollar in lost change. I held the trap door up as Lester climbed out, then he held it for me. It was a tight squeeze for both of us to be in the access channel at the same time, but it was only for a second. Lester listened for noise and then kicked the plywood panel out of the way. In a moment, we were both outside again. We quickly replaced the panel, making certain that it looked completely untouched.

For several days we stayed away from our new and very secret get-away spot. We went back on a day when we were short of money and looking for a solution. We were successful and split nearly fifty cents after sifting through the lint a second time.

Altogether, I guess we went into the vent less than ten times before the day when we got caught!

That day seemed just like all the other times. We were careful to make sure no one was looking at us as we removed the panel and quickly disappeared into the old window frame. We checked quickly for change, taking no more than ten minutes to sift through the muck on the floor and extract the lost coins. And then we tried to leave. The trap door would not open! We were trapped inside!

At first, we were just afraid. The fear became very real and very solid, and crept up the gullet from deep within the belly, creating a bilious taste in the mouth and a lump in the throat. We were in deep, deep trouble. We both tried to pry the door up but it was not moving at all. Then, as we gathered our wits, we checked it out more closely and discovered two heavy wires attached to the ends of the door and extended out of sight through two newly drilled holes in the floor, right next to the wall.

Someone had set an elaborate and very real "trap" to catch us, and catch us they did. Images of being pulled out of the vent by school or even civil authorities were making their way through both our minds. They were unpleasant images and in a few moments gave way to even worse scenarios where the authorities did **not** find us. Instead, we died and rotted away to skeletons in the dirty vent as our families grieved and searched in vain for some sign of us. We were very scared. Only then did we begin to look a bit closer at the construction of the trap we had triggered.

The wire that held us in was wrapped tightly around nails that were firmly implanted in the wood of the hatch cover. It had been wrapped that way with a tool, probably pliers of some kind. At first, it appeared that such a tool would also be needed to undo the wire. However, as we all know, necessity is the mother of invention. Lester and I first tried to use coins to remove the wire, but were not having much success. It was too difficult to get any leverage from so small an object. Then we came upon the idea of using our belt buckles. They worked much better, as the belt served as somewhat of a handle. It was still a time-consuming process and we nearly panicked as the bell rang, ending the lunch hour.

We doubled our efforts and, in just a few moments, were able to pry the remaining coils of wire from the nails. We climbed out quickly and raced for the door. We both knew that we were late! Whoever tripped the trap to catch us could easily surmise that Lester and I were the guilty ones.

As we reached the top of the first landing, salvation popped into view. There hadn't been enough time for the teachers to take the roll yet. There was still hope. Our future looked brighter as I pulled the little hammer from the wall, broke the glass, and pulled the lever that filled the halls with fire alarm music!

The entire student body vacated the school in a matter of three or four minutes, and with them, Lester and I. We had not been seen.

Later that week, I was sent downstairs to get a new eraser and a box of colored chalk for Mrs. Boatman. As I waited in the janitor's storeroom, I saw the two wires that came out of the ceiling and were wrapped tightly around a two by four at the top of a storage shelf. I thought of disconnecting them, but decided that it was all just a bit too risky. Lester and I never again entered the vent system of Aberdeen Elementary School. But we'd had an adventure and even made some candy money. There were no regrets.

34

Milking

Aberdeen was the home for some very successful business enterprises, in addition to the Nealy Honey Company. The IPG (Idaho Potato Growers) had a processing plant in Aberdeen where, strangely enough, potatoes were processed. Millions of pounds of potatoes were harvested and brought to this plant, where they were converted into countless cases of *Tater Tots* and French fries (both regular and *Krinkle Kut*), which were frozen and shipped to wholesalers far and wide.

There was also a factory that made potato starch. It also supplied an odor most foul on those occasions when the fumes from its by-products would waft through town. However, they were downwind most of the time.

One of the mainstays of the community was the Kraft cheese factory, a remarkable place where the milk from the surrounding farms was turned into *Velveeta*. Farmers would often come by and pick up the waste products of these businesses to be used as feed for their livestock. The whey from the cheese factory was always a premium, for it could be used to nourish calves, as well as to provide fine pig slop.

My father sold milk to Kraft for as long as I can remember. By most standards, it wasn't much of a contribution to the entire Kraft world. For our limited resources though, it worked out well. Every morning, the milk truck would come by and pick up the Stoker milk cans and leaving empties in their place. Milking the cows was something that had to be done at about the same times every day, early in the morning and then again in the evening. My dad didn't care for company as a rule, but once in awhile he would allow an interruption as he milked.

In the early days, Dad milked by hand, developing a skill that was impressive to see. If one of us walked into the barn as he milked, he would quickly re-direct the stream of milk in our direction. He could aim that stream of warm white liquid with uncanny accuracy across the entire breadth of our barn. We did not like getting squirted with milk and clambered to safety as quickly as possible.

Later, Dad acquired a milking machine, and we "automated" the milking process at the Stoker homestead. It was amazing to see the difference as two cows at a time were milked by the machines. The time it took to milk the cows was cut in half, at least.

Along with the milking machine, Dad bought a milk cooler and placed it in the old garage. It was a large metal chest that was filled with water that was kept just above the freezing point. After the cows were milked, the milk cans were deposited inside the cooler so the milk could be kept as fresh as possible. In the morning, someone would go out to the garage, open the cooler and one of the milk cans, skim the heavy cream off the top, and fill the pitcher for breakfast. Mostly my father used the cream. He would use it on his *Quaker Oats*, creating a layer of cream between his oatmeal and his sugar. The rest of us didn't like cream much and I guess it's good that we didn't.

That cooler had some other uses, too. We often used it in the summer, for it was an ideal place to keep watermelons until they were needed. There seemed to be melons floating in that cold, cold water all the time. Whenever the lid of the cooler was raised, it released a very distinctive, but pleasant odor. If anyone were ever to ask me what ice water smelled like, the odor from that cooler would come to mind.

The Kraft Company would leave cheese and sometimes other products on a regular basis. Every year, prior to the holidays, they would leave the most wonderful boxes of caramels. There were dark and light caramels, and each of them was individually wrapped in cellophane. They were a genuine treat in my house, and were doled out sparingly. Seldom was anyone allowed more than one at a time. These were the finest of candies, and when they were gone, the boxes made excellent pencil boxes.

I was always interested when my father spoke of his cows. There were phrases and procedures that I did not yet understand, such as "a fresh cow" or "a cow that has gone dry." But for the most part, I was able to learn from my father, and I was ready a few years later when he "passed the mantle" to me.

35

The Aberdeen Posse

One of the most beautiful things in Aberdeen was the Aberdeen Posse in full dress regalia. They were really called the Aberdeen Boots and Saddle Club, but mostly we just called them the "posse." It was made up of some of the finest horses and riders in the Pacific Northwest, to my way of thinking.

For as long as my memory is allowed to stretch, Herschel Vergus headed up the posse. He was the entire Aberdeen Police Department. He was a very large man—I mean a very, very large man. Because of that distinction, he was the butt of many a joke when he wasn't looking. The jokes weren't really as cruel and insensitive as you might think, for Herschel was really a well-liked "pillow" of the community. It was always said that Aberdeen had the largest police force in Bingham County, and that was a comment more about the weight of our policeman than the number of men.

Herschel had a beautiful palomino and some of the nicest looking tack in the entire area. When he sat astride that huge mount, he became something regal, something stately and beautiful, and his great weight was no longer an issue. There was only the melding of horse and rider as they performed.

Because our house was just up the road from the rodeo grounds, Mike and I were very aware of when the posse practiced. Every year, they worked hard to prepare a performance for the annual rodeo. Night after night, they practiced, just walking the horses through the routines at first, then increasing the speed to the trotting and cantering paces that would be used in the show.

Sometimes Mike and I would walk up the road and sneak in under the bleachers. We found a vantagepoint that afforded an excellent view of the arena and we could watch the posse practice without danger of being caught. It was exhilarating to see and hear the horses as they were put through their paces. The heavy breathing of the horses seemed to keep a cadence that turned the entire practice into a performance that was almost musical.

The posse practiced for weeks and as they sharpened their skills, the day of the big rodeo grew closer and closer. In the last few days before the big day, handbills began to appear on the streets. These were fresh versions of the weathered posters that had been up long enough to fade and blend in with the background.

A few days before rodeo day, trucks began to show up with the rodeo stock. It was fascinating to watch as the stock was moved through seemingly endless corrals and chutes into various holding pens. There were several different corrals—one for bareback broncs, another for saddle broncs. There were pens for the roping calves and separate pens for the bulldogging steers. Far more interesting than all of that, however, was the special pen—the one with eight-foot rails—the one that was used to house the Brahma bulls.

The bulls seemed to attract kids like sugar attracted yellow jackets, and I was no exception. As if their massive sinew and muscle wasn't enough to admire and stimulate conversation, these animals were bred with attitudes—bad attitudes. They were taught from "calfhood" to be as mean and ornery as any animal under the sun, and they seldom fell short of that goal.

The grounds required as much preparation as the performers. The closer rodeo day came, the more attention it got. There was an old water truck that belonged to the city that was called into service to help. Its tank was filled at the railroad depot and then it drove around the arena with water spraying from its rear as if it were a fountain in the park. Then a tractor and harrow were brought in to work the moisture into the soil. This process was repeated until the ground was perfect for the big event.

In addition to the actual grounds, the bleachers and grandstand were adorned with banners and bunting. The entire place became an attractive myriad of bright color, lending to the excitement that was building all through Aberdeen.

Strangers began to show up. They were mostly there to compete for prize money and traveled a seasonal circuit that included our little town. The Davis Motel on Main Street was filled quickly—all four units. Even the three motels in American Falls did a good business during rodeo days. Many of the cowboys came into town pulling their homes behind them. Dozens of little trailers and pickup campers were collected on the west end of the grounds. It became a small town unto itself, made up of folks who knew each other from the rodeo circuit. Most were friends and had no trouble getting along. They enjoyed themselves, especially in the evenings. I always felt drawn to the rowdiness and music that came from their encampment every night, but I was much too young to join in.

Rodeo Day brought crowds of people. Nearly half were strangers from out of town. There were really two shows. The preliminary rounds of each event were held during the day and then at night the finals took place. Our posse, the Aberdeen Boots & Saddle Club, performed at both events. The evening show was the best, though, because they galloped through several intricate maneuvers, including figure eights, with red and green flares. The horses were well trained and the men were well rehearsed. The overall effect was remarkable.

The names of the broncs were always fun, for they all conveyed a sense of foreboding. Names like Cyclone, Man-eater, Hurricane,

Buckshot, etc. helped support the impression that these creatures knew their job was to throw cowboys as far and as fast as possible.

The bulls, too, had names that were designed to strike fear into the average observer. The fact that they carried more than a thousand pounds of muscled mean helped to spread that image. They had names like Killer, Widowmaker, Terminator, etc.

Usually, the local heroes were eliminated early from the bronc riding, the dogging, and the roping competitions. And that went double for bull riding. The finalists were almost always made up of the regular circuit cowboys, though occasionally one of the locals would get lucky and make the evening performance. When that happened, the support of the community was deafening.

Aberdeen's girls always did well in the barrel racing event, and both genders did well in the relay races.

Mike and I would sit in the bleachers and scream for our favorite local cowboys and cowgirls. We thoroughly enjoyed the rodeo and also the popcorn and hot dogs that made the rounds of the bleachers. By the time we got home, we were hoarse and exhausted. We went to bed on rodeo night with dreams of being the prizewinner in future rodeos. In fact, I dreamt that I wore the belt buckle of the world champion bull rider. It was so much easier on the body to dream it rather than actually **ride** the bulls.

36

The Appendectomy

One day in my ninth year, I became very sick. At first, my mother thought that I was bothered by one of the normal childhood illnesses. They were quite common, normally resulting in an upset stomach, an inability to hold any food down, and a fluctuating fever. Usually, though, such an illness would run its course in a day or two and then I would feel fine. In fact, it was the only time I was able to have a soft drink, because my parents would splurge the family budget on *7-UP* to help settle queasy stomachs.

But this illness was different. When two days became four, then six, my mother contacted Dr. Rock and asked him to stop by the house and check on me. Dr. Rock was Aberdeen's doctor during that all too short period when we actually had our own medical person.

Normally, we had to go to American Falls and see Dr. Harms. And when he became too old, and could only deal with cuts and bruises, we had to drive all the way to Pocatello for medical aid. Dr. Harms staffed the hospital in American Falls and had the dubious distinction of having delivered me. In fact, Dr. Harms was present when most of the population of Aberdeen first saw the light of day.

Dr. Rock, though, for a time, ran a small clinic on Main Street in Aberdeen. Most of his work, however, was done in the homes of his patients. More serious maladies were treated at Schiltz Memorial Hospital in American Falls.

When the doctor stopped by the house that day, his diagnosis wasn't long in coming. I had an inflamed appendix and needed surgery at the earliest opportunity. My parents were instructed to take me to American Falls and get me admitted that evening. Dr. Rock called them from our house and told them to expect me. All the wheels were in motion to slice me open and remove part of my God-given innards and not one person had asked me for permission. I might have been angry about that were I not so ill.

That night, alone and afraid, not knowing if I would live or die, I was forced to face one of the most frightening and terrible procedures that my vivid imagination could comprehend. The sparsely furnished room was bleak and gloomy and only served to make the experience that much more frightening. I had only a few minutes warning and was unable to plan an escape. I was trapped. And when the nurses showed up for surgical prep, there it was, right in the center of a tray, as though it were a dessert for some fine dinner. But I knew what it was. I had seen it once before. It was an enema bag—and the sight of it almost cured me—almost!

Fear took over my consciousness and time became a series of warped images and strange procedures, all leading to the single operating theater in the small hospital, where the brightness of the lights brought me back to my senses. But it was short-lived, for a masked lady held a mask over my face and told me to count backward from one hundred.

One hundred….I wished they would shade my eyes….ninety-nine….I hope Dr. Rock was a good student in medical school….ninety-eight….do they wear masks so I won't know who they are….ninety-seven….why would anyone want to learn to count backwa….. .

When I woke, my mom was there and told me it was over and my appendix had been sacrificed for the greater good. For the first time in a week, I felt no nausea. That was a luxury that lasted but a short time. In just a few moments I was hit by multiple waves of stomach-churning stimuli. I was still a very sick boy.

I spent four days in the hospital before returning home to the sympathy of my sister and brothers. But I was not to have an easy time of it. The prize, the crowning achievement for me, was an ugly incision that was very impressive when shown to my siblings. It was red and raw and stood out like a relief map with its clamps. And it became redder and nastier as the next week crawled by.

I had an infection! Dr. Rock came by regularly to change the dressing, but some unseen creatures had found their way into the hidden depths of the open wound and it became very sore and painful. In fact, Dr. Rock described it as "a softball-sized pus pouch." He was such an articulate man!

Dr. Rock, after weighing the advantages and disadvantages of a return trip to the hospital, decided to lance the pocket of infection to provide me some relief. He also prescribed the latest miracle drug for controlling such things—something called sulfa.

From that time on my condition improved, and though it was a long time before I was running and jumping around, my wounds healed. I always wondered why we are given a piece of gut, each of us, with no apparent purpose other than to get inflamed and cause us to suffer physically and mentally.

37

The Tunnel Rats

Mike and I shared a penchant for major construction work from a very early age. We carried our natural instincts for such things to a normal fruition by our decision to turn my mother's vegetable garden plot into a safe and effective fallout shelter.

Fallout shelters and bomb shelters were a big topic of conversation in Aberdeen, especially after the nuclear accident at the atomic energy site in the desert to the northwest of us, near Arco. Some of the people in Aberdeen actually invested real money in backyard shelters, but my family hadn't that luxury. We had to settle for whatever my brother, Mike, and I could come up with.

Across the driveway, in front of the "shack" where the transient labor lived, was a large plot of ground that was normally used as a garden. It did not, however, get used all the time. It was during one of those times when it was not under cultivation that Mike and I built our most ambitious project.

It began as an ordinary hole in the ground, made with painstaking effort and by using a shovel from the garage. We took turns with the shovel, and after hours of work, had created a substantial hole. We were able to stand in it and ground level was nearly at our chest. We were spurred on by the smell of the moist Idaho earth that we had uncovered.

By mid-afternoon, our hole had been expanded to a rectangle about five feet wide and twelve or thirteen feet long. In the course of our digging, we discussed what we would do with the hole. We talked of abandoning our plan for a shelter and just pulling the garden hose across the lane, turning on the water, and creating a fine swimming pool.

In the end, though, we agreed to revert to the original plan and our shelter began to take shape. We went to the weeded area behind the labor house and its outhouse and retrieved some old planks that had once been doors on the old leaning garage. We huffed and puffed and moved them around to the construction site that had once been a garden. It was a struggle for two diminutive lads such as we were to properly place these large planks, but we remained dedicated to the task at hand and eventually succeeded in stretching them across the top of the hole we had dug.

We had to extend a small trench from the hole, gradually decreasing its depth until it would serve as an entrance into our new bunker. Once it was properly tested, we went to work, covering the planks with the mound of earth we had removed and piled nearby. In no time, our project was out of sight, completely hidden from view. We had created the ultimate hideout.

We were able to climb into our trench and slither back into the darkness, away from all earthly cares and concerns. But things were not perfect. We had to make some adjustments. The first thing we needed to do was arrange for the necessities of life. We needed light, food, and water if we were to have a legitimate shelter. And we needed a way to close up our entrance so no fallout could get in. And since we weren't quite sure what fallout looked like, we decided it needed to be a very special door.

We managed to sneak the flashlight out of the back room of the house without being detected, but that wasn't really enough. We finally solved the problem with the acquisition of a large box of blue birthday candles and a box of wooden Fire Chief matches. Then with a couple of spoons stolen from the same cupboard, we hollowed out several small cubbyholes in the dirt walls of our new fortress and firmly planted candles. When they were all lighted, there was a feeling of closeness and coziness that couldn't be achieved with just the flashlight.

After a few short trips to our bedroom, Mike and I managed to move our most valuable treasures to the new hideout. We had three cardboard boxes filled with crayons, *Little Golden Books*, tablets of paper, etc., all the things we would need to ensure that history would still be written even after the bomb.

For a door, we searched through the waste material behind the old outhouse and near the granary, but it was no use. There was nothing suitable. In a bold stroke, we solved the problem by removing a large section of plywood from inside the granary. It was used as a retaining wall to keep the oats in the huge bin until it was needed. By raising it slightly, enough grain came out from underneath to provide a shovelful or two for the feed buckets. That is, until we took the wall and made a door out of it. Then our grain covered the floor of the granary, much to the delight of the pigeons that roosted above and the field mice that lived underneath the floor.

We placed our new door over the trench and, with careful maneuvering, were able to pull it over the entrance behind us whenever we entered our underground room. It was far from convenient, but it was effective, to our way of thinking, against any fallout.

When Dad discovered that part of his granary wall was missing, our door was removed and returned to its rightful place. Mike and I received stern lectures and we no longer had a door. We continued to play in our hideout for several more days, but as the inside of the place dried out, it became dirtier and less cozy. One day, we got a cloudburst and the heavens opened, raining heavily for nearly an hour. Mike and I remained in our house, unaware of the devastation that was occurring in our tunnel home away from home.

We had to abandon our fallout shelter after less than two weeks. It was declared unsafe by my father and off limits. We didn't mind, though, for the inside had become little more than a mud hole, and all our books and papers were destroyed.

38

Red Wheat Peril

A farm is fraught with dangers of all kinds and ours was no exception. Hardly a day went by when my mother was not called upon to administer first aid to at least one of the kids, and it was likely to be more often than once a day.

Usually, the injuries were minor, and seldom serious enough to raise an eyebrow, let alone start a panic. They were common ailments, ranging from small cuts and scrapes to a variety of insect bites, and exposure to some of the more exotic flora of the area. Cuts and scrapes, while providing the necessary and all-important hematological evidence of our bravado, were easily treated. Tincture of iodine was used to wash these bleeding wounds and we could almost always count on it stinging with a greater vengeance than the original injury. And there was no one that could apply a more liberal dose than my mother, who would follow this cruel gesture with a blowing exercise, trying in vain to convince us that wind would reduce the stinging. It never did work like that!

For most of these wounds, *Band-Aid* management was all that was required, but once in a while, Mom had to reach way back into the cabinet and get the adhesive tape and gauze. The tape was in a metal container that had to be popped out sideways to provide access to the tape. We had to be careful not to bend the ring so that it would be available to snap back into place and continue protecting the surface of our adhesive tape.

For most insect bites and stings, we always had a collection of concoctions, each with its own advantages or disadvantages. We had everything from *Bactine* to calamine lotion. Sometimes they would provide some relief and sometimes they were no more than an exercise in futility. But we tried.

Things like thistles, poison oak, poison ivy, or stinging nettle, had no real treatment that would eliminate the misery completely, but we did the best we could.

Of course, all these things were what we called "outside" things, meaning they were visible on the body and could be covered, medicated, and would heal. But there were "inside" things that caused much greater concern. These were the things that brought nausea or fever or both. They were much more serious than the "outside" things.

One day, Mike and I, in the course of our travels around the farm, made a discovery. We were playing in the old garage, a building that had been used to store everything but automobiles for at least 30 years. It housed the milk cooler and all manner of tools and pieces of tools, most of which would never be used for anything. On this day, though, there was a stack of grain bags, several dozen, and they were right in front of the big door.

The grain was wheat and we became excited. Any kid knew that, if you chewed wheat in large enough quantities and for a long enough period, it became just like gum. What's more, the taste was pretty good too.

Mike and I took full advantage of our proximity to such a treat. We untied the loosely tied string that held the top of the bag closed and we each grabbed a side and opened it wide. We both reached into a bag and pulled out a handful of the wheat. It was a reddish color, but tasted just like any other wheat. We chewed rapidly, replenishing the wheat supply as needed, trying to reach the "gum" stage as quickly as possible. It wasn't long before we both had a cheek full of wheat gum, as if we had some sort of "kiddy" tobacco.

We both stashed some extra into our pockets for later and went on our way. Soon we both stormed into the house. We slammed the screen door, as usual, and headed for the sink, each of us wanting to be the first to use the "drinking" cup that always sat there for everyone to use when they were drinking water. We removed our wheat gum while we drank and laid it on the counter. As each of us finished drinking in turn, Dad came in and immediately asked if we had been into the wheat in the garage. He sounded upset, and we did not want to be in trouble, so we proclaimed our innocence and prepared to return to the yard for more interesting things. But Dad was adamant, and demanded that we empty our mouths. When he saw the gum, he knew we had lied.

He seemed more concerned about the wheat, though, than the lying. He turned to Mom and told her that the wheat we had taken was "treated." It was his seed wheat and had been processed and treated with herbicide to prevent insect attack prior to its germination. It was poisonous!

Mom leapt into action as though she had been fired from a cannon. The wheat gum was in the trash can in the blink of an eye. I hoped that would be the end of it, but I knew better. I failed to see what was so alarming. There was no way bug poison was going to affect a big kid like me, or one like Mike for that matter.

In a moment, Mom had mixed baking soda and warm water and was demanding that we drink. We balked, but she insisted and the nasty liquid began to disappear slowly as we both drank. She yelled at us to drink it all, every drop, and she seemed so excited that we did, without question. In just a few moments, both of us were in the bathroom, regurgitating right on schedule, just as my mother had planned.

Dad was on the phone. He had started to call the doctor in American Falls, but one of the neighbors had picked up **her** phone at the same time and they began to talk. Because of our "party line," there were three other homes that had access to our phone. Even when someone called for "28", our number, the neighbors sometimes got confused about the number of rings and answered our calls. We very often shared news with neighbors in this way.

Dad was talking to Mrs. Fuchs, who lived up the road and around the corner toward town. She advised him to just keep an eye on us and see if we got sick. Only then would we need a doctor. I guess it made sense to Dad because that is exactly what he did. He and Mom watched us. They questioned us about how much wheat we might have ingested. They encouraged both of us to vomit and clear our little poisoned bellies. We obliged at least once, and I think Mike went for a second time.

We did not get sick. We were fine, and eventually even my parents were convinced that we would not expire. Only then did Dad begin to lecture most firmly about leaving things alone and asking permission before we got into things. We listened and we learned. Most of all, we learned that when we ate the red grain, we would be forced to throw up—and that was not pleasant. Both of us made a solemn vow that day, and we have kept it from that day to this. We have avoided all red grain, with the exception of *Trix* and *Froot Loops*.

39

A Bike All My Own

I remember when I reached the point where I no longer could tolerate sharing a bicycle with my brother. We had a very nice twenty-four inch Schwinn that was not even full size. Santa Claus had provided it, but Santa had a way of expecting me to share many of the neatest gifts with my brother, Mike. Santa was wrong. Every boy needs a bike of his own.

I knew there had to be a solution to the problem. At first, I thought that I could just bully Mike into ignoring the fact that the bike was half his. That didn't work. Then I thought that perhaps I could trade something else for his half of the bike. That worked until my mother got wind of it and then the trade was declared null and void. My half interest in the wagon was returned to me along with a used box of 48 Crayolas and three white agates from my rock collection.

I didn't know how to solve the problem. One day, though, the solution came to me. I was walking home from school with Kevin Kirkman. We stopped by his parents' store, The Home Market, and as we sucked on *Tootsie Roll Pops* from the glass fish bowl next to the cash register, we talked with his mother.

Kevin wanted a new kind of bike, one of those fancy ones with brake handles and gearshift. It was supposed to have three speeds, but that made no sense to me since the speed of a bike is a direct function of the legs that are pumping away on the pedals. I began to see why Kevin had brought me into the store. He needed some support for his argument and I helped where I could. I knew deep down that Kevin didn't really need to argue with his mom because he always got whatever he wanted anyway.

The discussion was going well to my way of thinking until Mrs. Kirkman brought up the inevitable.

"What about your other bike? It's almost new."

Kevin was ready for that. "Steve wants to buy it. He already offered ten dollars!"

Well, as I said, Kevin was ready. I was not. I had said nothing about buying his bike. And I certainly did not have ten dollars. Nevertheless, something told me to play along.

"That's right, Mrs. Kirkman. I want to buy the old bike. But I have to ask Mom." I added that to give myself an escape route. As it turned out, I didn't need or want one. During the course of the next few days, I did odd jobs for my Grandpa Frank, mostly pulling thistles from the edge of the wheat field. He and I made a deal for the exact amount I needed to add to my "savings" so that I would have enough to buy the bike. Kevin spent that time first working on his dad and then in selecting just the right three-speed from the catalog. Once he had just the right picture of the bike he wanted, his dad took him to Pocatello and they found one just like it. As soon as he had the new bike, he called me. I was ready.

It was my first major purchase and I did it all on my own. I made my own money. I negotiated the deal (at least I told my mom and dad that I negotiated. In fact, I just paid the ten dollars.) I picked the bike up at the Home Market on Saturday morning. Of course, I had to pay homage to the new three-speed that Kevin sported, but that was just to be nice. Soon I was riding home in style. That must be what it feels like to cruise the streets in a limousine. I was in what Grandpa would call "hog heaven." I was in what my mother would call "tall cotton." I was traveling in style.

It was different riding a real twenty-six inch, full-sized bicycle. I felt like I had arrived! It was gorgeous, too, with a beautiful tan paint job, with green trim. It had a tank on it that resembled a motorcycle gas tank with the word '**Schwinn**' painted across its entire length. It was a great bike and I knew I had done well. I could hardly wait to show it off at school. I wasn't ready for the reaction I got!

I was feeling good as I rode my new bike onto the school ground. I felt good. I looked good. I could see that people were watching. I was proud to show off my new bike. I anticipated that I would have to handle several glowing comments as I placed the bike carefully between the stanchions of the bike rack. I was ready with thirteen ways to say thanks for the compliments, but I was taken aback by the reaction of the other kids.

"Whatcha doin' with Kirkman's bike?"

"Why ya ridin' Kevin's Schwinn, man?"

"Yer bike get broke down, Stoker?"

All the comments were like that. Everyone thought I was riding Kevin's bike or that I "borrowed" it so Mike could ride mine. Even when I explained that I had bought the bike and it was mine now, they referred to it as "Kevin's old bike."

It was an unbearable situation. All my excitement had been replaced by frustration. None of them understood at all. They didn't know what I had done to get that bike, the work I did for Grandpa or the discussion with my own parents to get permission. None of them could understand that it was my bike now.

That night after dinner, I took my bike across the lane to the garage. I closed the door as much as I could (it wouldn't close all the way) and opened Dad's toolbox. In a few minutes, I had removed the tank, the seat, and both fenders of the bike. With an old brush and half a can of old green paint, I went to work. I repainted that bike the most hideous mixture of colors that can be imagined. I decided to leave off the fenders and drive the bike "stripped for speed." I used so many colors on the tank that, had I been able to look into the future, I would have called it paisley. I wasn't sure myself whether I liked it or not, but I knew one thing. It was different than anything anyone else had.

When I drove my bike onto the playground the next morning, everyone noticed. Many liked the new look. Many did not. But they talked through two recesses and the lunch hour about Steve's bike! And later that week, fast and fenderless, Steve's bike defeated the newest three-speed in town by two lengths in a race from the Hiway Store to the Purina Feed Store, and a legend was born.

40

Uncle Gordon's Fairview Dream House

One summer I was called upon to help my Uncle Gordon fulfill a dream. It was his dream, exclusively his, and I envied him for being the dreamer. But when you watched his face as he explained it, it was hard not to get caught up in the dream as if it were part of us all. For a while that summer, his dream was as real as could be.

Uncle Gordon, my mother's younger brother, was married to Aunt Iris, and they had begun to add to their young family. They lived in the house on the "lower place", Grandpa Frank's other farm. It was a nice house, but Uncle Gordon wanted very much to have a home of his own. His opportunity came in a very unusual way. He bought a school building!

The Fairview School was located between American Falls and Aberdeen. There was no town there. In fact, there seemed to be nothing there at all. But a few hundred feet off the old highway, hidden in a wooded vale between highway and the lake, was a school. It had been used at one time, of course, but had been abandoned for years. Whatever students attended classes in that building were grown and gone.

The building was a remarkable piece of work. It had a wide set of concrete steps leading into the main floor. There was also a wide set of wooden steps leading to the large basement. By the standards of most school buildings, it was probably quite small, but for a home, it was a very large building.

The rooms on the main floor and one large room in the basement had stacks of school desks of all shapes and sizes reaching all the way to the very high ceilings. Some of the desks were large enough for adults, and had seats attached. They had desktops that lifted up, revealing a book storage area beneath. Other desks were very small and in groups of four or five in a row, sometimes more. Some of those were very small.

In addition to the desks, there were thousands of books scattered throughout the building. They were everywhere. Some were no more than shells of what they had been, but many were in very good condition. I asked Uncle Gordon if we might not take some of them home. When he explained that we were to clean them out of the building and burn them, I was ecstatic! It meant that I could hoard as many of those volumes as I could carry.

We began the task of clearing out the building by hauling desks out to the yard and stacking them so they could easily be loaded onto a truck later. It was not easy work, for most of them were connected together and it was difficult to navigate through the doorways and stairways with such strangely shaped objects. There were times when long assemblies had to be taken apart with screwdrivers and crowbars. We tried to avoid that, though, for it was too easy to damage them to the point where they were no longer useful. It was important to avoid damage, for the school district in American Falls wanted the desks delivered to them. It was part of the bidding deal that had brought the building to Uncle Gordon.

We used shovels at first to remove the dirt and dust, emptying them into buckets and hauling the heavy buckets outside and away from the building. One by one, until hundreds had been carted away, the buckets continued. Then we switched to brooms for a time, and then mops. The whole process took days, and the amount of matter removed from that building would have made the *Guiness Book of World Records*, I am sure.

During the cleaning period, Uncle Gordon allowed each of us to choose a desk for ourselves, to be hauled in his truck to our homes and given to us as permanent payment for our assistance. We were meticulous in making our choices. We examined everything, from storage space to writing surface, wanting to snag the very best for ourselves. I selected the very best I could find, and pushed, pulled and struggled to get it loaded onto the back of the truck. Mike and I chose fine desks, and were thrilled to get them. They were a wonderful bonus to go with the books I had hoarded. I had books on a variety of subjects. My favorites were the geography books with their maps. I loved maps. But I also had great books of Idaho and U.S. history, and even a terrific volume of *Grimm's Fairy Tales*. For months after helping my uncle, my poor mother secretly weeded out the collection of books until it was manageable.

After the cleaning, Uncle Gordon took a sledgehammer and began putting holes in the walls of the building; holes that would be doors and windows. It was an arduous task, as the walls were nearly three feet in thickness. In time, the new holes were framed and the old ones filled. The entire building began to take on a different look.

Those of us children that had helped in the early stages stopped visiting Fairview as more skilled workers and grownups took over the work that needed doing. We stayed at home, out of the picture, and in time, even began another school year.

The grain was harvested and the potatoes almost ready to dig when I next visited the old school. It had been completely transformed! It still had the outward appearance the original building had, but it was more colorful. But the real surprise was inside. The high ceilings were gone. The large area was divided into kitchen, bedrooms, living and dining rooms, and closets. The ceilings were lowered to about eight or nine feet. The floors were plush carpets and the decorating was first rate.

The old school had become a home, but even more. It was a showplace, a remarkable achievement, and I was so proud of my uncle for his dream and his determination. He had succeeded where lesser men would never have tried. And to this day, though the conversion has long since passed into other hands, I feel a pride in my Uncle for turning an old and forgotten country schoolhouse into a beautiful rambling ranch house.

41

Roller-skating

There were a lot of fads that came and went as I grew up in Aberdeen. I was inspired to take up roller-skating by the athletic antics of just a few of the other kids. There were some that could zip by at breakneck speeds, both frontward and backward. They could spin and jump and stop on a dime. I was envious of their skill and daring and could hardly wait to exhibit my own version of these qualities.

The acquisition of skates was not an easy thing for me. There was not a great deal of money floating around at that time, and my birthday and Christmas were both a half-year away. At first I thought that perhaps I could convince my mother of the importance of my owning some skates and, at the same time, point out the folly of waiting until mid-winter when roller skates would be of no use to anyone.

Needless to say, my mother was "underwhelmed" by my arguments and stood by her decision to not buy me skates. She did, however, leave a small door open with the suggestion that perhaps I could earn enough doing odd jobs to purchase my skates without her help. It was a neat idea, but easier said than done. The only people I knew had their own kids and all the work to be done was already part of their kids' chores.

I searched high and low for some way to make a few dollars. I became obsessed with the idea of owning my own skates. Images flashed through my head in the form of daydreams. They were images of me skating faster, farther, and smoother than any other kid at Aberdeen Elementary. They were daydreams in which I excelled in my natural ability to spin, and dart, and turn, and jump curbs. I just **had** to have those skates!

A breakthrough finally came in the Spring, coincidental to one of the rites of Spring that we always faced—shearing day, the day that the sheep had to be gathered together. The day they had to be penned in a special way so that the shearing crew that was hired could easily reach those woolies and wrestle them into submission for their annual haircuts.

Shearing day always brought a great deal of excitement. It was, in addition to being necessary for the health and well being of the farm, a social event. The womenfolk worked to provide a king's table for lunchtime, for sheep shearing crews have avarice appetites. In fact, those very appetites and the resulting sluggishness produced by midday engorgement were the very reasons why Grandpa Frank pushed so hard to get the bulk of the job done in the morning. He oversaw the herding, shearing, penning, and even cooking with the finesse of a chessmaster.

Every year Grandpa asked for volunteers to "tromp" the wool. Every year he assigned it to one of his younger sons. Once assigned, they did an admirable job. I had watched them in the past and I felt that it was time to pass the mantle. I asked Grandpa if I could "tromp."

At first, he just laughed. Then he asked me why I would want to do such a job. When I explained about the skates, he asked what the Valley Store might be asking for skates these days. I told him they were nearly five dollars and a skate key was an extra quarter. He looked out over the backs of his sheep for the longest time and then he agreed to let me tromp the wool. He said that if I stuck it out until the end of the day, he would give me ten dollars. I did, and the ten dollars was paid.

The very next day, after school, Mom took me to buy my skates. There were two types of roller skates, but I had no decision to make. My ten dollars was not enough to purchase the kind of skates that were already attached to their own shoes. So I bought the cheaper kind, the kind with little clamps that squeezed in over the shoe soles to hold the toes in place and then strapped across the instep of the foot to hold the remainder of the skate in place.

I loved my skates. They were bright and shiny, and the straps and wheels were dark blue. The night I bought them, I put them on again and again, turning the skate key on the bolt that tightened the clamp and adjusting it over and over again, looking for the best "feel." I spun the wheels with my finger and they just turned forever, as if there were no resistance at all. I could hardly wait to sail across the school playground, but I had to wait. Mom wouldn't even let me stand up with them on my feet. She said the linoleum would get dented, so she watched me closely all evening, ready to pounce on me if I disobeyed.

The next day, we left for school early. I buckled the straps of my new skates together so that I could drape them over my shoulder as I rode my bike.

I arrived at school more than a half-hour before the first bell and quickly surveyed the sidewalks and concrete surfaces around the school to see where the smoothest place might be to launch my new image. I decided on the basketball court. There was one basket there with an old rim and part of a metal chain net. There was no one playing basketball though, so I knew it would be great for roller-skating.

I sat on the south steps of the school and carefully connected my new skates to my shoes. I was slow and meticulous, somehow knowing how important it was to have a snug and secure fit. When I finally had them just right, I stood up. It was amazing how short everyone looked from my new height. Then I took my first step. Suddenly, It was amazing how tall everyone looked from my new low!

I was never so thankful for the padding on my rear as I was with that first fall, for it was fast and hard and I was not prepared to fall. After all, I was supposed to be racing and jumping and spinning. Not falling on my keester!

I had been humiliated, but I was only down, not out. I picked myself up and once again reached a standing position. This time, I held on to the wall at the edge of the steps and I put one foot in front of the other. I did it again. And again. I was walking. I even allowed myself to roll just a bit. No problem. I allowed both feet to roll. I let go of the wall and headed out toward the basketball court. Small steps, ever so small, as I moved away from the school into "no man's land." I was roller-skating. It wasn't pretty, but I was doing it.

As I gained confidence, I began to look around. Other kids were watching me. I increased my speed, discovered I was going too fast, and decided to cross my foot in front, spin once, and stop—facing the opposite direction. In my mind's eye, I could visualize my move and even the "ooohs" and "ahhhhs" of my audience. I felt good. I was in control. It was going to happen.

My mind's eye had absolutely no control over my feet and legs. I crossed my right foot and front of my left and initiated the spin that I knew would come. But it did not stop. I made at least four revolutions, my arms flailing in various directions as I tried to regain control. Then I landed on my hands and knees. Hard! My jeans were ripped as my knees sought a hold of their own in the concrete. My hands caught me, protecting my head from major trauma.

I sat there, all alone with my misery. Everything was hurt—my knees, my hands, my elbows, my shoulders, and my pride. I clenched my fists, just to see if they were there and to hide the blood from the abrasions. I did not want this to be a big deal.

I carefully removed the skates, got to my feet, and entered the school. I draped the skates over my shoulder as I rode home that day and put them carefully in the "back room," the place where everything was stored that had outlived its usefulness.

For a time, I wore the skate key around my neck and school, and let everyone think I did my skating at the church. Those from the church thought I skated at Cub Scouts. One thing was for certain. I never again tried to roller skate. In a few weeks, I set the skate key aside as I played "keepaway" and someone stole it. More power to them. I hope it unlocked **his** dreams.

42

Cub Scouts

I was a Cub Scout. That may not sound like much, but at the time it was the epitome of respectability. It was neat. It was cool. It was the thing to be. Scouts were revered among boys and I not only wanted to be a scout, I wanted to be a good one. It was a goal that was common among the boys in the town, and as soon as I was eligible, I joined.

I became a full-fledged member of Pack 21. I went to den meetings once a week after school. They were at Dean Tarpeel's house. His mother, Dorothy, was our den mother. She was a pretty little woman and wasn't much taller than we were. She was always smiling and had the energy of ten women. It had to be one of the best cub scout dens ever, and that's really saying something, because there were a lot of cub scout dens in Aberdeen. Behind potatoes, scouts were the principal export.

Mrs. Tarpeel always treated me like something special because I had learned so much about astronomy and she was interested in it too. We had many discussions about the planets and their order from the sun, etc. I always felt good when she seemed so impressed with what I could remember.

One time, we had our den meeting in the Tarpeel's back yard. It was an interesting yard, too, because of the rumor that they had a fallout shelter. I had heard that they built it after an accident at the atomic energy site near Arco, Idaho, northwest of Aberdeen. There had been a lot of publicity about it, not to mention the ever-increasing fears about communism and nuclear holocaust. Anyway, rumors were flying that the Tarpeel family was able to allay their fears with the construction of a fallout shelter. Many of us envied them. Others might have thought them a bit strange for worrying so much. Either way, they had an interesting yard, especially since I didn't see anything special there. If a shelter was there it was well hidden.

That backyard meeting was memorable for several reasons. It was the first time I ever tried to make my own neckerchief slide. I carved out a terrific Indian head and painted the finished carving in bright colors to accent the shape of the Indian's face. I was quite proud of it and used it for many years, passing it on to one brother after another.

The meeting was also memorable in that we learned how to bake a cake on an open fire by using a coffee can to make a reflector oven. We all ate what we baked, even though a few of the efforts were hardly palatable. Mine didn't turn out too bad. At least it cooked all the way through and it cooked evenly. OK, so there were a couple of flour clumps here and there. So what? It isn't easy using a fork as a beater.

The biggest event of that marathon meeting, though, came from the very back of the yard. Along the back of the property was a small ditch that carried the water for irrigating the Tarpeel's lawn (as well as every other lawn on that block). As our meeting wound to a close and interest in the projects began to wane, the boys got a bit rowdy and began horsing around on the ditch bank. It wasn't long before they had disturbed a nest of garter snakes and then the chase was on. Every boy in Aberdeen loved to catch garter snakes.

Garter snakes are basically harmless creatures and prefer to be left alone, but can be very useful as filler material for girls' dresses and even for the drawers in school teachers' desks. I had been catching and using them since before I started school. It was a simple procedure. It only required that a stick be pressed onto the snake until the captor could grab it between thumb and forefinger, right behind the neck. Then it could be exhibited in a variety of ways.

On that particular day, I was as quick as the rest of the guys to go after a snake. After all, what better way to impress the beautiful Connie Conklin than to be able to show proof of my abilities as a hunter and provider. I spotted a likely candidate for capture and leaped into the squirming mass of reptiles and cub scouts, anxious to make my mark.

I got my hands on the largest snake I could see and in moments, he was mine. He rolled and slithered and slithered and rolled, but I did not let go. I was bigger and stronger and braver than some old garter snake. That is, until he bit me. That's right. He bit me! Never had anyone I knew been bitten by a garter snake, but I guess these guys were pretty riled up. The snake latched onto the back of my middle finger and hung on. I ran across the yard to Mrs. Tarpeel and the snake was still hanging on. Before she could react, one of the other scouts grabbed the sides of the snake's jaws and squeezed and, only then, did the snake release his hold on my finger. They dropped him and he slithered away.

The skin was broken on my finger and a red welt had formed. It didn't really hurt any more than a clothespin would have, but I didn't let on. I played it for all it was worth as my cub friends gathered round to see my snakebite. For a time, I was the center of attention. When Mrs. Tarpeel finally applied some tincture of merthiolate and a bandage, I was almost saddened to have the wound covered.

The next day, even without the snake, I got the sympathy of several of the girls, not the least of which was the beautiful Connie.

43

The New Fire Truck

The fire station and city hall was located off Main Street, just around the corner from the Utoco Station. We had a fire engine and it had a bell and a siren, just like in the movies. It was, however, the oldest vehicle in town with the possible exception of Old Man Kramer's pickup. To me, I thought it a miracle that it even started, let alone made actual trips to fires and other emergencies.

The only time that old fire engine ever looked good was during the annual parade during July. It always led the parade and was cleaned up for just that purpose. With an all-volunteer fire department, that was the only time anyone made the effort. The rest of the year, it was often dusty and dirty, but it was always full of gas and ready to go whenever the town's emergency siren wailed its call for the volunteers.

Of course, the town siren was also used to mark the hour of twelve o'clock on every day except Sunday. I always wondered what would happen if a fire call came in at noon on one of those days. How would the firemen know to rush to the station?

Whenever the town's whistle signaled that there was a fire to be extinguished, the entire core of Aberdeen became an instant flurry of activity as the merchants and other businessmen of the town raced to the fire station and assumed their duties as firemen. Joe Darvik would be out the door and halfway across the Main Street before his customers realized just how long they might have to wait for service at the cash register line. Leland Tarpeel would leave his customers to their own devices when it came to checking oil and pumping gas. He was proud of his Utoco Station and didn't like to leave his customers to serve themselves, but priorities were drawn and there was no hesitation. Sometimes, his customers were right beside him in the race for the firehouse.

They came from both sides of the street—the Western Auto Store, The Valley Store, Wampler's Clothing, The People's Store, Wilde's IGA, and Mary's Cafe. And even though these people left their shelves unattended and their businesses open, there was never a question about its being intact when they returned. Whether after hot, dusty, dangerous hours fighting a haystack fire or a few minutes to douse some burning leaves that got blown too close to someone's house, the result was the same. No one stole anything. Most were patient enough to wait. Those that weren't would leave a note apologizing for their lack of patience.

Time finally took its toll on that old fire engine and it became evident that it needed to be replaced. Unfortunately, the Aberdeen budget could barely pay the expenses for gasoline for a fire engine, let alone buy a new engine. We were, after all, a very poor little farm town. For a time, the idea of purchasing a new fire engine was brought up at town council meetings and then quickly dismissed since there was no apparent solution to the problem. Meanwhile, time and again, the responses to emergency calls came closer and closer to the edge of disaster. It was only a matter of time until one of the calls would be a home instead of a trash barrel or a haystack.

The first real move to acquire a new fire engine was made by my Cub Scout pack. It might have had something to do with the fact that Dorothy Tarpeel, my den mother, was the wife of Leland Tarpeel, the volunteer fire chief. I don't really know. But the move was made nonetheless. We made contact with a fund raising organization and made arrangements to sell home fire extinguishers. They were state of the art cans, with the latest technology allowing them to be pressurized so that, when a button was pushed on the top, a white creamy gunk would come out and smother any small "around the house" fire.

Our fire extinguisher campaign was a big hit. We charged the obscene price of $3.00 for each can and we only paid fifty cents apiece for them. We kept no secrets, however, and the entire town knew of the mark-up. They didn't seem to mind, though, and they supported our effort to raise money to purchase a new fire engine. We went from door to door and were seldom turned away until the latter days of the campaign when people would invite us into their kitchens to show us the collections of extinguishers they had accumulated.

We raised a lot of money for the cause, but the most important thing we accomplished was in rousing the community to action. In just a few weeks there were bake sales, yard sales, garage sales, and even a farm equipment auction with the proceeds going to the fire engine fund. There were dinners and barbecues where the whole town was invited and charged a "plate fee" to help raise more money. There were signs made by the kids at school plastered in every window of every business in Aberdeen and some even managed to find their way to the storefronts of American Falls.

The town coffers began to fill ever so slowly at first, then enjoyed small spurts amid the periods of stagnation. Finally the announcement was made that the new engine could be ordered. We had done it! We had made enough to buy a new fire engine.

The whole town turned out for a ribbon-cutting ceremony when the new vehicle was placed into service. It was a red-letter day, to be sure, and a testament to what a community can do. We were very proud.

At the Aberdeen Days parade on the next 24th of July, our new fire engine led the way, followed by the old pumper, which was still brought out for parades, though good for nothing else. We would look at each other and grin in the knowledge that little old Aberdeen was probably the only town of its size with **two** fire engines in their parade. We were so proud!

44

Dwight's Bad Day

There were many ways to get into trouble at my grandparents' house and I think I managed to find them all. But I remember one time when the trouble belonged solely and completely to my Uncle Dwight.

Dwight was nine months older than I, to the day, and we were the best of friends. He was, however, one of the most luckless people I have ever known. That one summer day was enough to convince anyone of the truthfulness of that fact.

We had been playing all over farm that day. We had started by hunting frogs down at the slough. We caught several good specimens and were tiring of the sport when Dwight decided to take an unnecessary risk and try for one very large bullfrog among the cattails and reeds.

He stalked it carefully, moving slowly and quietly through the mud near the bank. The frog kept a jump ahead of him at first, but he was persistent. He kept stalking that elusive amphibian as best he could, completely unaware that he was being drawn into a very unstable section of ground. As he readied himself for the final assault, his shoes became firmly implanted in the mud and he pulled his right foot from the shoe as he pounced upon the frog. He lost his balance and went face first into the slough, arms flailing helplessly and both shoes staying in the mire.

When he came out of the water, he was covered with muck. He was also covered with insects, some of which couldn't even be identified! The mud had closed over his shoes and the disturbance in the water had removed all evidence that he had even been there. He poked around in the mud for five minutes until he was able to extract his shoes. Then he dragged himself, panting in frustration, to the bank, where he flopped into the foxtail and weeds—weeds that left him covered with burrs. A tar and feather job could not have been more effective. He was a mess, and on the verge of tears.

We went back to my grandmother's house and she came out and hosed him off. We all helped to remove the burrs. He was not a happy kid.

Less than an hour later, he was in a fresh set of jeans, had a clean shirt, and a pair of tennis shoes. Grandpa asked us to scout around and find some eggs. Most of the chickens were in the coop and their eggs were in the proper place, but there were a few chickens that had "flown the coop" and had been laying eggs all over the farm in various locations. It was our task to find those locations and retrieve the eggs.

We were quite successful for a time, finding eggs near the playhouse, the garage, under the apple trees, and in and around the haystacks. Dwight spotted two of the best laying hens sneaking under the wooden floor of the barn, through a large opening near the pigpen. He lay prostrate on the straw and stuck his head down near the opening to look for eggs. The sunlight was too bright to see anything, so he moved in close enough to get his head into the opening and out of the sun. After his eyes adjusted to the gloom, he spotted a nest just a few feet further under the floor. As he wriggled even farther into the hole, he startled a chicken that was still underneath and it nearly tore off his head as it came out through the opening!

The suddenness of the assault made him jump and he cracked his head on a huge beam that held the floor in place. He pulled himself out of the hole as a huge red bump formed on the side of his head. It was not a pretty sight.

He should have let it go at that, but now it was a matter of principle. He had to win at all costs and he returned to the hole under the barn floor with a new resolve. In seconds, he had managed to get close enough to reach the eggs. He grabbed the first, pulled it back into his left hand, and reached forward for another. Again he was successful. As he went after the third and last egg, his luck ran out. The two eggs in his left hand exploded! Then the third egg exploded in his right hand. They were old and rotten.

He looked like a trapped badger the way he backed out of that hole. He did it with the speed of a badger, too. Dean, Mike, and I held our noses to avoid the stench that emanated from his newly decorated shirt and we escorted him back to the house. Grandma came out and hosed him off. He was soon dressed again and we went to play. We were finished with egg gathering for the day.

For a time, we climbed around in the apple tree and threw crab apples at each other. The need for another source of "ammo" led us to the "monkey nut" trees on the far side of Grandma's garden, where we had a seemingly endless supply of throwing material. Soon, though, we tired of that game and returned to the apple trees at the end of the garden so we could "scarf" a couple of green apples for munchies. We would have been OK, too, but Dwight found a hole high up on the trunk of one of the trees and stuck his hand into it to see how deep it was.

Well, it wasn't very deep, but it was deep enough to house a hive of bees. They did not take kindly to the probing of Dwight's fingers and they responded as one. He dropped to the ground and began to run as they swarmed after him. It was like something out of a cartoon, the way the bees streamed after him. When he reached the grass of the back lawn, he tripped and fell and began to roll over and over in an effort to dislodge those insects that had gained a footing on his ample body. He was being stung and he was being stung a lot.

Grandma came to his rescue and began to hose him off, driving the bees away with the water. Once again, he had to dress in dry clothing, but this time, he had to wait while Grandma smeared his upper torso with calamine lotion. His left eye and both hands swelled to three times normal size as his crying finally dwindled to no more than a few sobs.

Grandma suggested that he remain in the house for the rest of the day, so we began a game of Monopoly. I guess his luck wasn't **all** bad that day, though, because he wound up with Boardwalk and Park Place and had a hotel on each. By dinnertime, Uncle Dwight was a winner!

45

The Home Market Caper

Lester Larkin was my best friend, without a doubt, but I had other friends with whom I grew very close. Kevin Kirkman was one of those friends.

Kevin and I went to the same church and became friends over a period of time. He was taller than most kids our age and had a blond crewcut that he kept adequately greased. He walked with the upper half of his torso bent forward, as if he were about to fall, but as near as I can tell, he never did. He had a slight speech impediment that did not bother me and an attitude that did. Much of the time, he seemed to have a chip on his shoulder. He was quick to anger and quick to fight, and seemed to always be on the defensive. He was just as quick to join in at play if the slightest of invitations was rendered.

Kevin's parents, Ron and Nell were an interesting couple. Ron was a very large man, even larger than the town policeman, Herschel Vergus. In fact, for a long time, Ron was a deputy of Herschel's. There were many jokes about Aberdeen having Idaho's largest police force. Nell was a nice lady with bunches of little wart-like things growing in the folds of her neck. I think they were called "skin tags" but I am not certain. They always fascinated me but, of course, such things were never pointed out or discussed.

The Kirkmans were, for the most part, merchants. They had several business enterprises over the years, but the one steady thing that was always there was The Home Market, their little store that carried a wide variety of items for sale in a very small space. Most of their business came from the sale of groceries, but they kept all sorts of oddball items that would be hard to find anywhere else, much of it catering to the wants and needs of school kids. The Home Market was strategically located on a side street between the school buildings and Main Street. Half the kids in town had to pass the Home Market a couple of times a day during the school year.

Sometimes, if I were with Kevin, we would storm through the store to the living area in the back where the Kirkmans made a home. On the way, Mrs. Kirkman would permit us to delve lightly into the penny candy boxes at the counter. I always took a jawbreaker, because they would last for hours if you sucked them just right and held them between the cheek and gum properly as soon as they were small enough.

When Nell Kirkman was having a real good day, we were granted leave to select a Sugar Daddy or a Black Cow. Once I even got a Big Hunk with a Cherry-O-Let and an Idaho Spud. I loved Idaho Spuds because they had shredded coconut on them.

I would come and go as I pleased between the store and the living quarters, because I was Kevin's friend. They made me feel like one of the family. They trusted me, and I betrayed that trust in the worst way.

It happened one Spring day when I was in the fourth grade. I got out of school and met my friend Lester at the bottom of the fire escape. We walked together to the Home Market and decided to go in and check out the "squirt guns." After all, it was that time of year and we children felt compelled to add as many colorful little water pistols to the teachers' collection boxes as was possible.

Lester and I greeted Mrs. Kirkman and began to browse the store. Lester and I were over against the wall when we whispered to each other and made the decision to steal something. Neither of us had money, and there were some brand new Duncan Yo-Yo's in the display case at the end of the aisle. I went over and chatted with Mrs. Kirkman while Lester filled his pockets and stuffed things down his pants. As soon as he was safely outside the store, I said good-bye to her and left. Then I met him outside and we ran into the alley behind the bank to divvy up the loot.

Lester had stolen two yo-yos, several packages of Double Bubble with baseball cards inside, a pack of Twinkies, two water pistols, and a ball. I took the Twinkies, a yo-yo, a green water pistol, and half the bubble gum. Then Lester headed for his house and I headed for home. Both of us swore a secret oath to never tell what had happened.

On the way home, it occurred to me that my mother would question how I had acquired these treasure, so I decided to hide them in the rafters of the old chicken coop and not even take them into the house. It was a clever plan, but did me no good whatsoever.

Lester was caught with the yo-yo right at dinnertime and he told the whole story to his mother. She called my mother and told her the story. And Mom told Dad. He was not happy. He ordered me to bring every item to him. I went out in the dark to the chicken coop and brought in the whole stash. At that point, my father began a very long lecture about integrity and honesty and how a man's good name was all he had of any importance. A good name and reputation was the only important thing you can have when you leave this world. Stealing from someone was the absolute nastiest thing a person could do.

There was much more. It was a long lecture, and he ended it by telling me that he would drive me to school in the morning and all the things I took would have to be returned. Then he sent me to bed. No one said good night to me, and my brothers and sister were not permitted to talk to me. I had a terrible time sleeping.

In the morning, my father was true to his word. He ordered me into the pickup and drove me directly to the Home Market. We sat in the pickup for about fifteen minutes before they opened and it was the longest quarter hour I ever spent with my father. He did not speak and would not look at me. I had a lump in my throat as big as an Idaho baking potato. It seemed like forever before that store finally opened and Ron came out to run his American flag up the flagpole at the corner of the store.

Dad handed me a five-dollar bill and told me that I was to take back the things I had taken and pay the full value for them, in addition to apologizing to Mr. & Mrs. Kirkman. It was the hardest thing I ever had to do. I felt like crying. My father was treating me like the scum of the earth, and I had to muster up an apology and get it out without breaking into tears. I did it. Barely! And Mrs. Kirkman said that I did not have to pay for the items, but my father was at the front door and told her that I must. She accepted the money and rang up a **NO SALE** on the cash register. She took the items and laid them under the counter. She said that all was square, but we both knew it would never be square again.

I could never look Mrs. Kirkman straight in the eye again after that morning. I always remembered the humiliation of that experience, even long after she forgot.

Lester's dad gave him a lecture, too, and made him go pay for the items, but he didn't have to give them back. As far as I know, neither of us ever shoplifted again.

46

Lucy's Fleas

On every playground in the land there are games played. For the most part, the games are similar, no matter where you might be. In Aberdeen, we played a lot of tag. In simple terms, a person was designated as "it." "It" would race around in a desperate effort to touch one of the other kids and transfer that dubious label. It was not a good thing to be "it." Once the label was transferred with a legal touch, the new "it" would be off and running.

There are, however, variations to this game. In the small town of Aberdeen, the variations were as cruel and insensitive as in any large city. One of those variations was called "Lucy's Fleas." It was just like any other games of tag except for the malicious tone and the intensity of the players in their efforts to **not** be the one designated as having "Lucy's Fleas."

Children are, without a doubt, the most intolerant of any group. That is the reason why, when faced with differences from the norm, they actually become hostile, and even openly cruel.

I was introduced to "Lucy's Fleas" long before I had a clue about the origin of the name. To me, at first, Lucy was an imaginary person of terrible repute and in the course of avoiding the touch of her "fleas" I came to be just as adamant about avoiding this imagined scourge as the rest of the children of Aberdeen.

One day, totally out of the blue, I found out the true history of the game. I saw Lucy. She was four years older than I and therefore, in a different school building and in a different circle of peers. One of the guys in my gang of friends pointed her out and announced that she was **the** Lucy, the one with the "cooties," the famous girl whose fleas I had been avoiding for a couple of years.

When I heard the news, I went to my uncle, Dean Slaugh, for verification. He confirmed that she was, indeed, the same Lucy. I was fascinated. I wanted to know more about this malady that Lucy had, for it had elevated her to a high status in my mind. Imagine having a problem so well known and talked about that a game of tag was named after you.

I followed behind Lucy and her younger brothers on the way home from school one day, just to see where she lived. I was surprised to find that she lived just a few minutes walk from my house. Lucy's family lived in a ramshackle house that had seen better days. Half the windows had not glass, but wood instead. Glass had been there at one time, but as the glass was broken, it was replaced with panels of wood, for glass was far too expensive.

Lucy and her brothers were from a poor family—very poor. Lucy's dad was a man that took odd jobs on the farms in the area. He was a big, friendly guy with a great smile that appeared often when he was around his children. His wife was equally friendly, but always seemed to be occupied with her housework, trying to make do with what she had in her efforts to make her family comfortable.

The children all went to school in a group, not separating until they were at the elementary school. Then Lucy and one brother would go on to the junior high. The other two boys went to the same school as I did, but were two grades behind me. None of the kids seemed to have any friends. They stayed close to each other. I didn't really understand why until much later.

I didn't dwell on Lucy's problems. I had investigated. I saw no cooties. I saw no fleas. I was as confused as ever, but I continued to play the game.

A few weeks later, I was playing on the lawn in front of the church while waiting for my mother when Lucy and one of her brothers walked by. Some of my friends began to taunt her. Soon the catcalls were flying from several sides. They had started with remarks about "Lucy's fleas," but soon included hateful and malicious remarks about the holes in their shoes and the homemade clothing they wore. That bothered me a bit because my mother made most of our clothes and I didn't know it was a bad thing. Of course, my mother always managed to buy regular material. Lucy's mother had only white muslin and flour sacks to work with, but the finished dresses were not unattractive. At least, I didn't think so.

In just a few moments, poor Lucy was crying and the children that hooted and hollered seemed satisfied and started off to do other things. But they were not permitted to continue their play. My mother and Mrs. Rees had come out of the church in time to see most of what had happened. They called all of us around in a circle and my mother gave us a lecture about differences in people. At first, she embarrassed me, but when she pointed out Danny's big ears, Lester's freckles, Kevin's speech problem, and my glasses, she began to make her point.

There were no miracles that day. No one ran after and apologized to Lucy. And "Lucy's fleas" did not disappear from playground games. But I think there were some changes—small ones that don't seem like much. I first noticed it when Lester included Lucy's little brother when we chose up sides for softball. Soon her brothers were playing in several different groups. And Lucy herself had even found a group of girls to pal around with. They were still poor and still dressed the same as before. As far as I know, the only difference was that just a few of the other kids in school became just a bit more tolerant of the differences that make us all unique.

47

Mike's Fifteen Minutes of Fame

Aberdeen seldom had real emergency situations, but sometimes they were inevitable. One summer day in the mid-50's, the volunteer fire department received one of the strangest calls of their entire history.

The Aberdeen Telephone Company was a small phone company that was owned and operated by my second cousins, the Matson family. It was a company that is completely independent of the huge Bell system, but one could hardly tell except for the strange line noises and the single operator that manned the switchboard. Emergency calls went directly to that operator and she, in turn, called the city offices and reported the situation as best she could. The city office was the location of the switch for the emergency siren. Once that switch was thrown, it set in motion a remarkable series of events.

On that fateful day, the siren went off on schedule to mark the noon hour. Scarcely ten minutes later it sounded a second time, and the merchants of Aberdeen leaped into action. In moments, the new engine was out of its garage and waiting as the latecomers rushed to hop aboard for the trip to the site of the reported emergency. Those already there were scrambling into their respective emergency garb; boots, helmets, and oversized protective suits.

In minutes, the engine was on its way, this time led by Herschel Vergus in the city police car, which happened to be nearby. That helped to ensure that traffic was out of the way. As they raced to their destination on the south side of town, the word was passed that this was not a fire, but the rescue of a child, and the protective dress was being relaxed even as the engine roared out onto the highway.

In just a quarter of a mile, the engine left the highway and turned onto Beach Road. They were on their way to my house. They were on the way to help my brother, Mike.

Earlier that day, Mike and I had played out in the fields, riding our imaginary horses the entire length of the road that traversed our eighty-acre farm. It started as our driveway, then passed the corrals, the granary, the barn, and then turned gradually to the left as it skirted the sugar beet field. It made a sharp right turn after the first bridge over the irrigation ditch and continued on through the middle of the wheat and barley fields, and the alfalfa field. Then it ended at the second beet field. It was a gravel road as far as the barn, but from that point it was a dirt road, its center marked by clover and weeds. Mike and I often used it for play, for we were able to actually stir up a dust trail with our imaginary horses. It was impressive!

After a morning of hard riding, we had a light lunch and then went out to continue playing. We did not go back to our horse riding game, but instead we decided to explore the outbuildings in search of something that would trigger an even better imaginary game. We found that something of interest in the barn, next to the bins where Dad kept the grain for the milk cows.

It was a milk can. Milk cans were very large and shiny cans with metal lids that usually had to be removed by striking them under the edge with a piece of two by four or a similar object. In this case, my father kept a small crowbar hanging on a hook from one of the barn's support posts. This was accomplished by using a small piece of rawhide as a hanger. Under normal circumstances, the lid would remain on the can and its cleanliness for the next milking would not be compromised. But Mike and I had different plans for that milk can.

We managed to remove the bar from its hook and we pounded and pounded, first under one side and then the other, until we were able to lift the lid from the can. At first, that was enough. We looked in the can, we lifted it, one of us at each handle. We turned it on its side in the straw. I got on all fours and stuck my head into it and yelled, enjoying the echo. It was fun. Then Mike took a turn.

He got on all fours, just as he had seen me do, and stuck his head in the can. He yelled too. But it wasn't enough. He wanted to try that great echo with a song:

"Tweedly, tweedly, tweedly, dee.
I'm as happy as can be.
Jiminy Cricket. Jiminy Jack.
You make my heart go clickety clack.
Tweedly, tweedly, tweedly dee."

It was a thrill for him to hear his voice amplified and reverberated by the milk can. But as his song ended and he tried to pull his head back out, it became all too evident that he was stuck.

I tried everything a big brother could do. I pulled on his feet, but that only pulled the can and hurt his neck. I sat astride the can as though it were a horse and encouraged my younger brother to pull with all his might. He tried his best, moving from one position to another, but it was to no avail. It was as if his singing had caused his head to swell. It was not coming out!

Mike began to cry. At first it was just a whimper, but it soon became a panic stricken bawling that alarmed me and I decided to go for help. I told him to stop crying and I would get Mom to help. Then I ran to the house and burst through the screen door out of breath and hardly able to explain to my mother what had happened.

We returned to the barn. My mother wasn't sure what had happened but when she heard the wailing, she quickened her step. Her presence seemed to allay Mike's fear somewhat, for the crying subsided to sobs as

Mom and I tried to work together to extricate him. We weren't any more successful than I had been alone, and Mom told me to stay with Mike while she called for help. She returned to the house as Mike renewed his bawling. He was crying so hard that the back of his neck was all red. It must have been a great echo for him to listen to.

Dad was away at a lamb auction in Blackfoot, so my mother called the operator and declared an emergency.

When the police car and the fire truck arrived, my mother was in the driveway to guide them to the barn. Behind the fire truck came the curious onlookers, and the reporter for the Aberdeen Times, our weekly newspaper. The entire driveway was congested with traffic as everyone sought access to find out what was happening.

Harold Larkin, my friend Lester's dad, and the town's only plumber, could not contain himself. He began to laugh. Soon, the entire volunteer fire department was in various stages of belly laughter, and my brother's crying took on a different tone as his emotions changed from abject fear to frustration and anger.

It took several tries before Mike's head was finally relieved of its oversized helmet. An application of axle grease finally allowed his head to slip from its trap. My mother hustled him off to the house so she could clean him up, but not before his picture was taken for the local press.

The following Thursday, Mike's legs were featured on the front page of The Aberdeen Times, but his face was still firmly ensconced in the milk can. I was so proud of my "celebrity" brother!

48

Shear and Shear Alike

Sheep shearing day came every Spring. It was a busy day, and full of very hard work, but we all looked forward to it. It was one of those events on the farm that took on the air of a celebration—an event.

My Grandfather Frank made arrangements far in advance with the crew that was to do the actual shearing, for their time was at a premium, and contracts had to be made to ensure that they would be available. Grandpa knew all the good crews and some of those that weren't so good, and so was able to dicker for a good price and an ideal time frame just by virtue of his reputation as a fair and knowledgeable farmer.

It was important to get a good crew for it made the difference between profit and loss in a very competitive market. A good crew could command top wages for its work, but it was not easy to be a good crew. It took a good deal of experience to learn how to shear efficiently without harming the animal. Of course, nicks and cuts were always part of the process, for the sheep seldom cooperated. A bad crew however, often turned the animals back into the corral with serious wounds, sometimes with profuse bleeding.

There were preparations that had to be made the day before shearing day. The sheep had to be gathered from whatever pastures they were grazing in and moved to the shearing location. Sometimes, that was at our farm, and sometimes at a neighboring farm. It was much more efficient to gather several herds together for the shearing and then the cutters only had to set up once.

For that year we had to move the sheep to Bill Darvik's farm, about half a mile to the north of us. Bill and his hired man had already prepared the "holding pens" by wiring dozens of four foot panels together and forming a maze of chutes and small pens. By using such a series of chutes, the individual farmers were able to keep their stock separated from that of other farmers. It also made the job of branding much easier, for all the animals were branded immediately after the shearing.

We were able to move our herd in a couple of hours. Those that lived several miles away took all day to get their animals to the Darvik farm. By the end of the day, thousands of bleating woolies were crammed together in very uncomfortable surroundings and waiting for the cutters.

The shearing crew arrived with the dawn and set up quickly. They used bed sheets to separate their individual staging areas from the chutes. That fooled the sheep into thinking that there was a wall between them. All the cutter had to do was to reach beneath the curtain and grab the leg of the nearest animal, then pull it under the sheet and onto his platform. It took great skill to hold the sheep with one's legs and one hand while operating the electric clipper with the other hand.

The clippers were special, with each cutter maintaining his own, carefully sharpening and oiling to keep it in optimum condition. No one ever touched another man's clipper. To do so would cause serious repercussions.

Clippers consisted of a hand-held unit that had a blade about four inches across. It was attached to a series of short metal tubes that contained rods and gears that could be traced back to an electric motor that plugged in near the ceiling of the shed. They hung up and out of the way, kept secure by a wire harness. By controlling a thumb switch at the handle, the cutter could turn the blade on and off at a moment's notice. The elaborate system of rods and gears permitted the cutter to move the clipper in any angle of attack without being restricted.

Beside the shearing platforms, and to the rear, was a small area where the fleece could be scooted over with one foot by the cutter as he worked. Another person would be ready to tie the fleece with a cord. The cord was made of twisted paper, but was a strong as any twine. The fleece was usually removed as one piece and the person who tied the fleece would be ready with the cord laid across both insteps, feet about a foot apart. Then the fleece was pulled onto the feet and folded over like bread dough against the legs until it was compact enough to pull the ends of the cord over it, cross them, flip the fleece, and then tie it off. Then the fleece could be passed along in a bundle toward the tromping rack.

The tromping rack consisted of tall scaffolding with a three-foot circle cut in the platform at the top and an iron ring slightly larger in diameter. The large "wool bags" were about ten feet long and three feet in diameter. They were made of burlap. The open end was painstakingly wrapped around the iron ring and then the bag was allowed to hang from the circle on the tromping rack. The bottom of it hung about a foot off the ground. Because the bag was so long, a portable stairway was needed to reach the top of the rack. It resembled the gangway at airports that are used to roll up to the passenger doors of aircraft. Such a stairway allowed the carrying of the fleeces up to the top of the rack, where they were put into the opening.

It was my job, as a tromper, to be inside the big wool bag. It was a job that had just a few drawbacks. For one thing, it was very claustrophobic, to be in such a tight place, unable to see out, and having freshly sheared fleeces being poured down upon my head. I would pull them down past my body and proceed to "tromp" them, packing them as tightly into the huge bag as I could. It required a certain degree of skill, for to properly pack such a bag, I had to march in a circle, keeping one foot in the center while turning and jamming the other as far down the side of the bag as I could. Over and over again, I tromped and packed and tromped and packed, trying to get as tightly a packed bag as possible, containing as many fleeces as possible.

As the clattering of all the clippers filtered through the burlap, I tromped. Eventually I would be high enough in the bag so that my head was in the clear. I always looked forward to that, for even though I loved the odor of the lanolin in the wool, it was nice to occasionally get my head out into the air. Besides, there were some sheep that were not the cleanest creatures and their fleeces brought different texture and different odor—not quite so pleasant as lanolin.

As the day wore on, bag after bag was tromped and packed. My grandfather was there with a huge needle and string to sew the bags closed once they were packed tightly enough. Then a two by four and fulcrum was used to lift the bag high enough to dislodge it from the iron ring and it was allowed to topple out the side of the scaffolding onto it's side. A tractor with a front-end lift was then used to stack the bags at the side of the building, tagged with each farmer's name and a count of the number of fleeces inside.

At lunchtime on shearing day, the noon meal was a special treat, prepared by my grandmother, my mother, and by the wives of the other farmers involved. It was a meal that could put Thanksgiving dinner to shame and was as big a part of the day as the shearing itself. The cutters would eat and eat and eat, then take a short break, Grandpa called "siesta time." Then, after inundating the ladies with compliments about their fine meal, they would wander back to their staging areas, somehow all getting there about the same time and starting the afternoon's work all at the same time.

Sometimes, the cutters made a contest of the job, racing to see who sheared the most, or wagering on who could shear a sheep the fastest and cleanest. Such contests were always fun to watch. As night came on and lights were turned on, the horseplay seemed to stop and they all concentrated on finishing the job.

Finally, long after sundown, the last fleece was handed me to tromp and the partially filled bag was folded over, sewn and tagged. The cutters dismantled their equipment and chatted with each other as they stored it away and prepared to leave for their next job. Sometimes it would be nearby and they would be happy about a good night's sleep. Sometimes they had miles to travel so they could be ready the next morning to do another day's work in another place. In such instances, they would sleep in their vehicles as they traveled. It was not an easy life.

I would go home to a bath and a good night's sleep, feeling good about the work I had done. I hoped that my grandmother's remarks about the benefits of lanolin on skin and hair were true. And I drifted to sleep under woolen blankets, wondering if anyone else had any idea of how much went into the making of such blankets.

49

The Time Capsule

Mike and I were inspired when we decided to make a time capsule. We were really no different than thousands of others that have asked the question, "When I am gone, what will I leave behind?"

Now there is no rhyme or reason why two boys that have yet to live their lives should be worried about what they will leave behind, but worry we did. There were lengthy discussions about the great loss the planet would feel if Mike and I were no longer a part of its make-up. We were, after all, the center of our universe. Perhaps our perception was a bit jaded, perhaps not.

We had several discussions of how we might leave our marks on the world. We discussed fortune and fame, and the likelihood that neither were options we could count on. We discussed the possibility that either of us might become stars of the sports world, perhaps even of the caliber of Jay Nelson or Ron Potts, who were part of all the excitement after Aberdeen High played their basketball games. Even that was risky, however, for such acclaim is usually temporary. We needed something more permanent; something that would ensure our legacy to the world. We decided to bury a time capsule.

There were several days of conversations before we made the decisions about what to include in our capsule. Idea after idea was mentioned, then abandoned. Finally we had enough items in mind to truly impress those future persons who might find our treasures.

The next thing we had to do was come up with a suitable container. At first, we used a shoebox from my parents' closet. It had been used to hold my dad's Sunday shoes, but we knew he wouldn't miss it. He always had water to turn, beets to cultivate, or sheep to care for whenever the family was preparing to attend Sunday meetings. My dad's most pressing tasks seemed to be on Sunday, at least until we were home from church.

As we stashed our treasures in the box and began to talk about where we should bury our capsule, we realized that the shoebox was not strong enough to protect our legacy from the elements. We needed something else. We finally decided on a Mason jar. It would be sturdy and protected from the elements. It had a metallic lid that we knew would last the many decades that would be required. We returned dad's shoes to their box and "found" a Mason jar in the back room. We were ready.

Our next decision was also a difficult one. We had to find the ideal location in which to place our time capsule. We had seen a news story about a time capsule that was buried in the corner foundation of a new skyscraper in New York, but we had no new buildings that we could use. We talked of burying our capsule deep in the haystack. If we were careful, it could be put between the bales after the first crop of hay. By the time the third crop would be stacked on top, our bottle would be far inside the stack. Then we remembered that the hay disappeared during the winter months, so we abandoned that plan. We finally decided on a site. We dug a hole right in the center of the old chicken yard at the end of the rundown old coop behind our house.

We dug for a long time, taking turns on the shovel. As we dug, we talked, reaffirming our decision to bury the jar far beneath the surface of the ground, away from weather and people and animals that might seek to ruin our project.

When the hole was finally ready, we placed the jar and its contents, with great ceremony, more than a foot below the surface of the chicken yard. We replaced the soil that had been removed, brushing away the area carefully to remove any indication that the ground had been disturbed. We even transplanted a weed right atop the spot to help hide it.

Mike had put his entire collection of bubble gum comics in the jar, wrapped carefully and secured by a rubber band. There were comics from both *Double Bubble* and *Bazooka*. He also contributed the saucer launcher that he had acquired from a box of *Corn Kix*. It had once launched a small disk far into the air, but it was broken and would no longer spin the disk.

I put in two baseball cards, one Duke Snider and one Bobby Richardson. Duke was a duplicate card and Richardson was a Yankee, so I knew I would not miss them. I put in some pennies, too, both copper and steel. And I added my brass neckerchief slide that had been part of my Cub Scout uniform. I never used it after I carved the new one with the Indian head. I included a code ring that had a secret compartment. It had come from a box of *Cracker Jacks*.

For a couple of days after burying the jar, Mike and I returned to make certain the site hadn't been fouled by some unseen enemy, but it was OK, and we finally stopped looking, agreeing to come back in fifty years and retrieve our trinkets.

One day we returned from school and discovered that Dad had torn down the old chicken coop and yard and made the area part of the pasture. All references we had used to locate our time capsule had been destroyed. We tried our best to locate it so that we might remove it to a safer place but we were unable to find it. I suppose it is in the safest place it could be, even now.

50

Even Bum Lambs Go To Market

Idaho winters were harsh, often with large accumulations of snow and frigid temperatures that lasted for days at a time. The lambing season was as predictable as that weather, and only when the winter season reached its worst would the lambing season begin.

Dad would watch the bulky ewes with the eye of a true shepherd, trying desperately to catch each one before it gave birth and move it into one of the "lambing sheds." Inside those sheds were hundreds of small pens, four-foot square cubicles designed to hold a ewe and her lambs.

If the new lambs were moved to those lambing shed pens in time, they had a chance to survive the experience. If not, the weather would claim its victims quickly. Sometimes only the lambs were lost. Sometimes both lambs and ewes succumbed. Then there were those rare occasions when a ewe would perish, leaving its offspring orphaned, bawling and hungry. There were also times when the ewe survived, but was unwilling to allow the new lambs to suckle.

Such lambs were called "bum lambs" by my father. He would wrap them in burlap and bring them to the house to be nurtured by Mike and me. Rarely would there be more than one "bum lamb" at a time, but sometimes there were twins.

We would prepare a cardboard box with the burlap "gunny sacks" and lay the poor waifs in the bottom of the box. They would shiver and shudder, partly from the cold and partly from fear. The stronger ones would make their displeasure known with a high pitched "Baaaaaa" that belied their distress.

We would rush around the kitchen in our efforts to feed the bum lamb as soon as possible, for we knew that if they did not receive nourishment quickly, they would die.

We heated cow's milk in a saucepan and then poured it through a funnel into a large *Pepsi-Cola* or *7Up* bottle. Then we would place a black rubber nipple on the bottle and begin the task of convincing the lamb that it was not only satisfying to suck on that nipple, but it was an absolute necessity. Most of the time, we had to force a small trickle of milk into the lamb's mouth before it was willing to make any effort to suck on its own. When the lamb finally discovered that the nipple provided a warm and tasty meal, they learned quickly to welcome it.

The orphaned lamb had to be fed every couple of hours at first, then less often. After a couple of days, it would be so eager to get the milk from the bottle that the bottle was nearly wrested from our hands. The lamb's tail wagged vigorously as it pushed and shoved at the bottle, as if it wanted to climb inside with the milk.

Once the lamb reached that level of activity, we knew the danger had passed and that it would live.

Most of the time, the lambs were returned quickly to the lambing sheds. Dad would help them adopt foster mothers by rubbing them with the placenta from a ewe that had just delivered, fooling the ewe into believing the orphan was its own. It was not difficult to fool the ewe. Except for the turkey, I think that sheep are the stupidest of all barnyard animals.

Sometimes, though, even when a lamb survived, it could not be successfully placed with a foster mom. I don't really know why. Perhaps there was a personality (or should I say sheeponality) clash. Perhaps the ewe thought it ugly, or too much like its father. In any case, the lamb would be given a pen of its own and we continued to feed it by hand until it was weaned and willing to eat grain with the adults.

We had to be very careful to avoid emotional attachments to those little creatures, for they were destined for "Lamb Chop City," but it wasn't easy. Like humans, they are very cute and cuddly until they get a year or two behind them.

Sooner or later, the lambs had to be taken to market. They were loaded onto the truck, bleating their disapproval at having to leave their mothers, and my father would take them all the way to Blackfoot. There they would be sent through the auction barn and sold.

It was sad to have to part with the bum lambs that we grew to love, even when we weren't supposed to. We knew, though, that it was all part of raising sheep, and we tried to be brave.

I enjoyed the times when Dad would let me go to Blackfoot with him, for it was exciting to see all the different animals at the auction. It was especially fun to see horses and pigs. Horses were so beautiful to watch and the pigs were always so funny.

It was fun, too, to hear the auctioneer do his job, spouting gibberish that made everyone's nervous ticks come to the surface as they scratched ears and flinched shoulders and scratched heads. And every time they did that, the auctioneer would point at them and give forth a new and even more vigorous stream of gibberish.

After the auction, my Dad would wait around and get his check from the office. Usually, it went well, and Dad was happy enough to stop for ice cream cones at the Dairy Queen by Snake River High School on the way home. There were times, though, that he would grump about and complain that the payment had not been high enough to pay for the grain those lambs had eaten. During those rides home, we passed the Dairy Queen without stopping, though I never failed to give it a stare as we went by. And I did that with the most pathetic and miserable face I could put on. I don't think it ever worked to change Dad's mind, but I tried.

51

The Utah Trips

We seldom left Aberdeen. However, each year, usually just before school started, Mom and Dad would pack up the car for a trip to Utah. I looked forward to seeing Dad's family. The trip took six or seven hours, but I always enjoyed it. My favorite thing was to look out the window at the mountains as we drove along their eastern edge. There are many beautiful mountain ranges that make up the Rockies, but the Wasatch Range is one of the more scenic.

We always took the same route south, and once we got through Pocatello, familiar territory disappeared. The small town of Inkom always brought a comment from my father about how its residents had to pay their "Inkom tax," after which we all laughed and tried to top that old joke. We passed McCammon and the turn-off to Lava Hot Springs. We passed Moreland and traveled over Malad Pass to the town of Malad, the last Idaho town before the Utah border.

For some reason that I will never understand, all the kids waited anxiously for that border. I guess it helped us realize that we were passing a milestone of some kind—that we were actually making progress in our journey to Grandma's house. It seemed the only thing that told us there was a difference, for Idaho farms looked much the same as Utah farms.

Once we crossed that state line, and almost before its "beehive" welcome disappeared to the rear, we reached the Tremonton crossroads near Tremonton, Utah, another famous milestone. It was a four-way stop sign where the bulk of the semi truck traffic came together. We always stopped at the Crossroads Cafe and had breakfast before continuing on through Brigham City, Ogden, Salt Lake, and on to Provo. It was a rare treat to get pancakes or French toast, and fried eggs and toast, and store-bought milk!

There were always landmarks and habits that I could count on. One of those was the canvas water bag that hung from the hood ornament in front of the radiator. Another was the Maddox Restaurant right at the edge of the mountains near Brigham City. It was nestled comfortably and inconspicuously amid the fruit orchards, and though I never ate there, I recognized it as a famous eatery for the area. It was obviously far beyond my father's budget.

Sometimes, though not often, Dad would stop at one of the many roadside fruit stands and pick up some apples or peaches for us to snack on. It was a special treat. But even with such treats, the fact that we had traveled several hours with a carload of kids began to cause problems.

"What's the next town, Dad?"

"David's kicking me."

"Scoot over to your own side."

"How far now, Mom?"

"Stop touching me!"

"Dad, I have to go. Bad."

"Mom, I don't feel good."

These were but a few of the comments and questions that brought reaction from the front seat, where Mom was trying to feed the new baby, Paul, while trying not to hit Becky in the face with an elbow. At the same time, the four of us in the back were fighting for whatever space we could attain. Dad tried to ignore the increasing din coming from behind him, but he had his limits.

Some of the problems were easy to deal with. Dad was quick to stop alongside the road so that we boys could relieve ourselves. If we were lucky, there were bushes that afforded a certain degree of privacy, but sometimes we were humiliated by passing drivers that never failed to honk their horns wildly to let us know that we had been seen and that they **knew** what we were doing.

The carsickness was common in such tight quarters, and the speed with which Dad could pull over and stop was incredible. If you were the one that had said, "I'm gonna throw up," you had better darn well be prepared to do so when Dad stopped.

My parents had stock answers that they bellowed from the front seat. Those answers were as predictable as the comments that caused them.

"Do you want to walk the rest of the way?"

"I'm gonna come back there. You don't want me to come back there."

"Someone is gonna get their ears boxed!"

"I don't want to hear another peep from back there."

"You should have gone before we left."

" I'll give you kids something to cry about!"

I suppose that if we analyzed these comments from my parents, we would have recognized that they were as ridiculous as the comments from the kids. However, through some kind of magic that we did not understand, they seemed to have the effect of quelling the disturbances, albeit only for a short time. Somehow, though, we always managed to get by, without injuring each other, and usually clean and dry.

As we drove south, I always began to look for *Lagoon*, an amusement park with a huge roller coaster. Once we passed that, I knew that we were nearing Salt Lake City and I always found myself hoping Dad would drive past the state capitol and the Mormon Temple Square. Such buildings were very impressive and I loved to drive by them.

There was a big arch with a seagull on it near the head of State Street. It was neat. It seemed that I could look out the back window forever and see the capitol dome behind us as we continued south to the Point of the Mountain, where we would pass the Utah State Prison. Dad would always tell how he and Grandpa Jack had worked on the crew that built the prison years before. The hair stood up on the back of my neck when I saw the guard towers and the tall fences with coils of barbed wire along the top. Sometimes there were even prison work crews along the roadway and that really made my heart race as my mind filled with imagined danger.

It took about an hour longer to reach my grandparents' home in Spanish Fork, and they always rushed from the house, smiling broadly with arms outstretched, anxious to encircle all of us as we spilled out of the car. Grandpa Jack, Dad's stepfather, would invariably pinch our cheeks and laugh as he followed the tortuous pinches with a vise-like bear hug. Then we would go into the house and gather round as Grandma Vera told us all about her ailments, her latest sicknesses, her doctor's visits, and her entire medical history. I was always amazed that she moved around so well and did so many things when she was so close to death.

In the evenings we chatted, watched TV, and ate ice cream. I always enjoyed that, for my appetite for ice cream was seldom appeased at home, though Dad would occasionally succumb to his craving for Butter Brickle or Maple Nut and always brought home enough for everyone.

The best part of our Utah trips, though, would come on the second day. That's when we visited my Uncle Max and Aunt Blanche's house. I always enjoyed playing with my cousins, Paul and Garth, and I was especially fond of the pool table in their basement. We played pool for hours, and I honed my skills with a cue to a level that would serve me well in later years.

Another great pastime was to run the few blocks to my grandparent's house, stopping along the way to buy candy at the store. Uncle Max always gave Paul and Garth enough change to treat their out-of-town guests, and I usually chose one of my favorite candy bars, a Black Cow or a Big Hunk, and sometimes I selected a jawbreaker from the jar on the counter to supplement the candy bar.

At Grandma's house, we were limited as far as amusements, but there were a couple of possibilities. If the season was right, we could scale the wall behind the house and raid the orchard there, eating our fill of peaches, plums and apricots. But the most fun was across the street at the school ground. There was an abundance of playground equipment, including some very high swings. We pumped ourselves as high as we could and then "bailed out," trying to gain as much distance as we could. It was a noble game, though we often bloodied knees, palms, and even our faces as we sought higher and farther goals than our competition.

Mike and I always slept over at our cousins' house on the second night, and played so long into the night that we were quite subdued when we left for home the next morning.

Usually, we took a different route home. Dad would take Redwood Road, a thoroughfare that circumvented the traffic lights of State Street in Salt Lake. It also provided an opportunity to turn off toward Tooele, where his other sister, my Aunt Bliss, lived. She and Uncle Marcellas owned a motel and a Western Auto hardware store there. And there was an entire new group of cousins to play with. I enjoyed climbing the mountain behind their home and found rocks high on the mountain that contained tiny fossilized fish.

We only stayed a few hours in Tooele, always having to go so Dad could get back to his water, his beets, his grain, the livestock, etc. Then we'd drive on to the Tremonton Crossroad and take the shortcut through Snowville. We entered Idaho on the back roads, driving through foothills and farms to Rockland, finally joining the familiar old highway near American Falls. Our trip would end less than an hour later as we reached Aberdeen and home. Dad returned immediately to his chores, Mom to her housekeeping, and Mike and I to the comfort of familiar games and toys.

52

Pulling Thistles

One job that we were able to do as kids was to pull thistles. It was not a job to be sought out, for it was a tortuous endeavor at best. Even with the best of gloves, long-sleeved shirts, heavy denim jeans, and high-topped boots, the tiny spines would find their marks. And they seemed particularly fond of the tender skin of pre-pubescent young farm boys.

There were many things that Dad asked me to do that I enjoyed, but thistle duty was not one of them. Dwight and Mike were no more enthusiastic than I, and we all dawdled as much as possible to avoid the task. Such tactics, however, were fruitless. The thistles did not go away until we made them go away.

Dad had no love for the thistles, but he didn't hate them either. He allowed them to flourish along the ditch banks and even in the grain fields. He drew the line though, when they attacked his precious sugar beets. A particularly strong stand of thistles threatened to choke out the tender young beets and my father would not permit that to happen. His resolve to destroy such an encroachment was so strong that he was willing to sacrifice his sons in an effort to rid the field of such a menace.

One day we were taken to the farthest reach of our eighty acres and introduced to the greatest crop of thistle I had ever witnessed. The plants were nearly as tall as we were, and their vivid purple blossoms served to accentuate the fact that they were almost ready to go to seed. If such a thing were allowed to take place, the thistle patch would be trebled. Dad would not allow such an event to be. As he left us in the field, his parting words were, "don't come in till every thistle is pulled and piled along the ditch bank. Then, after they dry, I'll burn them." Having said his piece, he gunned the old "Jimmy" pickup and left us alone, spitting out the dust from his departure.

We moved slowly into the thistle patch, hoping for a miracle, yet knowing there wouldn't be one. Finally, when we could think of no more excuses, we began the labor. We pulled thistles, big ones and bigger ones, ignoring the sticks and scratches as they accumulated on our hands and forearms, even our faces.

We stacked the thistles in the field and then, just for a change of pace, stopped pulling the nasty plants so we could carry our individual stacks to the bank of the irrigation ditch.

As the sun rose higher and the day heated up, the pile on the bank grew to very impressive proportions. We could see the results of our labor, too, as the patch of thistles became smaller. The success spurred us on and we worked hard. Even so, we felt the need for a break about mid-morning and we sprawled out on the ditch bank to rest.

It didn't take long for the water in the ditch to cast its spell on us, and all three of us soon shed our boots and socks and dangled our feet in the cool water. It felt terrific, but the nagging memory of Dad's decree tickled our consciousness, and we dressed again for work.

As we readied ourselves to attack the remainder of the errant weeds, almost in unison, we felt the urge to relieve ourselves, no doubt stimulated by the feet in the water. Of course, we were alone in a field, and modesty was not a problem. It should have been a simple thing for each of us to create his own private puddle, watch it sink into the soil, and return to work. Once again, though, simplicity avoided us.

Dwight and I peed quickly and uneventfully, but my younger brother felt a need to be creative. Young boys always take pride in the strength of their bladders and their ability to control those bladders. It's a skill that disappears with age, but for young boys, the challenges are endless. Mike was no different. For some reason, he was prompted to direct his stream in a high arc over the fence.

As a rule, such a maneuver would have been quite harmless, and even worthy of admiration. Mike's pride was as evident as his ability, but it was short-lived as the arc began to lose altitude and came into contact with the single strand of barbed wire that had been dubbed by its manufacturer as "The Weedburner." It was an electric fence!

I shall always remember the unearthly screech that exploded from the very depths of Mike's throat as he fell backward into that newly stacked pile of thistles. Just as memorable were the next few hours. He sobbed miserably as my mother's tweezers removed hundreds of tiny needles from his back and bottom while he lay on his very uncomfortable front. He was unaware that older men would someday undergo indescribable surgical procedures to accomplish the same effect that he had received by accident. His discomfort lasted into the evening and then all was normal.

The next morning we returned to the field and completed our task. The thistles were removed, and our electric fence remained dry and foreboding, though I noted my younger sibling cast several woeful glances in its direction.

53

To Catch A Thief

Gasoline was almost as important to the operation of a farm as the land and the water. Neither the little orange Allis Chalmers tractor nor the big red International Farmall could do any work without this vital fluid. The old Dodge truck, Dad's pickup, and even our car had to be fueled from large, rust-colored tank that stood beside our driveway between the house and the barn.

The tank was very large, and held hundreds of gallons of gasoline. It sat atop a large wooden frame of two by sixes that was held together with rusty old bolts. There was a long black hose attached to a nozzle, much like those at the service stations in town. The similarity ended there, however, as there were no gauges or electric pumps to deliver the fuel. The entire process relied on gravity, and that explained why the tank was mounted so high off the ground. Even so, the long hose, even when doubled over and locked in place with the padlock, was partially coiled on the ground.

I was too small to reach the lock or nozzle, and even Dad had to reach high above his head to unlock the padlock and open the valve. He often sat on his tractors as he filled them with gas. Later, in the field, he would use the square fifty-gallon tank on the back of his pickup to refuel the tractors so he would not have to disconnect their loads to return to the main tank. The pickup tank had a hand pump, and I often was called upon to work the handle as he monitored the progress of the fill-up from atop the tractor.

The pickup tank could be filled at the Utoco station in town, but whenever the large tank needed replenishment, Dad would call Leland Tarpeel and schedule a delivery from the big truck that could always be seen behind the Utoco station next to City Hall. Mr. Tarpeel would drive under the tank, use his own key to unlock it, and then pump the fuel from his truck into the tank. He seemed so happy and friendly, and always had a kind word for Mom when he dropped off the invoice at the house.

One morning shortly after Grandpa Frank came over to change the water on the beets, he and Dad discovered that the hose on the gas tank had been cut! Someone had stolen gasoline during the night, allowing the remainder of fuel in the tank to flow out onto the ground, making that rich Idaho soil even richer, and my father even poorer.

Dad quickly called Herschel Vergus, the town policeman, and he came to investigate. His investigation was short and fruitless. There were no clues as to who might have brought a car, under cover of darkness, right past our house and up to the gas tank. Dad was angry, to be sure, but my Grandpa Frank was furious. He could barely contain himself as he vowed that such an incident would not be repeated. He swore then that he would catch the culprits himself, without help from the local constabulary.

The next day, the Utoco truck came and refilled the tank. The ruined hose was replaced with a new one and Dad went back to his work. Grandpa, however, was not satisfied. At dusk, he pulled into the drive and right past the house. The trunk lid of his DeSoto was partly open, secured with baling wire. Grandpa parked in the drive and quickly snipped the wire with the pliers that always hung in a leather scabbard on his belt. He removed a roll of tin that he had transformed into a formidable trap. He had driven nails through the metal, about an inch apart and the entire length of the metal ribbon.

Grandpa wasted no time in stretching that metal strapping across the driveway and securing it at both ends. Then he took his irrigation shovel and threw dirt from the edge of the drive onto the metal, so that, in the twilight, it could barely be seen. The nails were not visible at all as the sky began to darken. Satisfied that he could do no more, Grandpa went home, stopping at the house only long enough to alert my parents to his project, and to warn them to keep us kids in the house.

For more than a week, Grandpa returned with the sun to remove his contraption from the driveway and store it in the old garage next to the milk cooler. He returned every night to replace it. He was determined to discover who had stolen the gasoline and he would not be swayed.

One morning we awoke to Grandpa's car horn. He was honking it to get my father's attention, but we all responded. There in the driveway, abandoned, was a metallic gray 1957 Chevy. It was a beautiful car, right down to the four flat tires! We often saw it on Beach Road, throwing gravel as its teenage driver sped by. It seemed almost like a stranded whale as it sat there, disabled by Grandpa's trap.

Mom called Herschel again, and he was there in minutes. There was no longer any doubt about the identity of the thief. Everyone in town knew the car and its driver. Herschel and Dad drove off in the police car. When they returned, we were told that the boy's father would be paying for a new tank of gasoline and would be punishing his son himself. Dad would not be pressing charges.

Later that day, The boy and his father came to retrieve the car. The boy sweated to change the four tires as his father looked on, prompting him with loud curses and yelling about how his son would pay such stupidity.

I found out later that the car was sold to someone in American Falls in order to get the money to pay for the gas and damage to the hose. I never saw it again, but I did see the boy on the school bus from then on. As far as I know, he never again had his own car for as long as he lived at home.

54

Aberdeen Holidays

Summer holidays posed somewhat of a dilemma to Aberdeen residents. It's not that they weren't popular. In fact, there were too many summer holidays to observe.

We observed May Day in school with a field day and sporting events. It was a lot of fun, but still the lesser of the summer celebrations.

We always had a great and somber observance of Memorial Day at the end of May, and that served to kick off the summer. The Aberdeen Cemetery fairly shone on Memorial Day. People came from near and far, some even with out of state license plates, and they always left sprays of flowers or wreaths. I was always amazed at the number of ways that flowers could be displayed. I always preferred seeing flowers the same way parents prefer their children—alive and in their own beds!

The conversations overheard at the cemetery seemed to be about other ancestors and other cemeteries—those not visited. Perhaps it was guilt. Perhaps it was just the events of the day that prompted such talk.

I always occupied myself by strolling aimlessly among the grave markers, looking for clever little comments carved into them and trying to notice any stories that might be interpreted from the names and dates. Most of the names were familiar ones, but there were a few that I did not recognize. Still, I was conscious of the fact that at one time or another, the dear departed had been part of Aberdeen.

Flag Day, too, was an Aberdeen event to be remembered. It seemed that nearly every home and business flew the Stars and Stripes. Flags lined the streets and proclaimed the patriotism of every resident. There was, in Aberdeen, a strong sense of patriotism that was unmatched anywhere else I have been. It was evident in the total participation of the Pledge of Allegiance at public gatherings, or in the presentation of the colors at local events. Even our national anthem was rendered, if not with talent, at least with enthusiasm and vigor.

Both Memorial Day and Flag Day brought active participation from the American Legion Post in Aberdeen. The Legion's paper poppies were in every lapel, part of every hairdo. Their honor guard and rifle salute at the local graveyard was the most exciting part of the day. Dad was always glad to be part of such observances. I felt a certain pride when he donned his legion cap and joined his comrades. Sometimes, though not often, he would talk a bit about his war experiences. Even Mom seemed to enjoy his legion activities on the holidays. Not so the rest of the year, when Dad would hang out at the Legion Hall for poker or pool. My mother only liked the American Legion on the holidays. The rest of the time, it was a bad influence and a waste of time.

Independence Day was great. No where else could so much be accomplished with so little than on our Fourth of July celebration. The townspeople bought up crepe paper for weeks in preparation for the floats they would build for the town's parade. Some of them were very creative works of art. The high school band always marched in the parade and played a Sousa march. They gave the entire event a certain atmosphere that could never have been achieved without a band.

After the parade, people would gather at the City Park and picnic or just visit. Even the farmers managed to spend most of day in town, except for milking and feeding times for their stock. In the afternoons, there were softball games and boating at the reservoir. When Sportsman's Park became more developed at the Aberdeen Boat Dock, many of the picnicking and ball-playing activities were held there instead of in town.

The highlight of the Fourth, though, was the fireworks show. The entire town attended. They carried lawn chairs and blankets as they sought the best locations from which to watch. They'd settle in at their favorite spots several hours before dark. It seemed an eternity before the city fathers felt it dark enough to begin the show, but it would finally begin, with a long pause between each shell in order to draw out every last "Ooooh!" and "Ahhhhh!" It was always a long and fun day, totally exhausting, but worth every ounce of expended energy.

Most small towns in Idaho had similar celebrations to the ones I have mentioned, for these are all national holidays. Aberdeen, however, had one more day of celebration. July 24th was Pioneer Day, in honor of the arrival of the first Mormons to Salt Lake City. The entire town celebrated it. Religion made no difference. It was another day of picnics, softball, boating, and visiting—much like the 4th of July. The major difference was that the Mormons usually had an outside stage set up and put on something called a "road show." They were always musical and a terrific showcase for local talent.

One year, the determination was made that it was just too expensive to have both celebrations, and a compromise was reached. The two July holidays were combined into one great day of celebration and called "Aberdeen Days." Besides saving money, it afforded a non-religious connotation to assure everyone, regardless of religious affiliation, the same degree of comfort. Most of us who were younger felt terribly cheated by this unwelcome turn of events. We wanted two separate holidays and thought it absurd to combine two glorious days into one.

I still return to Aberdeen in the summer whenever I can, usually right between holidays, so that I can attend the family reunions or high school reunions that are cleverly scheduled in the off weeks from the bigger holidays. It's a good thing, I suppose, that I no longer live there, or I am sure I would suffer from a heavy overdose of burgers and hot dogs each summer as I tried to be at each and every summer celebration. But sometimes on a summer evening, I can think back to the warm summer Fourth of July nights, when I would run around on the lawn at Grandma's house with my uncles, aunts, and cousins, carrying my own personal sparkler and whooping like a Confederate raider.

55

Canning

My mother canned lots of food. To be truthful, she bottled it, but the result was the same. We always had great things to eat that required no more than a trip to the storage room or pantry. But there were also some things that I would have liked to hide in the barn!

Often my mother and grandmother would get together for a day or two of canning. It seemed more hectic than their get-togethers for quilting, but the canning was much more interesting. Most impressive were the variety of aromas that permeated my grandmother's house—odors that caused salivary glands to kick into high gear and the mind to wander into some absolutely wonderful places.

Grandma's stove became the center of attention during the canning process. Every burner had a pot on it, almost giving the impression of a miniature city skyline, created with small pots and tall pots, thin pots and fat pots, all lending themselves to the illusion of crowded buildings. There were pots for boiling lids and rings, pots for boiling Mason jars, pots for full ones and pots for empty ones. The most important ones, though, were the pots that were used to cook down the food to just the right point for bottling.

Tables and kitchen counters were covered with fresh, sun-dried tablecloths and all the trappings for the canning were laid out in an orderly fashion, from pectin boxes to sugar canisters.

They canned all sorts of things. My favorites were the peaches, pears, and apricots. These were fruits that were not grown in the Aberdeen area, but Grandpa, Dad and Uncle Gordon would take trips in that old Dodge truck to a place where such fruit was plentiful—Utah! They would drive south to the area around Brigham City and stop at the fruit stands along the highway. They would pore over the hundreds of baskets available, rejecting some and quickly purchasing others, depending on the quality. Most of the baskets were bushel baskets, but there were smaller baskets called pecks. The truck would return with a mixture of baskets with a wide variety of fruits and vegetables.

I never got too excited about the vegetables. I didn't like most of them anyway. Besides, the carrots, peas, green beans all had to be prepared before they were canned and that meant that we kids were called into service, whether to peel carrots, shuck the husks from the corn, shell the peas, or break the ends off the beans. I didn't really mind the work because it was more a social event than work, but there was that nagging in my mind telling me that someday I would have to eat these things. Oh, the corn and carrots weren't so bad, but beans and peas were better fed to the livestock as far as I was concerned. I couldn't get too excited about canning things that would one day result in the famous "You can't leave the table until you clean that plate" line that my father was so fond of using.

Sometimes there were even worse things, like pickled beets and those nasty cucumbers, but the worst of all were tomatoes. I never understood how those awful squishy red things could even be considered as people food. I could not understand how something used to make a product as delightful as catsup (or ketchup, depending on whom you talked to) could also provide the clumps of nastiness that ruined soups and chili, robbing the wonderful meaty flavor of stews. Nothing caused me to retch more quickly than canned tomatoes and it sickened me to see my uncles and cousins eat them raw. I will admit, though, that even the tomatoes emitted a wonderful aroma as they cooked down in those canning pots.

Best of all were the fruits. We not only were spared the preparation, we often were given peaches, apricots, pears or plums to munch on. We could make ourselves sick on strawberries, raspberries, and cherries. Sometimes we even got some of Grandma's homemade bread with hot, "not yet canned" jelly spread liberally on every horizontal surface. Nothing could taste better than that! Homemade bread, fresh from the oven, is a truly religious experience!

I enjoyed eating peaches and apricots and using the pits as ammunition in our mock wars. When these battles were completed, it looked as though Grandma's apple trees had been shedding peach pits.

When the canning was finished, Mom and Grandma would divvy up the bottles and we would return to home to restock our shelves with the jars of newly canned goods. Pints, quarts, and even two-quart containers were lined up on the shelves in an orderly fashion. Mom was careful to move older bottles to the front so they could be used next. I must admit, though, that if I were sent to the back room for fruits or vegetables, I was not very reliable when it came to identifying them. I often returned to the kitchen with newer peaches, rather than the old ones that had darkened in their syrup. Or I would "mistake" corn for green beans. After all, it **was** dark in the back room.

It is funny in a way that, as I got older, peas and beans seemed to taste better and better, cucumbers and pickles became quite delightful fare with any meal. Even pickled beets seemed rather tasty at times. By the time I joined the navy years later, I even liked tomatoes in all its forms. And now I long for those times when I could just reach up and pull such wonderful home-canned foods from the shelf.

Now we buy such things from supermarkets, paying heed to the labels so that we can monitor our sugar, salt, fat grams, and calories. We complain about the preservatives and the carcinogens, and do our best to lessen the evil effects of these products on our fragile health. It seemed simpler then, and somehow safer, just to peer through the glass and see that, "Yes, here are the peas," and then heat them up in a pan to be served at the evening meal. The only thing we had to worry about then was if they would taste good or not.

56

Sputnik

The space race had a profound effect on our lives. Some of the changes, such as those to the school system, were perhaps too subtle for us to notice. Other changes were not quite so covert.

We were proud to be Americans. I don't know any boy that didn't reach a point of near worship when it came to Alan Shepard. He was the first man in the United States to actually go into space in a capsule and return to earth. The thrill of seeing him plucked out of the ocean was unparalleled in the annals of history. And when John Glenn actually went into orbit, science fiction became reality for many of us that frequented the Aberdeen library. We read Ray Bradbury, John C. Clarke, and Isaac Asimov, to name a few. We **grokked** *Stranger In A Strange Land* and fantasized about *The Martian Chronicles.*

As our country tickled the great beyond with its technology, we were proud and excited. But the earliest events that prompted all that activity occurred months and even years earlier. It all began with Sputnik.

Sputnik was a Soviet satellite that orbited the Earth several times a day, beeping its defiance toward our great country as if to say "you lose!" We were upset as a country, and appalled by the Soviets obvious lead in what was being tagged as the "space race." Politicians argued that we had become complacent. Educators spoke out about the downfall of our entire school system. Everyone had an opinion about why the Soviets had aced us right out of that "race."

I was not concerned about the political ramifications of Sputnik, but I thought about it a lot. Even on the playground at school, there were comments made about the Russians and their "spy" satellite. It became popular to call another kid a Russian if you really wanted to hurt his feelings, but you had to be ready to sport a fat lip if he chose to take offense.

One day after school, I had permission to go to Lester's house to spend the night. That was always a lot of fun, because Lester was the only child in his house. He had a room of his own, and lots of great things to play with, not to mention the well-stocked refrigerator. We could get a soda any time we wanted it. And we even got a glass of ice to put it in. Yep, good ole' Lester was definitely living in tall cotton.

I really liked Lester's dad, Harold. He was always so funny and he had a laugh that made everyone around him laugh as well. My favorite thing about him, though, was that he was a ham radio operator. He had a special place just packed with radio equipment. I thought it was fascinating. The walls of the room were lined with something called QSL cards. They were postcards with the call letters of other "hams" that he had contacted. They came from all parts of the world and I thought it was the neatest thing to be able to talk to so many people from so far away.

On that particular day, Harold was at home. He was a plumber and came home off and on all the time, depending on the work he had to do. Anyway, on that day he was already seated at his radio and turning dials. Lester wanted to go and play, but I was mesmerized. I watched Harold as he listened to a Morse code message and wrote it down as if he'd had it dictated to him. I was amazed as he handled his own code key, sending dots and dashes out over the airwaves as fast as he could. I found it hard to believe anyone out there could be copying his message but, sure enough, he got an answer and traded pleasantries with someone in Alaska. It was very exciting! He finished his exchange with a promise to send a QSL card through the regular mail. Of course, I wouldn't have known that, but Lester told me. He was almost as fast with the Morse code as his father.

When he had finished, Harold turned around and stared at us for a minute, then said, "You yahoos want to hear Sputnik?"

My heart jumped right into my throat, and even Lester forgot about going to play. We both nodded our heads and crowded in to hear whatever we could hear. Harold said it would take a minute and he had to change his coil from fifteen to ten meters or something like that. I didn't even know what that meant, but we watched him remove a little wire thing from the back of his radio and replace it with one of a different size. He turned it back on and began to hunt through the band with his tuning dial. The noise from the speaker on his desk changed several times. Sometimes it squealed and sometimes it was recognizable as Morse code.

Finally, he reached the spot on the dial that he wanted. He turned a couple of knobs and tuned it in as best he could. There it was—a definite signal—all the way from outer space.

Beep. Beep. Beep.

It was clear as could be, and I was as excited as I could be. I could hardly wait until I could get home and tell my parents that we had heard the Russian signal and that it seemed to be completely harmless.

I had no way of knowing on that night, that a few years later, after the space race changed leaders, I would be given the chance to serve on the backup maintenance crew for the air search radar system on the pickup ship for Apollo 14. It would be an opportunity that I would decline in order to avoid a lengthy family separation. I suppose even that trait was seeded and nurtured in me as I grew up in the small community of Aberdeen.

57

Ross Park

One of my favorite places to visit was Ross Park. I seldom had a chance to go there, but when I did, I loved it.

Ross Park is a municipal park in Pocatello, one of Idaho's largest cities. It was unique in that it bordered a high lava ridge and in addition to the hill itself, there were hundreds of huge boulders amid the heavy forestation. The entire park was riddled with paths that ran in and among the rocks and trees. It inspired the imaginations of my Mike and me, as we raced among the boulders.

The entire landscape was similar to that on the Roy Rogers show. There was one exception. While Roy and Dale rode Trigger and Buttercup, usually followed by Nellie Belle (the old west version of a jeep) and Bullet, it seemed they sped by the same rocks and trees several times in the course of a show. Ross Park, though, provided a wide variety of boulders and trees. That's what made it so much fun.

One day, we could be cowboys and Indians and I, riding my trusted Thunderhoof, made good use of the natural cover and often prevailed in the conflicts with my enemies. My ability to make galloping sound effects with my mouth was envied by all that played. My trotting sounds weren't very good, but then I seldom if ever slowed to a trot.

Other days, we played Robin Hood and left the paths to climb among the huge rocks, not realizing that we often put ourselves at risk. One slip and a fifteen or twenty foot drop to the smaller rocks below could well have been catastrophic. However, we were the most skilled of all merry men, and had no accidents.

At times, we could move from tree ranches to boulders or vice versa. We became very skilled at such maneuvers, as long as we waited long enough after lunch. It wasn't an easy thing to run and fight and climb on a stomach loaded with pork and beans, potato chips, and hot dogs.

The picnic area that stretched out at the base of the hill sported much less in the way of foliage and trees. There were still many trees, and nearly all the picnic tables were shaded for most of the time, but that part of the park was mostly lawn. On those weekend excursions that lawn was always strewn with a variety of blankets and lawn chairs and sometimes hammocks as people from all over the area came to relax and spend the day away from their normal routines.

At the north end of the park, and built right into the ridge itself, were the animals. It was Pocatello's only zoo, though it wasn't big enough or well stocked enough to be called a zoo. It certainly did not compare with the Hogle Zoo in Salt Lake, the only real zoo I had ever visited. Nevertheless, it was exciting to visit.

There was a large chicken wire cage that held monkeys. I don't know what kind of monkeys were there, but they were active and loved to do obscene things that caused my mom to blush and look away. Mike and I loved it. There were several other enclosures. One contained several white-tailed deer. They were boring to watch, except when they came to the fence to beg for food. Someone was always there to feed them, even though the signs along the length of the fence warned against it. It was here that I learned that white-tailed deer are partial to peanut butter and jelly sandwiches.

A large meadow provided forage for a few American bison. The sign said they were American bison, but they certainly looked like buffalo to me. I even called them buffalo, for I thought the name "bison" sounded silly.

There was another cage with a bear and another with bobcats. They were very interesting, but my favorite of all was the mountain lion. Even that lion had several names. The sign said it was a mountain lion, a cougar, and even was referred to as a puma. I thought it marvelous that the beautiful cat could be so many things. The best thing about that lion was that it looked so powerful. I was certain it could have ripped its way out of that enclosure in minutes. It chose instead to gaze upon the people that filed by, giving each of them a look that bespoke the intelligence of the beast, a look that proclaimed not only a tolerance for humans, but also a superiority over them. I have seen that same look many times since on the faces of house cats.

There was a road that split the park. On the opposite side of that road was a portion of the park that we did not venture into. There were several baseball and softball diamonds there. There was also a municipal swimming pool, but we never had the opportunity to swim there. Both might have attracted our attention had they been isolated, but the rocks, trees, and the "mountainous terrain" was too great an attraction. We could see ball fields anywhere, and so chose to play our imagination games with all our available time.

My parents were very patient and allowed us a lot of play time, but when Dad wanted to go, he got agitated when he had to climb rocks and circumvent trees to find each of us. He did so, though, locating each of us one by one and sending us to the car. In a way, it was almost like a good game of *Hide-and-Seek* as we each tried to be the last one found. After all, the last one found didn't have to sit in the car and wait.

58

Basement Homes

It was hard to find a basement house in other towns, but Aberdeen had a lot of them. I often wondered if perhaps the basement house was just an architectural phenomenon of Aberdeen and could not be found in any other location.

I didn't waste a lot of my time contemplating such questions, but I was curious and so, asked my Dad for an explanation. He took it in stride, as he did most of my dumb questions, but he did try and answer it. He explained that basement houses resulted from the efforts of families to build themselves homes in stages rather than all at once. Often, farming communities suffered as a result of both inclement weather conditions and large fluctuations in the prices paid for crops. That was why many folks who started building houses were unable to finish them and had to settle for adapting them to basement houses.

I could understand the reasoning, even at my young age, for even as young as I was, I had seen the damage that flooding and drought could bring to a farmer's money crop. It was not pretty. Sometimes farmers were forced to sell out and leave after a disaster of that sort destroyed not only their crops, but their confidence.

A basement house is exactly what it sounds like. It is a basement. Nothing more. It is created out of the shards of broken dreams.

Whenever anyone made plans to build a house in southeastern Idaho, the beginning of the project was almost always the same. The first step after a plot was located and procured was the excavation. A hole was dug to form the basement of the house and hold the foundation walls. Often, in those days, the basement was used for storage of a heating oil tank or even a coal bin. Storage of winter fuel in basements was common. In addition to the fuel storage, it was an opportunity to make use of the extra space for extra storage; or for actual bedrooms or pantries. The possibilities were only limited by imagination or budget—usually the latter.

I have seen a variety of basements and some were very impressive. I knew it was possible to finish a basement completely, with all the comforts of home. It is a good thing that such finishing was possible, I guess, because a basement house stopped there. After the foundation was laid and the basement roughed out, the main floor was built, providing a ceiling for the basement.

It was at this point that construction on so many Aberdeen houses was interrupted. Instead of putting up walls and rafters and roofs; instead of plaster and paint and shingles, the job stopped. Tarpaper was installed over the floor to keep out the weather and the wet and the basement house was born. A roof had been created for the basement and the only thing left to do was install a stairway to the ground level, frame it in, add a door, and then tar paper the whole thing.

It was difficult to tell there was even a residence there. The only thing that stood out was that tiny enclosure containing the doorway and the upper part of the staircase. In passing these strange, incomplete structures, strangers might have been confused by them, wondering why barns and outbuildings were so modern and complete while the basement house seemed to be ignored and destined to stay forever in a state of waiting.

I was bothered a bit by the basement houses. I knew several of the kids at school that lived in them, and I found myself feeling sorry for them. I thought it sad that many of us had entire houses and they were forced to live in basements. I never had occasion to actually go inside one of those houses. That may have remained the case had it not been for church.

My church had a program where a man and a boy would visit each of the families in the congregation periodically and just check on them, find out how they were getting on, and show them that people loved them and cared for them. I thought it a good program and anxiously volunteered to participate. I was teamed with Mr. Anderson, my scoutmaster. We were assigned to visit three families. We knew them all, but had not been in their homes. One of those families lived in a basement house.

As we pulled into the long driveway to that house for our first visit, I felt an extra tug of excitement at finally being able to see the inside of one of those strange houses. Mr. Anderson's car fishtailed through the snow as we battled our way up the drive.

A man emerged from the barn as we stopped the car. He carried a pail of steaming milk as he crossed the yard and held out his mittened hand to shake first Mr. Anderson's hand and then my own. Then he led us into the small covered porch area outside his door. The three of us removed our boots and we followed the man inside. He pulled a string that hung from a naked light bulb and we were able to better navigate the steep stairs that led into his basement home. We came from the dimly lighted stairway into a bright and cheerful kitchen.

The unmistakable odor of pot roast permeated the entire area, mixed with that of hot biscuits that warmed in the half-open oven. The lady of the house greeted us with a broad smile and an invitation to join them. We declined politely and apologized for arriving at mealtime, though we had called ahead and set the time. The invitation, the refusal, and the apology were without any awkwardness. The sentiments were sincere.

The lady of the house still insisted that we sit with them as they enjoyed their dinner. She poured two large cups of hot chocolate and set places for us. Only then did she call her own three children to the table. There were two pre-school boys and a girl about eight years of age. They scurried around momentarily as they sought their own places and then sat quietly, hands in their laps, until their father called upon the girl to offer thanks to the Lord for their meal. With arms folded and heads bowed, the young girl spoke a quiet prayer, not only expressing gratitude for the meal, but for her family, their home, and even for the visitors that shared the moment with them.

We made small talk during the meal, discussing the coming Spring, the successful lambing season, and even the daughter's schoolwork. It was a pleasant visit that had to end all too soon.

Mr. Anderson and I donned our winter coats, said our good-byes, and ascended the stairs to the outside. With a final wave, we went back down the driveway and headed for home. As I left that basement house that night, I realized that we had visited not just a house, but a happy home, filled with love. It made no difference whether their house was a mansion or a shack, a three-story Victorian or a basement house. It was a home, and I learned something about homes that night. Homes are made by the families that live there—and not by carpenters.

59

A Special Friend

Clyde lived just across the road from us. Actually, his house was not on Beach Road, as ours was, but rather on the road heading north from our driveway.

Clyde was one of the strangest grownups that I had ever seen. Oh, he had whiskers just like my Dad. He was big, too. Real big. I think my Dad would have looked funny in Clyde's clothes, because they were so big.

I didn't see Clyde very often, but he always watched us as we waited at the edge of the road for the school bus. He looked very sad and lonely. His mother visited Mom on very rare occasions and they would stand out in the yard and talk. Most of the time, Clyde stayed at home, but one day he accompanied his mother. He seemed genuinely happy to be with Mike and me. We were wary of him, because of his size and age, but he soon put us at ease with his laugh and his gentle manner.

We played with the Tonka trucks and plastic animals for awhile, making roads and houses and farms in the dirt. We shipped twigs and clods back and forth to bolster the economy of our make believe city. The twigs became logs, the clods became boulders of granite to be used in building new farms and houses and roads. We carted animals of all kinds to market, too. We didn't care that some of the cows, sheep and horses were blue or green. We didn't care that an occasional giraffe or lion or elephant crept into our livestock loads. We didn't care that we had chickens bigger than our cows or that some of our horses had to be hauled with soldiers sitting rigidly astride them, even in the trucks.

Finally, tiring of the tiny world we had created, we began to destroy it with violent truck accidents. Tunnels were caved in. Houses once again became rocks and sticks. The devastation was complete!

Only after the city was history, did we realize that Clyde was very upset with what we had done. He was crying. Mike and I both assured him that no one was hurt and that our city would live again, perhaps even in greater glory. It took a long time, but we were able to direct him away from the dirt pile behind the house. As soon as it was out of sight, it was forgotten. He was a happy Clyde again—ready to play something new.

We played for awhile on the rope swing that dangled from the "big" tree. Mike and I took turns in the tire as Clyde, with his great strength, pushed us higher and higher, until the branch above creaked in protest. Then we sat in the tire as Clyde spun it round and round, causing the long rope to knot itself as it twisted. He would turn us until he was exhausted, and then let go. He stood back and laughed boisterously as the rope began to unwind, gaining momentum until the rest of the world was no more than a blur to whichever of us sat in the tire. Then, after it stopped, we would climb from the tire and try to run across the lawn in a straight line, as our dizziness caused us to veer to the side and fall laughing to the grass.

When we tired of the swing, Clyde went to a bush at the edge of the yard and broke a branch from it. He grasped it near the ground and held it tightly as he twisted and bent it until it finally ceased to resist and broke in his hand. Then he pulled a small pocketknife from his overalls and motioned for us to sit with him on the grass.

We watched in amazement as he deftly used the knife to trim the tiny limbs from the branch he had broken. He cut slits in the bark and slid the bark from the branch, then began to carve spaces and indentations in the white wood. After a time, he replaced the strip of bark onto the stick, and using strings cut from the ragged holes in the knees of his overalls.. He used them to bind the bark back into place. With a quick flick of the wrist, he made a couple of small cuts in the bark. Then he looked it over carefully and offered it to me. I must have looked confused, but he put the end of the stick into my mouth and told me to blow.

I blew as hard as I could and was rewarded with a shrill, high-pitched sound that earned the attention of my mother, not to mention a howling reaction from my dog, Elvis. It was a whistle! A fine whistle!

Mike and I were both amazed and as he began to make another, we watched even closer, hoping to learn the secret of such a fine art. In a few minutes, Mike also had a whistle and we raced into the house, letting the screen door slam, as we rushed to show our new prizes to Mom. She, too, seemed impressed. Even Clyde's mother, who was visiting, seemed to beam with pride in her son's accomplishment when she saw our excitement.

Our visitors left soon. Mom went to her sewing supplies and returned with two pieces of yarn, one blue and one red. She made our whistles into necklaces, so that we could wear them around our necks. The different colors enabled us to tell them apart. I had the blue one.

Later, when we showed our whistles to Dad, he and Mom talked about how interesting that such a skill could be learned by someone as retarded as Clyde. I didn't know what retarded meant, and it was a couple of years later when I learned that Clyde had died. I was sad when I heard it, and looked for my whistle as if to jog my pleasant memories of this very special friend. It was nowhere to be found. I realized that day, though, that I had lost much more than just a whistle.

60

Gangland

The schoolyard at Aberdeen Elementary served as the stomping ground for two separate and distinctive gangs. These were not the types of gangs that one heard of in the larger cities of America, but they probably had the same roots. I suppose there has always been a need for people of similar interests and backgrounds to group together. It isn't necessarily a conscious effort. It just happens. And so it did with me.

Our gang roamed the playground in a group, acting rough and tough and full of stuff. There was not a definite leader, I don't think. Lester and I were kind of co-leaders, and probably the only ones that were in the group all the time. The others came and went, as their interests changed.

I don't think we intentionally harmed anyone. I don't think we even tried to intimidate anyone. But it did happen. It was hard to refuse the basketball court or the swings to such a large group. Other guys tended to just walk away and let us have what we wanted, rather than risk a confrontation with so large a group. We made use of that tendency.

The other gang was a much rougher group, led by a very big guy named Tony Valdez. He had the reputation of being the toughest and meanest kid in school. Even when he spoke to the teachers, we could sense a certain type of discomfort. Tony seemed to enjoy that power he had over the teachers.

The two gangs seldom got in each other's way. We had different interests to be sure. There was also an unspoken understanding that our gang would be seriously maimed should we ever fight it out. Such an understanding served us well, and we avoided confrontation on every level. Except for the day we both wanted the "ocean wave!"

The "ocean wave" was a piece of playground equipment that was the ultimate in thrills. To use it was such an enviable goal that first and second graders were not permitted on it at all. It was an honor reserved for the upperclassmen of the school.

The "ocean wave" was a very large pyramid-shaped thing that had a wooden bench around the outside, worn smooth by countless butts. There was a steel ring around the whole thing for the adventurous riders to hang onto. Several half-inch steel rods connected the seat to a central hub at the top. It gave the impression of an Indian teepee without a cover. At the top, where all the rods converged, there was a hub with a very large bearing. The entire assembly sat on a large steel post at the center.

The "ocean wave" could be pushed and pushed until it literally spun around that center pole with enough force to throw off its riders if they weren't very careful. The best part, though, was that once it started, it could be pushed and pulled into and away from that center pole. If enough force were used, the whole thing banged into the pole with a heavy clank, jarring the bones of anyone that managed to hang on to their seat.

Every recess there was a teacher assigned to playground duty. They almost always stayed near the "ocean wave" so they could render first aid if needed. They tried time and time again to get the riders to settle for much less of a ride than the apparatus offered. They seldom succeeded, although there were occasional instances when the "ocean wave" was chained for a day or two in order to punish those who defied the teacher's request for a mild version of an "ocean wave" ride.

One beautiful Spring day, both the playground gangs approached the "ocean wave" at the same time. Ordinarily, we would have shrugged and moved on to another activity, but on that day we knew we were there first. We were feeling our oats. We chose to fight for our right to be there.

At first, there were only words, cast back and forth as each group chose to better the other. The words became more heated and it was soon painfully clear that a fight was imminent. I looked for ways to get out of the situation and still maintain some degree of honor, but it was not to be. Tony Valdez brought the challenge to its apex.

"Ok, Stoker and I will fight. When I beat him, he and his gang have to go play with the girls and stay out of our way." Then he laughed. As he amused himself with his unfunny joke, I realized that I would have to sacrifice myself to this big Mexican kid. I glanced around, looking for the duty teacher, but she was nowhere to be seen. I had no way out!

My thoughts were interrupted when Tony's beefy hand hit the left side of my face. He had slapped me. Hard. It almost knocked me down, but I was just glad he hadn't closed his fist. As I raised my left hand to assess the damage, his other hand slapped the right side of my face, and my lip began to bleed as it sought the same space that my top teeth occupied.

I saw the right hand coming again and stepped back. His fingers whizzed by my face, so close that I felt the air they displaced. Tony lost his balance and fell. Instinctively, I jumped on him. I grabbed him by the neck and squeezed as hard as I could while, at the same time, trying to get a leg on either side of him so that he couldn't throw me off. I almost made it, too, but he was fast. Very fast. His knee hit me in the side and he scrambled free, but as he rose to his feet, I landed a slap of my own. My palm hit him solidly on the nose and it began to bleed profusely. Seeing him bleed fueled my anger. I swung again, knowing that I could win. Knowing that good would prevail over evil. Knowing that bullies are all bluster, and they weren't nearly as tough as they pretended to be.

Knowing all those things did little to help me. Tony proceeded to beat me up. When he tired of that, he beat me **down**. Then he beat me **sideways**. Finally, after he realized that he had won, he decided to let me live. He backed away and lowered his hands. My friends moved in to help me to the school so that I could use the bathroom and try to find out if I had a face left. Tony and his group piled onto the "ocean wave."

I was not seriously hurt. In fact, except for a cut lip and some very sore muscles, my ordeal could not be detected. Interestingly enough, Tony Valdez, from that time on, always treated me as he would a best friend. I'm not sure whether that was because I had faced him and he admired my bravado, or that he had beat me soundly and I was not a threat. Either way, we had an understanding that lasted throughout school.

By the time I reached junior high school, Tony had moved away. It was several years later that I heard he had been stabbed in a knife fight during a barroom brawl in Blackfoot.

61

Stamp Collection

I skipped from one hobby to another like a bee in a dandelion patch. After all, the cub scouts promoted collections to help young boys learn about life and the things around them. So, I collected things. At first I collected leaves, but they dried, becoming brittle and unmanageable. I switched to matchbook covers. They were everywhere and most of them even told a story, like what they advertised or a location that was unique. I found them lying on the ground and in the gutters of Aberdeen. I found them in small bowls on cafeteria counters and at the tables in Mary's Cafe.

I didn't save the matches. They were expendable. I just tore off the front cover and mounted it on the large piece of poster board that my mother bought for me at the Rexall Drug Store. Once that poster board was filled, I stopped gathering matchbook covers. I actually displayed the collection at one of the scout bazaars, but it soon found its way into a place of insignificance under my bed, where time and dust reduced it once again to something that looked like it belonged on the ground and in the gutters of Aberdeen.

At the age of eight, we made a rare trip to Pocatello to visit the dentist. I hated visiting the dentist and balked noisily when he attempted to use a drill in my mouth that might better have served someone searching for oil. The man lied every time, telling us that it wouldn't hurt and then doing all he could to be sure that it did. What's worse, he had the absolute worst breath on the planet, even worse than Half-pint, Grandpa's pony.

Mom always felt a bit guilty for subjecting us to the dentist and so, when we finished there, she was easily convinced that we needed something to compensate us for pain and misery. It was that possibility that kept Mike and me from running away to join the circus whenever the dentist was mentioned.

It was on one of these rare bribery trips that I acquired my very first stamp album. It was called an Ambassador, and was filled with illustrations of stamps from all the corners of the world. On those pages where a new country started, there were small empty boxes at each corner to mark the space for flag and coat-of-arms stamps, which were included with the album. I was diligent in getting them placed perfectly in the boxes and, as I did so, my album began to become a more colorful book.

Along with my coats of arms and flag stamps, there was a post-paid card that, according to the ad, could be sent in to receive a free bag of 1,000 stamps with which my collection could be started. I quickly sneaked a three-cent liberty stamp from Mom's stationery box, held my nose as I licked three-fourths of the glue from its back, and applied it to the card. I waited till just the right time to mail it.

Our mailman drove around in his own car, servicing the rural mailboxes for the entire town. It was interesting to see him drive, for he sat right in the center of the car seat and used his left hand and left foot to drive. His right hand stayed available to retrieve and deliver the mail from the boxes along the road. I never saw him sit behind the steering wheel. Mom always said we could set our clock by him, though, for his schedule was as rigid as his expression. I knew what time I could expect to see him coming from the Hansen place across from the rodeo grounds. I waited until he pulled away from their box before I ran into the road and placed the card into our mailbox, remembering to raise the flag so he'd know that there was outgoing mail waiting.

The reason I timed the mailing so closely was that I was afraid that my parents would find out I was sending away for stamps. I wasn't sure why I didn't want them to know, but there was something in the wording on the card that gave me a deep feeling of discomfort, something I felt my parents would not like, though I was not certain what it meant. In very small print at the bottom of the card was a statement that said a package of approvals would be sent with the free offer. I had no idea what "approvals" were, but I knew my parents would know and would **not** approve.

I watched for the mailman every day, and every day I ran to retrieve the mail. Mom must have suspected something, having seen my new interest in getting the mail, but she said nothing. Days came and days went and still there was no mail for me. I began to think that the H.E. Harris Company offer had been a figment of my imagination. Finally, nearly two months later, the package arrived!

The bag with 1,000 stamps was, indeed, a treasure! I spent hours looking through my album and matching the stamps with the proper places within the volume. The "approvals" however, were very special. Unlike the stamps in the bag, they had no paper attached from old used envelopes. They also had a certain something that made them special, I think because they were labeled individually and placed in their own separate little waxed paper envelopes, with a special price for each stamp.

Those approvals were of a quality far and above that of the free stamps, and the longer I looked at them, the more certain I was that they had been included with my shipment as a terrific bonus. I didn't dwell on the intricate details of the situation, or on the small print in the letter that came with them. My integrity remained intact, however, and I returned them in the post-paid envelope. I was sorely tempted to mount them in my album, but common sense prevailed. Unfortunately, the next time I received approvals in the mail, common sense took a back seat to greed and avarice.

This shipment of approvals came from a company called Capitol Stamp Company. I had not ordered anything from them. Mom said that I was probably on a mailing list. I wasn't quite sure what that meant, but it sounded important and if it meant getting free stamps in the mail, I was all for it. I promptly removed the approvals from their presentation envelopes and mounted them in their appropriate places throughout my album. Then I threw away all evidence of the mailing. I just knew that if I ordered nothing and I received something, that something was mine to keep. No question!

Several weeks later, a knock on the front door brought the "angel of death." We seldom had visitors on the farm, and when we did, they always came to the back door. Front doors in Aberdeen were used as fire escapes and little else. Another thing, we never had visitors wearing suit and tie. But that day was an exception.

A solemn looking man stood at the door and spoke in hushed tones with my mother first, then my father. Occasionally, they glanced in my direction, but I could not read their eyes. I didn't know what they were doing.

After a time, Dad went to the kitchen and wrote a check while Mom kept the stranger entertained on the porch for a few moments. Dad gave him the check and he left. I was still puzzled as I watched his car disappear down the road, but I was not to be kept in the dark. Dad called me to the kitchen and I could tell by the tone of his voice that he was not a happy dad.

The man had been from a collection agency. He had come to collect forty dollars for the stamps I had purchased. As my father explained it to me, the man had agreed to forgive the debt when he discovered that I was so young. However, my father is a stickler for honesty and integrity. He insisted on covering the debt. My father was also a stickler for punishment whenever it was warranted, and he certainly felt that it was warranted after my stamp caper.

62

Indian Jim

My Dad usually had a very good relationship with the people he hired to help on the farm. Indian Jim was no exception.

Jim was a very attractive young man, a Navajo Indian. He often spoke of his home near Gallup, New Mexico, and how much he missed being with the rest of his family.

Mike and I loved to be around Indian Jim, as we called him. He seemed to enjoy our company and was always willing to include us in conversation. We, in turn, followed him around whenever we could, eager to hear stories of faraway New Mexico and Arizona. We hung on every word as he told us about life on the reservations and how the Indians lived. His descriptions of homes and activities among his people filled our imaginations with grist for our own play. We spent hours pretending to live in clay hogans and working on imaginary rugs and jewelry. We paid no mind to the fact that such work was delegated to the women on the reservation. It was interesting, and therefore fair game to our own variations.

Indian Jim headed a crew that worked first for Grandpa Frank and then moved on to other farms in the area. He lived, however, in the labor house across our driveway and so, was accessible to us in the evenings. He often lighted a small fire in the dirt yard in front of the labor house and stared into it as he smoked his pipe. Mike and I envisioned that pipe as a peace pipe that could only have been of great historical value and we often lurked in the shadows so we could smell the aroma of whatever tobacco blend Indian Jim might be using. Sometimes he would be somewhere far away and he did not notice that we were there. We would sense his desire for privacy on those occasions and return to our own side of the driveway after a few moments.

There were, however, some times when Indian Jim would be fully aware of the two young wide-eyed boys that hovered at the perimeter of the firelight. He would invite us to step into the circle of light and join him. He did so with great pomp and ceremony and it was an enjoyable game for all of us. Then he would leave for a moment and return with some sort of meat from his one room shack and then painstakingly whittle some roasting sticks with the hunting knife that always hung at his side. As Mike and I sat close to the fire, warming our food, Indian Jim would make us feel that we were eating rattlesnake or wild boar, or even coyote. It seemed that his stories would actually change the flavor of the meat that we cooked.

One day Mr. Lords, the town banker, called my dad and informed him that there were "irregularities" in the checks that my dad had written to his workers. Dad left for awhile and returned with Herschel Vergus, the town policeman, and Grandpa Frank. The presence of a police car in our driveway was enough to captivate the attention of Mike and me, but we were unable to figure out what was going on.

There were angry words and Indian Jim was ordered to take his crew and leave the labor house. Herschel advised him to go back to New Mexico and avoid Idaho altogether.

It was late that night before I realized what had happened. Indian Jim had added some numbers to the amount of the checks that Dad had given him. I could tell from my Dad's tone that it had been a serious crime that might well have resulted in Indian Jim's having to go to jail and be away from his family even longer than just the summer. I understood more than my dad realized about the crime, for I had learned what forgery was from watching Dragnet on television. The serious look on Sergeant Friday's face told it all.

Grandpa Frank and Dad had agreed not to press charges, instead banning Indian Jim's crew from working in the area and sending him away. I am not certain why they did that. Perhaps it was because Indian Jim's family needed him so much. Perhaps it was because my dad and grandfather had such a great respect for the Navajo nation. Or perhaps it was because Indian Jim had been so good to the two little boys from across the driveway.

We missed Indian Jim and we still held him in high regard, but not as high as before. He now took a back seat to Cochise, Chief Joseph, and Geronimo. They would not have done such an unpardonable thing to my dad.

63

A Fair Day

Aberdeen Public Schools (as if there were any private ones) seldom had field trips. It may have been that it lacked a budget for such frivolities and it might have been that there weren't that many interesting places to visit. In fact, an Aberdeen field trip would probably have been a visit to a **real** field!

There were rare occasions when a school trip **was** planned. One of those times was when a bus was used to take interested kids to the Eastern Idaho State Fair in Blackfoot. On opening day at the fair, students and children were granted special discount tickets and Aberdeen provided a school bus so that we could take advantage of that generous offer.

I loved bus trips and all that they entailed. It was fun to join my friends and classmates on such trips, and the bus ride itself was often the best part. There was a party atmosphere, and we came up with a variety of ways to amuse ourselves. The only requirement was that our activity be noisy and rowdy.

Sometimes we'd sing along with the bus radio, as loudly and boisterous as possible. I have to admire the drivers chosen for those trips, for their tolerance was far above and beyond the call of duty. Then again, perhaps they were deaf. They didn't seem to mind the din.

The first order of business in Blackfoot was to attend the parade that kicked off the weeklong celebration. It was exciting to see so many high school bands from the area and all the floats from every conceivable organization, from the Future Farmers of America to Union Pacific. As far as I could tell, it was also the only time that local and state politicians ever joined the general populace. Funny how a few pieces of candy thrown at the crowd during a parade served to get the same people re-elected again and again.

Once the parade through the streets of Blackfoot was finished, we re-boarded the bus and headed for the ultimate goal—the fair! We took a back way into the fairgrounds, parking somewhere far from the fair itself. We parked amid horse trailers and pickups that had license plates from exotic, faraway places—places like Texas, Arizona, and Oklahoma. Our bus got free entry to the fair. At least that's what they told us. I always thought the long walk from that parking area, dodging horse "biscuits" and mud puddles, more than made up for any parking fee we may have saved.

As with any fair, the midway was the greatest attraction, with its food and game booths, and wild rides of every imaginable type. I was no different than most boys my age, but I had been taught by my father not to trust **any** of the game booths. In fact, my father referred to them as "gyp joints," and always punctuated that phrase with horror stories of how diligently they strove to separate innocent farm boys from their hard-earned dollars.

Still, I was fascinated with the apparent ease of tossing rings over bottle tops or knocking down a stack of cast iron "bottles" with a softball. They even had booths where you could shoot basketballs or just choose a string to pull in the hope that one of the big prizes was attached to the other end. I wondered, too, what could be so difficult about tossing a coin onto a plate. It seemed so easy. As I watched others play, I seldom saw anyone win anything larger than a tiny token gift and yet, throughout the fairgrounds one could see large guys and girls carrying stuffed animals almost as large as they were. It was a mystery to me where these things came from.

I enjoyed strolling through the commercial buildings and in seeing all the demonstrations. I was mesmerized by the "hawkers" who managed amid stacks of beautiful vegetables, to use the latest in slicers and dicers to turn those "veggies" into works of art. It wasn't the product that fascinated me, but the smooth and flawless delivery of the demonstration. I had the feeling that most of those people could do the entire demonstration and read the newspaper at the same time. I suppose that comes from years of saying exactly the same thing over and over again.

I also took delight in carrying around a paper bag with strong corded handles to collect all the free brochures and samples. There were rulers and yardsticks, complete with names of farming machinery companies or feed stores. There were books of matches that advertised products and services from all types of businesses located throughout southern Idaho. There were calendars, notebooks, and gadgets of all kinds. They were designed primarily to advertise, and though all the booths knew that kids were not the customers they were trying to reach, they were well aware that each kid had a home. I guess it was considered good business to get your advertising into a home, no matter how it was done. Because of that, vendors were willing to quickly place items into my paper bag and move me on down the line.

It was upon returning from one of those trips that I did one of the most stupid and potentially dangerous things I have ever done.

The bus arrived back in Aberdeen much later than had been anticipated. I chose to walk home and, as I walked I went through some of the candy I had acquired during the day. I strolled leisurely homeward as I swung my new yardstick with "International Harvester" imprinted on the side. It was like a sword, and a swung it at whatever I passed, pretending to be a cavalry officer aboard my imaginary horse, Thunderhoof.

As I passed the Star Theater and the grain elevator and then crossed the tracks to the east side of town, I discovered the book of matches in my bag. I cannot remember what they advertised, nor can I remember what possessed me to light them all at once.

I removed a match and struck it along the black strip at the bottom. After it ignited in flame, I touched it to the rest of the matches and they burst into flame. It startled me and I dropped them. I was at the edge of the street and near a vacant lot west of the Lutheran Church. Well, the lot wasn't entirely vacant. It was occupied by a summer's growth of wild weeds and grass. It was thick with the vegetation, all of it dry and thick.

The grass near my feet started to burn instantly. I recovered quickly and tried to stomp out the flames, but they skipped quickly to an area too large for me to deal with. The fire was getting bigger and moving quickly.

I panicked and took off for home at a dead run. I didn't stop until I was there. I burst through my front door at the same time the city fire siren sounded. I was terrified!

I told my mother what had happened and she told my dad. He jumped in his pickup and drove off to see what had happened. He didn't return for the longest time, but when he did, he brought good news. No one had been hurt and no buildings were lost. However, he explained that the fire had burned a very large area, right up to a private home on the south side of the lot. The Lutheran church had been threatened and even scorched on the side, but it had been saved.

I was relieved and vowed to my parents that I would never play with matches again. And I meant it. I was never so scared!

The following Thursday, when the weekly edition of *The Aberdeen Times* came out, there on the front page was a picture of the blackened field and an article about how the fire had been started by a minor playing with matches. I was grateful that my name was not in the article, for I did not wish to advertise my stupidity. I never told anyone about my starting the fire and the incident passed into history with no repercussions, except for the fact that I can bring those feelings of terror and futility to the surface easily. The memory is vivid. I think that perhaps that memory has been my punishment for pulling such a stupid stunt.

64

Junior High School

My fifth grade teacher was Mrs. Bickett. She was an impressive looking woman. She carried herself with authority and confidence, and she commanded respect whenever she spoke. However, that respect was born of fear—fear that disappeared when she turned her attention to other things.

She was sometimes referred to as Picket Bickett, but more often, the students just called her Eagle Beak. I know it wasn't a nice name, but it seemed so apropos, considering the nose that she looked down as she addressed her students. It was a remarkable proboscis, not necessarily unattractive, but it did seem to draw the gaze of all who looked at her.

Mrs. Bickett was of strong German stock. She had been teaching for many years and it was destined that she be at her post for generations to come. In a sense, she **was** Aberdeen Junior High.

Fifth grade was exciting. I had put in my time in the other building, and my promotion to fifth grade had moved me to junior high school. The junior high building was one step closer to the large green building that housed Aberdeen High School. I knew there were four years more to wait, but the mystery of high school was there to be dreamt of and dwelt upon.

Mrs. Bickett had a very definite routine. Our class started the day, as we always had, with the pledge of allegiance. Mrs. Bickett always called on a class member to lead the class in this ritual and it seemed to me to be much more meaningful with the stern look of Eagle Beak at the head of the class. It just seemed more American somehow.

After the pledge, the routine of Mrs. Bickett took a definite turn.

She read from the Holy Bible. Not much—just a verse or two. Then she gave a moment of quiet time so that those who wished to pray could do so. I don't know how others felt about verse reading and prayer time, but I always liked it. I was well aware that Mrs. Bickett was a Mennonite, and that her faith did not necessarily agree with my own. My mother had taught me, however, that there were many different sects that worshiped God in many different ways. She stressed that our heavenly father hears all prayers, regardless of who prays them. I took a great deal of comfort in that knowledge, and enjoyed the opportunity to participate in the Morning Prayer.

I liked Mrs. Bickett. She was about as stern looking as any teacher I had seen, but after a time, it was easy to tell that she liked all of us and cared about our progress, both in school and in life. One of my favorite things about her was that she refused to treat us as children. She had told us on the very first day of fifth grade that children went to the elementary school. We were now in junior high, and because of that, we were young ladies and gentlemen. From that day on, she treated us as such, and it felt good.

The building that housed our junior high school consisted of a long hallway that surrounded the gymnasium that was located in the center of the building. That gymnasium was the center of our school and the center of all activity in the school.

It was a small gym, but it had a personality of its own. There were two rows of spectator seats on each side at floor level. At the south end of the gym was a blank wall. At the opposite end was the stage. It was a stage built high above the floor of the gym in order to permit the storage of folding chairs underneath.

The folding chairs were made of wood, and were stacked on large drawers that pulled out onto the gym floor to allow the quick transfer between auditorium and gymnasium. The drawers were on small wheels, similar to those of a shopping cart and just as efficient. The drawers never failed to go askew, making it necessary to push and shove and pull and tug from several angles in order to get the cumbersome thing back into its rightful place.

High above the gym floor, on each side, was another row of spectator seats. The only access to those seats was from the stage at the north end of the gym. At the end of the walkways on each side were some locked doors. There were rooms off those walkways and I was fascinated with them, for I never saw anyone go in or come out of those rooms. When I asked someone about them, I was told that they had been classrooms in the past, but were now used for storing old desks and books and such. That information only served to stimulate my imagination, for it was like having locked and very dark dungeons right in my school.

Sure, the locked rooms were on the second floor and dungeons are supposed to be deep in the ground, but I allowed for the difference without difficulty.

One night after school, when I was supposed to be rehearsing for the class play, *Alice In Wonderland,* I sneaked up those stairs off the stage and crept the length of the gym to one of the doors. It was unlocked!

My heart pounded in my chest as I opened the door. It creaked slightly and I was hit in the face with a strong musty odor old. I smelled the oldness within that room and wrinkled up my nose at it as I let my eyes grow accustomed to the light. I was excited, for I was about to uncover the mysterious contents behind that locked and secret portal.

Gradually, I reached the point where I could make out shapes first and then more detail. Finally, I could see into the room. I stared for the longest time and then slowly closed the door, being very careful not to draw attention to myself. Once again, I crept back along the walkway, high above the gym floor. I tiptoed down the steps and returned to the stage and the rehearsal. I had not been missed. I had gone on an adventure, and had returned without being discovered. I had answered the burning question about what was in the hidden room.

I now knew beyond the shadow of a doubt that the room contained "old desks and books and such."

65

Camp Little Lemhi

I was very active in the Boy Scouts of America. Camping was one of my favorite things to do, and I went on numerous informal camping trips. I enjoyed them thoroughly and had a good time, but there was one thing that always bothered me. I only went to the formal scout camp once.

It was exciting for me as I prepared for a week away from home. My troop was to spend two weeks at Camp Little Lemhi, near the border between Idaho and Wyoming. It was beautiful country and I looked forward to it. But there was much to do if I was to be equipped and ready for such a camp.

One of the first things I needed was a sleeping bag. I had been camping many times, but had always borrowed one of the sleeping bags from my grandparents' house. This time, though, their sleeping bags would not be available. Besides, my parents decided it was about time for me to have one of my own. We looked at some great bags in a couple of sporting goods stores in Pocatello, but we finally bought one from J.C. Penneys. That did not surprise me, for my mother always shopped there if at all possible. It was possible for scouting things, for it was the only place I knew of that stocked Boy Scout supplies.

It was fun getting ready for camp. I got a new "mess kit" and some utensils. I had a good scout knife already. I must have packed and re-packed several times during those last few days before we were to depart.

My scout troop piled into two cars for the trip to camp. It was a tight fit with all the equipment, but we didn't care. We were finally on our way. We headed north, through the familiar country between Aberdeen and Blackfoot, and then on through Idaho Falls. I think it was a town called Ririe where we turned off from the main road and turned eastward. It was a beautiful drive through Swan Valley. When we finally reached Palisades Reservoir, we had to cross the dam and backtrack a few miles to Camp Little Lemhi.

I was impressed with the beauty of the camp. At its center was a small lake, surrounded by the staff cabins and the camp store. At the edge of the lake was a small wooden pier lined with canoes. We had to drive around the lake to reach the parking area near the camp store. The drive served to intensify the excitement of the entire troop. We had finally arrived at camp.

We unloaded the cars as Dale Matson, our scoutmaster, went in to find out where we were to go. The driver of the other car waited until he returned and then left for home, leaving Dale to handle the whole group of rowdy scouts.

All the campsites at Little Lemhi were named after Indian tribes. We were assigned to the Navajo Camp. We lined up with our equipment and plunged into the pines, following the little rustic wooden signs that were scattered through the area. The trail was narrow, but well worn. As we hiked, Dale told us that Navajo Camp was farther away than any other camp and that we should enjoy the fact that no one would be running by **our** camp to reach the lake and the camp store.

We passed smaller trails that branched off. Beside each one was the name of a different Indian tribe—Comanche, Apache, Seminole, Blackfoot, Sioux, etc. Every name we saw seemed to me to be better than Navajo, for who ever saw a movie about brave and fearless Navajo warriors? I secretly wanted to be at one of the camps like Apache or Comanche, whose famous warriors and leaders had been scattered through my reading and television as I grew up. The only thing I knew about Navajo Indians was that they worked with my grandpa and they thinned sugar beets. It was very disappointing!

We finally reached our campsite, the Navajo Camp. It was more primitive than some of the ones we had passed and that was okay with us, for we wanted to "rough it" as best we could. We spent the afternoon setting up tents, unrolling our sleeping bags, and arranging our things for a week of fun. I shared a tent with Jay Jackman, one of the older scouts.

Once the camp was set-up, we were anxious to cook and eat, but Dale thought it best that we get oriented to the entire area. He lined us up and led us back to the lake. We visited the camp store and, the fifteen dollars I had brought was burning a hole in my pocket, I kept myself from buying anything. I was, however, a bit envious of some of the guys that thought nothing of buying a soft drink and chips, or even some of the scouting items that were on sale.

The week went well, with much to do and learn. Even so, there were highs and lows. My favorite thing was the overnight hike to Red Ridge. We could see the ridge high above us and it was intriguing. Our troop, with a camp guide accompanying us, left the Navajo Camp and took a trail of several miles to that ridge.

The guide had a habit of stopping every few minutes, turning toward the column that followed and shouting, "Is everybody happy?" By the time we got ready to make camp for the night, we had spent half our time walking and half our time answering that silly question. Of course we were happy! We were hiking in the mountains!

We were introduced on that hike to dehydrated food. Everything we ate came in a bag carried by our guide. I must admit, the Minestrone that we had for dinner was quite good, but the eggs that we had for breakfast the next morning left much to be desired. They were terrible!

By mid-morning we were gazing down upon the tiny Little Lemhi lake from atop Red Ridge. We had conquered the obstacle. It was great!

By mid-afternoon, we were back at our camp and exhausted. Half the troop fell asleep early and they missed dinner. I was **not** one of those. I never miss dinner.

The dark part of the week was that I didn't swim well enough to meet the minimum scout standards. Over and over again I tried and failed to go the distance. To be truthful, I think I was destined to fail because for some reason, I was afraid to swim that far out into the lake.

Because I could not meet the swimming standards, I was not permitted to do the overnight canoe trip on Palisades Reservoir. Oh, I helped load the canoes on the trucks and helped with the other equipment. I helped unload everything at the reservoir, too, but I had to ride in the truck to the place where the canoers would be camping. It was disappointing to miss that canoe trip and even worse to suffer the humiliation of being one of only two that couldn't swim. I was not a happy camper.

The greatest thing that happened to me at scout camp was the discovery of "boondoggle." I don't know if there is another name for it. It's a plastic, flat string-type stuff that comes in a variety of colors. I spent my entire stash on the stuff, and I forced myself how to learn to braid and weave it into some great items. I made key chains and bracelets and headbands. I enjoyed doing it. I returned home with a "boondoggle" something for everyone in the family.

I also returned home with several rolls of Kodak film. My mom had allowed me the use of her Brownie, and I made good use of it. Although my pictures were in living black and white, I still treasure them. They bring back memories of a time gone by; a time of fun, learning, and camaraderie that I shall always cherish.

66

The Fads

As I grew up in Aberdeen, fads would come and go. The popularity of certain dances, products, and even quirks in the language of the young people would increase and decrease as if it were riding its own roller coaster. Such fads came in like gangbusters, rode out a short period of popularity, and then disappeared forever.

Changes in the language were brought about by changes in society itself, and Aberdeen probably received such changes long after they disappeared from the general population. The "beatnik" era of the 50's was an interesting phenomenon nationwide, but had little effect on an Idaho farm town, except for a belated effect on the language. Kids began to punctuate their sentences with the word **man**.

"Where you goin', man?"

"I went to the show last Saturday, man."

"You got your arithmetic assignment done, man?"

This not so subtle intrusion into the language of the young must have been very irritating to the parents, but to the youth of Aberdeen, it was all part of being "cool!" For the most part, this change in the language was short-lived and disappeared, giving way to other verbal abuse.

The need to be "cool," however, did not disappear. It was always there and it is there even now. Of course, there are variations. Thirty years after trying to be just "cool," something was added and the kids became "cool dudes" and "cool chicks!"

Quirky language took new turns constantly. A snaggle-toothed cartoon cat was probably the cause of everyone putting the word **even** at the end of his or her sentences.

"I'm not going to go to class, **even**."

"I had no ideas for that writing assignment, **even**."

The "even" on the end of the sentence had no purpose, other than to be stressed and said at a painfully slow rate. Later, the word crept into the middle of the sentences, but was stressed much more than any other word.

"I don't **even** like that girl."

"There's not **even** a reason to stay awake past midnight."

The changes in language were constant, none of them lasting very long, but instead each one gave way to the next "fad talk."

Other fads came and went and they were fun to witness. Many involved clothing and hairstyles. Many involved products. There was one very big fad, though, that might well have been the craze of the century. It showed up in Aberdeen almost overnight. In a matter of just a few days it was in nearly every house. Everyone had to have a hula-hoop!

My house was no different from any other. We just **had** to have a hula-hoop. We couldn't live without one. I suppose my mother realized that, because it wasn't long before she brought one home from the store. It was a bright orange and just looking at it caused excitement. It was beautiful!

At first, Mike and I took turns, trying to make the hoop go around as we moved our hips. It looked so easy on television. We were slightly disappointed to find out that it took practice. The hoops did **not** stay up without a coordinated effort. It didn't take long, though, before we were doing well and even trying a few tricks. It was too bad that we had to share, because everyone wanted a turn every time, but we managed to learn how the thing worked.

In time, we acquired a couple more hula-hoops and I even learned how to do three at once. I learned how to do one on each arm as I did one around my waist. I learned how to make the hoop rise to my neck and then go back to my waist without stopping. I reached the point when I thought myself somewhat of a hula-hoop expert. That's why I volunteered so readily to enroll in the hula-hoop competition at the school's annual field day.

I practiced and practiced in preparation for the big contest. When the day finally arrived, I was ready. When the contest finally started, I was eliminated from competition in the first round. Other kids could make those hoops defy gravity, do magic tricks, bring in the mail, and all kinds of other things.

I was never so happy to see a fad disappear and go away.

67

Reptilian Tales

Snakes were a necessary evil in the Aberdeen area. For the most part, their contribution to the ecosystem was, if not appreciated outright, at least tolerated. They served as control over several species of rodents and the like that would surely have overrun the farming industry had the snakes not kept them in check.

There was a diverse assortment of snake types in the area, and most of them were quite easy to ignore. Garter snakes were kept as pets sometimes, but even they remained relatively inconspicuous as they did their magic with the pest population.

However, there were cases where the farmers and the snakes came to direct confrontation with each other and even all out war.

The fertile soil of Aberdeen was a blessing provided by centuries of volcanic activity. It provided one of the best growing mediums in the world, to be sure, but it did have it drawbacks. With such recent volcanic activity there was also an abundance of lava rock. The local farmers removed as much as they could, but sometimes there was more rock than could be removed. Such "rock piles" dotted the landscape of the area. Though not useful to man, they served as a haven for various types of flora and fauna, with one of the most prolific being the Western Diamondback rattlesnake.

Every kid in town learned to avoid the areas where the rattlers lived, or at least how to navigate those areas carefully enough to avoid confrontation.

Farmers plowed and cultivated around the rock piles, often losing time and destroying machinery parts if they tried to work the ground too close to the rocks. Every once in awhile, a farmer would decide that a rock pile could be extracted and would work to do so, expending a great degree of time and money to recapture another acre or so of usable land. In a way, such determination accounted for the success of the Aberdeen farmers, as year after year there was a bit more land under cultivation and fewer piles of lava rock.

One year one of the farmers encountered a natural snake pit that threatened his entire farming operation. His land was overrun with rattlesnakes, much more than the few that popped up in other areas. He was able to trace the snakes to one of the lava rock piles on his land. As he investigated further, he found that several feet below ground level was a large chamber that had been created by differing rates of lava cooling eons before.

The chamber was almost a cave, and its floor was in motion with the writhing bodies of rattlesnakes. There were hundreds of them. They were also sunning themselves on and around the rocks nearby.

The man threw a rock into the chasm and was amazed at the deafening sound that emanated from the nest as hundreds of snakes, startled by the rock, rattled their protest.

I first learned of the snake pit from *The Aberdeen Times*, our weekly newspaper. There was a picture on the front page of a couple of boys from my class holding pitchforks adorned with dead rattlesnakes. There must have been forty or fifty, and the article said that they hadn't even tried to kill the snakes in the pit. Those snakes in the picture had been killed in the nearby rocks.

The farmer tried everything he could think of to rid himself of those snakes. He tried to gas them at great expense. The result was disappointing. He tried to eliminate them by pushing a large wood fire into the pit with a bulldozer. It didn't work either.

Many of the kids from town went out and tried to kill the snakes. Many were killed, but it seemed to have little impact on the total population of the pesky reptile.

The farmer was almost at his wit's end when he made the decision to dump and entire truckload of some kind of petroleum product into the pit and ignite it. Black smoke filled the air and it seemed to burn forever, but it worked. Of course, it didn't get rid of all the snakes, but most of them were eliminated and his farm was restored to normal operations.

It would be several years later before such a popular snake story became news in Aberdeen. That happened when nearby construction forced a colony of garter snakes to move into my grandmother's house. She was living alone and not at all happy about the company, but I think that she enjoyed the national attention it brought. All three networks did reports. Paul Harvey called. Hers was a lead story in *The Weekly Reader*. Most of the school kids in the country heard about my grandmother, the "Snake Lady" from Aberdeen.

68

Sixth Grade Poet

At first glance, it seemed that my transition from fifth grade to sixth grade would be quite simple. Even my teacher had the same last name. Mrs. Bickett was my fifth grade teacher and Miss Bickett was my sixth grade teacher. They were in-laws, I think, but entirely different.

Miss Eve Bickett put many more demands on her students than did my previous teachers. She was a strict disciplinarian, too, but I didn't mind. I liked her and she was an interesting teacher. A couple of times a week I also had another teacher, Mrs. Fugate. It was the first time I had multiple teachers and I sort of liked it, even though it forced me to learn what was expected of me from two different personalities.

Another thing that was different about Miss Bickett's class was that we had several seventh graders in it. I had never been in a mixed class before, but it didn't seem to cause any problems. They had their own books and work to do and we had ours.

I was never very great at doing homework. Usually I was able to slide through with a minimum of effort and didn't even pay attention to schoolwork outside of school hours. One time, however, that habit caused me some trouble.

I had been assigned a poem. Miss Bickett had told the entire class to write a poem of at least sixteen lines. They were to be entered in the Women's' Club contest. Well, I ignored the assignment. I was not interested in entering a poetry contest. And I was not interested in writing a poem. Real men did not write poetry!

Miss Bickett collected the poems the following day after making the assignment. Since they were all passed to the front of the room, I figured that I was home free. She would never notice that her stack of verse did not include one written by me. Oh, how wrong I was!

It was only a matter of minutes when Miss Bickett called me to her desk and told me to sit in the "hot seat" that she kept at its side. She lowered her glasses to the tip of her nose. She let the small gold chains attached to each side of those spectacles sway for a moment as she stared over the top of her lenses. She did **not** look happy.

"Steven, I cannot find your poem."

I stammered for an instant, not really saying anything. I tried to adjust myself to a more inconspicuous position in that most uncomfortable chair as she went on.

"Did you even **write** a poem, Steven?"

I nodded slowly, watching her eyes as I moved my head from side to side. "No, I couldn't think of anything to write about."

She pushed her glasses back into a normal position and smiled. It was kind of a sideways smile that did not indicate humor or happiness or any of the normal things that smiles are supposed to be associated with. She pointed at the books on her desk: a dictionary, some textbooks, and some others I didn't recognize.

"Steven, what do you see there?"

"Books," I answered, too quickly.

"Then you will write a poem about books. You will write sixteen lines about books. You will do it at recess. You will remain in your seat during recess until you are prepared to hand me a completed poem. Am I understood?"

I nodded again. She motioned for me to take my seat again. Later, just before the bell rang for the afternoon recess, she placed a sheet of lined paper in front of me, as if to remind me that I would not be going outside.

As the class cleared and everyone went out to play, I wrote "*Books*" at the top of my paper. I remember thinking that if I were reading a book instead of going to school that I would be happier. I wrote a first line.

"*Books open a wonderful new world for me.*"

I continued to write the required sixteen lines, as fast as I could while trying to keep to the subject of books. I finished it with enough time to enjoy about fifteen minutes of the twenty-minute recess. I hurried up, placed it in front of Miss Bickett, and stood quietly as she read it. She nodded and told me to go ahead to the playground and I was out the door in a flash.

It was a couple of weeks later that I got the surprise of my life. Miss Bickett read my poem for the whole class. Then she announced that it had been the winner of the first place award for the Fifth School District and would be entered in the Idaho State Poetry Contest. Best of all, she gave me a check for fifteen dollars. I looked at it over and over again. It was very official looking and had beautiful writing. It had an imprint for the Women's Club. I was very proud of myself.

Several weeks passed and I had almost forgotten about the state contest. I guess I just thought it was over. But it hadn't been over. The results came back to our school and I sat at Miss Bickett's desk as she opened a brown manila envelope.

There was no check inside, but there was a letter for Miss Bickett and a certificate for me. I had won the third place award for the entire state. I was so excited!

My ego got such a boost from that experience that I have continued to try and write poetry ever since. I have learned to enjoy it. I have also learned that men do write poetry. They always have.

69

Giving The Finger

Aberdeen Public Schools began its school year much earlier than most other school systems. Like many other schools, they made allowances for "snow days," teachers' conference days, holidays, and other similar and predictable interruptions to academia. Unlike other school districts, they also made allowances for the harvest. School let out in October, usually for about two weeks, for what we called "spud vacation."

Spud vacation was an absolute necessity for a town like Aberdeen, for when it came time to harvest sugar beets and potatoes, every farmer felt the need for extra help. The only pool of labor they could tap for such assistance was that consisting of school kids.

At harvest time, there was a need for manpower to drive tractors, trucks, and other more specialized harvest machinery. There was a need for people to ride the back of potato diggers, hands flying as they tried to remove clods, vines and culls from traveling up the "elevator" chains. Those chains carried the material from the digger and dumped it into the trucks that crept slowly alongside in the field.

The fully loaded trucks would then travel the county roads as fast as they could safely be driven so that the potatoes could be deposited in storage facilities as quickly as possible. Storage was usually completed with the deposit of the truckloads in a potato cellar. Potato cellars come in various sizes, but they usually consisted of very long, half-buried trenches. The roofs of those cellars were varied, from elaborate metal Quonset-style roofs to the more common ones made of wire and baled straw, covered with tons of earth. Either way, they provided insulated protection from the harsh elements of Idaho winters.

The cellars required special crews, too. The trucks backed down into the narrow openings into the cellars and their loads were emptied into special elevator equipment called "pilers" that were used to create massive potato piles as tall as twenty feet or more and evenly spread across the breadth of the cellar. It was an effective way of storing potatoes, but it was also important to store them as clean as possible.

Once again, just as in the fields, crews manned the machines, picking out clods, vines and whatever tubers might be questionable due to rot or discoloration. It was a vine-picking job in such a cellar that afforded me my very first real harvest job. Technically, I was too young to work, for the law required that a child be fourteen years of age. The man that hired me was a good friend of my father's and chose to ignore the law. Most of the farmers ignored that law during the harvest anyway. The jobs had to be filled.

I worked in an elaborate cellar in town. In fact, it was more like a warehouse than one of the normal cellars, but the routine was the same—unload the trucks, pile the potatoes, and get as much dirt and vines out of them as possible.

Potato trucks have a V-shaped bed with a conveyor chain running the length of the bed where the "V" came together in the middle. The conveyor was operated by a small electric motor mounted at the rear of the truck. It had to be plugged in by the cellar crew to one of the extension outlets.

The weight of an entire load of potatoes would have been far too heavy for the small motor to handle. To solve that problem, fitted boards were cut and laid across the bed and just above the chain from front to back, preventing the potatoes from resting on the chain. As the truck was unloaded, the boards were removed one at a time, from the back, to allow the chain to carry the potatoes out the rear of the truck with a minimum of effort. Sometimes the boards turned sideways or jammed. When that happened, someone had to work very hard in the truck to get the chain running and the spuds moving.

The end of the chain at the rear of the truck hung over the hopper for the piler, which carried the potatoes up to the desired elevation and deposited them. It was my job to try and keep the spuds moving, while trying to remove vines and clods.

As we neared the end of a long day of about twelve hours, we were getting ready to unload the very last truck of the day. When I plugged in the motor at the rear of the truck, it whined but did not start the chain. One of my co-workers climbed into the truck and helped the driver clear out some of the load by hand. Then they found a board that had been askew and corrected the problem. I tried the motor again and the chain almost started, but it didn't. Two of us decided to grab the links and pull to help get the engine started. It worked. The chain began to rapidly dump spuds into the hopper of the piler.

The only problem was that my glove had become caught in the sprocket that drove the chain. My left hand was pulled through a very unnatural half circle around the sprocket. Worst of all, the index finger on that hand remained inside the glove for that circuitous trip around the sprocket! It really hurt! I didn't know until I removed the glove that the end of the finger had been pinched clear off. I was not feeling very good.

My finger had been pinched so completely that it pinched it closed and it was not bleeding. It was also about two inches wide. One of my co-workers grabbed the glove with the end of my finger in it and rushed me to his pickup. He drove like a madman to the doctor's office. I guess I was lucky to have had that accident during one of the rare times when we had a doctor in town.

The doctor quickly looked at the mass of tissue in my glove and determined that it was crushed and unusable. Then he began to examine my finger more closely. As he pressed against the sides, it was like opening a floodgate and blood shot against the wall. I was **not** feeling well!

He worked meticulously to pick out each and every bone fragment and clean the wound as best he could. By the time he had cleaned it, my father arrived. I listened as the doctor expressed a couple of options to my dad. He explained the nail bed was gone and most likely the first joint was damaged. He recommended that my father permit him to sever the finger below the wound at the middle knuckle. He stressed that it was the only way to make certain the finger healed evenly and cleanly.

My father thought long and hard before saying anything. Then he looked at my finger and mentioned that it seemed the roots of a nail were still intact. The doctor said that it might be possible, but not likely. My dad didn't listen. He asked the doctor to bandage the finger as it was, saying that if it were necessary to remove it later, then so be it.

It took a long time for that finger to heal. At first, I had to make regular trips to the doctor for dressing changes and cleaning. After a while, the doctor advised my mother how to care for it and my mom and her trusty bottle of hydrogen peroxide took over.

In time, the nail grew back and over the top of the shortened finger, providing a thick protective covering over a most sensitive spot. I always wondered how my father knew. I am still grateful for his insight!

70

Moving On Up

The time came when my parents decided that it was time to move again. Unlike previous times, though, the move was to a different house in the same town. We moved into Grandpa's "lower place."

Uncle Gordon had completed the conversion of the Fairview School and his family had moved into their new and beautiful home. They had vacated the house at the lower place and, since it was bigger, and closer to much of the work that my father had to do, it seemed logical to move in. After all, there were eight of us now, and the one bedroom house on the other farm was just a bit cramped, even with the clever arrangement of bunk beds and children.

In a way, the new house afforded little more on the ground floor than what we had already had—a living room, a kitchen, a bedroom, a bathroom, and a closet. Actually, on closer inspection, some differences were there. There was more than just the one closet, the rooms were larger, and there was also a back room between the kitchen and the back door that provided storage. In addition to that, there were porches both front and back, a luxury that we hadn't enjoyed before.

There was something else, too. We now had a basement. Most of it was space for a coal bin and a furnace, but it was a gold mine for storing and stashing things and it provided the perfect place for Mom's supply of home-canned food.

The real treat was a second floor. We had never had one before. Through a door off the living room, near the entrance to my parents' new and private bedroom, one could gain access to the stairway to that second floor. At the top of the stairs, a small room was made into Becky's bedroom. To the left, a much larger room provided a place for the five brothers.

The boys' room had a double window that overlooked the front yard and porch roof, while Becky's room had a window that overlooked the back. The ceiling of these rooms was flat in the center and then each side sloped downward along the rafters. There wasn't much headroom. We didn't complain though, for to have three bedrooms now instead of one was indeed a new and wonderful experience.

About halfway up the stairs, one only had to turn his back to the stairs and there was a "secret door" that opened with a couple of hook and eye latches to reveal an attic above my parents' bedroom that would serve well for storage. It had a window, too. In fact, it was a better window, for it was overlooking the south pasture and you could see into the distance, whereas the other two windows had so many trees in the way that there was little to see.

For the first time since I could remember, our bunk beds were broken down into individual beds and there was enough room to place them all and still have room for a bookcase, a table/desk, etc. It was a great thing to have our own room, and we were excited about it.

Our greatest excitement, though, came when we realized that we were indeed farther out in the country and had a whole new world in which to run and play. There was an old garage, an old chicken coop, lambing sheds, haystacks, corrals, an old boxcar that served as a granary, and best of all, a huge red barn with concrete floors and even a working shop inside. It had an immense loft that wasn't used.

Access to the barn loft was through a trapdoor in the ceiling of the main part of the barn. We had to climb a makeshift ladder fashioned by nailing rough-hewn boards between the studs. The loft had a homemade gym set up in it, with weights, etc. There was a "gunny" sack hung from a rope that was filled with grain and used as a punching bag. It was great! The only drawback was the hundreds of pigeons that felt the loft was theirs and theirs alone. Even so, we managed to share it with them without much trouble, just an occasional "gift" that was delivered from above when we weren't being very alert.

Beyond the corrals were several acres of old farm machinery that provided another great place to play. There were some things so old that I couldn't even figure out what they might have been used for. Some of the machinery was for harvesting potatoes, but new and improved methods had long since been discovered. Besides, Grandpa Frank had stopped raising potatoes and decided to devote his lands to sugar beets, grain, and hay.

There were eighty acres of farmland, and more of sagebrush and pasture. To the south of the house, amid the sagebrush and "monkey nut" trees, there was a small canal that carried water to several of the other farms in the area. It's best feature was a waterfall. It was called Cooney, though I have no idea where the name originated.

Cooney would become a special place for us. It was far away from the house and right in the middle of a terrain of nothing more than sagebrush and lava rock. It was a place of play and refuge from parental eyes and passers-by.

Far to the north of the house, along a ditch bank between fields, was a lone tree that, for some reason, I found fascinating. I couldn't understand why it was there, for all other trees had been removed to allow for the cultivation of the land.

Our new location was one of wonder and exploration, of new things to do and to enjoy. We adapted readily to the new house and farm, but it took a bit longer to get used to the idea that I could no longer take a bike to school. I began to ride a school bus again. It became more difficult to spend time with my friends for my new home was too far away.

My brothers and I were very creative, though, and we found a variety of ways to entertain ourselves.

71

Having A Blast in Aberdeen

Dynamite was plentiful. It was as easy to acquire in Aberdeen as candy. There were laws on the books, though, about who could buy dynamite. The most important of those laws was the requirement that the person who purchased it must be twelve years of age!

The Aberdeen Hardware Store, right there on Main Street just north of the town center, sold dynamite. Of course, it had to be purchased in parts. It cost twenty cents for a stick of dynamite. A blasting cap and a fuse were a nickel apiece. A few words with the clerk at the hardware store, and a basic understanding of how to use those parts could be had and understood.

There was one year that using dynamite became sort of a teenage fad in Aberdeen. There were several kids that were buying it and using it as though it were leftover firecrackers from the Fourth of July. I was not one of those kids, but I might have been if thirty cents had been easier to come by.

Every day at school there were new stories circulating about what so-and-so had done with dynamite the night before. Most of them had to do with comparisons of how big a hole the blast could make in a potato field or how easy it was to move lava rocks.

One of the more interesting stories had to do with two guys that went out to Sportsman's Park and "fished" with dynamite. They would toss the lighted stick into the reservoir. If the timing was right, they were treated to a huge plume of water that often drenched them. The by-product of that experience was the fish that would float to the surface to be gathered up and taken home for dinner. This method wasn't legal, of course, but the chances of a game warden being anywhere around Aberdeen were about as remote as the chance it will have its own TV station.

My Uncle Dwight had his own wild experience with dynamite. It happened down at the slough, that great slow-moving drainage ditch where we often went "frogging." Dwight had an overwhelming desire to find out if the explosive made a larger hole in mud than it did in dryer ground. He carefully placed the charge and then lit the fuse. He knew that it would not be wise to remain for the show and so he started to climb toward the safety of the bank. However, the sides of the ravine were nearly as muddy as the bottom was, and he slipped back down into the mire.

Dwight realized that time was running out and tried again to scale the bank. He slipped a second time! Now he was beginning to panic. He got a running start and literally flew up the bank, receiving assistance from friends above who grabbed him and pulled him the few remaining feet to the edge. It wasn't clear whether it was the hands of his buddies or the blast from below that helped him sail over the edge to safety. He made it just in time, but not without the experience of seeing his almost-shortened life flash before his eyes.

As I mentioned before, I could not participate in the dynamite fad, but I did get my chance to use it the following summer, when I took a temporary job for the Aberdeen-Springfield Canal Company.

I was hired to assist Joe Lipman, a man that normally patrolled the canal banks on his motorcycle looking for problem spots. However, I would not be helping him with that. Instead, I was to help him clear out lava rock for a new canal branch near the Duffin farm northwest of town. It was just for a few days, but it was exciting.

Most of our day was spent in placing dynamite charges to clear out tons of lava rock. Joe used a portable jackhammer to make holes in the rock. He taught me how to judge the position of the charge and how best to place it. He taught me how to place caps and wire. We didn't use the same kind of fuses as the kids in town. We connected the wires between charges and ran them far away to a sheltered area, usually the pickup, to be connected to a magneto with a plunger at the last minute. That way we could set off all charges at once.

The most important thing that Joe taught me was how to stand when the blast occurred. Yes, we would stand. He explained that people who huddled behind something with their eyes closed were in danger of being hurt. Instead, we stood behind the pickup, and when the plunger was pushed, we stood way back, hands on hips, looking straight up. Actually, the hands on the hips wasn't a part of the training, but Joe did it with such a sense of style that I chose to learn it the same way.

The reasoning behind that funny stance became all too sensible as I gained experience. The chances of flying rocks being shot toward us were slim, and even if they did, the pickup was there to stop them. The real danger was that our charges were placed in positions designed to clear the hole. Most of the material was blasted high into the air. Because of that, we looked straight up, prepared to step to the side if we saw any chunks of rock headed our way. Joe said it was important for me to keep a cool head and just use the baseball skills I had to dodge anything coming out of the sky. It was apparent that he hadn't watched me play, but I was still as careful as could be.

The job only lasted a few days. We cleared nearly a half-mile of rock, making it movable enough for the bulldozers and other heavy machinery that was brought in to finish what Joe Lipman and I had started.

The dynamite fad disappeared as quickly as it had surfaced. I'm not sure why. Perhaps the kids involved were beginning to get some sense of how stupid their activities were. Perhaps they just got bored with it. Perhaps a few phone calls from concerned parents changed the way the hardware store sold its dynamite. Nevertheless, Aberdeen got through the period without any reports of injury or death. Rather remarkable to my way of thinking!

72

Up, Up, And Away

Warren Hollingsworth was one of Dad's best friends. The Hollingsworths lived in a beautiful new home across the road from my grandparents' house. It was a nice home that replaced the dilapidated structure that the Gonzales family had lived in when I was younger.

Although the Hollingsworths visited my grandparents, I didn't really pay much attention, because that was adult stuff. I tried to avoid adult stuff as best I could.

I think, though, that my dad became Warren's friend because they frequently met for sport, conversation and gossip in the town's cultural and social hub—the eight-lane bowling center—The Spud Bowl.

I didn't know that Mr. Hollingsworth had an airplane. Had I known, I might have found a way to lobby for a ride, for I loved airplanes. Every time a plane flew over, Mike and I would run out of the house to look. It was really exciting when those with more than one propeller would fly lower than normal on their way to the Pocatello Airport on the other side of the reservoir. The **real** thrill, however, was when the airplane flying over was a "jet." That would make it a red-letter day.

One day, Mr. Hollingsworth invited Dad to "go up." He added that Dad could bring me if I was interested. I was.

We met Mr. Hollingsworth at the Aberdeen Airport, which is little more than a long wide piece of blacktop with a couple of protective sheds, a gas pump, and a wind sock that looked as though it had seen better days.

I stood by and watched as Mr. Hollingsworth and Dad pushed an old, faded red airplane from one of the sheds out onto the blacktop. I even joined Dad to help push the wing around so the plane was facing north. Then Mr. Hollingsworth jumped up on the wing and opened the door. He pulled a seat forward and Dad boosted me up so that Mr. Hollingsworth could help me into the rear seat and fasten the seat built securely across my middle.

As the two men remained outside, cranking up the propeller, I began to realize that I was really going to leave the ground and fly. The butterflies began to do somersaults in my stomach as first Mr. Hollingsworth and then Dad climbed into the cockpit in front of me.

I couldn't see much of the instrument panel from where I sat. My seat was much lower than theirs was and they blocked the view. All I could do was think of the cloth fabric that covered the plane. Until a few minutes before, I had thought all airplanes to be some strong metal, but this one was covered with cloth much like that my mother used with her sewing machine.

When the engine sputtered and then started, the plane began to vibrate and I had thoughts of its breaking apart and killing us all. Then the throttle was increased. The noise and vibration increased considerably. Dad turned in his seat and yelled to me that we had to wait until the engine warmed up before we could go anywhere. I craned my neck to see the engine heat gauge on the front panel and I could see its needle crawl toward a green mark that I instinctively knew marked the point where we could fly.

The needle had not yet reached the green when the plane began to move to the north end of the runway. Mr, Hollingsworth had to look out the side window because he couldn't see over the front any better than I could. When we reached the end of the blacktop the plane turned and faced south. Once again we waited. It was almost tortuous waiting for that needle to reach the right spot. I felt as though I would like to jump from the plane and run away, as far and fast as I could. All of a sudden, flying didn't seem like such a good idea!

Finally, everything started happening at once. We lurched forward and began gaining momentum. Almost immediately the rear of the airplane lifted up and suddenly we could all see out the front. I was pushed back into my seat as I watched the long runway get shorter and shorter. We seemed to be fishtailing a bit and it was not a good feeling.

Suddenly the ride became smoother and I watched as the blacktop beneath us got farther and farther away, then was replaced by a gravel road, then a wheat field. Then my stomach made a strange move as the aircraft banked to the left and I was looking straight down at a farmhouse and barn and corrals. They looked so small!

I was flying and it felt great. I wriggled from one side of the seat to the other, trying to look out both sides at the same time so as not to miss a thing. I saw the Bickett house and our house and the Clayton house and the highway. Another bank to the left and we were over Aberdeen. It was indeed a small town. We banked to the right and passed over the University Of Idaho's agricultural experiment station and then followed the road for a minute until we were over Sportsman's Park and American Falls Reservoir.

Everything looked so different. I was fascinated! For the first time in my life, I saw what was on the other side of the reservoir. We were flying over the Fort Hall Indian Reservation. After a few minutes, we turned back toward the reservoir. Once we were out over the water, Mr. Hollingsworth decided to play games.

I didn't know at the time, but Mr. Hollingsworth had done the same thing to my Dad the first time he flew and had also done it with others on their first flights. He seemed to take delight in causing his rookie passengers to "lose their lunches." As he started his maneuver, I could see the sparkle in his eye. I knew he was having the time of his life trying to show me the time of mine.

He explained that he was going to fly straight up until the engine quit. I did **not** like the sound of that, but there was nothing I could do. My entire body went taut as we started upward. I was gritting my teeth, no longer interested in what was outside the window. I was only aware of one thing—total fear!

I could feel the plane shudder as it slowed and then the engine noise stopped! The front of the plane nosed over and then quickly aimed itself toward the water below as my stomach lunged into my throat! It seemed as if we were heading straight to our deaths and then the engine started again and we pulled out into straight and normal flight once again.

Dad and Mr. Hollingsworth started laughing at me. It must have been very funny to them and I am certain that the look on my face was exactly what they expected. I did notice, though, that even my dad was a bit green around the gills. He had been through a stall before, but it still got to him, too. I could tell.

By the time we landed back at the airport, my stomach was almost back to normal. Still, it felt very good to feel the earth beneath my feet again. I had flown and, except for the stall, I had enjoyed it thoroughly.

By evening the flight seemed like a dream, but even so, it was a dream that marked another milestone in my life. I had been flying in an airplane! Imagine that!

73

When Gypsies Speak

He came to our school for just a few weeks. His name was Peter Rankin and he was the most interesting person I had ever met. He sat behind me in Mrs. Chambliss' class and we talked almost as often as we breathed.

Peter was a gypsy. I had almost no understanding at all of what it meant to be a gypsy, but I certainly enjoyed hearing about all the things they did. I suppose I might even have been a bit jealous of Peter and his exciting life had I not been so busy soaking in the stories and tales that he told.

Peter Rankin was not a pretty person. In fact, I would have to say that he and ugly were very close friends. His head looked as though it belonged on a full-grown man, while his body looked as if it had been stunted somewhere around third grade. He walked with a limp. His arms were so long that he looked like an orangutan as he stalked down the halls at school. The clothes he wore were brightly colored, even more so than the attire of the Navajo women that lived nearby during my more formative years.

Nevertheless, Peter's clothing and physical appearance became secondary to the light in his eyes and the skill with which he could tell a story. And boy, could Peter Rankin tell a story!

During our lunch hour and during recess, groups of kids would huddle around Peter to hear his tales. He acted as though he was an adult, handling the attention gracefully and proceeding with his stories as if they had been told hundreds of times. His voice took on a deep timbre for a boy, and his accent and excitement served him well as he talked.

He told about living in the French Alps. He told about living in Paris. He told about life in Spain. He talked of the many schools he had been enrolled in and the many places he lived across the United States.

There seemed to be an inexhaustible supply of names of small towns and descriptions of schools as he spun his tales of travel and excitement.

His barrage of information entranced me. I ate it up. I had an even better opportunity than most to hear Peter, because he sat behind me in class. Mrs. Chambliss constantly had to tell me to face the front and get to work, but the pull of Peter's adventures was just too strong to resist.

When I went home at night, I talked about Peter Rankin. I repeated his stories and his philosophy of life as best I could for my younger siblings. Most of my sentences started with "Peter Rankin said...." My mother finally grew tired of hearing about Peter Rankin and she told me that she would hear no more. Not long after, Mike told me that if he heard another Peter Rankin story that he would throw up. I began to get the hint and stopped telling them all the great things I was hearing.

I still listened at school, though, and I continued to enjoy the tales as much as ever. I just kept them to myself.

One day I noticed that Peter seemed a bit "down in the dumps." He was short tempered and depressed. He seemed quick to anger and he told not one single story. During lunch, I sat down next to him in the gym and asked him what was wrong. At first, he didn't seem to want my company, but in a few minutes he was telling me the whole problem.

He was leaving Aberdeen. His large family was moving on to Blackfoot where his father had a new job. Peter was very unhappy about leaving so soon after he had come to us, but he was used to it. He explained that he would get over his disappointment, but that he truly envied the rest of us because we had homes that were permanent and friends that were permanent and an entire town that was permanent.

The next day, Peter's desk was empty. He was gone! Just as rapidly as he came into our school, he left it again. I was still stuck there, but with a much better sense of the true value of being stuck.

74

Hunters

I was not much of a hunter. It wasn't because I fell for the gentle pleading in the eyes of a deer. It wasn't because I had some noble sense of doing the world wrong to take the life of a poor, defenseless animal. It wasn't because I was avoiding some negative social stigma. The truth is, I never really had the chance to become the hunter I dreamed of being—that cross between Davy Crockett and Kit Carson, with just a bit of Jeremiah Johnson thrown in for spice.

Dad went hunting once in awhile, but not often, for he had trouble getting away from his work long enough. He **did** manage a few deer hunts where he would leave for a day or two and come back with enough venison to last the winter. I remember how proud he was of his new .308 caliber rifle and the scope that went with it. He also bragged a bit about his shooting, describing how his bullet had cut the throat of his prey well enough that it was "bled out" before he got to it.

My Grandpa Frank and my uncles were hunters. They met each new hunting season with an excitement and anticipation that I could not share. They, too, had their stories—one about the famous shotgun maneuver near the slough that netted both a pheasant and a duck with the very same shot. I guess it **was** rather remarkable. It was also an accident. No one knew that when the bead was put on the pheasant, that a duck was leaving the slough at the same time and far in the background.

There was another story, too, about a shotgun going off by accident and barely missing one of my uncles. It was the result of carelessness, to be sure, and I am certain that neither Dean or Dwight would want me to say who was at fault. They knew better, too, because Grandpa Frank was a stickler for teaching proper gun safety and his lessons said nothing about digging the barrel of a shotgun into a snow bank.

I never did go on a deer hunt. I wanted to, but it never happened. I did love the taste of venison, though, and enjoyed the "deer burgers" that we had when I was younger.

The only hunting I ever did with any success was for pheasants. Aberdeen was famous for its abundance of Chinese Ring-necked Pheasants. They were plentiful, and any kid that had reached the age of twelve and had the four dollars for a license could go out during the pheasant season and bag his limit. That limit was usually four birds a day.

Dad showed me how to properly clean a pheasant and prepare it for the frying pan. As far as I am concerned there is no better taste than that of a properly prepared pheasant. Perhaps that is why I took more of an interest in hunting them than in hunting duck or any of the other birds.

I used my father's twelve-gauge shotgun when I went looking for pheasants. It was probably a bit big for me, but I managed. I didn't need to spend a lot of time beating the bushes anyway. Pheasants were everywhere.

Because the pheasants were everywhere, Grandpa and Dad stressed safety when we hunted. They weren't really that concerned about our handling shotguns, for we had been taught well, but the concern was for the most dangerous thing of all—out-of-town hunters!

They came from many places, but most of the time, I think they were from Pocatello. Perhaps my view had been jaded by my Grandpa Frank, who was perfectly willing to paint a big red "**COW**" on the sides of our livestock in the hope that some of these "furriners" could read. Hardly a season went by that we didn't lose a ewe or two to those trigger-happy nincompoops from parts unknown and unknowing.

There were some nice ones who, regardless of their stupidity, would come to the house and admit to the destruction of one of our animals. They would offer to pay damages, and Dad or Grandpa would readily accept the offers. At times they seemed surprised when their money was accepted, as if they thought the mere admission of guilt was compensation enough. It was as if they had no concept of the fact that a farmer's livelihood depends largely on his livestock. Nevertheless, they paid.

More often than not, though, the culprits that murdered our livestock would escape by some back road and be doing the same thing elsewhere before we realized there had been a loss. These pillars of big city society seemed to view farmers as some sort of subspecies of the human race, incapable of thought or reason. They acted as if the farms were there for their pleasure and sport, like a golf course or a country club. Despite my grandfather's attempts at educating them through the use of signs on every other fence post that said "No Trespassing," or "No Hunting," it seemed that each and every one of them thought the signs were for someone else.

Once we were in the front yard, discussing the condition of the roof with Grandpa. We were about to recover the shingles with a combination of linseed oil and graphite to make it a bit more waterproof, a bit blacker and a whole lot more attractive. As we were getting advice from Grandpa Frank on how to best get started, a man came walking into our lane from the gravel road. He was dressed in all the fancy store-bought hunting regalia that established his identity as one of the out-of-town hunters.

My dog, Lucky, was not about to allow a stranger to gain access to the yard without a challenge. He ran to the edge of the yard and placed himself between the man and us. He began to show his teeth and growl about as fiercely as such a gentle dog could.

The man stopped, then hollered to us, "I would like to borrow a jack and lug wrench. My buddies and I have a flat tire about half a mile down the road. Would you please call off the dog?"

My grandfather answered without hesitation. "Why don't ya just shoot him like you've done to everything else around here that draws a breath?"

We started laughing. Dad told me to take Lucky around in back of the house. He told the guy to get in his pickup and he'd take him back to his car and help him change the tire. We all got a pretty good laugh out of what Grandpa said, but you could tell by his eyes that he hadn't really been trying to make a joke. He meant every word. His disdain for city hunters was obvious, at least to me.

The pheasants were really the only things I hunted for its food value. But it was not the only thing I hunted. My favorite beasts to hunt were jackrabbits. They were miserable, crop-destroying rodents and I despised them. I carried a .22 caliber single-shot rifle with me most of the time and often stopped on the back roads and picked off rabbits. I was not interested in eating such a thing, but left them instead for the magpies and the hawks.

I would often shoot starlings and sparrows out of the trees near the house for the cats. I also shot rattlesnakes.

I suppose, in retrospect, I feel a touch of regret for killing the sparrows and the starlings, but never have I regretted the slaying of a rattlesnake or a jackrabbit. I consider such action as a benefit to humankind. I guess I always will.

75

Love Can Hurt

Seventh grade is a stressful time for all young people, especially the boys. It is a time of changing physiology. It is a time of growing pains and social upheaval. Most of all, though, it is a time of raging hormones!

Hormones are tiny things, invisible to the naked eye, that permeate the control center of a boy's brain and do serious damage. Oh, I suppose they are there in most people to some degree or another once adulthood rears its ugly head. But in boys, somewhere around twelve or thirteen years of age, they take over. I was no different.

Almost overnight my entire philosophy of life changed. No longer was baseball more important than girls. No longer was camping more important than girls. No longer was music more important than girls. No longer were food, sleep, or air more important than girls.

Almost overnight those obnoxious, giggling, quivering masses of flesh became attractive, beautiful vessels of wonderful personalities that prompted even the most bashful of boys to become obnoxious, giggling, quivering masses of flesh.

I feel it is necessary to explain the way hormones work in a young boy. You see, they begin to accumulate slowly, and they disguise themselves so as not to be recognized. They take up residence in the deepest recesses of the brain and wait. Once they realize that they outnumber all the "common sense" molecules, they mass into large armies and take up positions in the most important parts of the human mind. They set up entire garrisons in the eye, ear, nose, and throat department and begin to cause the victim to see, hear, smell, and speak differently around the female of the species.

It is frightening, to say the least. Once the position has been established, a one-sided war is declared, and the complete destruction of the "common sense" is unavoidable.

In most cases, an amazing appreciation for girls occurs, and more often than not, each boy focuses on one particular example of femininity. I am sorry to say that I was no different. I am sure that I was unconscious, but one day I noticed that the absolute embodiment of perfection was sitting across the room from me. Her name was Toni Crowder.

I had known Toni for quite a while and had always thought her to be a bit stuck up and quite obnoxious. But now she was different. She was witty and sweet and funny and beautiful. She was smart as any girl in my class and got terrific grades.

Toni had dark hair, almost black, that cascaded down over her shoulders. It was kept away from the sides by gold-colored combs most of the time. The bangs made a perfect frame for a perfect face. Well, OK, it wasn't perfect. There were some flaws, but they were perfect flaws. There was a beauty mark below her left eye that couldn't have been placed in a better spot by an expert. There were a few freckles, too, just to keep the beauty from hitting me all at once. She had fabulous teeth and natural red lips that made it look as though she was wearing lipstick. And then there were the eyes. She had the most gorgeous green eyes I had ever seen. Geez, how could she have been there all year without my noticing?

We had exchanged words in the past, usually barbs of some kind, often over who got the better grade on some assignment. Once in awhile she even stuck her tongue out at me from across the room if I answered one of Mrs. Chambliss' questions correctly. In fact, we had even fought over who was going to use the drinking fountain first.

Once the hormones did their thing, though, it was obvious that I had wronged her time and time again. Of course, she deserved to drink before me! Of course, she was the better student!

For some reason, we became very close. Once we spoke to each other with civil tongues in our heads, we began to talk more. In a matter of a few days we even sought each other out during recesses and lunch periods. We spent those times walking or sitting with each other, just talking about things in general. Each of us enjoyed the other's company. At times we even passed notes in class and I would pull them out at home and read them again and again. They were just ordinary notes, but they were from her and that was special. I was very careful not to let my loud-mouthed siblings know what was happening. I thought that matters of the heart should remain in the heart, not on the lips.

I knew all along that I was much more in love with Toni than she with me. Oh, I was someone to talk with, but she didn't think of me as a boyfriend. I tried not to think of her as a girlfriend either, but it was difficult considering the fact that I even dreamed about her.

I will never forget the Field Day that year. Our school always celebrated the first day of May with a field day celebration where all the kids took lunches and picnicked on the football field. There were athletic events that awarded ribbons, such as the fifty yard dash, the baseball throw, the high jump, etc., but that year I sat on the grass and shared my Twinkies with Toni Crowder. It was the best field day I ever had. As the hour approached for me to catch the bus and go home, Toni removed her necklace and gave it to me. It was a gold chain with a heart pendant and her gift of it to me was indescribably special. I thanked her and gave her a hug. Then, just before I ran to catch my bus, I kissed her!

I was love-stricken to be sure. All the way home, I tasted Toni, and she tasted as good as she looked. I stashed the necklace in a very secret place, away from the prying eyes of my family, and moped around for the weekend.

When Monday came, Toni and I still walked and talked at lunchtime, but we never again kissed. We were never again as close as we were on that field day in May. Summer vacation began a couple of weeks later and before the next school year began, Toni had moved away. I never saw her or heard from her again. Geez, she was beautiful.

I wonder whatever happened to that heart pendant and chain.

76

Big Hole

There were many places in the area where the boy scouts could go and camp. There was the mountainous terrain above Indian Springs or the quiet isolation of the desert to the west. There was the swampy area near McTucker Creek at the north end of American Falls Reservoir or the sandy and rocky terrain west of American Falls itself. There was, however, another area along the reservoir that I remember best. It was an isolated spot away from the main roads and out of sight from the boat dock at Sportsman's Park or even from the main part of the reservoir. We called it Big Hole!

It was really named Big Hole years before the scouts ever went there. It was a part of the Snake River, by virtue of the fact that it was a hidden inlet off of the main body of American Falls Reservoir. It was well known by the best fisherman in the area as a place where fish were plentiful and could be caught at all times of day or night. It was for that reason—the good fishing—that it was called Big Hole.

Had we gone camping in late Spring or Summer, we may have had to share the area, but we didn't go then. Our outing at Big Hole was made in December! We were to camp and practice survival skills, and the obstacles we faced were far different than at other campsites that we frequented during the summer months.

We gathered at the church for the short drive to Big Hole. We waited in the foyer because it was cold and breezy outside. Finally, we hurried to load the vehicles that would take us. In a way, it seemed daft to go out into the snow to camp when we all had nice warm homes to sleep in, but we were scouts and we looked forward to the adventure.

When we reached our campsite we started a fire, even before trying to set up our tents and get ready for the night. Unlike other campfires, this one was made in a special way, so that we could all heat up lava rocks to use in our tents later. The fire was much bigger than normal and spread out more. Because of that, it had to be watched closely, not that we thought it would get out of hand. After all, there was snow covering everything.

To prepare a place to sleep, we had to first find an area large enough. It wasn't an easy task, considering all the lava rock and sagebrush, but we eventually found enough clearings for everyone. Of course, the older scouts got the good spots nearer the fire, but we younger ones didn't complain. That's just the way it was.

The snow was dry enough so we could use a broom to sweep the areas clean and put down our ground covers. Those covers were usually heavy canvases, but some had plastic sheets. Then we pitched tents, a job made more difficult because the ground was frozen and it was hard to get the stakes driven into it. Then we rolled out our sleeping bags inside. We were finished.

The whole troop gathered around the fire and we prepared for our evening meal of beans and hot dogs. Afterward, we continued to huddle close to the flames for warmth as we drank hot chocolate by the gallon and sang songs, trying to ignore the cold and have the best time we could. We told jokes and stories and drank more hot chocolate.

Finally, it was time to "hit the sacks." Each of us used gloves to carry the large lava rocks to our individual tents. They had been warmed for hours by the fire and would serve us well during the night.

I place two of the warm boulders at the foot of my sleeping bag and clamored into it as soon as I could. I only removed my boots and outer parka, for it was very cold and the more layers one wears, the more comfortable he is. I scooted myself down a bit and put my feet against the hot rocks. They began to warm immediately. I was surprised. The rock thing worked. They stayed warm for most of the night and it made for a very comfortable sleeping arrangement. I felt cozy and warm and went to sleep quickly. Unfortunately, the comfort would not last.

The entire camp was so miserable by two in the morning that no one was asleep. Oh, the rocks were still warm. Even the sleeping bags were as cozy as ever. The problem was the hot chocolate!

Time and time again, each member of the troop, after waiting as long as he possibly could, had to drag himself out of his sleeping bag. Each had to don his clothing and coat and boots, and then leave the camp area to relieve himself. In the history of the world, there could not have been so many bladders filling so often so fast. Sleep was impossible!

Finally, somewhere around five in the morning, we just gave up, stayed dressed, and built up our campfire again. We tried to use it to keep us warm, but temperatures in the teens and a stiff breeze made even that impossible.

By the time we finished breakfast, everyone was mad at everyone else. Tempers were short and all were exhausted. Still, we tried to make the best of it. We split up and went exploring in the rocks and caves along the coastline of the reservoir. Normally, all those caves would be underwater, but in mid-winter the level of the lake was so low as to make the whole place unrecognizable.

Most of us had fun doing the exploring. Some of the others actually cut into the ice on the lake and fished. By late afternoon moods were better again and everyone seemed happy.

As we prepared the evening meal, someone suggested that if we had another night like before, we might all kill each other before morning. Ideas were kicked around and discussed. Then someone suggested breaking camp and going home. We had planned on doing that first thing in the morning anyway, and so there was little resistance to the idea.

We finished eating quickly and broke down our camp more quickly than I had ever seen it done. We hiked out to the place where the cars were parked and we went home.

That night, as I lay in my nice warm bed, I made a life decision. I was never again going to camp out in the winter. It just wasn't smart.

77

Our Little Acre

Dad gave us an acre of sugar beets. Actually, he didn't give us the beets. He gave us the plot where the beets would grow. He plowed and harrowed that acre along with the others in the field. He planted our acre at the same time he planted the others in that field. Several times during the season, he set up our old orange Allis Chalmers tractor with the beet cultivator. When aboard that tractor and cultivating the beet field, he also cultivated our acre.

I don't want to leave the impression that we kids did nothing for our beets, though, because we worked very hard on them, trying to make them into the best acre of beets on the farm.

Usually, Dad would irrigate our beets, too. However, though he was the expert, and projected the image of being completely capable when it came to opening culverts and tending the water, he did elicit our help. I don't think he needed it. In fact, I'm certain that he did not. But the point of our having an acre of sugar beets was subtler than just a gift of a part of the crop.

Dad was trying to teach us about responsibility. He wanted us to appreciate just exactly what must go into a farming operation in order to get something out of it. He wanted to instill in us the same type of work ethic that his father had taught him. Because of that, Dad was willing to tolerate our incompetence as we tried to make the water spread through the rows of beets in **our** acre as well as he did it with the rest of the field.

We watched as the beets began to break through the soil and grow. It wasn't long before they were large enough for thinning.

Beet thinning is a hard job. The beet planter places a continuous row of seeds and the beets begin to grow in a long line. If allowed to continue that way, the plants are too numerous and too close together. They rob each other of the precious nutrients and become little scrubby things all wound around each other and not good for much of anything, let alone sugar production. So they must be "thinned."

There are mechanical thinners that, when mounted on a tractor and properly run through a beet field, will thin beets. The mechanical thinner, though, is unable to do more than just a cursory job as its blades rotate and swipe away at a predetermined rate removing everything in its path. It leaves multiple plants and is questionable to say the least. For that reason, people must do the hard job of polishing off the job the mechanical thinner started. On our little acre, **we** had to do the thinning.

We went to the field, armed with short-handled hoes and a file to keep the blades sharp. We also carried plenty of water in Mason jars, for we had been warned that it would be a long, dry day.

Dad gave us short-handled hoes because of our inexperience. When the handle of the hoe is only twelve inches long, the person using it is forced to bend down low enough to get a good look at what he is doing. It is also easier, from that slumped position, to reach down and pull one of the double plants out with the fingers. If attempted with the hoe, it usually resulted in destroying both plants and leaving a space. Too many of that kind of space would cut into our profits.

The more we thinned, the bigger that acre became. For some reason, we thought we would be there about half a day. It took three. Three days of bending over and fine tuning our acre of sugar beets. We ached from the bending. Our hands were blistered from the handles of the hoes. In my case, I had an added problem. My tee shirt had ridden up as I bent over and I had a three-inch wide band on my back that was blistered from sunburn. I was in terrible pain.

A few weeks after the thinning job, we had to go and weed our acre of beets. Weeding was a bit easier, but not much. We **were** permitted to use long-handled hoes. That was much easier on the back, but it still required a lot of bending, for the beets were getting bigger, and the leaves had to be moved aside to find those hidden weeds that were up close to the plants, robbing them of that money-making nutrition.

We worked hard, trying to make our acre the cleanest of them all. We joked around and tried to stay in good moods as we worked. The most popular joke came in many variations, but had the same theme—a theme my mother would not have appreciated. We made comments about being "hoers," about "hoers" making more money, about living in a "hoer" house. OK, it was a cheap play on words but we were desperate. We needed every laugh we could get.

The day finally came when we no longer had to do anything with our beets. They were dug and harvested along with the rest. They were loaded into our truck and hauled to the "beet dump" in Aberdeen.

The beet dump was a beehive of activity during the harvest. It was located at the rail yard. Trucks were lined up from all over the area, waiting for their turn on the scales. Each truck, after it was weighed, would pull up onto a loading ramp, and once the cables and machinery was properly connected, tipped on its side and emptied into a huge hopper. The beets were carried up a series of elevators and dumped into train cars. After the beets were dumped, the trucks righted, and the equipment disconnected, the trucks would drive off the ramp and pull under another conveyor where the dirt and garbage that had been in the load would be returned to the truck. Then it would be driven back to the scale a weighed again, so that the "tare" could be deducted from the original weight. This is the process by which payment was determined.

Aberdeen didn't rate a train engine of its own. It was just a small town at the end of a branch line from Blackfoot, so when a train car became filled with beets and an empty car had to replace it, it was often done by hand. I was fascinated to watch one man with a specially designed lever with a very long handle, just stick it under the wheel of a train car and begin to move it by pulling down on the handle. It was amazing to me that a lever could do so much.

After dumping, Dad would return to the field, shovel the tare from the truck, and then start digging beets again. The digger was probably the most expensive piece of equipment we had. It dug the beets, chopped the tops off, and dumped them into a hopper. Then move them up an elevator and into the truck. It was quite an operation.

Eventually, the beets were harvested. Some time later, Dad received his check from the Utah-Idaho Sugar Company and we all waited as Dad figured out our individual shares. We each received about forty dollars for our acre of beets. It felt good, but it was obviously not the thousands we had spent while dreaming of what we would do with our "wealth."

Dad just said to take note about how difficult it was to make money farming. We took note.

78

Tonka

We always had a lot of cats around. I don't know if anyone ever bothered to count them. It would not have mattered anyway, for the numbers were constantly changing. They came and they went—most of them nameless.

Our cats were wild. Most farm cats are. They live off field mice and other rodents, birds, and who knows what else. They do the farm a great service by helping to keep the rodent population down. They are not really pets, but an integral part of the farm they live on. In order to keep that balance, it is a good idea not to feed the cats, for once they begin eating the easy meal, they begin to get lazy. After all, why chase down a mouse, if all one needs to do is to hang around the back door and wait for table scraps?

At our house, we fed the cats. We gave them the table scraps. Of course, with six kids, even table scraps were scarce. But we gave what we didn't use to the cats. After every meal, the cats would be hanging around the back porch to see if anything was left. Usually there was very little, and they fought for what they could get. We were quite sure that they would still do their job and go after the rodents.

One day, in the deepest, darkest corner of the old chicken coop, Mike and I found a litter that had been born to one of the older female cats. She wasn't very tame, and not happy about our intrusion into her world, but intrude we did. There were six kittens and we decided that Fate had provided a pet for each of the kids. We chose our kittens and named them.

I was the oldest, so I chose first. I picked an ugly little tortoise shell kitten to be mine. She wasn't pretty by any stretch of the imagination, but she seemed feistier and more active than the others. In fact, she bullied them, and I liked that.

I named her Tonka Wa-Kon. I had seen a Disney movie about a wild horse that was caught and tamed by an Indian boy played by Sal Mineo. He had named that great stallion Tonka Wa-Kon, which meant "brave one" or something like that. Eventually, that great horse was part of history when it became part of the U.S. Cavalry and was the sole survivor of Custer's Last Stand, the massacre at the Little Big Horn. I liked the movie and I liked the name, so my kitten became Tonka!

I spent a lot of time holding Tonka, letting her become comfortable with me. She accepted me, but still she had that wild streak that would not go away. She grew quickly, and was larger than the other cats. In fact, she showed little tolerance for them at all. Whenever they came near her, she cuffed them and they would scamper off.

My younger brothers and my sister didn't really pay attention to their kittens. In fact, they weren't even interested. It made no difference, though, for the kittens grew up to be normal farm cats, just like all the others—except for Tonka.

Tonka was a very big adult cat. She looked like a cougar as she stalked and killed her prey. Unlike the other cats, Tonka did not turn away from a challenge. On several occasions I saw her make off with kills that might have been surprising were it not Tonka. She even went after pheasants and rabbits. I often wondered how such a wildcat wound up in a litter with a bunch of normal kittens.

Tonka remained wild. Once in a while, she would allow me near her. She would even allow me to pet her, though the expression on her face was one of tolerance, nothing more. None of the other kids could get close to her. Even the dog kept his distance.

She was with our family for many years. She grew tamer as she began to have litters of her own and she let her kittens hang around the back porch with the others. Even then, she seemed to sit back from the group, unwilling to accept any handouts, for it seemed as though she knew she was the ultimate cat, a huntress, and a symbol of pride and prowess for all of "catdom" to admire.

79

Sax, Lies, and Audio Tape

One of the greatest things about being in the seventh grade was that I was allowed to take band. Most kids were not interested in band, but I was. For one thing, twice a week it meant going to the high school and having a band class with the music teacher there. Also, common sense told me that if I were at the high school taking band, I would **not** be in junior high, doing something boring.

One of the first things I needed to do was to choose an instrument. Mom tried valiantly to guide me to something like a flute or a clarinet. I am certain that she wanted to keep the investment as small as possible, so that when I grew bored and tired of band (somewhere around the first week), that it would not be such a terrible financial loss when I quit practicing and gave it up.

I did **not** want to play the flute, the clarinet, the piccolo, or any other of those instruments that were dominated by the female of our species. Such instruments were for girls. I knew it, and I knew that all my friends knew it. I would not play a girl's instrument!

My mother took me to Pocatello to Fawson Music, the only place in the area where band instruments could be purchased. I think she believed that, if I saw the new clarinets and the shiny flutes, perhaps I would change my mind. What she didn't count on were the shiny trumpets and cornets and saxophones. She didn't count on the drums either.

I had about a hundred dollars of my own and knew that my Mom would have to make up the difference on whatever I chose. We spent a long time looking at different instruments and finally, after choosing the trumpet, then changing to drums, then being talked out of that, I chose the alto saxophone. It seemed respectable enough, not strictly a girl's instrument, and yet girls could play them, too. The car dealer tactics of Lee Fawson supported me as well. He owned the store and hovered over my mother like a vulture.

So I began to learn to play the saxophone. The squawks and squeaks started to become, if not musical, at least tolerable. I was in the band to stay. I practiced and did not quit.

I was disappointed when the band started practicing in the gym at the junior high building and we no longer went to the high school, but by then I was into it and I accepted the change easily.

That day at Fawson Music when I bought my saxophone, I saw something that I just couldn't seem to get out of my mind. It was something new—a tape recorder. Oh, I had heard of them, and even saw a Wollensak portable at school once when the high school choir was putting on a Christmas show for our junior high. I had not known, though, that they were so accessible to the general public. I wanted one in the worst way. And that's how I finally wound up getting it—in the worst way.

When I first mentioned to my family that I wanted a tape recorder, they mostly just laughed. What a ridiculous idea! What did I need one for? It's far too expensive. Why would I even consider such a thing? Every possible reason for being non-supportive was jumping out of everyone's mouth. I just dropped the subject.

By the time I brought up the topic of my buying a tape recorder again, I had thought it out and devised a more viable plan. First, I had put away a few dollars. I would be making more, and my parents were always more receptive when they knew I was committing my own money to whatever idea I had. I had already bought my own stereo. It was a Magnavox portable record player and had a remote speaker. It did justice to my steadily increasing record collection.

To get permission to buy the tape recorder, I had to make several promises and tell a lie or two. I promised to buy it myself. I promised not to buy so many records, using the argument that once I could tape songs from the radio, my uncontrollable spending on records would be curbed. My parents worried about my spending so much on rock and roll, and they listened to that argument.

I promised not to be selfish with a tape recorder and to let other family members use it. Then came the biggest lie of all. I told my mom that our bandleader had recommended we use a tape recorder for playing back our practice sessions and hearing ourselves play. It was an out-and-out lie. He had never mentioned such a thing, but I thought it sounded good, so I used it to convince my mom that I absolutely **needed** a tape recorder.

One day, I finally had the money and convinced Mom to take me to Pocatello to shop for a tape recorder. Although I am certain that she was never fooled by my weak attempts to fool her, she took me to Pocatello and we shopped.

We looked in many places and at many different models before I finally bought one. I also bought some five inch reel tapes to use on it. The first thing I did when I got home was to get all my family to talk into the microphone so they could hear what they sounded like. Then I went to work on a more pressing project—recording the latest hits off my mother's radio. It required that I be left alone. Otherwise, my noisy brothers' voices came across on the tape.

I made a great many tapes with that recorder, but one thing I never did. Not once did I ever record myself playing the saxophone.

80

Cooney

South of our house, across the pasture, three fences, and just a short walk through heavy sagebrush, was a most exciting and wonderful thing. It was a waterfall! It was cold and wet and beautiful, and it was ours! No other kid in all of Aberdeen had his own waterfall.

Of course, by most standards it was nothing. Even I had seen better waterfalls, some in Yellowstone Park and some in less famous parts of the Rocky Mountains. Even Shoshone Falls, on the Snake River, was a favorite picnic spot. It was always advertised as being higher than Niagara and was only two hours drive down-river from American Falls, another impressive cataract. But our waterfall, insignificant as it was, was all ours.

For as long as I can remember, our waterfall had been called Cooney. Not Cooney Falls. Just Cooney. I never did know where the name came from, but I used it as often as I could, for we loved to go there and play.

Cooney was just part of a huge irrigation ditch that branched off from the large canal near the airport to the west of us. It supplied water for all the farmers in that one square mile where our farm was located. The ditch twisted and turned its way through the sagebrush and lava rock and monkey nut trees to points far beyond where we were allowed to go. However, the waterfall—Cooney—was on our property, and we made the most of it.

Usually, we would spend most of our time in the water below the falls, using a footbridge as a place to slide in and climb out of the murky water. Sometimes we would just lie on the wooden bridge and take in the sun. When the heat became too uncomfortable, one only had to roll off into the water to cool off. And cool it did, for the water was cold and fast moving. It felt terrific on those hot summer days.

Sometimes we would spend hours in the water, just playing with the water skippers that, for some reason, could walk on water and not sink. We would laugh and play "King Of The Hill" off the bank, or just walk up and down the course of the ditch in the waist deep water, feeling the soft mud between our toes and enjoying life to its fullest.

Sometimes we would play "cowboys and Indians", filling the air with imaginary bullets and arrows as we scrambled for safe haven behind the sagebrush. We used the numerous sheep trails to get around in that wild area as we pretended to ride our fabulous imaginary horses into battle. As always, my trusted Thunderhoof was but a tongue click away whenever I needed to move fast and low through the countryside.

Ultimately, though, the greatest thrill was in proving we were brave and daring souls by climbing that waterfall. It was a challenge that, once thrown down, could not be ignored. If someone refused to accept the challenge to climb the falls, his manhood was in question. His ability to hold his head high would be seriously impaired, and he would be ridiculed and persecuted for his cowardice for hours.

Climbing the falls was not an easy task. It was perilous for many reasons, not the least of which was the slimy green moss that adorned the lava rock that jutted out from the precipice at odd angles. It was those rocks that provided both the handholds and footholds that permitted the most daring of us to actually climb the falls.

Another obstacle to climbing the falls was the sheer weight of the water as it hurtled over the top and crashed on the rocks below, causing a spray that stung the skin and made the slime-covered rocks even more perilous than they would have been. Oh, it was gloriously dangerous!

I took pride in my ability to traverse the rocks time and again without serious injury. I had learned the secret places under the water that one needed to know to be successful. I knew where and how I had to cross from one side to the other to avoid the big bruises and bleeding scrapes that seemed all to regular an occurrence with my brothers and uncles.

Many an afternoon was spent at Cooney, watching each other's bare bottoms glisten as we took turns climbing the falls. We were comfortable and happy in that secluded little spot and for years it served as our "secret place", where we could go and not be bothered with adult intrusion of any kind.

81

Ashes to Ashes

I loved life on the farm. I am just as certain that I did not know how much it meant to me during the time I was living it. There was always so much to do, so many things to keep track of and to worry about, and I watched as my father worked from before dawn until long after dark. Even so, we were a happy family, and we never wanted for the important things of life.

To be honest, my father expected much less from his sons than many of the others in town expected from theirs. Dad seemed to prefer to do most of the work himself. I often wondered why that was, and to this day, I'm still not sure. Perhaps he felt that if a job was to be done correctly, that he must do it himself. Perhaps he wanted to give us better opportunities for our own lives and thought that by leaving us alone, we would develop other interests. Perhaps he just liked the farm work so well that he kept the majority of it to himself. I don't know.

I do know, however, that my life on the farm was unique. It was a wonderful experience, fraught with a myriad of personal experiences. I watched as my father turned dirt into beautiful fields of well-tended crops. I watched as the grain was harvested and divided, some into seed, some into feed, and some for sale to the mill to be used by the people at large for their bread, their tortillas, their cakes and their cookies. As Grandpa Frank said, "even good whiskey requires good grain."

I watched as sugar beets were harvested and sent to the trains to be transported to factories that would provide the sweetener for nearly every kind of food my mind could imagine.

I watched as the sweet smelling alfalfa was cut, dried, baled and stacked to provide food for the farm animals.

I watched as sheep were shorn and the wool sent off to be turned into clothing and blankets. I watched the lambs go off to market to provide chops for the masses or "rack of lamb" for those fancy restaurants. I watched the milking of the cows, and the marketing of the milk to the Kraft factory in Aberdeen, where it could be turned into ice cream or butter or caramel candy. I watched other cattle go to market to be turned into hamburger and T-bones, and rib-eyes and Porterhouse's and Prime Rib.

All in all, I loved the crops and the harvesting. Most of all, I loved the animals, from the Holsteins that had to be milked twice a day, to the sheep that were "dumber than dirt." I loved the calves and the lambs. I even loved the dogs and cats that chose to share our farm.

Animals on a farm are plentiful and, contrary to what some believe many of them do not live idyllic lives. Of course, we were not barbarians. We tried to make them as happy and comfortable as possible. However, at times nature just took over and the poor beasts were left to the mercy of fate. This was especially true of sheep.

Each year we lost several of our ewes, especially during the lambing season. Sometimes we even lost some lambs. It was sad, but a fact of farm life that we had learned to live with, and we dealt with it as best we could.

If a ewe died in the lambing sheds, it took a lot of strength and energy to remove it. Usually, if Dad had time, he would tie a length of twine around the feet of the corpse and drag it out of the sheds. More often than not, Mike and I were given the task. Neither of us enjoyed touching dead animals. We would use a stick to raise the leg of the animal enough to loop some baling twine around it. We always used a longer piece than Dad did, because we needed enough rope to make ourselves a sort of harness so that we could tug and pull the heavy load through sheds, corrals, and gates until we reached the edge of the lane.

That lane was an extension of our driveway that circled one end of the barn, crossed in front of the old boxcar that served as a granary, and the area where Dad parked the two tractors, the hay baler, the beet cultivator, and other equipment that he used to farm. Farther on, that lane passed several pieces of old farm machinery that was no longer used, such as hay rakes and forks and plows, etc.

At the end of that road, it made a tight circle and joined itself so vehicles could easily turn around and head back toward the house. In the center of that turn-around was a rocky area that held so much buried lava rock there was no way the land could be used for planting. That was the area where we disposed of the dead animals.

Mike and I were given the job of moving those dead beasts all the way out to the rock pile and dumping them. We would enjoy that task, for even though we had to deal with the dead, it afforded both of us an opportunity to drive. We would take turns, but I was the oldest, so I got to be first. Sometimes we would use one of the tractors, always the orange Allis Chalmers, because Dad didn't like us to drive his International Farmall. Usually, though, we would use Dad's pickup.

We tied the corpse to the rear bumper and dragged it all the way to the rock pile. Once there, as I made the turn, I tried my best to pull the animal directly over the center. Sometimes there were other animals already there, in various stages of decay. We always tried to burn the animal cadavers as soon as possible, but they did not always burn completely. At such times the maggots and the gore, along with an indescribable odor, was nearly enough to cause one to lose one's last meal in a most undignified manner.

We always had to go to Dad and get the key for the bulk gas tank that was used to gas up the farm machinery. We would unlock the padlock and carefully pour some gasoline into an old five-gallon oil can that we kept near the old boxcar granary's front door. Then we would return to the rock pile and saturate the dead animals with gasoline. Then very carefully, we would light a match and throw it onto the wooly mass. The fire would flare up suddenly and engulf the whole area. Each time we did it, we hoped that it would last long enough to destroy the whole thing, for we did not want to face maggots and gore on our next trip to the rock pile.

Strangely enough, I found the process of burning the animals to be very interesting. Not only could I learn about the internal anatomy of the beasts, I was completely fascinated by the way that maggots and rot occurred. I certainly did not think it pleasant, but it was the processes that intrigued me. Oh, there was one pleasant aspect. That happened when the animals were burning. Once the wool was gone and nothing was left but the burning flesh, the air was filled with the smell of cooking meat, not unlike a barbecue. It made me hungry when I smelled it, yet like my father, I never ate mutton.

82

Indian Springs

One of the great pastimes of my youth were those times when the family would pack up and go to "the nat." School outings took place at "the nat." Church socials were held at "the nat." But best of all were the family picnics.

"The nat" was a natatorium. It was built up around a natural hot spring that sprung right there in the midst of the grain fields that covered the rolling foothills of the mountains southeast of Pocatello. It was less than a mile to the freeway that had recently been built to connect Twin Falls and Pocatello. It was only another mile or so to American Falls, the county seat of Power County. Yet, even with such close proximity, it almost seemed to hide in a small vale of trees that were completely hidden from the main road and only barely visible from the narrow paved road that connected Rockland with American Falls.

It was called Indian Springs, and the greatest of its attractions was that large swimming pool and it's surrounding dressing rooms. There was but one entrance to the pool, through a small gift shop where pool users could pay their fees, receive a key to a dressing room, check their valuables, and even rent swimming suits to use.

Inside the pool area, and to the left, there were restrooms containing large shower areas. Near the entrance to the restroom was a springboard mounted out over the pool, about four feet off the water. Directly across from it was a solid diving platform, with different levels and steps going up the back. All around the perimeter of the pool were individual changing rooms. They had very colorful doors, painted different colors to help assist the swimmers in returning to the correct rooms when changing back into their street clothes. As if the numbers weren't enough!

I was always a bit self-conscious when using the dressing rooms, for the bottoms of the doors to those little cubicles were several inches above the concrete and it was easy to see people's feet as they removed their street clothing and donned their swimwear. I was very aware that people might see my underwear under the door as I removed it. It was very disconcerting.

The pool was large, with depth numbers painted on the sides from the shallow end to the deep, where the water was eight feet deep. A rope stretched from one side to the other usually separated the two ends. I spent the majority of my time in the shallow end for I was not a good swimmer. Years before, I had taken lessons at that very pool, coming on a school bus early in the morning and participating as best I could, but I scarcely learned to dog paddle well enough to save my life, let alone actually learning to swim. I was more concerned then about whether or not I had a dime so I could buy some salty shoestring potatoes to eat on the bus as we went back to Aberdeen.

Outside of the pool area, across the parking lot, was a nice shaded picnic area, with grated grills for cooking burgers and hot dogs. There were long picnic tables that could be moved so as to accommodate large groups if necessary. To the west were several pools that contained colorful fish and frogs. They were inundated with lily pads and a constant source of entertainment to all of us kids as we tried to capture fish or frogs.

I remember one specific incident when we had a large family gathering at the "nat." I had already finished my swim and was getting ready to go out to the picnic area for lunch. As I walked along the edge of the pool toward the entrance, I saw my Aunt Mildred trying to get her own kids out of the pool for lunch. For just an instant, I watched her face, as she became aware that her daughter, Berta, who could not swim, was below the surface of the water nearby. Berta was struggling weakly. Aunt Mildred was nearly hysterical. I jumped into the pool, clothes and all, and lifted Berta up to her father, who had responded to his wife's distress.

Berta was frightened, but she was all right. Her parents took turns holding her as I pulled myself out of the pool. It had been a shallow area, and I am sure someone would have pulled her out in time, but I had done it. Later, as I munched on a hot dog, Uncle Rob stood at my side and thanked me for "acting quickly and saving Berta." Now, years later, the incident has been forgotten by almost everyone. However, I remember it for two reasons. First of all, I enjoyed the feeling of being a hero, even for a moment, of my family, especially Uncle Rob. Secondly, I still remember what it felt like to spend the rest of that day squishing around in my wet shoes and socks.

83

Someone Else's Chores

Calvin Stevens was one of my best friends. Actually, he preferred to be called Cal as we got older. I guess Calvin was just too childish for him. Yet, I remember one time when childish was exactly what he was, and it cost me dearly.

Calvin and I often spent time together in the football field after school. All the buses were lined up at the edge of the field and those of us who were still in junior high school had to wait nearly twenty minutes before boarding the buses. The delay was caused by the longer hours of the high school. I guess the school officials thought it better that no one board the bus until it was actually time to go.

One day, during that waiting time, several of us were wrestling around on the football field, playing "keep-away" with various objects that fate provided. One of those objects just happened to be Calvin's blue baseball cap. Now I was not the one who took it, but when it mysteriously appeared in my hand at the same time that Calvin appeared in my face, I knew instantly that I was not the one to return it to him.

I scrambled as he reached for his cap, and he kept coming. In a matter of moments we were rolling on the ground and I was trying to use my body as best I could to shield him from the coveted cap. It worked, too, but in the scuffle, Calvin's glasses were knocked to the ground and we both rolled onto them. The crunch was deafening and brought the entire game to a quick end.

A very near-sighted Calvin groped around on the grass until he retrieved his mangled spectacles. He squinted at me in disgust as I handed him the blue baseball cap. He huffed and puffed as though he were the Big Bad Wolf himself, and then off he stomped, haughtily stretching himself to the full extent of his five foot two inch height.

Soon the buses were opened for boarding and we streamed onto ours, quickly taking our seats and anxious to get home. Calvin avoided me. I could tell he was upset. I thought about it as we dropped him off. His was the first stop on the highway south of town. I rode for another mile to the Airport Road, then west a mile before I got off with my sister and brothers and the Claytons. Then all of us meandered the last quarter mile to our homes on foot as the bus continued southward.

By the time I had said good-bye to Chick and Wallace Clayton and walked the rest of the way to my house, my mother had already received a phone call from Calvin's father. Apparently it had been a very angry call and in turn it made my mother angry at me.

Calvin's father had told my mother that I broke Calvin's glasses and that he was holding me responsible for their replacement. He further demanded that I come over to his house and do Calvin's chores, since Calvin could not see well enough to do them himself. My mother had agreed.

Mom told me in no uncertain terms that I was to change out of my school clothes and take my bike over to the Stevens home, do Calvin's chores, apologize to Calvin and his family, and then return home to face whatever my father decided to dish out as punishment. I was not thrilled at the prospect and I felt that further explanation would exonerate me. However, it was evident that my mother was not in a mood to discuss the incident, so I changed and left for Calvin's house on my bike.

As I rode the two miles to Calvin's house on my bike, I became more and more angry that he had made me out to be the culprit. He had been as guilty of wrestling as I was. My mood was not improved when I arrived at the Stevens home and saw Calvin, with his terrible near-sighted eyes, watching cartoons on television as his father made preparation for taking me out to do Calvin's chores. My parents had taught me to respect my elders, and so I refrained from telling Mr. Stevens what I thought of his plan. Instead, I listened as he directed me on what and how to do the chores that should have been done by his son. Even though I was unusually irritated by his Canadian accent and arrogant manner, I held my tongue and went about completing all the work he gave me to do.

I finished at dusk. Mr. Stevens was out in the barn milking his cows, so I knocked on the back door of the house and told Mrs. Stevens that I was finished and about to leave for home. She invited me in. When I came into the light of her kitchen, she asked me to sit at her table for milk and a cookie. I took the opportunity to tell her my side of the story about what had happened when the glasses were broken. Mrs. Stevens called Calvin, asked him if what I said was accurate, and he confirmed it. His mother gave him a nasty look and told me to head on home. She gave me two cookies to eat on the way and I retrieved my bike and took off, anxious to get off the main highway before it became too dark to be safe.

I was angry at Calvin for several days after that night, but his parents talked to mine and explained that they would pay for the new glasses because Calvin was as much at fault as I. My father didn't even bring up the subject. It was forgotten soon after, but I will always remember that night that I had to do the someone else's chores, without compensation or even an apology.

84

All I Want For Christmas

The anticipation of those annual visits from Santa Claus was almost more than I could bear. It seemed like an eternity between those fabulous Thanksgiving dinners at Grandma's house and the ultimate night of nights—Christmas Eve!

As the month of November came to an end and we crept into December, the local stores began to decorate for the big day. The Valley Store took on a festive appearance with new lettering that looked like frost had been sprayed. It provided a wintry accent to the dollar signs and bargains that the lettering touted. Christmas decorations seemed to pop up overnight on everything from the hardware store to the American Legion Hall. I suppose that, for a small, town, Aberdeen did as well as most in bringing the Christmas spirit to the season.

In my earlier years I was obsessed with seeing Santa Claus and conveying to him my every wish and dream for that perfect Christmas. I was not at all concerned that he seemed to be in several places at once, nor that he closely resembled one of our neighbors. All that was explained away by my grandmother, who said that it was such a busy time of the year that the real Santa needed help from others, who dressed up like him. She assured me that any messages given to the substitute Santas would reach the real Santa, but I had my doubts. Something about them just didn't seem to inspire confidence in either their memories or their ability to pass on those important messages that they were given.

One of these Santas was always at my church, and he always passed out small paper bags that contained a variety of hard candy, peppermint sticks, peanuts that were still in the shells, and a popcorn ball. I looked forward to that bag of candy each year for it was quite a treat.

I had many good Christmases, and though my messages to Santa didn't always get to him, he seemed to know me well enough to substitute some very fine things. I remember one very special Christmas when I wished for and received a long gray plastic truck. It had a speaker on the trailer that swiveled, but best of all, there was a long cord attached to a microphone so that I was able to make announcements from the speaker on my truck. It was a marvelous toy!

Christmas in Aberdeen was very special. The schools decorated thoroughly, with everything from a big tree in the main hallway to the hundreds of pieces of creativity that adorned the walls and windows. They were made with crayons, construction paper, white paste, scissors, and whatever else might have inspired the creator.

At home there was always a big, lighted Christmas tree in front of our biggest window. That evergreen smell permeated the house and did as much to add to the holiday spirit as anything. There were candy trays put out with fudge and divinity and popcorn balls, and even some peanuts and oranges. My mother made her "pepper nut" cookies and I snacked on them until I could not eat another.

Sometimes carolers would come by the house and sing, and our cookie and candy trays were passed around them in thanks for their performances. They were usually cold and their breaths could be seen as they sang. Sometimes they were even snow-covered, but one thing I noticed was that they were always smiling.

I remember another Christmas very well, not for what I received, but for something that was given to my sister, Rebecca. I was a little older then, and very conscious of the sidelong glances and secret message that passed between my parents in the few days prior to Santa's arrival. I tried my best to hear and learn all I could, knowing that such secrets were of great importance to us, but I couldn't quite figure out what was going on. All I knew was that my father was spending a good deal of time away from home and that my mother seemed very interested in how well he was doing whatever it was that he was doing. She seemed a bit nervous during those last hours before Christmas, as if my Dad's job would not be done.

For a long time, Dad had been coming home late and Mom was not saying anything about it. I knew he had many things to do and lots of animals to watch and care for, but it was unusual for Dad to be late for supper. He almost always made it for supper, but that year, in those days before Christmas, he was late nearly every night.

I was curious, but I didn't dwell on it. I became caught up in the excitement of Christmas. I tried hard to be good and not let any of Santa's elves catch me treating my brother badly or not doing what I should. I wrote letters to Santa, hoping to convince him to bring my favorite dream on Christmas morning. Sometimes it worked and sometimes it didn't, but I always tried. And by then, I knew exactly where to leave his letters!

That Christmas morning was a good one. I cannot remember, though, what Santa left for me because the only thing that sticks in my mind about that year was the beautiful blue and white girls' bicycle that adorned our living room. It was for my sister, Becky. It had plastic streamers at the ends of the new white handle grips. There was a bow on the handlebars. It had big fat new tires and a new seat. It was not, however, a new bike. It had been lovingly restored from a piece of junk. My father had used his welder, his grinding wheel, and his other tools, as well as his skill and perseverance, to turn an old rusty wreck into a gorgeous piece of transportation for his only daughter.

Nothing was said about its being "used." My sister loved and used the bike for a long time.

That was the year that I learned what Christmas really meant.

85

Step By Step

There are events in our lives that we can identify as having forever changed the course of our existence—events that have a profound effect on who we are, the way we think, and the goals we set for ourselves. Such was the case when my beloved Connie Conklin left Aberdeen.

For years I had worshipped her. I dreamt of her. I planned our lives together over and over again, constantly changing each detail to make the intertwining of our lives more and more glorious!

Of course, Connie was aware that I loved her. How could she not be aware, seeing as how I became such a blithering imbecile whenever she was near me. Still, she tolerated me and often even welcomed my attentions. On those occasions we would walk and talk and laugh and we delighted in each other's company. I was as love stricken as any burgeoning young pre-teen could be.

Although my devotion to Connie had been steadfast and true from the time she entered first grade until she reached junior high, her attachment to me was erratic. There were times when I was, without a doubt, her one and only boyfriend. Other times, I was but a good friend and confidante. Then there were the dark times when she seemed to hate me. I never understood those changing moods.

I, too, was moody. I was especially moody on the day that I heard my father telling my mother that the Conklins would be moving away. I was crushed! I left the house and went out to find a place to feel sorry for myself. I was soon huddled in a corner of the granary and wondering why such a terrible thing had to happen. Later, as our families said good-bye to each other, I was tongue-tied. I did not know what to say or how to say it. All I could do was look at Connie and feel a sense of loss unlike anything I had felt before.

The Conklins moved to Orem, Utah. It was another state and a great distance, but I knew that my grandparents lived in Provo, just south of there, so I felt hope. I hoped that I would get to see her again.

It was many months before the chance came to see Connie again. It happened on our annual trek to visit Dad's parents. The trip went much as they always did. We visited grandparents, aunts and uncles and cousins that we had only seen a handful of times in my young life. We had a good time and for the most part, Connie and her family didn't even enter our minds. However, as soon as we began to pack up for the trip home, I remembered almost with a panic, and mentioned it to my parents.

It was then that I found out my parents had intended to visit the Conklins all along. They had timed our departure so that we could spend a few hours visiting them and still have time to get home the same night. It took only a little while to find their new address once we arrived in Orem, and for once, I chose to sit with Connie rather than to play with her older brothers while just wishing I had stayed with Connie.

We talked of Aberdeen as I tried to update her on all her old friends. I told her stories about what they had been doing, intertwined with what I had been doing. She seemed interested and I rambled on, painfully aware that she had the most beautiful eyes I had ever seen.

After awhile we decided to go for a walk and we sauntered slowly down the street as we talked, oblivious to traffic or other pedestrians or anything but each other. For the first time we talked of our feelings for each other.

We held hands, each of us reaching for the other. There was some hesitation, but the awful awkwardness I had always felt around her was no longer a problem. For the longest time we just walked, saying nothing, until we reached a street corner where Connie suggested we start back toward her house. We turned and started back. We walked slower, feeling each other's warmth through our fingers.

About halfway back to her house, we stopped together, as one. Nothing had been said for several minutes, but we both knew that we would kiss.

It was a wonderful moment, filled with emotion, as we held each other and shared that one, lingering kiss. It was not like the grade school pecks on the cheek at all. It was different somehow, and she responded warmly, putting her arms around me and leaning into me. It lasted an eternity and yet, it was over all too soon.

We heard the honking of the car horn. Dad was ready to leave for home. We separated and walked hurriedly back to her front yard. My family was already loaded up and my Dad was talking to her father through the car window while Mom was talking to her mother on the other side of the car. I jumped quickly into the back seat and rolled down the window to say good-bye to Connie. I wanted to reach for her again, but didn't. I was aware that my brothers, sister, and even my parents would not miss such an act, so I held it in check and just whispered a weak good-bye. Connie turned and went to her front porch. She turned and waved, then disappeared inside the house.

The pain that welled up within me was unlike anything I had ever experienced. My emotions were going every which way, as if they had been blown asunder by dynamite. I was ecstatic. I was sad. I was thrilled. I was crushed. We had shared a very adult moment, and I longed to make it happen again. The opportunity, though, had passed.

Soon we were on our way home. Dad chose to use a little known short cut through Snowville, Utah and the back roads through the rolling hills that was to come out near American Falls. It was faster, but not as comfortable a ride.

I was glad when the sun went down, for soon it meant that no one would be able to see me in the darkness. I would be able to let the tears come without having to explain them. Until that blanket of darkness came, I stared out the back window at the mountains that receded behind us. I knew that Connie was living near the base of the biggest of those mountains and somehow I still felt linked to her through them. Finally the gathering darkness was too much and I could no longer see them. I turned and faced forward again, letting the tears come, silently suffering my loss.

My mother had, as she always did, turned the car radio to a lively station to help keep my father awake as he drove through the darkness. Our shortcut was one of isolation, without other cars to help keep one awake, and I welcomed the music. I listened to the words to the songs and they seemed to be written for me. They seemed to say what I felt. One of them came on several times during the remainder of that trip:

> *"Step by ste-ep…I fell in love with you…*
> *Step by ste-ep…it wasn't hard to do…*
> *First step—a sweet hello…second step—my heart's aglow…*
> *Third step—we're on the phone…Fourth step—we're all alone*
> *Fifth step—we're on a date…Sixth step—stayed out late…*
> *Seventh step—we took a chance…one kiss and true romance…"*

The song made me both happy and sad. I knew now what true romance meant. I knew what the song meant. But I had been cheated out of some of those steps by circumstance and distance.

Gradually, Connie became a pleasant memory. She would return to Idaho when her family moved again to Pocatello. My family would again visit hers. I would still marvel at how beautiful she was, but I was never to feel the same way about her as I did on that crowded, but lonely drive back to Aberdeen so many years ago.

86

Alcho Chumley

I suspect that there is one in every town—one of those special people that actually become part of the town. Aberdeen certainly had one. His name was Alcho Chumley. We all pronounced it as "Elko," like the city in Nevada, but I never knew whether that was correct or not. Either way, he answered to it.

Alcho could be seen often on the short Main Street of Aberdeen. He could be found there during any season or any weather. I often wondered if he even had a home. He just seemed to be a permanent fixture in the basic make-up of the community.

Alcho was the scruffiest looking man I had ever seen. He had a wild growth of beard that looked as though it was a patch of weeds rather than whiskers. It was mottled and rough looking and covered his face and neck, giving him a totally unkempt appearance. He added to that by wearing clothing that looked as though it was gleaned from someone's trash. In retrospect, I realize that might, in fact, be exactly where he got them. He wore Levi jeans, too large for him. They had large cuffs folded at the ends of the legs. Those cuffs were the only indicators of how nice the material had been, for the rest of the jeans were threadbare and full of holes. He wore plaid flannel shirts in an equally sad state and usually more than one.

The most memorable thing about Alcho's appearance were his shoes. They always had twine wrapped around them to hold the soles on, even in winter. Most of the time, that didn't seem to bother him, but I am sure that the winter brought more misery than we could detect.

Most of us had been told early on that Alcho was mentally retarded. There was also a story going around among the school kids about how he had been hit in the head with a baseball bat by an older brother more than forty years earlier. We never doubted the truth of that story.

Sometimes in the course of our play, the kids would call one another Alcho or Chumley whenever someone wanted to convey that they were witnessing some sort of mental incapacity. It may have seemed cruel, but I don't think cruelty was intended at all. The words were used more as adjectives than as barbs or name-calling. In fact, Alcho was treated with a certain degree of respect throughout the community. That respect probably resulted from the treatment he received from the townspeople.

One only had to watch Alcho for a while to see that the townspeople took care of him. He was taken under several wings a day as far as I could see. It was not unusual for a local farmer to invite him into Mary's Cafe or the Spud Bowl and buy him a meal. He had more offers for cups of coffee than he could possibly accept, and yet he accepted. Sometimes people would just automatically buy an extra cup to go as they left an establishment and hand it to Alcho before they drove away. He always seemed to appreciate the gesture and never failed to thank the benefactor.

Alcho Chumley had no steady job, but he was in constant demand for odd jobs around town. Even my father hired him once or twice and that was really something, since my father preferred to do his work himself. Alcho was always doing some kind of odd job, and he was always given a fair wage for his work, sometimes even more than fair. He was a hard worker, but needed to do work that didn't take too much thought. He could work for hours without even taking a break.

If he wasn't working, he was usually easy to locate. One only had to look for the dark wool stocking cap that he wore, regardless of the season. If you couldn't find Alcho in a matter of minutes, you could rest assured that he was doing some odd job for someone somewhere.

I think that Alcho might also have been an alcoholic, though I didn't witness anything personally other than a good relationship with the regulars at the Rainbow Bar across from the Aberdeen Hardware.

Occasionally Alcho showed up with a new shirt or trousers or even shoes. It didn't happen often, but it did happen. On such occasions, everyone knew that someone had made a move to help him replace his worn out things. As always, the town took care of him.

Alcho Chumley was still walking the street in front of the People's Store the day I left Aberdeen for a navy career. It was natural that he should be there, for he had always been there as I grew up in Aberdeen.

I never saw him again, but years later when I returned to Aberdeen to bury my father, I was reminded of him.

I was standing with my brothers. Full military honors had been rendered for my father by the American Legion. Afterward, both my mind and body wandered, and I found myself staring at a large headstone a few feet away. The name on it was Alcho Chumley! I felt sadness at seeing that he had passed away, but even then I realized that someone had taken the trouble to mark the spot with a fine marker. It occurred to me that, even in death, Mr. Chumley had friends, an entire community that recognized him as a person that belonged—a true citizen of Aberdeen!

87

A National Pastime

Aberdeen was an avid supporter of Little League. I suppose it could be said that it provided respite for the entire community from the hard farm work that went on day after day. It was a distraction, and it was fun—even for someone like me. You see—I was a terrible baseball player.

I was assigned to a team called the Cowboys. The owner of the People's Store, the father of a good friend, coached it. Our coach was a great guy and made sure that we all got to play. Even me! I was grateful for that, because as I loyal as I was to the concept of winning, it was very difficult to remain happy and contented from the bench as I watched everyone else having fun. Therefore, on those short occasions when I was put into the game, I tried to concentrate more on the kindness and encouragement of my coach and less on the disgusted looks on the faces of my teammates.

There were three other teams in Aberdeen, the Pirates, Indians, and Russetts. There was also a team from Springfield, the Jets, and a team from Grandview, the Comets. They were two very small communities north of Aberdeen. In fact, except for a store and a post office, there was little in either town, but the nearby farms. Springfield had an elementary school, but except for that, all the kids attended Aberdeen Schools.

Most of our games were played in Aberdeen, but occasionally we would travel to Springfield to play the Comets or the Jets. The Comets were from Grandview, but they had no baseball field there. That is why they used the Springfield ballpark.

We had some terrific athletes on our team. Scott Thornhill was our pitcher during my first year. He was a great pitcher and an even better hitter. I admired him for his ability, but seldom talked with him. He was older and definitely a better player and so I kept to myself. I noticed, however, in those rare moments when I played in my right field spot, that I was more concerned about doing things right for Scott than for anyone else because I did not want him to be mad at me.

Later, after Scott became to old for the league, our first baseman, Darrell Satterfield, became our pitcher. I moved from right field to first base, perhaps so I wouldn't be required to throw the ball very much. I am not sure. Actually, I had learned how to catch the ball and I did quite well at first base. Satterfield was a great pitcher and one of several good hitters we had.

I enjoyed Little League as much as anyone, but there were only two very memorable moments in my short-lived baseball career. The first moment happened during a game where I was playing first base and Satterfield was pitching. We were up to bat in the last part of the last inning. My friend, Ross, had walked when he came to bat and somehow had managed to get to second base, so we had a runner. We had two outs and we were behind by one run. As I came to the plate for the fourth time in that game, it was easy to hear the groans from onlookers. I had struck out three times and there was no reason not to do it again. I understood the groans and I was aware of my own limitations. It was not a happy bunch that watched me approach the plate.

Just as I was about to leave the on-deck circle, Satterfield ran out from the bench and put his arm on my shoulder. He looked me in the eye, spit on the ground just like a pro, and told me to get hold of one and put it out of the park. He must have seen my incredulous look or sensed my fear because he continued with "just pretend your out in that cow pasture of yours and keep your eye on the ball."

I kept that in mind as I stood there at the plate and watched the first pitch come whistling by. It was a strike and I hadn't even swung. I decided that I would do just as Satterfield had suggested. When the second pitch came, I swung that bat as hard as I could. My hands stung as I realized that I had hit the ball. Then I saw it, sailing high in the air toward left center field and going very deep. As the outfielders ran for the ball, I woke up and ran for first base. When I got there, our coach was behind the base and waving me on. I ran. I ran as fast as I could run, around second and on to third base. Satterfield was there and he waved me toward home plate. As I headed for home plate I could see the catcher getting ready to catch the ball. I decided that I would not likely get such a hit again and I was going to make that one count.

I slid safely into home a full two seconds ahead of the ball and the game was over. I had done it. I had actually hit a home run. I had won the game. I was lifted up and got so many slaps on the back that it was hard to breathe. It felt wonderful to get all that attention. I was on top of the world for the rest of that day. It was great. At our very next game I struck out three times and flied to short. Oh, well, miracles seldom last.

The other memory was not as pleasant. We were playing the Pirates and we were without our pitcher. Satterfield was sick. We began the game with me at my normal place at first base. Ross, the coach's son, was pitching. He was pulled shortly after the game began because he just couldn't get the ball over the plate.

Our coach asked for a volunteer. I raised my hand immediately. I had been pitching against the garage wall at home for a long time and I almost always hit my target. I was confident that I could do the job and I suppose that the coach could see that confidence in me. He moved me to the mound and I pitched the rest of the game.

I was happy at first, realizing that I had been right. I was putting the ball right over the plate every single time. I had no control problem whatsoever. In fact, my pitches were so good that the Pirates treated them as though they were having batting practice. I think every batter got several hits that day and my coach left me there to handle the humiliation as best I could. I think that was the longest game of the year. It certainly was for me.

We lost that game 24 to 6!

I never volunteered to pitch again, but I had a renewed appreciation for those that did.

88

The Bannock Peak Encampment

Camping with the boy scouts was one of my favorite pastimes. There were many memorable campouts during my years as a scout. One of my favorite places to go was into the mountains above Indian Springs, north and east of American Falls. Indian Springs was a naturally hot spring that had a natatorium built around it. It was often used for family gatherings where we took advantage of not only the swimming pool, but also a very good picnic and barbecuing facility. It was great for picnicking, but true camping required a wilder and more isolated area.

There was a good gravel road into the foothills from Indian Springs, but it soon turned into a dirt road, with two tire lanes and substantial vegetation growing up between them. The condition of that road was dependent on the weather. A good rain could render the road impassable for several days and during the winter months, there was no use even trying to use it.

The road wound through the foothills like a snake as it went higher and higher. In a matter of minutes, the foothills with its farms and fields gave way to a more rugged terrain and the trees closed in around the roadway. Farther on, the trees became thick tall pines and the road was completely shaded, even dark. The road began to make switchbacks in order to gain the increased altitude. It followed a stream for the most part, but even then we were only afforded occasional glimpses of the running water as the trees and brush became very heavy and hid the stream from view.

It would have been fine no matter where we decided to pull over and set up our camp, but we had a favorite spot, near the place where one of the service roads branched off to the east. It was near the road, but hidden from it and had a large enough flat area to accommodate several tents. The stream there was clear and cold, covered with watercress. Some of us ate watercress like candy, enjoying the mint-like flavor.

We were a scout troop that had formed some very routine habits during our times together. Setting up camp was done easily and quickly, before anyone was permitted to do anything else. The troop was like a well-oiled machine as the older boys helped the new kids until every tent and sleeping bag was in place. Wood was gathered, enough to keep a fire burning far longer than we needed it. Buckets of fresh water were fetched from the stream, as a large fire ring was built and a fire started. Part of the water was put on the first substantial coals. It was to be used for washing dishes later.

Our scoutmaster had one requirement for every new kid in the troop. He had to bake a cake over a campfire. It was not an easy task, but it was a lot of fun watching them as they huddled over the creative ovens they had made, mostly with the good advice from the older boys or even the fathers. I had a five gallon honey can that I had molded into a nice reflector oven. It worked well, and my cakes were always at least edible. Much of my success depended on the fire, not the oven.

Several cakes were started as soon as camp was set up. Those not baking disappeared into the surrounding area, not really with any purpose in mind, but just to enjoy the wilds of nature and see what was there before it was too dark to do so.

As the sun dipped below the horizon, supper was begun, each of us cooking food from our own packs. We also used our own utensils and pans. The only thing that was a community effort was the dishwater.

It became quite crowded around the fire at suppertime as each boy prepared his meal. We could easily have had two fires, but our scoutmaster felt that it was important for us to learn how to cooperate with each other. It usually worked out fine, too, except on those rare occasions when someone's food would get dumped into the flames because of an over-eager companion. Even then, there was a contingency plan, for the scoutmaster brought lots of extra food for just such an occasion.

I always went camping with an ample supply of bacon, eggs, ground beef, potatoes, and onions. I also had some canned pork and beans, just in case. On rare occasions when I could afford it, I also liked to carry some beef jerky to snack on. I enjoyed cooking about as much as anything we did, perhaps because I enjoyed eating so much. It was also nice to make a meal in the quantity I wanted and not have to worry about whether my brothers would grab the last piece of bacon or take the last of the potatoes.

I always cooked bacon first, so I could use the grease for other things. My favorite thing was to fry hamburger and diced potatoes together. Sometimes I would break some eggs into the mixture just for fun and that tasted good as well. After I ate my fill, I washed my pan and camping utensils and hung them on a line outside my tent to dry for the morning meal. It was important to clean them well to avoid a midnight visit from some critter that was investigating the food odors in the camp.

After everyone had finished eating and things began to slow down, we gathered round the fire to talk, tell stories, and sing. It was always a fun and relaxing time. We often used that time to roast marshmallows. Some of the guys brought the necessary ingredients to make s'mores, which were roasted marshmallows, sandwiched between Graham crackers with a square of Hershey's chocolate. They were delicious, but I thought them to be too much trouble. I liked to just char the marshmallows into a black "crispy" and then eat them right off the stick.

Late at night, it was time for snipe hunting. We were always sure to talk about it a lot as we had dinner, so as to build up the excitement level of the new guys. By the time we were ready to go on the hunt, they were primed and ready. We gathered together with potato sacks and flashlights and gave out some last minute instructions about the importance of doing things just right. Then we'd leave as a group and head for the darkness, getting far away from camp as possible and climbing into the hills where the heaviest brush was located. We all knew that snipes lived in the very heaviest foliage possible. It didn't matter that we scratched ourselves up in our eagerness to lend credence to the hunt.

When we were far enough away, we found a likely spot and left a couple of guys holding the bag open, warning them firmly about the need to keep their flashlights off and their mouths closed. Then we took whoever was left and posted them in remote areas to wave their lights and yell to frighten the snipes into running frantically through the brush and hopefully into the bag that had been so scientifically placed. Once the new guys were busy with their assignments, the rest of us found our way back to camp. We resumed our position at the fire, where we quietly listened to the din in the distance and marveled that those new guys could be so stupid as to fall for such a trick. Of course, discussions of previous snipe hunts were taboo, for we didn't want to be reminded of who the gullible participants had been in those.

When the weary and embarrassed snipe hunters eventually returned to camp, we would wander off to our tents to sleep. I was often surprised at just how restful it was to sleep in those mountains. I always awoke early, refreshed and ready for a new day. That way I could beat the crowd to the fire and finish breakfast early.

We liked to climb mountains during the day, and spent the major part of the day doing so. There were several high peaks in the area, and though the climbs were always steep and strenuous, it felt wonderful to stand at the top and add a "name stone" to the small pile of rocks that were stacked on top telling the history of that particular mountain.

Getting down was much faster, because we could utilize the still snowy areas and slide much of the way. We usually were able to do that without mishap, becoming human toboggans as we streaked down the sides of the peaks until rocks and trees prevented us.

On one of those treks, I found a very large rock, several inches in diameter, that I just had to keep. It was beautiful, gold-colored quartz, the biggest of its kind I had ever seen, and I just had to have it. Because of that rock, I had a terrible time trying to get down the mountain. It was very heavy, but I made it back to camp with the rock intact. My brother and I enjoyed it for a long time as it sat on display in our crowded bedroom.

89

Comes A Horseman

I loved horses. It was no secret. There were drawings of horses in various poses scattered on every school notebook I'd had for years. Other people doodled in other ways. I drew horses.

Walter Farley was my favorite author after H.G. Wells and Edgar Allan Poe. I had read all the Black Stallion series and Island Stallion series, making good use of my library card. I had read every other book I could find that dealt with horses. Richard Hagerman and I had become friends, finding a common ground in our love of horses. He drew them better than I, and he studied horse magazines, learning all he could. He taught me much of the terminology of the equestrian, from "fetlock" to "furlong."

I had been to the rodeo many times, and seen the beautiful animals put through their paces by the Aberdeen Boots and Saddles Club. I even had some experience myself, having learned to appreciate that nasty-tempered little cocoa Shetland pony that Grandpa Frank had stabled at our house. I had the bite marks to prove it.

It was no accident that one of the first things that attracted my attention after we moved to the "lower place" was a horse. It lived in the pasture across the road, just to the south of the Clayton's house. The Claytons were a successful family that operated a large farming enterprise that included a modern dairy barn and hundreds of acres of potatoes, hay, and grain. They had more Holstein cows than I could count, and they had that one horse. It was a beautiful palomino named Prince.

For a long time, I admired Prince from a distance. He was a beautiful golden color, with a white mane and a white tail that hung all the way to the ground. Most often he could be seen standing quietly in the pasture, leisurely grazing, just standing there as the world went by around him. Occasionally, he would walk to a point near the road, or even trot up to the fence, showing a bit more interest in the goings on around him. When that happened, I paid him more attention than usual, too, because I could see him better.

As time passed we became good friends with Chick and Wallace Clayton. I was a year older than Chick, and Mike's age fell in between them. We often found time to play together. They had a sister, Gertie. She was in my class at school, but she was not one to participate in our games. Sometimes we played baseball in either their pasture or ours. Sometimes we'd swim, or play hide-and-seek in their cornfield. But my favorite thing was when we would play with Prince.

There were two older Clayton boys, and they were supposed to be sure that Prince got exercised. However, they always seemed to be busy doing other things and never got around to it. One day, Oscar Clayton, their father, showing just a bit of displeasure with the older boys, gave the job of exercising Prince to Chick and Wallace. I was excited for them, though they seemed less than pleased.

At first, they didn't really do much with Prince, but a couple of days later, their father's gentle reminder seemed to inspire them both. I was able to help them as they saddled Prince and readied him for an afternoon of riding. Prince didn't like having a bit forced into his mouth, but he soon accepted it, and once in place, he was ready to be ridden.

The first one to mount Prince was Wallace, and he showed off for the rest of us by slapping Prince's rump and running him to the pasture fence and back. The Chick had a turn. He was kinder and just had him the horse trot around in a circle a couple of times. Then it was my turn.

I hadn't much experience with a fully-grown horse, and so I listened as both Wallace and Chick flooded me with instructions. Do this. Don't do that. I was certain that I wouldn't remember any of it. Still, I put my foot in the stirrup and swung onto Prince's back. I was nervous, and I think he sensed it. He seemed to fidget. I took the reins and started out at a walk. Chick yelled after me to hold the reins more loosely. I loosened them and Prince broke into a trot, nearly breaking my teeth. Soon, though, I was moving with him instead of against him and the trot became quite comfortable.

My turn was over all too soon, but I had thoroughly enjoyed myself and looked forward to the next time I would have the chance to ride that magnificent animal. I even dreamt of riding as I slept that night and it was a good dream.

My next opportunity came a few days later. The Clayton boys had been working Prince every day and they were growing tired of it. They actually came to my house and recruited me to help. I went willingly, anxious to ride again. That day, I learned to put the horse through his paces, from a walk to a trot, then to a lope, then a gallop, and then a run. He responded well to my signals and I felt at home riding him. I was having the time of my life.

I guess my comfort and ability to control the horse was noticed, because Harold, the older brother, asked me one day if I would be willing to ride the horse over to the Hagerman's place and back. He wanted to show the horse to his friend, but he also wanted to show him his new Ford Starliner, and he couldn't take both.

I agreed instantly, thinking I might get to show off in front of my friend, Richard, while Harold and Richard's brother visited. I saddled Prince all by myself and was soon astride him and waiting for Harold to open the gate for me so I could go out on the road.

I enjoyed that ride very much, walking sometimes, but galloping almost as much. Richard was not at home, so he didn't get to see me ride, but it made no difference to me. I was just having a great time.

Harold followed me back from the Hagerman's in his car, honking once in awhile, trying to get both the horse and me flustered. However, we did fine, and I got back safely. Harold showed me how to groom the horse and rub it down before putting it back out to pasture. We also gave him a generous helping of oats from the milking barn. He seemed to enjoy that.

That was the last time I rode Prince. The older Clayton boys took over his exercise regimen again and I was never invited. It was just a short time that I was able to bond with that beautiful beast, but it was glorious!

90

The Boy Battle

I didn't fight much. I would like to be able to say that it seemed stupid to me. I would like to be able to say that there was no point to fighting. I would like to be able to say that my problems were all resolved through the use of a rapier wit and smooth talk. I would like to be able to say all those things, but I cannot. For a time, fights seemed to plague me like a persistent cough. No matter how hard I tried, fighting was unavoidable.

I cannot remember specifically what started these fights, nor can I remember many of the fights themselves. Once they were finished, they were finished, and the participants went about their business as if they had just been jogging or something. However, one fight—one long and furious exchange—looms large in my memory whenever I think of those days at Aberdeen Junior High School. For reasons that I never understood, it was not a normal fight at all.

I had little to do with Dan Lessey. In fact, we didn't even share any friends. He was a year behind me in school and the most obnoxious person on the playground. He was loud and boastful and took delight in verbal barbs thrown at almost anyone that would glance in his direction.

One day, during the luncheon recess, I was engaged in a game of "horse" on the basketball court in the playground. There were several of us in the game and we were having a good time. I was sinking my shots and doing well in the game. I was not bothering anyone, least of all Dan

Lessey, but there he was. For some reason, he began to taunt me as I took my shots.

At first I just ignored him, assuming that he would tire of his game and move on to some other hapless student in another part of the playground. I was wrong! My lack of response only served to throw fuel on the fire and he stepped up the insults a notch, casting aspersions on people that I cared about, both family and friends. He added comments about my basketball prowess and me. Well, whoever said "sticks and stones may break my bones, but names will never hurt me" had not had Dan Lessey throwing the names.

I was beginning to get somewhat irritated. I began to respond to his barbs by going into a slow, but rapidly increasing burn. I started suggesting other things he might do to occupy his time, such as joining the elementary school kids on the other side of the high fence. I let him know that, in my humble opinion, his wit was much more in line with that of the first graders. He responded by questioning my parentage and I threw the basketball at him!

Well, he didn't see it coming. It hit him right in the face, causing a spurt of blood from his nose and fire from his eyes. He came after me in a fury and before I knew what was happening, we were rolling on the ground, each of us throwing ineffective punches at each other as we struggled to gain the advantage.

Dan got the first break, ending up on top of me and sitting astride my chest, pinning my arms to the ground so that I couldn't move. He sputtered and fumed, managing to mumble a few obscenities through the blood that was running down his face and onto mine. We were about the same size, and I struggled to free myself, wanting desperately to exact revenge for the things he had been saying. He was just as eager to beat me for hitting him with the ball.

I gained some leverage and almost threw him off me. I tried it again, and then again. It was no use. I was pinned very securely. He was straining to keep me there, though, and I struggled, not letting him rest. I got my chance when he leaned over to make sure that his blood was hitting me in the eye. I smashed against his face a second time—this time with my forehead. It hurt terribly, but it knocked him off me and I reversed our position quickly. In a flash, I was astride him and pinning his arms to the ground. We continued to fight—each of us exhausted and yet we fought on.

At first, the other kids egged us on. They loved to watch a good fight. Each of us had our rooting section, but there was no time to listen or acknowledge their hoots and hollers. We were locked in mortal combat and not paying attention to the cheering section. That is why we were so surprised when Mr. Pierce and the principal, Miss Bickett, pulled us apart. All the students were gone. The bell had rung and we had missed it!

Both of us, bloodied and trying hard to catch a breath, were marched into the office and seated firmly in chairs in front of Miss Bickett's desk. She stared at us for a long time and then lectured us soundly. Neither of us was permitted nor were we asked to tell our versions of what started the fight. Miss Bickett was not interested!

Our parents were called and both of us were taken to American Falls to be stitched up. We went to the same doctor, sat in the same waiting room, and yet we said nothing to each other. I got stitches in my left knee and at the corner of my mouth. Dan had a split lip and it was stitched as well. The doctor decided that the cut on his forehead would heal without stitches.

The next day at school, Dan came up to me and offered his hand. I shook it and all was well. We never again had a problem, each of us having earned the respect of the other. A few years later, we worked closely together as the two of us both moved sprinkler pipes for the same boss. We became good friends that year.

91

McTucker Creek

I will always remember my first trip to McTucker Creek with Grandpa Frank. I was always excited when I was able to accompany Grandpa on those special outings. McTucker Creek was no exception. I always got caught up in the excitement of preparing for an excursion with Grandpa, and I even looked forward to the smell of stale cigarette smoke that seemed to permeate his DeSoto. There was always a stop along the way for bait, too, that would result in all of us getting a chilled bottle of Nehi Orange or a fizzy bottle of 76 soda.

I was accustomed to the trips to Springfield Lake, but on this day, we drove right past it, and into unfamiliar territory for me. I enjoyed seeing new and different places and spent most of the time staring out the window. I watched the farms roll by as we drove on toward Blackfoot and I found myself wondering just how far we were going to go.

I didn't have long to wait, for Grandpa Frank soon left the highway and turned onto a gravel road. As we drove eastward, the land became more marsh-like and the farms disappeared. The graveled road gave way to a dirt road that had received little in the way of maintenance. Grandpa slowed the DeSoto to a crawl as he navigated the puddles and ponds that increasingly encroached on portions of the road. Soon we were all alone with the trees and the creek and Grandpa Frank found a spot where he could pull the car off the road and park.

McTucker Creek was a large stream. It was larger than some rivers I had seen. It was so deep that there was no chance we could get to the other side, and at several points so wide that I could not have reached the other side with a rock. All along the creek were inlets to standing pools and ponds. There were some places where the water just swirled around in a circle.

We fished from the bank for awhile, using the fly-fishing technique that Grandpa Frank had taught us. I caught nothing, but had some bites and a bit of excitement. Grandpa and Dwight had each caught a fish. Grandpa had some sort of whitefish that I did not recognize and Dwight had a rainbow trout that was quite enviable.

When we had tired of trying that first spot, we decided to branch out and find that "special fishing hole" all on our own. I found what I considered to be a likely spot, but had no more luck than before. Nevertheless, I was determined to keep trying. I did, too, until I heard a yelp and a holler from Dean. The yell came from somewhere beyond the heavy brush to my left and so it took me a few minutes to detour around that brush and locate him.

When finally I saw Dean, I could hardly believe what I saw. He was fighting a fish—a very big fish! His pole was bent nearly double as he tried to land whatever beast had connected itself to the other end of his line. Just as I reached the spot where Dean was furiously trying to stay dry and still hang onto his pole, Grandpa and Dwight emerged from a thicket on the other side of Dean. Grandpa took one look and sent Dwight back for the net.

Dean fought the fish for what seemed like a very long time, but finally Dwight returned with the net and Grandpa got into position to capture the fish as Dean walked it upstream along the bank. He soon had it netted, but even then Dwight had to help him lift it to the bank.

Dean had hooked a fish that must have weighed well over thirty pounds. It was huge! For a moment we were envious of his good fortune, but that envy gave way to sympathy as the fish was emptied from the net and we all got a good look at it. It was a carp! It was, as Grandpa Frank called them, "a trash fish." It was not a fish that could be consumed.

The beast that had been extracted from the water was killed and disposed of. Grandpa Frank said that such fish destroyed the nesting areas of the good game fish and that it should not be returned to the water intact. That explanation was good enough for me, but I truly think that Dean wanted to eat it, regardless of what kind of fish it was.

As it turned out, that was the last "catch" of the day. Oh, we tried at a couple of places and for more than an hour, but after the carp event, our hearts just weren't into it anymore. We finally went home.

I enjoyed fishing at McTucker Creek, but it was hard to get to. The next time I went back was one of those rare occasions when my father was able to break away from the farm duties long enough to go with us. That was a special time for me, one of only two times that I fished alongside my Dad.

92

Strawberry Mouthwash

I suppose that nearly every young boy tries new things, some of which would bring immediate disapproval of his parents, had they known. I was no different, I suppose, except that I think my conscience suffered much more than the average kid. I hated defying my parents' wishes and the guilt I felt when I did so was horrendous! So it was when I first attempted smoking!

I had always been taught that smoking was a bad thing. It went against the advice of my religious upbringing. It went against the advice of my parents and my grandparents. To be honest, it made no sense to me. I could not see the purpose for burning a weed and breathing in the smoke. I even wondered how such a ridiculous pastime was even begun. Where in history did someone get the idea that it might be fun to eat smoke?

There were, however, some other dilemmas that I had to deal with. Grandpa Frank smoked, and I loved the smell of his tobacco. He forbade his own children and grandchildren to smoke, and yet he did it himself. It was a bit confusing to me. My father also smoked, though I never saw him do so. It was no secret, though, for we could smell it on his clothing, mixed with the barnyard odors of hay, both fresh and processed. If there was any doubt about his smoking, it was dispelled by my mother, who often made rather snide comments to him about the habit, irritating him and usually eliminating any happy vibes that might have been in the house. Such comments always seemed to increase the tension, and that heavy feeling hung in the air like a heavy fog, making things very uncomfortable.

It was inevitable that I would try smoking. After all, I needed to know just what the big thrill might be. I had wondered for a long time and had never had the opportunity to try it, if one could call that an opportunity. That opportunity came one summer day when I found my father's stash of Lucky Strikes in the trunk of the car.

I stole a handful of cigarettes from the pack, thinking that I may need some extras if it was as much fun as some people made it look. I stashed them in a hiding place in the granary and waited for an opportunity to get my hands on some matches. That chance came later that same day as I rode in Grandpa Frank's DeSoto. He always had matches lying on the seat and I knew I could steal a book of them without their being missed.

I did nothing more that day, but the next morning after Dad had left for the fields, Mike and I sneaked out to the granary, got the cigarettes, and then disappeared even further from the house. We decided to go out by the old potato cellar, away from the hay and straw, to light up our first cigarettes.

We were as secretive as we could be, feeling a great adrenalin rush as we prepared to defy not only parental advice, but religious advice as well, for we had both been taught the evils of smoking in Sunday school. Even so, we were determined to discover wherein the magic of smoking lay, and we solemnly lit up.

At first, the lighting was difficult. Neither one of us knew that it was easier to light if you sucked on the other end at the same time. We soon discovered that secret, however. I did it and was rewarded with a lung full of smoke, causing me to cough and wretch at the same time. After a moment to collect myself, we got another lighted for Mike. The two of us sat there in the dirt, trying to appear sophisticated as we made an effort to blow smoke rings and even make smoke come out through our noses, an exercise that brought absolute misery along with even more coughing and retching.

We both felt very ill, very quickly, and decided to snuff out the cigarettes. We buried them there on the hill at the side of the potato cellar, along with the extras and the matches. Smoking was not cool!

As we headed back toward the house, we were painfully aware of the nasty taste in our mouths and the horrible smell that seemed to be on all our clothing, in our hair, and especially on our hands. We needed a plan.

We stopped at the cow's watering trough and rinsed our hands and faces. Then we held our heads under the faucet and got our hair soaking wet. Our crew cuts would dry quickly. Last but not least, we headed for Mom's garden.

The garden was our only chance to rid our mouths of that stench and the horrible taste that went with it. We had both thought that some radishes would do the trick, but when we got to the garden, we saw that there were no more radishes. We decided on strawberries, and we huddled behind the corn stalks, shoving strawberries into our faces as quickly as we could pull them off the plants.

I think the strawberries worked, because Mom said nothing to us. In fact, we seemed to have gotten away with the whole thing, except for the fact that Mom went out to harvest her strawberries and most of them were gone. She finally decided that some birds of some kind had taken a liking to them and eaten them. Mike and I kept quiet.

93

Sheddy Sheds

There is no doubt that cleaning lambing sheds is one of the most disgusting, stinking, degrading, miserable jobs on the planet. My father, with his infinite wisdom and sense of fairness, always assigned that duty to Mike and me.

It happened every Spring. Dad would dangle a financial carrot in front of us and we, in a semi-stupor, would move slowly toward the sheds, pitchforks in hand, and begin the two week task of removing all that had collected there during the long winter months. During the lambing season the straw bedding was placed there by my father, over and over again, as the ewes would come to term and deliver their tiny little bundles of joy. Dad moved them out of the lambing sheds as the lambs became strong enough to endure the harsh climate. Then he would spread out more straw for the next lucky tenants.

By the time Spring arrived, the floors of these sheds were several inches thick, sometimes more than a foot. But the floor was not just straw! Sheep have a way of adding their own bit of magic to the equation. They provide various bodily fluids and solids that combine with the straw to form an entirely new substance—a substance that has the consistency of cement on its surface, while hiding a much more pungent and softer material underneath.

We had two sheds, each of them about forty feet wide and perhaps three times that in length. The walls were built of wood. There were wooden rafters as well, covered with a thick canvas roof. All along the centerline of the shed, bare light bulbs hung, with long strings attached so they could be turned off and on, as they were needed. Even with every light on, the insides of the sheds were dimly lighted, especially back in the corners and at the sides where the light was of little consequence.

Mike and I took our time preparing for the misery to come but come it did. After we procured our forks and wheelbarrow, we started digging away at one of the entrance doors. We worked quickly at first, trying not to let the smell bother us as we removed the hardened top of the "floor" and exposed that juicy and pungent material underneath.

As we removed the gunk, we loaded up wheelbarrow after wheelbarrow, taking turns pushing the loaded barrow to the far side of the corral and dumping it. That way we each had a chance to grab a few gasps of fresh air from outside the sheds. It took a dozen or so loads before we could even tell that we were making progress.

The work was back breaking, miserable, stinky, degrading work. The smell of the freshly disturbed sheep manure was almost more than the human body could endure. It permeated the shed, stinging the eyes and causing the nose to rebel in whatever manner it could. We were not alone, however, as the flies buzzed our heads and did touch and go landings on the manure like seagulls on a freshly plowed field.

It was just a matter of hours until we adapted to the smell and to the work. We must have adapted, for it didn't seem nearly as bad as when we began. Oh, the smell was still horrible, but something about it was almost attractive in its acridness.

When lunchtime came, we quit and went in to the house for more than just lunch. We lobbied heavily to my mother to let us take her radio, the one she had received as a birthday present, to the sheds, so that we could listen to music as we worked. We were tired of just talking and complaining to each other about how miserable we were.

Finally, Mom relented, and we returned to the job only after plugging in that radio after securing it high on a shelf at the end of the shed, so that we would not accidentally knock it down.

The work went faster with the music. Both of us worked faster and stayed happier when we could sing along with the latest hits of the day. There was, however, one song that demanded that we stop work and pay close heed to, singing along as best that we could. It was *Cathy's Clown* by the Everly Brothers and we both loved it.

Mike and I worked on those sheds for several days, raising the elevation of the corrals by a couple of feet as we lowered the elevation inside the sheds. We were tired, dirty, and ready to sleep at the end of each day, but we were also proud of the fact that we had made a difference. We had made a mark in Dad's world. He had needed us and we were there. When the job was finally done, Dad paid us in real money, the same as he would have paid a hired hand. It felt wonderful!

94

Coyote

The Aberdeen area supported a variety of wildlife. Jackrabbits and pheasants were plentiful. Several species of snakes could be found, as well as several types of waterfowl.

There were seagulls everywhere, especially in the Spring, as scores of tractors pulling plows turned the soil in preparation for the planting to come. The cacophony that came with the seagulls as they circled over the heads of the farmers was almost loud enough to drown out the noise made by the tractors.

Some of the more exotic fauna inhabited the desert to the west and seldom became an integral part of our lives. They had their space and we had ours and usually we had no interaction. There were pronghorn antelope on that desert, and rodents of all kinds, creating a veritable horn of plenty for the hawks and even eagles that hunted there.

One of the most misunderstood and hated animals also flourished on that desert. It was the coyote.

Coyotes were plentiful on the desert and lived primarily on rabbits and smaller rodents, but every once in awhile they would encroach into someone's farm and cause trouble. The biggest problem occurred when one of them decided to kill a sheep. In addition to being a financial burden on the farmer, a coyote that killed a sheep always came back and killed again, finding it a much easier thing to do than hunt.

Because of that tendency to kill livestock, there was an ongoing reward offered for coyote pelts. The Aberdeen-Springfield Canal Company paid handsomely for the skins. At least that's what I had been told. Although I hadn't personally seen it, I heard stories of the confrontations between coyotes and man. Such stories always seemed to end with the animal's carcasses being hauled over to the Canal Company in someone's pickup for identification and payment.

I'll never forget the summer that Mike and I found the coyote puppies! We were out near Cooney, the waterfall, and playing cowboys and Indians. As we ran through the sagebrush on imaginary ponies, we heard a whimpering sound that, at first, scared us. It took a while to get up the courage to investigate, and when we finally did, it took an even longer period to find the source of the noise. Every time we got close to the sound, it stopped.

Finally, deep in the heaviest brush, we found a coyote den. Actually, it was a converted rabbit hole, I figured, but coyotes weren't fussy. Near the entrance to the den, hidden in the brush, was a mama coyote. She looked as though she had been shot and came home to die. It didn't look like she had been there very long, but it was certainly long enough to distress her pups. There were three of them, and they were not happy. I swore they spit like cats when they first saw us, but I suppose it wasn't quite the same. They made it clear that we were not welcome.

We ran home and got a couple of grain sacks, a length of rope, and some gloves and returned to the den to retrieve the pups. In a few moments and after some harmless bites and scratches, we had all three pups bagged. The bags were tied off at the top and we carried them back to the house.

We let the pups loose in a small enclosure that we made in the old chicken coop and then set about to make a permanent place for them. We found a wooden box near the door to the barn, and some old window screen in the old garage. We stretched the screen over the top of the box and secured it tightly with several nails, making a movable flap at one end to use as an access port. That flap was fastened by hooking it over a clasp on the outside of the box.

We donned the gloves again and transferred the three coyote pups to the box. We put them on our back porch and spent the rest of the day trying to get them to accept some milk from the kitchen. They didn't seem to want it at all. They didn't even try at first, and then finally I got one of them to lick some milk from my fingers. The other two just wouldn't do it. By the time Dad came home, they seemed quite weak and sick, but the one that had taken the milk was just a bit more active.

Dad looked at the pups through the screen and listened to our tale of how we had "rescued" them, but he wasn't at all happy about their being kept there on his porch. We followed him into the house, as he explained why we should not have interfered with the pups. He was adamant in his view, and explained that they were wild beasts and that wild beasts are best left alone for nature to deal with, as it will. Then he expressed his opinion that the pups would be dead by morning, because they could not accept captivity. He was partly right.

Early the next morning we hurried to the back porch to check on the pups, not knowing what to expect. They were lying very still in the bottom of the box. Two of them had died during the night. The third was asleep beside them, but became quite active when we arrived. We removed the two dead animals and returned them to the same bag we had brought them in. Then we fed the other one. This time, he drank from the bowl. He had a good breakfast.

After our own breakfast, Mike and I took the two dead pups out and buried them. We were sad but realistic. Dad had predicted their deaths and they had died. It was just a fact that we had to accept.

Once the pups were buried, they were forgotten in the midst of our efforts to tend the one that had lived. We named him Wiley, and over the next couple of weeks he grew into a strong and very active pup.

Dad continued to express his disapproval, making certain that we remembered that the coyote was still a wild animal, and would carry the instincts of a wild animal no matter what we did to it. We were determined to make it a pet, however, and we spent hours trying to cuddle it and pet it and feed it. Sometimes it accepted the attention quietly and sometimes it responded by growling and snapping at us. At no time did it seem very friendly. At least, not like our dogs had been.

One day we decided to try and change the pup's diet. We cooked some hamburger and offered it to the pup, which he accepted readily. He ate every morsel, but threw it up again a few minutes later. Then we tried raw hamburger meat and had some success with that. It was eaten and not returned.

The pup grew very fast, or so it seemed, much faster than a dog puppy would have grown. Dad told us that the reason was because nature needed to give wild animals a chance to take care of themselves as soon as possible. Whether that was true or not, the growth was real. Soon the pup was too big and too active to remain in the box, except to sleep, and we tried to get him adjusted to a leash. He hated that leash and fought it every minute, chewing and snapping and biting as though it was an enemy to be destroyed.

Dad watched our efforts closely as we tried to tame that coyote, but he had kept out of it, letting us try. Finally, though, he stepped in. He sat down on the porch and explained to us that no matter what we did, the coyote would not be tamed. He seemed to realize that we wanted to be the only kids around with a pet coyote. He also realized that we had grown very attached to the little guy and that he needed to choose his words very carefully as he told us that the pup should be destroyed.

We listened in shock as he told us how the pup had been spoiled now, and could not survive in the wild, and yet it could not be kept in a box or a pen of some kind, for that was foreign to every gene in its body. I think we knew that Dad was speaking the truth to us in the best way he knew how, but we were stubborn and refused to accept what he said. As he finished and rose to go into the house, he turned and told us that we had brought the pup home, and that it was up to us to decide what to do about it.

Another day went by as Mike and I discussed what to do. It was not an easy thing to talk about, because the conversation kept circling around the issue and coming right back to one thing—the pup had to go! Finally, we acted. Mike got the pup while I went into the house and got the .22 caliber rifle that Dad kept in his closet. We were solemn as we walked slowly out beyond the barn, out of sight of the house.

Mike held the leash as I aimed the rifle at the pup's head and prepared to shoot him. But the pup looked at me and I balked. We had been feeding and petting that coyote for the longest time, and there was just no way I could just assassinate it like that. It was just too hard!

Both of us were teary-eyed and wishing that Dad had been there to do the deed, but we knew, too, that he expected us to handle it. After a time, we took the pup to the edge of the pasture fence and discussed letting him go. It was only a short run to edge of the sagebrush. Once there, he would be out of sight and gone.

We knew that we were fooling ourselves with such thoughts. We knew that Dad was right about his not being able to exist in the wild, with no mother to teach him, and just enough trust in man to make him inept at what he should do best—kill for food. We knew the pup should be killed. But we also knew that he needed a fighting chance, both for our benefit and for his. So we decided to let him go on the other side of the fence and give him a running start.

It probably wasn't any more of a fighting chance than shooting him right there on the leash, but both of us needed to feel that it was. We removed the leash and set the pup over the fence. He wasted no time at all in running for the sagebrush, as I used a fence post to steady the rifle and took aim. My mind raced with thoughts in the next few moments. I could let him go by missing the shot and then Mike could say that I tried. I could just refuse to shoot, but the images of him tearing up sheep or chickens just because he was too tame to hunt in the wild was too much.

I fired and my aim was true! As the report echoed, the running pup crumpled and lay still.

We climbed the fence and ran to him. He was dead. Both of us cried openly as we carried the pup back and buried him next to his brother and his sister.

We had learned a hard lesson. Dad had given us the leeway we needed to learn it well. We never again tried to tame a wild animal!

95

A Pig by Any Other Name Is Still A Pig

We never had hogs. Well, almost never. My father was not the least bit interested in keeping pigs. Now don't get me wrong. He loved those well-done pork chops that my mother would occasionally fix for dinner. He adored bacon, and ham, and most of all, a good pork roast. However, Dad made no bones about his distaste for the process of raising such animals. He considered them to be dirty, ill behaved, and much more trouble than they were worth.

Occasionally, Grandpa Frank had pigs at his place. I used to enjoy going out by the barn and hanging my arms over the fence as I watched the pigs. I enjoyed the sounds they made when they were fed, and I especially took delight in their complete lack of manners as they fought over every morsel.

There was only one time that we had a pig on our place. Even so, I think it was with some misgivings that my father gave my younger brother, David, permission to keep a sow as a project. He built a small enclosure for her near the entrance to the barn. It was made from the same four-foot panels that were used to make the temporary lambing pens. It was none too sturdy, but it seemed to do the trick. David's hog was not ambitious enough to try and escape. She wasn't even as interesting as the pigs I had watched at Grandpa's. At least they moved around and fought over food. David's had no others to fight with and she was far too lazy to move much. As near as I could tell, she just lay there.

David named her Norma. I don't know why, but I can venture a guess. I only knew two Normas in Aberdeen and either one could have justifiably been the namesake for such an animal. We tried to get David to use another name. Grandpa had one named Rosebud and we thought that was nice enough. We offered other suggestions, but David was adamantly determined that if he was going to take on the task of raising the pig, that he had every right to expect us to honor his request that she be addressed as Norma.

David was dedicated to Norma's care. He was diligent in his efforts to keep her fed and watered. He worked especially hard to make certain that her bedding was always freshened with the best of our straw. He talked to her, too. Oh, he knew she couldn't understand him, but he also sensed that she enjoyed the sound of his voice.

Norma grew quickly. Too quickly! It wasn't long before we knew why. Norma was going to have a family!

Now, Dad was none too happy about the prospect of having more pigs. He thought that he had already gone above and beyond all fatherly duties in accepting just the one pig without protest. Now he was faced with a dilemma. He began to stress the auction in Blackfoot as a great place to sell young piglets. In fact, he stressed it in nearly every conversation he had with David.

Of course, David was ecstatic! He could barely believe his good fortune. You'd have thought he was going to be the father. He could hardly wait until the hog came to term and delivered, providing him with a whole family of the little porkers. He talked of little else for the next few months, making him quite obnoxious to those of us who did not care one way or the other.

One morning Dad came in from the milking with the news that Norma had begun to deliver her piglets. David raced out to the barnyard to tend to her. Although there was little he could do to help, he stayed with Norma through her delivery, talking to her in a soothing voice and encouraging her.

Each time that a new piglet saw the light of day, David raced for the house to make the announcement. It began to happen so often that I went out to investigate for myself. It was true! Norma was lying on her side, suckling an entire family, while at the same time more family was coming!

By the end of the day she had finished her job. There were fourteen piglets! Fourteen! No one I knew had ever seen a sow deliver as many. What's more, they all seemed healthy. But that didn't last.

My father's theory, and it was a sound one, was that poor Norma just didn't have enough milk to support such a large family. For that reason, she took it upon herself to trim it down to size. Whether it was intentional or accidental, we couldn't tell, but during the next few days several little pigs died. It appeared that Norma laid on them.

David handled the losses well, but we all began to wonder if any of the piglets would survive. My father suggested that perhaps it would be of some benefit if David included some bottle feeding to supplement Norma's milk supply. David took on the task with a vengeance, determined to salvage as much of his brood as possible. Dad gave him some warm cow's milk at each of the two milkings each day and David got it into the piglets.

It seemed to do the trick. The "hogicide" stopped!

There were only five little pigs left, but they prospered. They grew into a group of happily squealing animals and David was proud of them.

When they were weaned, Norma was taken off to the auction and sold. A few weeks later, all five of the fat little pigs were also taken to the auction and sold. David made quite a bit of money. He had worked hard and been quite successful with his project, so much so that several of us kids tried to get our father to let us try to raise pigs. Dad, however, stood his ground and allowed no more pigs on the place.

In retrospect, I think my father made the right decision. After all, along with his inherent disdain for pigs, Dad knew that we were busy with school and church activities. He knew that none of us would be able to devote the necessary time and energy for animal care. The truth is, most of us would never have done as well as David, because we all knew that he was a natural farmer and we were not.

96

The Desert Rats

West of Aberdeen, and east of the largest "primitive area" of pine forest and mountains in the United States, was one of Aberdeen's best kept secrets. It was one of the most unique desert landscapes in the world. And it was well hidden.

To visitors, there appeared to be nothing to the west of town but more farms, much like any other direction. However, if one traveled north or south, they would eventually reach other communities. If one picked an easterly path, they would soon come to the American Falls Reservoir, part of the Snake River. But to the west were no towns and no rivers, just miles and miles of nothing. At least that's what we wanted people to believe! We liked to keep our desert private and unspoiled, to be used by the residents of Aberdeen for our own municipal purposes.

After a few miles, the gravity irrigated farms that lay to the west of Aberdeen gave way to larger fields that were irrigated by sprinkler pipes, fed by wells and pumps that dotted the landscape. A few miles further and such farms became less desirable. They began to be interrupted by "rock piles", hillocks of scrub sage and lava that had proven too great a task for the determined farmers that tried to reclaim land from the elements. As the rock piles became more plentiful and rugged, and the tilled land became less evident, the terrain finally gave way to nothing but sage and lava, populated by coyote, antelope, jackrabbits, rattlesnakes, and a variety of birds and insects.

Farther out, the lava became completely dominant, creating strange and wonderful shapes and formations that had no equal. In every direction were more recent reminders of the volcanic period that had created that rich, Idaho soil. There were caves and lava tubes scattered throughout the area, creating a virtual amusement park for those of us that knew how to use such a godsend.

When I was small, I had heard the legends that had been passed down about that desert. I knew the story of Liar's Cave in every detail.

According to the story, the local boy scouts had, for many years, made regular outings to a cave near the edge of the lava flow. The entrance was nearly vertical for about ninety feet. The only way to gain access was to be lowered into the hole by rope. Once inside, the cave branched out in several directions. That made it great for exploring.

The story tells of a time that three boys went to explore the cave on their own. A rope was secured at the top and the other end dropped down the hole. The first boy hurriedly climbed down the rope, only to find the other end of it tied securely at the bottom with a perfect bowline knot. It frightened him so much that he tried to climb right back up the rope. In his haste and disregard for his friend, who was trying to come down, he fell and broke his leg.

One of the other boys had to go all the way into Aberdeen for help to get his friend out of the cave. It took a long time and the trapped boy suffered for several hours. That incident was the reason given when someone asked why our boy scouts no longer went there. There seemed to be a strong reluctance to formally sponsoring a cave trip, so some of us decided that we would form our own group and not worry about formal sponsorship.

We were a small group, and called ourselves the Desert Rats. We thought the name rather clever since we went to the desert to crawl around in holes, sticking our noses into places where, perhaps, our noses did not belong.

Lester Larkin and I were the permanent members of our group, while most of the others came and went. We would use any excuse to head for the desert, for we loved the adventure of possibly exploring where no one had ever been. We also had Grandpa Frank's stories to encourage us. They were not of gold or hidden treasure or anything quite that exotic. His stories were about Indians. They were good stories, too, and inspired us to keep alert for artifacts that could be traced to the old tribes of Chief Pocatello and the Bannock and Shoshone Indians.

We went into Liar's Cave dozens of times. Not once did we find any mysterious knot tying or ghostly moans or groans. Yet we perpetuated the legend by repeating it to everyone that we knew, especially with those that chose to come with us.

We found and explored many caves in our excursions of the lava beds. Each had a personality of its own. Many of them had marvelous ice formations resulting from years of slow leakage into its darkness. Many of the caves had inhabitants. Several provided homes for animals and nearly all had bats. We avoided bat areas whenever we could because bat guano was not something any of us enjoyed nor chose to include in our exploration.

One day, a man came to our desert and changed things forever. His name was Jim Papadakis, and he was from Arizona. He had heard the legend of Liar's Cave and had come all that way to see for himself. He saw what he thought to be a great chance to become wealthy and he invested all he had into developing that idea.

Somehow, this man gained legal access to a large parcel of land containing Liar's Cave and though he may not have known it, several nearby caves. He moved a long trailer out to the site and proceeded to work on his project. For several months he could be seen working with pick and shovel, and even dynamite, as he altered what Nature had built. He couldn't be seen from close proximity, however, for the first thing he had done was erect a fence that was splattered with "No Trespassing" signs.

Many of the residents of Aberdeen resented the intrusion of Mr. Papadakis. Our Desert Rats were at the top of that list. The man had come into our area and taken it like a thief. Then he had the gall to restrict us from its use, without regard to our years of tradition. We watched in horror as he desecrated our favorite cave with his trailer, his tools and even his presence.

One day, on the main highway between American Falls and Aberdeen, a large sign appeared. It was homemade and hand-lettered with the words "Crystal Ice Cave." There was an arrow pointing toward the South Pleasant Valley Road. The man was in business, not only directing traffic toward our previously isolated area, but even insulting us all by renaming the cave.

Aberdeen buzzed with the news of the opening, but I did not hear of anyone that had actually visited the new attraction. With all the opinions I heard, there wasn't a single story from anyone that had actually been there. Even so, I did not choose to go myself either, for I was not about to support Mr. Papadakis in his endeavor. I still felt anger and disgust at his being there.

It was several months before I went to the Crystal Ice Cave. During that time, the handmade road sign was replaced with an official brown sign from the highway department, with an additional line giving the mileage to the cave. Brochures for the Crystal Ice Cave had been showing up at tourist stops along I-15 and even the newer Idaho road maps had an 'X' out on the lava beds with the Crystal Ice Cave label.

I needed to satisfy my own curiosity and convinced Lester to accompany me on a trip to the desert. We drove the well-known route out on South Pleasant Valley Road. For more than twenty miles, things were the same. Then we got to that old church at the end of the paved road. It looked odd out there in the middle of nowhere, but it served to mark the point where we always left the good road and drove over the little rutted and rocky dirt road that wound its way toward the lava beds.

In the past, we could see the lava rising above the rest of the terrain off in the distance. It was about five miles away, but the winding dirt road we had always used added about twelve miles to the trip. Well, we could still see the lava beds in the distance, but the road had changed. It had been improved. It was still a dirt road, but now it was freshly graded and widened. The two deep tire marks with the weeds and grass in the center had been replaced with a good and wide road, where oncoming traffic could actually pass each other without one person having to find a pull-out.

A few minutes later and we were there, parking in a crude but level parking area. We walked up a new pathway toward the trailer that sat near the cave. At the trailer, a lady sat behind some folding tables that had been set up and displayed a variety of volcanic rocks and geodes, and even some arrowheads and pieces of pottery. Each item had a price tag on it. A large sign behind the lady offered cave tours for a dollar and a half. We purchased tickets from the lady and then waited.

There was a family that had occupied the only other car in the lot. They had Colorado plates and they were perusing the rocks on the table while we waited. In a short time, Jim Papadakis himself appeared at the trailer door and stepped down. He greeted us along with the family from Colorado and began to talk as he led us down a path toward the cave entrance, an entrance that must have been a hundred and fifty feet from the hole we had always used.

We followed the tour with interest, as we took note of all the work that had been done. Papadakis had built a nice walkway of crushed lava. It must have taken forever just to do that. At the new entrance to the cave, he had installed a heavy glass door.

Papadakis kept a running dialog going throughout the tour. He explained how he had dug and blasted his way into the cave to provide a path that, even though steep, could be safe and convenient. He explained that the glass door was there so as not to interfere with the internal temperature of the cave. As we followed him down the steep pathway, he pointed out various interesting formations, explaining how they were formed and even how history was affected by the surrounding lava flow. He explained the difficulty he had in installing lights every few feet with as little impact on the cave as he could manage.

Finally, nearly a hundred feet below the surface and probably three times that in steep pathway, we emerged into a lighted chamber adorned with ice. It was the same chamber we had entered so many times before, but we came in from the opposite side. The placement of the lights created a beautiful effect as it illuminated the ice. Both Lester and I were impressed.

At the conclusion of the tour, the family from Colorado bought some souvenirs from the lady at the trailer, loaded up there car, and drove off. We hung back a bit and struck up a conversation with Mr. Papadakis, telling him of our exploits. We stayed for a long time, asking and answering questions. He told of his efforts and problems and we pointed out some other caves in the area that he hadn't known about. It was a pleasant visit and I decided I liked the man.

As we drove back home that day, we came to the conclusion that there was plenty of desert out there for the Desert Rats, and that there was no harm in sharing that little piece of it with the rest of the world.

97

I Was No David

There is a distinct difference between a slingshot and a sling. The boys around Aberdeen used both, but more often than not, the slingshot was the weapon of choice.

A slingshot is made with a forked stick. It had to be a good one, and so demanded that the builder do some serious hunting. He also needed to endure some trial and error before making a final selection. One needed a very sturdy fork—strong enough to hold up under the pressure of the rubber that would be used on it, and large enough where the fork came together to provide a good handle. Only then could the user be as confident and accurate as possible when firing a volley of stones.

Of course, there were various methods of building a good slingshot. The easiest was to use large rubber bands, but the preferred method was to use rubber cut from an old tire inner tube, tying it securely with layer upon layer of string, thereby securing it to the forked stick. A piece of canvas could be used to hold the rocks, but it tended to tear easily with heavy use. The best material for that piece was leather. An awl or one side of a pair of scissors could be used to put the necessary holes in each end of the leather piece, and the rubber was just poked through and looped before it was attached to the forked stick. Leather held up very well, and made the very best of slingshots, as good as anything that ever dangled from the back pocket of Dennis the Menace.

A sling is completely different. It is simpler to construct. One only needed two lengths of rawhide and a small leather pouch in the center to hold the missile that was to be fired. I preferred a sliding loop on one end to make it snug to my middle finger, though I knew others that chose not to use such a loop. I found that it permitted a quick recovery should you encounter a "misfire."

Both weapons were effective, but required a good deal of practice. It was much easier to learn how to use a slingshot. It was easily loaded, held, and fired by almost anyone and done so with a certain degree of effectiveness, though accuracy required experience.

There were store-bought slingshots, but they were expensive, and cheaply made with rubber bands and what looked like heavy wire as a handle. They did not hold up, however, under the stress and strain of heavy bombardment.

I preferred the sling. It was a good deal more difficult to master, but once I learned how to use it, I became lethal. The greatest difference, I suppose, between the slingshot and the sling was that the latter used centrifugal force to propel its load rather than elasticity. When properly used, the stones went farther, faster, and were quite damaging to whatever target was selected.

I practiced incessantly. At first, my rocks went flying in just about any direction, much to the chagrin of my younger brother, who realized that to be anywhere near me might be endangering his own well-being. Gradually, I learned to control the direction of my "ammo" and in time, I even reached a point where I could demonstrate a relatively high degree of accuracy when using the sling. I could knock over tin cans more often than not. I hit fence posts and bottles and trees. I even learned to hit the side of a barn.

I considered myself an expert with a sling. In the Bible, the story of David downing Goliath with a sling was one of my favorites. David was one of my heroes. I could imagine myself taking on giant after giant as they challenged my territory. Of course, my giants were likely to be telephone poles.

I soon tired of constantly knocking down tin cans that had to be set up again. I had put my mark on nearly every fence post on our eighty acres and even the corral fences. I had even marked the tree trunks around our front yard. I was beginning to run out of things to shoot at. I decided to search for something new and different, so I went for a long trek, all the way to the corner where our road met Airport Road. Then I headed up the hill toward the Aberdeen Municipal Airport. I just knew there would be something good to shoot at there.

Along the way, I kept my eyes peeled, searching for good ammunition along the gravel road. I stopped often, picking up rocks of just the right size, weight, and shape for my sling. I kept them in a drawstring bag that hung from my belt. Once it had held a terrific collection of marbles, long since disappeared. I am sure that each of my brothers absconded with their fair share. But now, it held "sling ammo," a job no less important than marble storage.

I reached the airport with a full bag of "ammo." Our airport consisted of two small hangar-like Quonset sheds, each large enough to hold a private plane. There were also a couple of other planes tied down nearby, their wings tethered to steel rings embedded in the new black pavement that the city fathers had so generously provided. There were no people there at all.

I put a stone in my sling and swung it in a circle, slowly at first, then faster. I released one end of the string and whipped the stone toward the windsock at the top of the nearest hangar. My aim was true and the sock slowed down the rock. It dropped to the roof of the shed and slid slowly down the side to the ground, making the only sound there. I just thought, "Oh, boy, I killed a giant sock!" I wasn't too excited about that experience.

I looked for another target and settled on one of the big, blue glass things on top of the power pole in front of the gas pump. I knew they were insulators and had some reason for being there, but I had also seen them up close and knew they were very hard to break. I didn't think there was a chance one of my rocks would break such large ones, anyway. I just wanted to hear the "tingey" sound when I hit it. I was very wrong!

I dashed off two quick shots and though I came close with both, they missed the insulator. I was more careful the third time, remembering to begin slowly, watch the angle, and release at just the right time. I hit that insulator squarely and it disintegrated! Pieces of it flew everywhere, and sparks flew even more! I had done something very bad. I hadn't meant to, but I hadn't thought it through. I hadn't even considered what might happen if the insulator broke.

I looked all around, feeling about as guilty as humanly possible, but still hoping against hope that I would not be discovered. I knew there was no one within a mile and yet I looked. I even kept looking as I ran for home as fast as I could run. Thoughts raced through my head just as fast. What if someone figured out that I had done it? What if someone came along and saw me running down the road away from the airport and then put two and two together later?

Fear of discovery made me jump the fence at the Bickett place and cut across their pasture, away from the road. I gave no thought whatsoever to the red and white mound of muscular meanness that lay directly in front of me. I had forgotten about the Bickett's Hereford bull! Then suddenly he was there.

In retrospect, I know it could not have been true, but it seemed as though he blocked out the entire horizon. He was a massive piece of flesh, rumored to weigh nearly a ton, and it was clear that he did not like sharing his space with a scared kid. He started my way and I knew instinctively that it was not to greet me. I veered to the east and so did he. I headed west and so did he. He was after me!

I wondered if I could slay the giant beast with my sling, then realized quickly that I had no chance of doing that. All I could do was run, and run I did. I had run over half a mile and yet I cleared the fence and sailed into the Clayton's garden, making a perfect twelve-point landing. The bull came to a stop and glared at me as I dusted off my black and blue body and walked leisurely home. I only wish that the coach could have seen just how well fear could make me jump.

That night, I stashed my sling in a dresser drawer and never used it again. I was relieved to see that the insulator had been replaced a few days later and that no one ever knew what I had done.

98

The Overnighter

The great tree far out in the field to the north of our house always fascinated me. It stood as a sentinel over the acreage of sugar beets and alfalfa. It stood alone, on acres of open farmland, rising from near the ditch bank as if to defy all the forces that had labored over past years to clear that land of trees. For some reason, it seemed very appealing to me, perhaps because it stood apart from all our other trees and, perhaps just because it stood out from the rest of the landscape.

That old tree must have been there for many years, because it looked old. There was a lot of dead wood and its branches reached far out over the fence—so far, in fact, that my father had to duck his head when his tractor came near the edge of the field there.

The tree had provided the only available shade for us the year we worked our very own acre of sugar beets. Work crews that went out into those fields to haul in the hay or to harvest the grain used it for the same purpose. I suppose that if the truth were known, many a lunch or refreshing drink of ice water was consumed under the wide spread branches of that old tree.

One day Mike and I decided to go camping all by ourselves, and we decided that the best place on the farm for us to go was to that tree. It was far away from the house and outbuildings, it had an ample wood supply for a campfire, and there was just enough of a clearing between the irrigation ditch and the fence for us to put up our little pup tent and build a fire ring.

As we prepared for our outing, we became more and more excited about the prospect of spending the night away from home and cooking our own food. Both of us had been on scout outings before, but this was an independent trip, with just the two of us. Because of that, it had a special significance. We would be on our own!

We left the house with all the ceremony of a troop of soldiers. We said our good-byes, got last minute instructions from Mom, double-checked our packs to make sure we hadn't forgotten something, and then we were off. We chose to hike down the gravel road to Airport Road, then turn right and go until we reached the turn-off into the farthest corner of our farm. From there we would follow the dirt lane for a time and then climb over the fence and follow the ditch bank to the old tree.

It wasn't necessary to go that far. We could have crossed the newly mown hay field in a direct line. We were, however, young adventurers and we chose to make the longest hike we could. Even with that effort, we reached the tree in about thirty minutes.

We swung our packs from our shoulders and put them on the ground. Then we sat down beside them for a much-needed rest and to discuss the course of action we would take in setting up our encampment. We had planned the outing based on our memories of what the clearing was like and now we needed to make some adjustments.

It was obvious that things were not exactly as we had remembered them. For one thing, the clearing wasn't nearly as large as we had remembered. We decided that one tent was enough. We could both fit in it. That would leave room for a nice fire on the other side of the small clearing. Another thing we hadn't noticed before was just how lumpy the ground had been. There was no way we could sleep in such a place, so we set about looking first for something with which we could smooth out the surface to a more comfortable texture.

There were dozens of dead limbs and branches lying beneath the tree and we had no trouble finding sticks to use as tools. The two of us worked quickly to break down the high spots and fill in the low ones. It worked well, and we were soon ready to pitch a tent.

It took extra work and more time than we expected, but we soon had a nice little camp set up. It was exciting for us, because for the first time, we were camping without any adult supervision. There was no one there to tell us when to eat or sleep, or when to do dishes, or what to do. It was a feeling of freedom that was almost euphoric. And we were enjoying it to the fullest.

We put a six-pack of root beer into the nearby ditch to keep it cool. Then we untied our sleeping bags and rolled them out. Instead of putting them in the tent right away, we used them to lie down and relax. We lay on our backs and talked as we gazed up through the tree branches and watched the clouds go by. They seemed to move faster as they passed over our old tree. I cannot remember what we talked about. I only recall the deep feeling of serenity and peace that I felt as my younger brother and I waited for the coming dusk.

Sundown was like an unspoken signal that gave us permission to start dinner. We had already gathered a supply of dead wood and broken it into kindling. We used some of it to make a small fire, and as soon as the coals were ready, we started our foil-wrapped potatoes. We opened a large can of pork & beans and put it next to the fire to warm.

As we dug into our packs looking for the hamburger meat that Mom had wrapped for us, we found that she had included some other surprises. There was a large bag of Clover Club Potato Chips and two packages of Twinkies. What a treat!

We ate the Twinkies while we waited for our hamburgers to cook. It was OK to do that because we were masters of our lives at that moment. There was no one there to protest our eating dessert first.

We enjoyed several burgers, slathered with mustard and ketchup and onion rings. They were the best I ever had! We ate our baked potatoes with as much butter as we could remove from the wrapper. It was already half melted, but most of it went on the spuds. They, too, were delicious. And it didn't matter that we also ate potato chips with our baked potatoes, for we were in charge of ourselves.

We roasted wieners on sticks and ate them without buns, just dipped them directly into the mustard or ketchup and eating them "fondue" style. We each drank two root beers, still cold from the ditch water where they had been stashed. Then when we thought our bellies would hold no more, we roasted marshmallows and ate them as we talked.

Later, after we had cleaned our dishes with ditch water, as the fire died down to just a few flickering embers, we sat there in the dark and just enjoyed the stillness of the night. It was only interrupted occasionally by the sound of a car on the airport road, but the field of grain between the road and us muffled even that.

We could see the lights from home, and even from the Clayton house, and the Bicketts, and even the Wedels and the Darvik places down the road. They all seemed much farther away at night. For just a moment I felt very lonely, but the feeling passed quickly.

We carefully doused the coals of our fire and dragged our sleeping bags into the tent. We went to bed much earlier than we would have at home, but we went to sleep easily.

The next morning, we rebuilt our fire and cooked bacon and eggs for breakfast. Then we broke camp, packing everything carefully and making sure we didn't leave a mess. We took a shorter way back to the house, cutting across a hay field and coming out near the rock pile at the end of our drive. Then all we had to do was follow the road in to the house.

We had enjoyed a great time out by that old tree, and in later years, when I would visit, just looking out across the fields of well-tended crops brought back vivid memories of that one night so long ago.

One summer, while visiting Aberdeen for a family reunion, I drove by the old "lower" place. It had long since passed into the hands of strangers, and that old tree was gone. I will miss it!

99

Lava Lake

I always enjoyed fishing. Grandpa Frank did his job well. He instilled in me a love of the sport, a love that I was never able to satisfy. From that very first time on the banks of Springfield Lake, Grandpa encouraged me to participate and even to excel. He was the consummate angler himself, and was eager to share his enviable wealth of knowledge with his sons and grandsons.

Sometimes we fished for hours with no more result than a sunburn and exhaustion. Other times we were quite successful, returning home with our catches, showing them off to the younger children and the womenfolk. The children "ooohed and aaahed" at the proof of our fine fishing skills. The women tended to show little interest, thinking only that these odious things needed to be cooked and served at the earliest opportunity.

Springfield Lake was, by far, the most popular place to fish. It was easily accessible and one could get there and fish for awhile, even after a long day of work or school. However, when there was more time, there were other opportunities for some fine angling. I had two favorite spots, places where I liked to go as much for the trip as for the fishing.

One of those places was McTucker Creek. It was uniquely foreign to me. Also it was wild and isolated. I seldom, if ever, saw anyone else around when we made those rare excursions to McTucker Creek.

My other favorite place to fish was Lava Lake.

Lava Lake was a great place to fish. There were two very good reasons for that. For one thing, it was the only place I knew of in Idaho where there was not a limit to the number of fish you were permitted to take. A second reason was that it was so easy to catch fish there. They seemed to be innumerable and they always seemed to be hungry for whatever baits or lures an angler chose to use.

There was also a slight drawback to fishing at Lava Lake. It was a relatively long drive to get there. I enjoyed the trip, but we were not able to make it very often, and that was too bad. It was a wonderful place to fish.

Grandpa Frank knew a shortcut to Lava Lake and one day he showed it to us. Until then, we had always gone nearly all the way to Blackfoot and then turned west to Arco on the highway, nearly doubling back for forty miles and wasting lots of time. The shortcut that Grandpa Frank took us on was called Tabor Road, but it was much more of an antelope trail than a road. Nevertheless, it cut nearly ninety minutes off the trip and so was worth the risk of being stranded in the middle of nowhere.

We were very aware of being stranded because it happened to us once. Grandpa Frank was tooling along that dirt road, minding his own business, when that old DeSoto sank to its axle in wet, squishy mud. It seems that a sprinkler pipe had been leaking and drenched the road. To Grandpa, that was an unpardonable sin and he took revenge swiftly. He opened his trunk, took an axe from beneath a burlap bag, walked about 150 feet up the line and hacked a brand new hole in it, thereby diverting the leak. Only then could we use the shovels he always carried to dig the car out of the mud.

We were delayed for a time, but soon on our way, Grandpa singing one of his little ditties while the rest of us wondered at his good mood. Soon we were once again enjoying the trip.

I found the trip interesting because we passed Atomic City and the National Reactor Testing Facility and that always intrigued me. Arco was an interesting little town, too, with lots of touristy doodads to shop for if the mood hit me. At Arco, we turned south toward Craters of the Moon National Monument, but Lava Lake was there on the right, just a few miles down the road, almost hidden in lava formations and sage. In fact, it would have been easy to miss if one weren't watching for it.

There was a large turnout along the road with room enough for several cars to park, and we did so. Then we took our gear and found a comfortable place along the edge of the lake and began to fish. The lake was unlike most in that it was right in the middle of lava rock. There were no grassy areas, nor were there sandy beaches. Just lava rock! And yet, the fishing was excellent.

I would have preferred trout, but trout were **not** the catch of the day at Lava Lake. It was filled with perch. Perch are also a fine fish for eating, but there are a few things about perch that I didn't like much. One thing was that they seemed to fight less than trout and that sort of spoiled the sport of the catch. The second thing was that they have some sort of spiny fins and skin, and so they need to be skinned rather than scaled. I never did like that task.

Perch had there "up" side, too. They took the bait and there were lots of them. We were fishing at a lake that had no limit on the number of fish you could take in a day. We always had a load of fish after a day at Lava Lake. In fact, our best day there netted 97 perch in about five hours. There were four of us that day and we made a good day of it.

Of course, the ride home always seemed to take much longer than the other way, but I guess that was natural, once the fishing was over. It was nice to have fresh perch in family-sized quantities. That was much better than catching a single trout and then having the family stare at me as I ate. But then again, maybe it wasn't.

100

Milestones

There are many milestones in a young boy's life, but perhaps there is none more significant than obtaining a driver's license. It is an event that is dreamt of, prayed for, and anticipated as much as any other.

I was ready and anxious to take my driver's test for the first time. The State Of Idaho required that I be fourteen years of age to receive my daytime license. At fifteen, I would also be permitted to drive at night, but first I needed that daytime license. I studied the state booklet and prepared for the test. I went out on the back roads around Aberdeen and practiced with each of my parents, neither of them very enthusiastic about my reaching my goal.

My parents made it very clear to me before I even took the test that the acquisition of a driver's license entitled me to nothing. It granted permission from the state to drive legally, but I still needed parental permission and I was not to assume that it would be granted on demand or very often. I was told, too, that there was no vehicle in the family with my name on it and not to assume that I could control theirs.

My birthday finally came and I took the test. I was nervous, but I did well and received the license. The first day I did not ask to drive. I did not want to appear over anxious and immature to my parents. However, that night I took out the license from my wallet several times, just to look at it. I could hardly believe it. I finally had my license!

My first opportunity to drive any significant distance did not come for a few days. Then one Sunday, after church, my mother let me drive home. The other kids ribbed me a bit, but I did okay and everyone survived the experience. No lives were lost. The car incurred no damage. All was as it had been before I drove. Mission completed!

It was frustrating to say the least, but I was not allowed to drive much. It became a regular thing for me to drive home from church on Sunday, but there were very few other opportunities. I reached a point where I hounded my poor mother to let me drive every time she left the house. Once in a while, she would agree and I would get a chance to hone my skills. I never drove with my father in the car. It was an unwritten rule. If Dad was with us, Dad did the driving. There was no sense in my even trying to change that.

As the weeks turned into months and the Winter into Spring, I added experience to my driving history in little bits and pieces. I thought about driving much more often than I actually drove.

I was nearing the end of the eighth grade. Soon I would be graduated from the eighth grade and ready to enter high school in the Fall as a freshman. As I became more and more involved with the graduation ceremony at Aberdeen Junior High, I became more and more aware that the graduation itself was another milestone in my life.

On the morning of my graduation ceremony, Dad made a big announcement. At least it was big to me. I was to be given the use of his pickup after the ceremony. Alone! By myself! With no parents!

I was excited. First of all, my Dad trusted me with his pickup. The significance of that was overwhelming! The pickup was not the car by any means, but it had a personality of its own. My dad loved it. He called it "The Green Hornet." It was a '56 GMC pickup, but he always added that it had a '58 Buick engine in it. It was a nice little truck. It was peppy, comfortable, and had a floor shift, so there was a lot more driving to it, and driving was what I longed for.

After a ceremony that lasted far too long, I lingered for a while at the school, making small talk with friends and their families. Dad came up to me and placed the keys to his pickup in my hand, adding that I should be home at a reasonable hour and that I should drive sensibly. It must have been one of the most difficult things he ever did.

Lucky for me, the ceremony had taken place in the morning, so I had hours with which I could enjoy the pickup. When I got into the cab I felt the strangest sense of power. I also felt the weight of trust and responsibility that Dad had given me. I began to drive.

I drove the streets of Aberdeen over and over. I offered lifts to my friends. I drove to the beach. I drove to Sportsmen's Park. I drove out on the desert. I drove north, south, east, and west, covering as much territory I could in the time I had. I parked at the City Park and talked with people. I went to the Spud Bowl to see who was there. Once I even talked with my dad. Mom had given him the car.

I drove and drove, stretching that great experience out as long as I could. I put a lot of miles on that old pickup that day, but I put them on safely and slowly. I broke no laws. I drove as responsibly as I could. And when the sun dipped below the horizon and I knew that I had but about thirty minutes left to drive, I drove slowly home, savoring the last few moments of a great day.

When I entered the house and returned the keys to my dad, he took them without much comment and without any derisive remarks. He never mentioned the miles I put on or the nearly empty gas tank. My great day ended with my being treated like an adult and for that, I was both grateful and proud.

There are many milestones in a young boy's life.

I was about to begin an entire new season of my life as a high school student. I was a licensed driver. I had lived more than fourteen years and had many small adventures. I knew that there would be many more to come. There would be other milestones. There would be other adventures to write about and to remember. But the day I had my father's old green pickup all to myself was one of the greatest gifts I have ever received. On that day I was not just one of the kids, but a real person. My father recognized it even before I did. That day, and many days since then, I was acutely aware of one wonderful and marvelous fact of life. I was my father's son!

Afterword

I hope you've enjoyed just a bit of the legacy that Aberdeen afforded me through those early years. Of course, I continued to live and experience even more as I went through Aberdeen High School and participated in the activities of community, church and school. High school, however, is an entire new ball game! I look forward to sharing some of those high school memories soon!

— Steven C. Stoker

About the Author

Steven C. Stoker was born and raised in Aberdeen, Idaho. After graduation from Aberdeen High School, he attended Ricks College in Rexburg, Idaho. While at Ricks, he studied music and elementary education. After one year at Ricks, he enlisted in the U.S. Navy.

Steve attended a variety of Naval technical schools and served in Vietnam during four campaigns. While serving in Illinois as an electronics instructor, he attended classes of Southern Illinois University and graduated in 1980 with a bachelor's degree in Occupational Education. He was retired early from the Navy as a Chief Electronics Technician in 1982, with a 100% service-connected disability. After retirement, he continued to work with the Navy as a civilian instructor at Service Schools Command, Great Lakes, Illinois, where he taught for 8 years.

During the San Diego years, Steven met and wed his wife and they had two daughters. In 1990, he retired for good and the family moved from Illinois to Arizona, where Steve does genealogical research using the computer and writes while Peggy, his wife of nearly 30 years, maintains a comfortable home and serves as a volunteer for a variety of civic groups.

Steve's two daughters, Kimberly and Christy, have completed college and are enjoying their own lives and recently, Steve is learning how to enjoy being a grandfather.

9 780595 196531

Made in the USA
Columbia, SC
10 January 2021

30595115R00231